SHERRILYN
KENYON
AND DIANNA LOVE

CINDY
GERARD

LAURA
GRIFFIN

DEADLY
PROMISES

POCKET STAR BOOKS

New York   London   Toronto   Sydney

Pocket Star Books
A Division of Simon & Schuster, Inc.
1230 Avenue of the Americas
New York, NY 10020

This book is a work of fiction. Names, characters, places, and incidents either are products of the author's imagination or are used fictitiously. Any resemblance to actual events or locales or persons, living or dead, is entirely coincidental.

Just Bad Enough copyright © 2010 by Sherrilyn Kenyon and Dianna Love Snell
Leave No Trace copyright © 2010 by Cindy Gerard
Unstoppable copyright © 2010 by Laura Griffin

All rights reserved, including the right to reproduce this book or portions thereof in any form whatsoever. For information address Pocket Books Subsidiary Rights Department, 1230 Avenue of the Americas, New York, NY 10020

First Pocket Star Books paperback edition October 2010

POCKET STAR BOOKS and colophon are registered trademarks of Simon & Schuster, Inc.

For information about special discounts for bulk purchases, please contact Simon & Schuster Special Sales at 1-866-506-1949 or business@simonandschuster.com

The Simon & Schuster Speakers Bureau can bring authors to your live event. For more information or to book an event contact the Simon & Schuster Speakers Bureau at 1-866-248-3049 or visit our website at www.simonspeakers.com.

Text design by Jacquelynne Hudson
Cover design by Lisa Litwack. Photo © Arcangel Images.

Manufactured in the United States of America

10 9 8 7 6 5 4 3 2 1

ISBN 978-1-4391-9111-8
ISBN 978-1-4391-9112-5 (ebook)

Contents

Just Bad Enough

SHERRILYN KENYON
AND
DIANNA LOVE

One

Jeremy Sunn stood next to the gazebo in the middle of the park and glanced around the festival to be sure no one saw him where he normally wouldn't be. Not on a Sunday off. Working undercover required patience, persistence, and . . . popcorn. He tossed a fluffy kernel into the air and caught the buttery delight in his mouth then eyed the Greek water-maiden statue.

The one he'd been lusting over for the past hour.

More like three weeks.

He'd staked out a lot of things in his undercover career with the BAD—Bureau of American Defense—agency, but never a woman for purely personal interest.

No one at the Festival of Emperors paid attention to him, probably because he'd dressed in jeans and a gray T-shirt instead of period clothing. Roman soldiers and women in togas hustled around trying to buy up the last deals of the day. The mid-July event drew traffic from across metro Atlanta to the historic square in Marietta.

And no one strolling past the water maiden in the

last hour had noticed why that one statue was different from the other three, besides being the only female sculpture.

But he did.

Beneath all that caked-on makeup beat the live heart of a flesh-and-blood woman. One he had to get an answer from before heading back to work on Tuesday.

Hell of a way to squander his last day off for a while and ancient history wasn't his forte, but he lived only a mile away and *she* was worth standing here waiting for the festival to end. He hoped.

A simple yes or no.

One answer had the power to . . . eat a hole in his gut.

Sweat trickled down his neck but he couldn't be as hot as that water maiden posed silently amid three massive concrete sculptures of Greek gods.

CeCe Caprice just pretended to be a statue. She could go for hours without moving a muscle when she performed.

He could attest to how hard she trained daily at his gym in Marietta. Yep, every inch of that shapely body wrapped in a toga and posed with a baby doll also coated in white plaster was very much a living, breathing human . . . and one hot female.

That he couldn't touch, damn it.

Correction. Wouldn't touch. Not if he found out she really had meant to give him a "back off" signal yesterday after spending the afternoon planting some damn flowers in her yard.

At least, that's how he'd read her odd reaction when he asked her out to dinner. Now he was starting to wonder if he'd jumped to the wrong conclusion when she hadn't actually said the word "no."

He'd never pressed a woman for anything so he'd backed off. Quick. Then regretted it when he missed her for the past twenty-four hours. He'd gotten used to sharing iced tea on her patio for the best part of three weeks, had never spent that much time just talking to a woman. The females he met were only interested in what he intended to do to their naked bodies.

But CeCe had hung on his words. And laughed at his jokes.

He hadn't even kissed her or had dinner with her.

Twenty-four hours of no iced tea, no talking, and no smiles. He missed her. Couldn't get her out of his mind for one day.

A woman had never spun him inside out like this.

Lust used to be fun, and short-lived. Not obsessive.

Three weeks at home recuperating from a leg wound— a souvenir of his last mission—hadn't turned out anything like he'd expected. Limping to his mailbox the first day at home he'd expected nothing more exciting than his standard fan mail from bill collectors.

When the screen door on the rental house next to his burst open and CeCe strolled down her driveway, the first thing he'd noticed was the sweet belly button winking at him between a red half shirt and white shorts.

He'd thought one of his teammates from BAD had sent him a get-well-soon girl. No way could that little bombshell be his honest to God next-door neighbor.

His luck had never run *that* hot.

But she was indeed a new addition to the neighborhood.

For the first time since moving there he regretted having to leave as soon as he healed.

CeCe had destroyed any operating brain cells he'd possessed the minute she smiled at him. Blue eyes had sparkled bright as sapphires tossed up in blazing sunshine. Every time she turned her head, he fought the urge to touch the wavy auburn hair that brushed her shoulders.

He woke up at night thinking about that thick mass spread across a pillow. His pillow. His bed.

But CeCe wasn't the kind of woman you spent a couple of steamy nights with then walked away. He'd be the first to admit he came by women easily only because the women he met saw him as nothing more than a short-term sexual buzz. Something to hold them over until the real thing came along. He'd accepted that for years as a trade-off for not having to spend his life entirely alone.

Hell, he wasn't long-term material. Not with his criminal history or his current occupation that required going back to prison on a regular basis.

And it wasn't like he could tell a woman he got arrested and thrown in the joint as part of his job description for BAD.

Which was why he should be looking for fast, fun, and forgettable instead of waiting to talk to CeCe here, the one place she couldn't disappear in her house and ignore him. He'd tried to do the same, to forget CeCe, but he'd spent three amazing weeks pretending he had a normal life because a sweet young woman shared iced tea and talked to him. She made him want a normal life. He just didn't know how to go about making it happen. Of all the women who had climbed in his bed, he'd never desired one like he wanted CeCe, and he hadn't even held her in his arms. Spending time with her felt too damned good not to try again to ask her out. To try to keep her.

No mission had turned his gut inside out like this.

He officially went back to work undercover in two days. Before that happened he would know where he stood with her. Had she turned down the date because she'd *really* had plans with her brother or because she wouldn't date a neighbor?

He only wanted a date. A dinner, movie . . . hell, he didn't know. Anything. Something.

But if CeCe told him no today he'd respect her decision and walk away . . . then ask BAD to relocate his residence while he was gone on the next mission so he wouldn't have to face coming home to find another man on her patio.

Popcorn crackled inside the bag he crushed in his fist.

Damn it, he'd never been in knots over a woman before.

"Hey, J!" a familiar male voice yelled.

Jeremy groaned. What the hell was Blade doing here? He stepped away from the side of the gazebo he'd been leaning against and turned to find Blade covering the fifty feet between them with long strides. Most people thought the skinny six-foot, four-inch guy got his name from having a body that moved through crowds like a black knife slicing water, not because he'd carried a switchblade since grade school.

After being busted in a chop shop raid and doing a stint in prison, Blade returned home to start a legitimate body shop business. Rehabilitating a cat not to hunt mice would be more realistic, but he'd been straight for a year and swore he was going to stay on this side of the law. His Denzel Washington smile, charismatic tongue, and ever present sense of humor drew women faster than bees to a hive.

Jeremy met him when they landed in the same cellblock in a Florida correctional institute after Jeremy got picked up for possession of stolen goods. BAD planted the merchandise and dropped the dime on him via a snitch so Jeremy could expose the identity of a nasty guy who had tortured and murdered three teens who refused to steal for him.

A dirty, but rewarding, job most days.

"Whatcha doing here?" Blade glided up in blue jeans and a red T-shirt sporting a motorcycle design. "This ain't your playground, dog."

"Boning up on ancient history." Jeremy peeked at his water maiden to make sure CeCe hadn't come out of her comatose state yet, but she hadn't so much as blinked.

"Speaking of boners, I got something right up your alley."

"That's not what I said."

"But it's what you're thinkin' about."

"How do you figure that?" Jeremy crossed his arms.

"Your eyes are open." Blade broke out a grin that destroyed any chance of staying pissed off at him.

Labeling Blade a "close friend" stretched the definition only because a true friend gave unconditional trust. Jeremy had learned at birth that anyone, even family, would eventually turn their back on you.

However, when it came to extending trust to someone other than Jeremy's teammates in BAD, Blade was that rare exception.

"Now that we've determined your state of mind," Blade continued with his line of trash talk. "Glad I spotted you. I got a sizzlin'-hot babe you don't wanna miss, right over there."

Jeremy looked in the direction Blade hooked his thumb over his shoulder. Two voluptuous smiling beauties dressed in costume were walking toward them through the middle of the park.

"Who're they?" Jeremy hoped his unchecked irritation hadn't come through, but introducing him to any woman right now was really bad timing. The last thing he needed was for CeCe to come out of her trance and see him flirting with another female.

But Blade noticed the smallest things sometimes and Jeremy wasn't ready to let him know about his infatuation with CeCe.

"That black diamond in the Cleopatra outfit is Cleo. She's *mine*." Blade waggled his eyebrows. "That redheaded seductress is Shelilah." He drew out the name *Shuh-liii-luh* in adoration.

"Shelilah? Is that even a real name? Did they have Shelilahs in Roman time?" Weren't all these statues of emperors from Rome?

"Details, details. Her name's probably Sheila." Blade beamed one of his on-the-move smiles at the women and lifted a finger for them to wait a minute then turned to Jeremy. "Come on, man. You're my lucky charm. These two are perfect. Right up your alley—hot women looking for some quick action then leaving tomorrow for Florida. All they want are a couple man toys for a night."

A disposable date.

Jeremy had been disposable from the first hours of his life when his mother tossed him into the closest Dumpster. He hadn't fared much better in all the foster homes after that. The only place that ever wanted to keep him had been juvie. He'd learned skills in there that put him on a path to fast money and hard time.

But all that stopped with BAD, or at least changed, since he now committed crimes only when ordered to for a mission.

Jeremy shrugged. "I'll pass, but thanks anyhow." He had only forty-eight hours left and intended to spend as much time as he could with CeCe *if* she gave him the green light.

This was his only chance. He could be gone for a week or a month.

By then, CeCe could be in someone else's arms.

"Are you crazy? What's wrong with you?" Blade growled and hooked his thumbs in the corners of his jean pockets. "I ain't seen you with a skirt in two weeks. Thought you were healed."

Three weeks, actually, to be exact. But who's counting?

"I'm healed." The wound in his thigh was sore but he could function. "Like you said, none that you've *seen* me with." Jeremy glanced over at the CeCe statue, no idea what possessed him to want a woman who said she'd just moved away from home for the first time. She had a quick wit and wasn't the least bit meek. Too sweet to be worldly or a quick fling . . .

"Come on, J. Get out of that damn funk you've been in. You don't come charm these women I'm gonna revoke your badass license." Blade grinned, which meant his devious mind was up to no good. "In fact, I'll tell everyone in the hood you done turned pansy-assed on us and can't get it up around a knockout woman no more."

"You bite, you know that? Let's go." Jeremy resigned himself to making small talk until he could find a way to get out of Blade's deal without insulting Shelilah and before CeCe left the festival, or saw him first.

Then what? Stroll back over to the statues when she came out of her trance and pretend he *happened* to be at the festival and, oh, what a surprise to run into each other?

Pansy ass.

SAM THE MAN clawed his way over a chain-link fence, dropped, and hit the ground running. Georgia humidity soaked his black open-collar shirt, his new one, damn it. He gasped for air, dodging between older clapboard houses just off the square in Marietta.

Quick glance back. They weren't close. Keep moving.

The neighborhood canine chorus grew with every yard he disturbed. Sam toed a foothold on a rear gate of one yard and plunged into an unfenced one, finally.

A rottweiler lunged, teeth bared, but the six feet of sturdy chain attached to one honkin'-big doghouse held while Sam sprinted past.

He burst from the narrow alley between well-tended aging homes and slowed to a quick walk. Cars were tucked bumper to bumper along both sides of the quiet side street. Shouts and barking from behind meant his tail was gaining on him. Time to make some serious mileage. He broke from the manicured yards thick with landscape and raced down the sidewalk. Clutching the photo card he had to deliver, he cursed the friend he'd trusted.

The friend who'd set him up.

But since no one could be completely trusted, Sam had taken the precaution of a backup plan. Never knew when a deal would suck toilet water.

Starface's two armed thugs hard on his ass pretty much flushed his day down the sewer.

Trusting the feds to come through in time had been a gamble to begin with, but maybe he should have set up the meet spot in advance. Now he was looking at bad odds, because the feds probably couldn't get to him in time. He'd sent a text message on the run for them to meet him in Marietta Square. The crowds milling around some damn festival there today would cover him long enough for the feds to snatch him out of sight.

But when Sam reached the square in sixty seconds he doubted even Superman could make it here in time.

He sliced across Church Street to where the crazy-looking event was winding down, the crowd thinning. He slowed to a fast walk as he entered the historic square, searching for a spot to hide his prize. All the tents would be picked up tonight.

Damn, no help there.

The smell of fresh popcorn fattened the air. He had to be careful not to draw the attention of off-duty cops working the event. They'd get him killed and probably a few of them, too. Sam zigzagged against a sea of teens bundled in groups and couples strolling, oblivious of any danger. Some of the patrons wore shorts but others were in togas. Huh?

A dumpy Caesar wannabe glared when Sam bumped the short bastard's bone-thin Cleopatra.

Sam clutched the tiny photo card, thinking. The feds would stick out like the Blues Brothers in this crowd *if* they were here, which they weren't. He needed a plan C at this point and slowed, searching for a safe spot to hide the memory card that was no bigger than a quarter. He passed an eight-foot-tall train engine replica packed with kids using it like a jungle gym.

Couldn't hide the card there. Rushing ahead between tents protecting displays of pottery and paintings, he passed vendors packing their wares.

Nowhere showed promise. Damn it all to hell.

He had to dump this card fast.

At the far end of the park he burst into an opening, almost taking a header into one of four life-size sculptures. The area had been arranged as a garden with white concrete-looking statues of Roman-like figures.

This statue garden offered him a slim salvation. For now.

Sam quickly sized up each sculpture. Which one was the best hiding place? He shoved his shoulder against the closest concrete emperor. That heavy sucker didn't budge, which meant whoever owned these would probably send a crew out tomorrow to pick up the statues with a crane when the crowd wouldn't be a problem. But this emperor didn't have a cut deep enough in the folds of his robe or in the rocky-looking base for Sam to drop the small digital photo card into.

Get caught with the goods and he'd die for sure.

Best plan he had was to dump the package then come

back later to retrieve his property. Or hope the feds miraculously showed up to save him if he got nailed by Starface's men.

Worst case, Sam would buy some time if Starface did catch him—a real possibility. He'd only give up the card if all other options disappeared. Letting the photos and video stored on this memory device fall into the wrong hands would unleash a mob war like none before.

He'd be the first casualty.

Sam eased over to a statue of a woman with a baby and long tulip leaves sculpted around the base. Deep crevices in the leaves would hide the small plastic case. Perfect.

"The park will close in ten minutes," screeched from a speaker on top of a pole.

"Take care of my booty," he whispered and made a bare flick of his fingers to toss the card into a deep fissure between a leaf and a stem.

He breathed a heavy sigh of relief for five yards and scooted between two large panel trucks. A quick glance past the other side and he started to move.

Strong fingers bit into his shoulder.

Sam froze, then turned to face the ugly mug of Dorvan, who appeared to be in the running for "Bone Breaker of the Year." Dorvan's shorter sidekick kept his back to the two of them, obviously watching the area so no one overheard them.

"Where's the memory card?" Dorvan asked casually.

"I didn't get it. Things fell apart at the meet." Sam licked his dry lips, wishing he could cause a disturbance, but he didn't trust the police not to shoot him in an altercation.

"Starface won't be happy."

"Swear I don't have the card." Sam figured the feds would be all over this place in another five minutes. "Tell you what. Give me a day and I'll come up with it."

A *click* sounded. Dorvan jabbed a knife tip into Sam's neck. Sam hissed at the sharp pain. His day was definitely going to shit.

"Let's go somewhere you can show me you don't have it." Dorvan jerked Sam along by his collar.

Not the response Sam had been banking on. A throbbing pulse hammered his skull. He would be searched, right down to body cavities.

"THE FESTIVAL OF *Emperors has now ended and the park is closing.*"

CeCe heard sounds as if they echoed through a long tunnel. A male voice talking a minute ago about . . . what? Now, a bullhorn-type announcement. Her thoughts bounced around until she realized she'd reached the end of her physical limit for standing still but her concentration wouldn't be broken. Discipline came from hours of practice . . . and growing up in a cautious environment. She never dreamed she'd get so good at this when she took up yoga two years ago to use as a mental lifeline.

Or that her new skills would offer her a way to support herself and a chance at a new life in a new location.

Drawing the first deep breath in almost two hours, she flexed her fingers from their stiff position. Sharp needles of pain shot through her numb limbs with each move.

Click. Whirr. Click. Whirr. Click. Whirr.

What was that? She rolled her head to one side, paused,

then to the other side and wiggled her toes. Her skin screamed for moisture, a shower to wash away the white powder coating. Step by step, she eased her body out of the deep Zen state she'd entered to perform her routine.

"I'm from the newspaper. You can talk now can't you?" a male voice said.

Oh, if he was a reporter the sound must have been a camera.

CeCe stretched her stiff face and cracked open her eyelids. She closed them again then forced the heavy lids to lift, squinting until her pupils adjusted to the fading afternoon light. The matte finish makeup made blinking a chore.

"Of course." She smiled. Her voice always sounded rough after a long state of calm, but she loved this job.

And loved finally being on her own at twenty-six with a chance at a normal life.

"I'm with the *Atlanta Journal-Constitution*." A fortyish man in dark slacks, white collared shirt, and an Atlanta Braves ballcap over short hair stuffed his camera into a green bag on the ground then pulled out a pad and pen. He had kind eyes that matched the photo on the media ID swinging from the lanyard around his neck. "Mind if I ask you a few questions?"

"Not if you don't mind me moving around while I answer." She shifted her weight, loosening up her leg muscles, and felt the crack in the top of her base give so she spread her feet on each side of the center to keep from damaging the area further. She *had* to find someone who could repair fiberglass this week.

CeCe tossed the baby doll statue to the ground so she could keep flexing her hands.

A woman walking by stopped short, stared in surprise at the doll, then at CeCe, then seemed to figure it all out before she shook her head and continued on.

Normal reaction when a person saw a statue move.

"No problem. You do whatever you need to do." The middle-aged photographer had a notebook out, pen ready in his stubby fingers. "I took a shot before you woke up. Is that what you do? Sleep?"

"It's more of a deep meditative state I learned in yoga." Hours and hours and hours of yoga that offered therapeutic escape and a way to survive. CeCe stretched one leg muscle, then the other.

"Have you done this a long time and do you work for a company?"

"No. I've been doing this for about a month. I contract from a company called Double Take. They're in Atlanta. Will this be in the paper for sure?"

"Yep. Be in tomorrow's. I'm going to take a couple more shots of you while you stretch."

"Sure." CeCe smiled inside, thrilled to show the owner of the company she was an asset. She'd get a copy of tomorrow's paper for the owner of Double Take. In this troubled economy, the newspaper article would be free promotion. Maybe get a couple copies she could send to her family in Canada. All at once her enthusiasm bottomed out. Her family hated any contact with the media and had always warned her about staying out of the public eye, but she was now officially a nobody and living an anonymous existence in a new country. She just had to be careful with her answers.

No one here would recognize her since she'd been hidden away most of her life and the only way anyone would know of her family was if they were in law enforcement or were a criminal.

She avoided both.

The reporter lowered the camera to hang from a strap around his neck. "What's your name and where do you live?"

"Cecelia . . . Caprice." When would that name come easily to her so she didn't hesitate each time to make sure she said her full name correctly? She'd better get used to it. Besides, Caprice was her true last name, the one she'd had at birth.

"I live in Marietta," she answered. Along with some sixty thousand residents, so no significant details shared there. In spite of her new freedom, she'd been raised in a cautious environment and taught to divulge only specific information when asked a question.

"Has yoga been a hobby of yours for a long time?" he asked over his shoulder then clicked his pen several times, muttering something before he squatted down to dig through his bag. "Hang on a minute."

A hobby? Hell, no, yoga had never been something as simple as a hobby. She'd first started ten years ago, as a way to survive her mother's death and deal with the dangers associated with her family. The discipline had kept her sane in a world where her every move was orchestrated and every word had to be thought out and edited before speaking. Impulsive had never been part of her vocabulary, which hadn't been easy as hormones had taken over her body.

She wanted impulsive, damn it.

CeCe kept stretching and squelched a frown at the word "hobby," which reminded her of Jeremy Sunn, her sexy neighbor. He'd hobbled over to where she'd been washing her dual-cab pickup truck and hosing off her statue base the day after they met at the mailbox and asked if she statue-modeled for a hobby.

What was it with men?

Just because she didn't sweat and grunt at her job didn't mean she wasn't working. Did Jeremy think owning a gym was a *real* job? An image of that ripped body sweating and grunting as he lifted weights in the gym sent a bead of perspiration trickling down between her makeup-caked breasts.

CeCe mentally whitewashed that picture before her camo makeup turned molten and puddled at her feet. She'd never seen him during the first two weeks she'd lived in the neighborhood, then he showed up one day, limping. He'd been hurt on the job but never explained how and she hadn't pressed him. Guys do stupid things when they get in a gym around other men. Jeremy might be embarrassed to explain how he got injured.

She'd decided to join his gym to do her daily yoga routines, but to be honest she suffered another hour of workout to see Jeremy a few extra hours a day.

For someone who had been a major flirt during that first meeting at the mailboxes, Jeremy was all business at his gym, polite to women and sharing a quick joke with guys. At first, she'd been grateful over the remote decorum he maintained there since she had to keep her distance from *any* man in public. But her gratitude slowly turned an evil green color when she noticed the other women ogling him and overheard their seductive comments about his beautiful body.

Yoga did little to smother her irritation.

CeCe had never enjoyed the freedom to flirt with a guy. Not if she wanted to see him a second time, which was why she made the most of her exclusive time with Jeremy when they were both home by asking him to help her around the yard and making him iced tea.

Anytime she was sure her brother wasn't expected to visit.

Her little adventure had been going great until she'd almost accepted a date with Jeremy after he'd spent yesterday afternoon planting pansies in her yard.

A breath before she'd screwed up and said yes, she'd heard a big sedan engine rumbling nearby that could have been her brother. In a moment of panic over her sibling catching her alone with a man, she'd rebuffed Jeremy with the excuse she had plans with her brother. Then her brother hadn't shown up after all. Talk about feeling like an idiot.

Jeremy had politely backed away.

But those vivid green eyes of his had dulled with the rejection. She hadn't seen him in a full day—a lifetime without his smile and rich voice.

She should have used her I'm-looking-for-a-husband spiel the first time they met, which usually obliterated any male interest for good and spared a man having to face her brothers.

The men in her family loved her but were so overprotective she was sure they'd forced one guy they hadn't approved of years ago to disappear. Yoga had become her life to combat loneliness, her only defense against curling into a ball of despair over feeling trapped. She doubted Jeremy would pass her family's test of "acceptable" men for her to date. They wanted her to find someone who was no threat, someone who would accept whatever she told him about her past and never dig beneath the surface to discover the truth behind the DeMitri family in Canada.

The minute any of them met Jeremy in person they'd know he wasn't a man to be easily fooled or controlled. They'd never find Jeremy selling furniture or running a grocery store. He ran his life and world by his own rules, a prime alpha male—not dating material as far as her brothers were concerned

She envied the hell out of him.

She'd have to bide her time another couple of weeks until Vinny—one of her three older and dangerous stepbrothers—left. He would, once she convinced him she was safe living on her own. When he went back to his wife and kids in Washington, D.C., she could finally accept a date without worry of interference. Until then, no dating and she couldn't let Jeremy know how much she wanted to be with him or what she'd really like to do with that buff body after hours in his gym, late at night with her favorite chocolate-amaretto sauce . . .

"Ma'am, did you hear me?"

"Huh?" CeCe blinked and stared, embarrassed. She'd forgotten the reporter.

"Sorry about that. I had a call from my wife."

She hadn't heard any phone ring.

He lifted his pad to write. "My last question was if you started yoga as a hobby."

"No, I committed myself to mastering yoga from the first time I tried it. Yoga requires dedication and discipline to reach a point of immersion so that you can stand without moving a muscle for hours." CeCe lifted one foot then the other, testing her muscle response before she risked stepping off the two-foot-tall base.

"I watched you earlier today and couldn't catch you moving at all. What's the longest you've been that still?"

"Two hours and fifteen minutes." She judged the distance to the ground where she wanted to land then moved her foot to take the step.

The base creaked. The crack shifted her balance. She lost her concentration for a second and wobbled but had almost recovered when a male hand appeared in her line of vision.

The hand had long male fingers and was attached to Jeremy.

What was he doing here?

What if her brother saw him this close to her?

CeCe was so busy looking for Vinny she lost her balance, flailing her arms.

"Careful." Jeremy caught her at the waist as she toppled forward. "I've got you."

That deep voice rumbled across her psyche with such assurance she fought off a sigh. Strong hands did have her.

She should have been relieved at his assistance, but her pulse ramped into high gear at being so close to Jeremy. Touched by him. Lean muscle filled out his six-foot-two body nicely.

Better than nicely.

She missed his warm scent she'd breathe in whenever he worked shoulder to shoulder with her in the yard. Smelling him this close was so much better. The women in the gym saw only a tall, blond male with sparkling green eyes. She saw the edge beneath his casual facade, the keen look in his gaze and the unyielding planes in his face.

This was a man with hidden layers and secrets.

Jeremy turned as he lowered her, handling her weight with an ease that confirmed he got plenty of return from his investment in a gym. She'd inherited her mother's five-foot-seven height, but not her mother's determination to keep her weight down.

Life was too short to pass up banana splits.

But she worried about his leg injury even though she'd noticed him adding a series of workouts on the leg exercise equipment this past week.

She stared up into a face that was a study in tanned skin over sharp angles. He'd been gifted with handsome lips that CeCe had felt only in her dreams. Heat swirled in those lightning green eyes, holding her prisoner.

Her lungs refused to expand.

Jeremy's fingers moved up an inch, touching her abdomen, and lit a slow-burning fuse for fireworks waiting to go off in her lower half. If he could do that just by holding her at the waist, she could only imagine what he'd feel like skin to skin.

What he could do with that sexy mouth.

When her feet touched earth again, she was close enough to get a whiff of his aftershave. He smelled masculine, virile . . . potent, something that could be called All Night Fantasy.

A wicked blend a man wore to lure a woman to a dark place.

She had a very dark bedroom and a few slippery fantasies to match.

"You okay?" Jeremy asked softly, then grinned.

Pure rascal.

What she wouldn't give for just one night with that grin.

When she didn't answer, his smile softened into concern. "Did you get too warm up there? Your makeup is smudging."

Too warm? More like she might combust if she didn't get away from him.

The reporter's face popped into view over Jeremy's shoulder, reminding her she had an audience.

Not to mention *Vinny might show up*.

"What are you doing here?" CeCe jumped out of Jeremy's grasp, flinching over the pained look that chased across his face for an instant. He'd never ask her out again if she acted like a witch. "I mean, uh, I'm surprised to see you."

"I was in the area." Jeremy shrugged, but his eyes narrowed as though he was cautious, and who wouldn't be after the way she'd just acted?

Damn it, why couldn't life be simple? Her reaction wasn't her fault. Just a safety precaution to protect him if anyone was watching. She didn't want Jeremy to just disappear one day.

CeCe held up a finger for him to give her a minute, then turned to the reporter. "Do you have any more questions?"

"Can you hear anything while you're in this deep state?"

A flicker of some man's voice crossed her mind. What in the world had he said? *Take care of my booty*.

She pondered for a moment before answering. "Yes, bits and pieces. I probably hear more than I realize, but the words may not register until later. Anything else?"

"No." He handed her a business card. "This will be in tomorrow morning's paper."

"Thanks." When the reporter left she turned back to Jeremy. "Sorry. I didn't mean to sound unappreciative, but I'm slow to come out of that state so I may be weird the first few minutes." She couldn't get involved with him—yet—but she didn't want to run him off either. Yeah, she realized that might sound contradictory, but she really liked Jeremy. Enough that she didn't want Vinny and her brothers to hurt him.

Which meant no dating right now. Surely Jeremy would give her another chance in a few weeks.

She flicked quick glances around them, watching for any sign of an aggressive Italian male built for championship wrestling heading their way. Jeremy was just as beefed up as Vinny, but she doubted he could take on all three brothers, which was exactly what would happen if Vinny, the attorney in the family, sent out a call to arms.

"That's okay." Jeremy's face eased back into happy as if he accepted her ridiculous excuse for acting like a Chihuahua on acid. "I'll have to get tomorrow's paper."

Idiot that she was around him, she just smiled, happy to see him. He had a rugged outdoorsy look, like a buff surfer with that white-blond hair falling to his collar. But she'd grown up around a pack of alpha males and knew when she entered the heat zone of one.

When Jeremy wasn't joking around, he had a powerful aura about him that warned others not to step into his arena unless they were up to the task. Some women might miss what hid behind the charming window dressing.

The wind stirred his hair in a loose and free way that made her wonder how he'd look in the morning after a night of hot sex.

With a body like that she'd bet on an endless night.

"You'll be famous," he added.

Reminding her about the photo brought her back from mental wandering. "I don't think so. How famous can someone made up to look like a statue be?"

"I'd know it was you even under all that makeup."

A tingle of regret over the picture and article inched up her spine. She didn't want fame and her family might not be happy that she'd talked to a reporter. *Stop obsessing and don't overreact.* Besides, it would probably just be a dinky article buried under weekend events. Her identity had been hidden under layers of caked-on makeup. And layers of Vinny's expert paperwork.

CeCe picked up the baby doll. When she turned back to her fiberglass base, Jeremy was studying it.

"You've got a crack in this thing," he muttered.

"Someone backed into my stand at my last event."

He lifted the sculpted base, not seeming to mind the white powder he'd gotten on his hands from her body makeup. "Where's your truck?"

"I have a hand cart to move that with," she protested, then took in his arched eyebrow and unrelenting expression to mean he only wanted directions to her truck. She finally pointed. "Over there near the theater. Last spot before the railroad tracks."

This was the first time he'd spoken to her since she'd

given him a lame brush-off for his dinner invitation. The look of disappointment in his face had eaten a hole in her stomach.

Was a normal life too much to ask for?

One not built around lies.

CeCe walked companionably beside Jeremy, sneaking peeks at his confident stride and casual manner.

He almost seemed . . . shy? No way. Just laid back today.

Why couldn't she have a man like him in her life?

Because her family wouldn't accept a clean-cut upstanding citizen like Jeremy and she wouldn't accept a man they approved of, so she couldn't win either way.

Didn't mean she had to live like a monk, did it?

Jeremy placed her fiberglass base in the truck bed then dusted the powder from his hands. When he turned to her this time his smile made her swallow hard.

She craved this man.

A long horn blast from the railroad tracks entering Marietta warned everyone a freight train was approaching and would pass through downtown not fifty feet behind them.

"Look, CeCe, maybe we could . . . " Jeremy hesitated as if the words in his head were waiting for a sign of encouragement.

Long white guardrails lowered into place with warning bells clanging at a deafening level. Automobiles stopped on each side of the crossing. The ground vibrated as the lead engine raced by dragging a string of loaded railcars. Loud rumbling prevented any conversation for a few minutes.

Her heart jumped at the desire pulsing through Jeremy's eyes, the male interest he didn't try to hide. But if she let him finish that sentence they'd both be disappointed with her answer.

After a minute of metal-on-metal pounding the caboose blew past, sucking the noise down the tracks with it.

Jeremy opened his mouth to finish his sentence.

"Ah, gee!" CeCe snapped her fingers.

"What?" Jeremy looked as alarmed as she sounded.

"I just realized I'm going to be late."

"For what?"

Answering that question was going to give her night-mares, but she had no choice. "Drinks at a friend's house. She wants me to meet—" *Just say it!* Use the one line that would put Jeremy off for a couple weeks, because she couldn't keep doing this over and over. *Say I have a girl-friend who wants me to meet a guy she thinks would be a good match for me.* CeCe had been raised around lies. Why were these so difficult to tell?

Jeremy waited, expectantly. "She wants you to meet . . . who?"

CeCe opened her mouth to give the right answer, but instead said, "Her friends . . . she, uh, wants me to meet her girlfriends."

His face relaxed.

She accepted the stab of guilt that cut her in half over leading him on but couldn't bring herself to completely destroy the light of interest in his gaze. Not after three weeks of getting to know Jeremy. Three weeks of heaven.

She'd never laughed so much. Once she got him to open up, he'd shared stories of setting up the gym and the people who worked for him. It was as if he'd never shared those stories with anyone else. She'd never spent so much time alone with a man who wasn't family and realized she felt safe with Jeremy.

If not for her overzealous stepfamily of men who had sworn to her dying mother they'd protect CeCe, she'd enjoy getting to know Jeremy much better.

Jeremy opened the driver's door on her dual-cab truck where the interior was covered in plastic. When she gained her place behind the wheel amid much crackling noise, he leaned in the opening and said, "See you . . . tonight."

As if he meant to do exactly that.

Be still my heart.

Hormones were going to get her in big trouble if she stayed in that rental house so close to him. Vinny would never have approved the lease if he'd realized just what kind of man lived next door to her. The little old lady who owned both houses had assured Vinny her other renter—Jeremy—was a quiet man who traveled often and kept to himself.

A sweet guy who never brought women to his house.

God forgive her, CeCe had jumped on the speculative look in Vinny's face the first time he glanced over at Jeremy limping around his yard. She realized Vinny had made the mental leap that Jeremy was gay. CeCe did everything she could to keep her brother convinced her neighbor was no threat to her.

Vinny might not be so at ease if he ever met Jeremy in person. He'd recognize another alpha and figure out quickly that her attractive next-door neighbor was not gay.

Not by a long shot.

Oh boy, had she screwed up or what?

If her defenses didn't hold up Jeremy would be in

trouble. Her brothers took overprotective to a whole new level and enforced a no-engagement rule with a .357 Magnum.

But she hadn't moved here to live in hiding the way she had at home. The minute she convinced Vinny to return home to D.C. permanently she would rush next door to invite Jeremy on a date that would end up at her house . . . in her bed . . . with her.

Until then she had to keep away from him.

TWO

Jeremy wheeled his Tahoe sport utility through the side roads heading home from Marietta Square and trying to beat CeCe back by taking the quickest route he knew. He felt like a teenager with his pulse racing, but he intended to arrive home in time to unload her fiberglass base and find out if he'd imagined that bedroom gaze she'd just given him.

Maybe he wasn't the only one experiencing the attraction between them.

Maybe she wanted to give him a shot.

Or maybe he was just hoping that look she'd given him meant she wanted to lick him from head to toe.

All Shelilah had wanted was a set of skilled hands to stroke an itch.

When Jeremy politely backed out, Blade had shaken his head at him and led the two women to his car with the intent of appeasing both females tonight.

Jeremy didn't care. Blade could have all the women in the world . . . except CeCe.

Whoa, hold it. That smacked of sounding . . . possessive.

A date. That was all he was trying to accomplish with Cece, to start.

Swinging into the driveway of his ranch-style brick home, he parked, not wasting time to stuff his truck in the garage.

CeCe pulled into her driveway a few seconds later.

Jeremy jumped out and reached the driver's side of her truck bed in several quick strides. He lifted the base from the back.

"I can unload that," she complained, climbing out of the truck and leaving a dusty white trail. Her garage door finished opening with a groan exposing the single-car storage space cluttered with packing boxes that prevented parking inside.

Jeremy ignored her. "Where do you want it?"

CeCe sighed then pointed at a spot in her garage with a chalky outline left from where she'd obviously stored the fiberglass unit before. He carried it over and dropped the base into place. The overhead fluorescent lights flickered on.

When he turned around CeCe was standing next to the switch by the door to her mudroom. White-dusted hair fell loose from the twisted-up 'do she'd worn earlier. Sweat drizzled along her face and streaked the coating over her shoulders.

She'd wiped most of the makeup off her face, revealing her eyes and lips. "I look like a bad Halloween costume."

"No, you look . . . sweet." He stepped closer and used a finger to lift a lock of powdered hair that had broken free and pushed it behind her ear. "And sexy." She didn't move.

He trailed the same finger down her neck and across her shoulder.

She shivered.

Damn it, he wanted this woman. She wasn't the kind of woman to date casually. For once, he considered that a good thing if she said yes, which was why he had to get it over with and ask her out. The sooner he got an answer, the sooner he'd either be in heaven or licking his wounds and leaving a day early for the BAD headquarters in Nashville, Tennessee.

The overhead fixture in the center of her garage flashed on and off, then made a sizzling sound.

"I'll have to get a bulb out of the attic," she mumbled, still not moving. Her eyes were locked on him, but he couldn't tell if she was daring him to take the next move or preparing to back away if he did.

"It's probably not a bulb." He lowered his hand. She might be more receptive if he gave her time to shower first.

She blinked, coming out of her daze to look at the light. "No?"

He angled his head around to look at the fixture. "Acting like a transformer."

"Figures," she grumbled. "Because replacing a bulb would be something *I* could do instead of bothering Miss Betty."

Jeremy smiled in agreement. He never bothered their landlord with repairs either, just took care of everything himself.

"I've got some spare parts from fixing one of mine," he offered, then added casually, "Why don't you get a shower and I'll swap out the transformer?"

The indecision in her face was beating the hell out of his ego. One minute she had eyes that called to him like a sultry siren and the next she was clearly backing up.

Then, bright as a ray of sunshine, CeCe broke out a smile that drew him in faster than a suicidal moth to a flame.

"That's a great idea. I'll get cleaned up quick." She'd clearly made some decision. The siren was back when she gave him a smoldering look that ran all the blood in his body south.

His cock twitched in response.

But did her response mean she'd go to dinner with him tonight? He had two days. Tick, tick, tick . . .

When she spun away and opened the door to her mud-room, he stopped her with, "CeCe?"

She paused and looked over her shoulder. "What?"

He didn't know why he had to constantly push limits, but that had been his nature since speaking his first words and Jeremy wanted a straight answer now. He couldn't take guessing any more. He had to know he wasn't misreading those heated looks.

If all she wanted was friendship, he'd fix her light and leave her alone. Forever.

"After I get this done," he said, pointing up at the lights, "you can see your girlfriend . . . or have dinner with me."

She chewed on the corner of her lip, another moment of indecision that rankled him so he decided to push all the limits at once. "Dinner . . . at my house."

Her lips parted in surprise then a clash of thoughts conflicted in her face before she finally settled on a decision that cranked up the wattage on her smile. "I'll bring the wine." She disappeared inside.

Jeremy stood there a moment, not believing she was really going to have dinner at his house.

Tonight. Alone with CeCe.

When the fog cleared from his mind, Jeremy jogged back over to his vehicle and pressed his garage opener.

He heard opportunity calling with her enthusiastic rush to shower. Jeremy was not one to pass up any opportunity that looked like CeCe Caprice.

DINNER . . . AT MY *house*.

Jeremy's words played over and over in CeCe's mind like a favorite tune.

She could have said no, should have said no. But all she could think was *Why not if I'm careful?*

When she finished toweling her hair she lifted a hair dryer then changed her mind. Drying the wavy mass never helped so why waste that time?

Cece brushed her teeth, smiling over her luck. He'd solved her dilemma. She hadn't wanted to risk inviting him to dinner in her house for fear of an unexpected guest—Vinny—showing up and couldn't very well have suggested to Jeremy she'd love to have a date on the condition of it being after dark and inside his house with the doors locked.

Jeremy would have thought she was psycho or way too forward.

She'd heard enough around the gym to know Jeremy didn't accept dates from female members who asked him and none of the girls she'd spoken with mentioned him having been in a serious relationship. Sounded as though he didn't monopolize a woman's time, which would normally be a positive trait for her situation.

What would it be like to have a man like Jeremy wanting to monopolize her time? Heaven.

Stop dreaming about the impossible and just live in the moment for once.

She leaned close to the mirror, inspecting her face where scrubbing the makeup off had left her skin red-blotched in places. She could take the time to put on new makeup once she told him she'd come over *after* dark. But if she didn't get back to the garage soon, Jeremy might finish fixing the light and go home. She didn't have his phone number and didn't want Vinny to show up with her standing at Jeremy's door.

Vinny would come over to meet Jeremy. Bad move.

She wasn't expecting her brother, but he hadn't been around the festival or at least she hadn't seen him. Her sixth sense warned her he was due to drop by unexpectedly.

Vinny was one of those insane people who got up before daylight so he normally stopped by early. If she orchestrated it right, she'd run out and get Jeremy to agree on the time then scoot him home before anyone saw him inside her garage.

She brushed her damp hair back and grinned at the mirror.

Tonight with Jeremy. She couldn't believe it. Chills skittered over her skin at the possibility of kissing him . . . just as an appetizer.

She pulled on a knit-and-lace top that stopped short of where her white running pants hit her hips. The lace was too much, too girly. Yanking that off, she dug out a powder blue sleeveless top, eyed it once in the mirror, and hurried to the garage.

When she opened the mudroom door to the garage, the last splash of sunlight had disappeared. She could just see Jeremy's hands moving. He stood two rungs up on a stepladder and was snapping the plastic cover back over her light fixture when her feet touched the cool concrete floor.

She saw him much better as he climbed down.

He'd taken off his shirt. Oh, mama.

"You're back in business." Folding the stepladder, Jeremy stood it against the side wall. He walked over to where she was glued to one spot and reached past her shoulder toward the light switch.

When his chest moved close to her face, she inhaled his scent and wanted to lean forward another inch to touch her lips to his skin. To taste him.

But she didn't move at all.

The light blinked on and glowed almost as bright as the smile he beamed at her.

What should she say? She sucked at casual conversation and had little experience intimately with men.

"I owe you one for that," she joked, then cringed at how stupid that sounded. "Thanks."

"Anytime." Green eyes narrowed in pure devilment studied her. "You look . . . refreshed."

She lowered her chin, glancing at herself like a dimwit who had forgotten what she'd put on.

The overhead light flicked off, leaving them in a dark garage except for the haze of twilight filtering from the dusty evening glow. Her eyes adjusted just as he touched a finger under her chin and lifted, drawing her gaze to his.

She ran her tongue along her lips and Jeremy's eyes sparked with heat.

One kiss. Just something to give her a little confidence for tonight.

Jeremy eased closer, soaking up her personal space without taking a step, and cupped her face. "About that IOU. Mind if I collect now?"

"I'm all for paying my debts promptly," she whispered, short of breath at the prospect of . . .

He lowered his head, gently touching his lips to hers. Slowly sweeping across in sweet nips then firmer. The tempo built, his tongue teasing, tasting her, asking for more one tiny move at a time.

She leaned into him. His long fingers spread across her face then moved to the back of her head. He wrapped an arm around her and she moaned at the feel of his muscled body when they touched. She wanted to climb inside that incredible body, feel him everywhere.

She opened her lips, raking his tongue with hers, playing. He tasted sensual, hot, and all male. She pushed her hands up the warm skin on his naked chest then reached around his neck, fingers driving up to fist his hair.

He held her at the small of her back, firm yet gently.

She ached to be with this man.

No way would one kiss be enough.

If the thick evidence of his reaction rubbing against her middle was any indication, she'd bet one kiss wasn't enough for Jeremy either. Talk about a confidence boost.

His lips pulled away from her mouth to torture the skin along her neck.

Even though the garage was dark, she didn't want to risk Vinny showing up and catching them together.

If she stopped Jeremy long enough to get inside the

house would the moment be ruined? She'd been intimate with one man, well, actually a boy in high school. And he'd moved away five days later. She had no doubt her brothers had found out and spared his life but they made sure he left town.

Jeremy's hand stroked up her back and she sighed. He kissed her again, taking her breath.

She had to protect him, but his kisses were intoxicating her to the point she couldn't think clearly. The smart thing to do would be to stop this before it got out of hand and walk away.

But if she did, CeCe had a quick flash of worry she'd miss her opportunity with him. He'd keep asking only so many times before a man like Jeremy moved on. In spite of how much she'd tried to deter his interest and talked non-stop about nothing significant, he was still here and kissing the curl out of her hair.

Her heart thumped fast as a machine gun with the trigger pegged. If she wasn't careful Jeremy would walk away with her heart in his hands.

Right now, his hands were driving her crazy to the point she was about to forget her first responsibility—to get them somewhere out of sight.

CeCe murmured, "Maybe we should—"

The rumble of a large automobile engine approaching sobered her quickly. She recognized the sound of that heavy sedan and jerked her head back. "Oh, crud. You have to go!"

"Why?" Jeremy lifted his head but held on to her.

She shoved at him and glanced at the end of the drive-way where Vinny's headlights shined on their mailboxes when he parked along her curb.

"It's my brother. Go home," she hissed at Jeremy.

The engine cut off and a car door opened then closed.

Jeremy's hands fell away and he stepped back.

His withdrawal bruised her soul. She whispered, "I'm sorry."

He started to walk past her and paused, leaning close to her ear. "I'm not." He pecked a kiss on her cheek.

When he sauntered out of the garage she just stood there. The outside lights controlled by motion detectors flicked on. But Jeremy didn't turn toward his house.

Vinny was lumbering along her driveway until he stepped around her truck and paused when the security lights flashed on.

Jeremy walked up to her brother and extended his hand. "Don't think we've met. I'm Jeremy, CeCe's neighbor."

CeCe couldn't breathe. No, no, no. Stay away from Vinny.

Her brother eyed Jeremy then sighed and shook his hand. "Vinny. What are you doing here?"

"Fixing her garage light and taking a look at her cracked statue base."

"If you fixed her light, how come it's dark in there?"

CeCe opened and closed the mudroom door to the garage. Then she flicked on the fluorescent lights, which shined brightly.

"This is great," she cooed, wishing she'd taken some acting lessons in school. "Thanks, Jeremy."

Jeremy turned to her as she emerged from the garage. "I already moved your statue base to my garage. Got a friend who owns a body shop. He'll fix the crack in the fiberglass."

She did not want to owe him any more favors. Not if it meant treating him so poorly every time her brother showed up. "That's nice of you to offer, but—"

"I'm leaving Tuesday morning on a business project that'll take a while, but I'll have the base returned to you before the end of the week." Jeremy nodded at Vinny with, "Nice meeting you," then walked to his house.

Not a swish in that butt.

"He didn't get fresh, did he?" Vinny stared hard at the house next door.

"Him?" CeCe forced a laugh. "He comes up with fresh *ideas,* like the other day when he helped me arrange my new flower bed." Jeremy hadn't even known the flowers were pansies or had a clue about planting them. But he'd smiled the whole time like he enjoyed himself.

Where was Jeremy going Tuesday morning? And for how long? A "business project" sounded like one of those long trips the landlady had mentioned.

"I dunno," Vinny muttered, unconvinced. Just as she'd figured, he started doubting if Jeremy was gay the minute he met him.

"You're the one who told me he'd be a good neighbor," she reminded her brother.

"He don't look too swishy to me."

"How would you know? You've never been around gay men."

"You got that right."

"Well, the ones I know from Jeremy's gym are all buff and very nice. Professionals who treat me with great respect . . ."

"Okay, fine, whatever. I don't need a lecture on being

PC." He finally turned his attention back to her. "I got to leave tomorrow morning early for a meeting in D.C., but I'll be back tomorrow night."

She had to bite her lip to keep from cheering. One night, and a day, without a Doberman chaperone. Taking a breath to calm her excitement, CeCe said, "Sounds important."

"Family business."

She tried not to frown and hoped "family business" wasn't something not quite kosher going on. But she really didn't want to know what.

"You be okay tomorrow?" he asked.

Her heart thudded in her chest. "Sure," she said as calmly as she could to keep from piquing his interest. She'd have tonight with Jeremy. She'd be more than okay.

Vinny sent another sharp look at Jeremy's house but must have decided he posed no immediate threat to her.

She smiled. He had no idea the threat she posed for Jeremy the minute Vinny drove away. But that gave her just one night if Jeremy was going somewhere this week. Crud.

"Let's go get some dinner, sis."

What? CeCe let out a strained breath. Her libido was screaming, but if she passed on dinner without a good excuse he'd get suspicious. "I'd love to. Let me grab some shoes and I'll be right out."

She ran into her house, digging around for a phone book. What if Jeremy's number wasn't listed? Her cell phone rang. When she answered, it was Jeremy.

"Where'd you get my cell phone number?" she asked.

"You wrote the flower order I picked up for you last week on a business card with your number."

She slapped her head. What a dunce. "I'm sorry, but I

can't make dinner. My brother asked me to eat with him to discuss something." Liar, liar, life on fire. Would Jeremy ask her to come over later for a nightcap? That's what always happened in the movies.

The silence that followed squeezed her heart.

"That's fine." Jeremy didn't sound like it was fine. "I'll make sure Blade gets your fiberglass base back by the end of the week. Bye."

"Bye." The phone clicked in her ear.

She couldn't believe she'd blown her chance.

SAM THE MAN shivered in spite of the muggy air still heating Atlanta at midnight. Every move he made hurt. Busted skin under his puffy eyes and cuts crisscrossing his chest still oozed blood. Threatening his balls had forced his hand.

He wasn't a fucking CIA agent for crying out loud.

If he hadn't been double-crossed he'd have delivered the goods without even getting his shoes dirty. The fool that screwed him was dead for sure. Only person Starface had ever kept around for more than a year had been Dorvan and even he was dispensable if the bone crusher screwed up.

Sam didn't give two shits about any of them. He hoped stalling just a little longer would give him one last shot at getting out of this alive. The FBI had to be in this area, searching for him. Had they scoured the area and given up, thinking he was gone for good?

"Where'd you put it?" Dorvan led the hike through Marietta Square where little stirred in the park area of the square just after midnight.

"Told you. In the goddamn statue." Sam squinted

into the dark, peeking everywhere Dorvan's light stroked the terrain. But no hint of the FBI's presence registered with him. *Come on guys, be here.* He'd run out of options and finally agreed to show Starface exactly where he left the memory card before Dorvan got to try a new way to make him talk. Perspiration pebbled across his lip. Sam's new black shirt stuck to his skin where blood had soaked through and dried.

"Which statue?" Starface ground out the question, thick with threat.

Sam drew a painful breath. "Girl with a baby. Had a bunch of leaves around the base. Right over—" What the hell? "It's gone," he whispered, not believing. A knife poked his ribs. He flinched at the new cut.

"Look, I swear it was here," Sam babbled. "Dorvan, tell him. You stopped me right after I dropped it. Tell him."

The thug shined his beam over the area. "You know, I think he's right. There was a little statue right here." He shined the light over the ground. Grass was still depressed from the base. "Yeah, there was another one here."

Starface stepped in front of Sam. "Better not be fucking with me. You stuck it in a statue that isn't here?"

"I swear. I wouldn't bring you out here just to piss you off." Sweat rolled down Sam's face and dripped off his chin. A stream pooled along his bound hands. He swallowed, panting.

Starface appraised Sam for a moment, then nodded. "I believe you. Move out."

Sam's breath wheezed out in relief. He stumbled behind Starface who walked away from the square and down a side street then turned between two buildings.

"I'll get it back, make everything right, okay?" Sam offered. "Whatever it takes to make you happy, you got it."

"Really? Anything?" Starface stopped next to a Dumpster that smelled nasty where bums had pissed beside it. The star-shaped birthmark on his cheek puffed when he smiled.

Sam took that as encouraging. "You got it. Just say the word." He grinned, seeing a light at the end of the tunnel.

"Dorvan. Make me happy."

Sam's mouth opened, but Dorvan's gloved paw clamped over his lips. A sharp pain seared his chest where Dorvan shoved the blade deep. Double pain when the blade jerked out. Sam crumpled, his head bouncing against the gravel and dirt, throat gurgling. He tried to breathe, scream. Nothing.

Starface snapped his fingers at Dorvan. "Find that statue. Get my memory card. We got forty-eight hours to deliver it."

Sam stared at the empty alley.

The memory card with damning photos and a video . . . now someone else's problem.

Tears ran from his eyes. His heartbeat slowed. Each harsh breath rattled in his chest. Starface watched him, clearly waiting to make sure dead men didn't talk.

Screw all these bastards. Sam clenched against a racking pain and forced a smile at the asshole just to worry him.

It worked.

Starface's confident smile lost shape.

Blood poured from Sam's mouth. He was drowning and couldn't say another word if it would save his life. He closed his eyes, prepared to wait for Starface at the gates of hell.

Good fucking luck to whoever had that memory card now.

JEREMY TAPPED HIS fingers on his chest. Sleeping would be nice, maybe even possible if he could get that kiss with CeCe off his mind.

Was she sleeping? What was she wearing? Anything?

He covered his eyes with his hand, listening to the ceiling fan swoosh around in a steady rhythm. She'd changed her mind the minute her brother showed up. That said a lot, almost as much as the fact she'd been clearly unhappy when he introduced himself to her brother.

Then the excuse for bailing out of dinner.

He'd been brushed off before. It just hadn't cut quite so deeply the other times.

His cell phone vibrated against the nightstand surface. He stretched across the bed, noted the time on his alarm clock was after midnight, and answered the phone. "Sunn."

"Jeremy? Did I wake you?"

He knew that sweet voice, but CeCe sounded distressed. "No. What's up?"

"I heard a noise in the backyard and . . . I'm afraid."

"I'll be right there." He shoved the phone between his shoulder and ear on the way up and yanked on his jeans lying across the foot of the bed. "Don't open the door until you know it's me." He hung up and zipped his jeans then grabbed his Walther P99 from the nightstand, heading for the sliding door to his backyard.

Cool air trailed behind him when he stepped into the humidity so thick he could almost carry it. He made a quick scan around his backyard that was still as a crypt. He leaped over the fence separating their yards and walked around until he felt certain nothing alive was nearby.

Before reaching her patio door, he shoved his weapon between the waistband of his jeans and his back then tapped.

The curtain inside moved, then the door slid open.

He stepped into the dark kitchen and heard her back up a couple steps. He could just make out her pastel robe—covered shape from a nightlight glowing in the hallway behind where she stood. "Are you okay?"

"Not really."

Jeremy moved forward then paused. "No one is out there."

"I'm still scared," she whispered. "Don't leave me alone."

The sound of her voice was enough to jack up his pulse, but he turned rock hard at the plea to stay with her. Good thing it was dark in here or she'd see how badly he wanted to take her up on that invitation.

He was worse than a dog.

She wanted comfort and he wanted her.

"Jeremy?" Her voice lowered a notch, husky. Just keep destroying his restraint with every word.

"Yes?"

"Would you hold me . . . for a while?" She took a step closer.

How was he going to do that and not touch every inch of her? His groin throbbed, heavy with desire.

But his conscience kept interfering. "How about if I promise to keep an eye on your house tonight?" *In between cold showers.*

"I'd really rather you stay *here* . . . tonight."

He could smell her fresh shower and sweet feminine scent. His senses sharpened in the dark, every nerve ending begging to feel her. The fine hairs along his neck lifted, warning him of a threat far more dangerous than a felon with a weapon.

If he held her close right now, she'd know exactly what he had in mind. Back off while he still could.

"Not a good idea," he warned on a tired sigh.

"*What* isn't a good idea?" She stepped close enough that their toes should be touching. His eyes had adjusted to see her better. She wore a long silky robe, something pink that shimmered when she moved. Wavy hair fell loose around her shoulders. The tiny heart-shaped face turned up to his with naked longing.

He wasn't even going to address her last question. "Go to bed, CeCe, before I do something we'll both regret. If you think I can stay here tonight and keep my hands off you, I'm telling you right now I'm not that damn noble."

"Fair enough." She lifted her hands to the front of her robe and let the sheer material slide off her shoulders to pool at her feet. "I'm not that innocent."

He should be dead, because this was either heaven or hell, depending on what happened next.

Three

CeCe held her breath. *Please don't leave*. A dinner date would have been so much easier than this, but that kiss in the garage convinced her to take a gamble with Jeremy when Vinny destroyed her evening.

She believed Jeremy would understand once she explained her situation to him. Just not right this minute. Maybe once they had a chance to know each other she could tell him a little about her life. She hated lies and didn't want to sleep with a man she couldn't tell the truth to.

But he wasn't saying a word.

She'd die of mortification if he turned her down right now. She'd never tried to seduce a man and if she didn't get her hands on Jeremy tonight her window of opportunity would slam shut as soon as Vinny returned tomorrow night.

And she'd lose her nerve.

If standing here almost naked in a short pink camisole top and lacy underwear wasn't vulnerable feeling enough, she'd just exposed herself emotionally.

Jeremy turned away from her and headed for the sliding glass door.

Her heart squeezed with disappointment.

But the door whipped to the left, closing. The lock clicked shut.

Then he returned to her. And stood very still, inches away, but so close he should be able to hear her heart pounding with hope.

"Jeremy, I—"

His hands cupped her face, silencing her next words when warm lips descended on hers. What an amazing mouth.

She was going to fold faster than a poker player with a bad hand if this was the prelude to what was to come. CeCe clutched Jeremy's waist then slid her hands up the warm skin covering taut muscles across his back. She'd almost fainted at the sight of all that sculpted body on display when he rushed in wearing only jeans.

Capable hands moved down her shoulders and behind her back, pressing her closer. His tongue brushed past her lips, sparring sweetly with hers.

She shivered at his touch, his strength and gentleness.

He was being damn careful with her. Did that mean he wouldn't go any further? She had one night if he was leaving Tuesday and wanted all of him tonight.

Then she prayed he wouldn't forget her while he was gone.

She hoped she wasn't making a wrong move, but she shifted her hands between them and climbed her fingers up his chest where his muscles quivered from her touch. That encouraged her. She grasped his shoulders and pulled herself up against him until she felt the solid ridge in his jeans.

He was definitely up for more than kissing.

She made one sensual rub, then another.

A growl vibrated from Jeremy. Heady excitement rushed through her at the prospect he wanted her as much as she wanted him. She smiled and ground her hips in what she hoped he'd think was a seductive way.

Jeremy reached down and scooped her up until her legs hooked around his waist, then his kiss deepened, demanding all her attention. He was so beautiful. Muscles rippled beneath her fingers with every move. He held her bottom with one hand and her head with another, his mouth refusing to give an inch, overwhelming her with his kisses.

She tightened her legs, sliding intimately against him.

Jeremy lifted his mouth from hers. "You better have a condom somewhere in this house or we're walking to mine just like this."

"B...B..." She couldn't think.

"Bedroom?"

"Yes."

He swung her around, moving with the stealth of a large jungle cat in the dark. His mouth found hers again, turning her insides crazy hot. When he entered the bedroom she blushed at the candles burning. Would he think it was silly or too romantic?

He slowly lowered her to the bed and brushed his knuckles across her cheek. "You're even more gorgeous in candlelight."

She sighed or maybe the room did.

"I want to see all of you," she whispered, tentatively.

Jeremy stood up, reached behind him, and laid a Walther P99 on the nightstand. She shivered at the smooth way he handled the weapon. Total confidence.

"I'll put this out of sight if it bothers you," he said, pointing at the gun.

She shook her head. "I grew up with guns in the house." In fact, Jeremy would be surprised to know how quickly she could break down and reassemble the one on the nightstand.

But right now she was more interested in the barrel inside his pants. "The only thing bothering me is you so far away."

He smiled and unzipped his jeans. Candlelight glowed across his golden skin, highlighting muscles carved to perfection. Not an overdone bodybuilder, but a modern-day Adonis with a powerful build softened only by honey-blond hair brushing his forehead.

When he peeled out of the jeans she lost her breath.

He'd dressed commando. Impressive.

Jeremy dropped down over the top of her, supporting his weight with his forearms.

She inched back at the untamed look in his eyes.

"Should have run when you could have," he teased. He moved farther on the bed, still towering over her, but paused as if checking to see if she'd changed her mind.

CeCe shook her head slowly and smiled. "I'm all yours for the taking."

A feral gaze lashed through those simmering green eyes.

He slipped an arm under her back and lifted her up, moving her higher on the pillow, then pushed her hands above her head to grasp the vertical bars in the brass head-board. "Don't let go."

Don't let go? She didn't dare ask why for fear of him stopping.

He ran his hand down her throat, over her shoulders, across the silky top barely covering her breasts in this position. His fingers lingered, slipping beneath the material to trace a path around one nipple.

She tensed, waiting, but he didn't touch the sensitive bud.

His finger drew circles slowly down to her navel, then paused. He lifted the edge of her camisole and shifted the thin material back and forth across her taut nipples. A fiery sizzle shot straight through her, erupting in a frenzy of wet heat that pooled between her legs.

She clenched, needing him to touch her everywhere.

The silk drifted back in place when he released it.

Her heart raced, anticipation taking her breath.

His fingers lightly raked the exposed skin around her navel then across the front of her lace underwear. His lips followed behind his fingers, kissing and nipping her skin.

He touched the inside of her thigh and slipped a finger under the edge of her panties.

She tensed, waiting for him to touch her most intimate spot. When he pulled the lace aside, he lowered his head and kissed her then ran his tongue across the fragile skin.

She gripped the bars and arched, crying out at the wave of pleasure that seared through her. He stopped before the sensation crested and kissed his way back to her breasts.

"I want to touch you," she panted.

"Not yet, sweetheart." His lips grazed her abdomen,

kissing lightly and murmured, "I love the feel of your skin. So soft."

He lifted her silky top, slowly, letting the material feather the tips of her breasts again, then slid it over her head. Tears stung her eyes at the exquisite pain.

Then his mouth covered one breast.

She'd expected relief, not blissful torture with a razor edge. His tongue toyed with one nipple, slowly driving her mad. A hand covered the other breast, then his thumb scraped gently across the beaded tip.

She arched, shaking with need for more, but he kept her dangling on that painful edge.

Jeremy moved slowly up to her mouth and the kiss was fierce this time, consuming and possessive. His thick erection rubbed against her stomach. She lifted up, pressing against him until he hissed and lifted away. She opened her eyes to see the muscles in his neck corded, tense from the strain of holding back, taking this slow.

She'd waited years for this chance and didn't want slow and easy. She scrambled to think of some way to shake him up so he'd stop being so careful. "I'm . . . wet for you."

His whole body shuddered. "You're killing me," he muttered. He lowered his head and suckled her breast, then moved his fingers inside her panties until he pushed one inside her. She inhaled a sharp breath and moaned on the release.

He drew the wet finger out and caressed her folds, teasing the one spot where her body begged for relief. He'd barely touched her when she exploded into a thousand sparks, her mind and body screaming with release.

And he wouldn't let her stop until she collapsed.

"Good God, woman."

"What?" she panted.

"I almost came just watching you."

She basked in the thrill of his words since that's all her boneless body had the energy to do.

He stretched out beside her and ran his fingers over her face. She kissed his palm. He turned her toward him and kissed her, his lips sweet now, gentle.

There he went being careful with her again.

"That's not it, is it?" she asked.

His hand stilled.

She reached down and grasped the smooth skin stretched tight over his penis. He growled and clenched at the touch. Slowly, she stroked her hand down, then upward to the damp tip.

Jeremy let out a harsh sound. "Where's that condom?"

She sat up and shoved him back on the bed playfully. Her heart thumped in a wild rhythm. To cover her nervousness, she just smiled and hoped she could do this correctly. Reaching over, she opened the nightstand drawer with shaking hands and dug around until her fingers touched foil. She moved back to Jeremy and straddled him.

Then fought with the foil packet.

She was going to embarrass herself if she couldn't at least open the damn condom. Large hands covered hers. She met Jeremy's gaze, terrified she'd see him laughing. He didn't say a word or smile, just opened the package, tossed it aside, and handed her the condom.

The last time she did this with a boy—and he *was* a boy—who wasn't quite so well endowed.

CeCe drew a breath, then took her time sheathing Jeremy, careful not to move too fast and scratch him with her nails. He was so silent and rigid by the time she finished, CeCe looked up to see if he was okay.

A line of perspiration beaded his forehead.

"Is something wrong?" she asked.

"No." His voice sounded raw. "I don't think putting on a condom has ever felt so erotic."

That had to be the nicest thing a man had ever said to her. She smiled with a sassy toss of her head.

Jeremy hid his surprise over her flash of boldness. She'd shocked the hell out of him when he stepped into her kitchen and found her waiting for him like a birthday gift wrapped in silk. CeCe Caprice had another side of her he'd never have expected. He'd guessed she hadn't done this much and watching her fumble with the condom removed any doubt. He would bet she hadn't been intimate with a man more than once or twice.

What she lacked in experience she made up for with unbridled enthusiasm. But what had triggered this for tonight?

Why had she blown him off and now . . .

She lifted herself up over his cock.

He lost all concern about why and grasped her hips, easing her down and sliding himself inside her. He gritted his teeth at the ragged pleasure of being surrounded by her tight heat.

Her eyes widened with a range of emotions, from surprise to shock to pleasure, with each inch he lowered her down his shaft until she dropped her head back, tightened, and moaned.

If she kept that up, he'd be looking like the one with little experience. He'd never met a woman who exploded so quickly. Just a touch.

She leaned forward again, her hands on his chest and a wicked gleam in her eyes. Without a word, she lifted up then down. He gripped her hips and met her stroke for stroke, every muscle in his body holding back, fighting to make this last.

CeCe quickened the pace and gripped his chest. He moved a hand until he could tease her with a finger. She arched sharply, tensed, and came again.

The woman was incredible.

He stroked deep inside her, coming right behind her. The force of his orgasm lashed through him sharp as heat lightning. His body clenched with a last powerful thrust. Rough breaths shuddered from him. The blinding surge of energy slowly abated.

That had been pretty freaking amazing. Not what he'd imagined at all and he had a healthy imagination.

She fell forward in a heap on his chest. Chuckling, he wrapped her in his arms, unable to do more until he got his breath back. CeCe was one incredible woman.

She'd been nervous as a cat in a room full of rocking chairs when he'd walked into her kitchen, trying to seduce him when it was obvious she had little experience at inviting men into her bedroom. Maybe something important had come up with her brother that she'd felt took priority over a casual dinner.

Jeremy could understand that, even though he had no family. Never had. But why had she called him over here late tonight? Because he said he was leaving in two days?

They still could have gone to dinner tomorrow. Unless she had plans.

In spite of this late-night gift, CeCe was no quick roll in the sheets.

She was a nice girl and sweet . . . and hot as hell.

Why question his good fortune?

Because he couldn't suppress a chiding voice that said this was all he'd ever be to any woman.

The contented sigh that slipped from her warmed his heart. He reached over and pulled the spread across her when she shivered. He'd rushed over here ready to take on any threat only to find she was the real danger.

She fit in his arms. The idea of keeping her there felt right. What was he going to do after this when he'd be gone in less than two days now?

He rolled her to the side and wrapped his leg over her, tucking her close. Unwilling to let her go now that he had her.

In the past, he'd spent a few hours in bed with a woman then got antsy, ready to leave. Not caring who his bed partner saw next. He'd had plenty of those encounters, but in fairness to both players all those women had been just as happy to treat him like another throwaway memory.

Walking away from CeCe wouldn't be so easy and he sure as hell didn't want to think about another man touching her.

CeCe was the kind of woman who would want more from a relationship.

He rubbed a hand along her back. The thought of having her to come home to felt . . . nice. He wasn't ready to get overly serious, but dating the same woman more than twice had its merits. If CeCe was willing to make love with him didn't that mean she'd want more too?

That she'd be here waiting for him when he returned from his next mission?

On the other hand, why hadn't she gone out with him before this? That question hadn't entered his mind when she was standing half naked in the kitchen trimmed in pink.

Maybe all she did want from him was sex.

He stopped rubbing her back, considering that possibility and dismissed it just as quickly. In spite of her temptress routine tonight, CeCe wasn't that kind of woman. She clearly didn't want her brother to know about this, but that wasn't so hard to understand when Jeremy considered her lack of experience with men.

CeCe was sincere. She wouldn't bring him into her bedroom tonight just to send him packing in the morning.

Four

If CeCe bent over and stretched in front of him one more time, Jeremy couldn't be held accountable for his actions.

He yanked the towel from around his neck and wiped perspiration off his forehead that had nothing to do with a vigorous workout he'd just finished on a circuit in his gym.

Nope, it was the erotic display going on across the room where CeCe faced a wall of mirrors.

His gaze strayed to where she'd found a corner to do her yoga exercises, but *that* move didn't look like yoga. She kneeled on the mat facing the mirror and raised her arms above her head then leaned back, way back, arching. Her breasts stretched the pale blue jog bra tight.

Then she arched even farther and twisted.

Reminding him of how she'd looked once last night.

The worn denim jeans he was wearing had always been his favorite because they were so comfortable. But it was feeling uncomfortable and crowded as hell beneath the zipper.

Jeremy gritted his teeth and turned around to the drink cooler he'd been working on before his control snapped and he stormed across the gym to strip her naked. He'd run errands all day so he could come in late to avoid suffering through the yoga routine she did every afternoon without fail.

Like either of them needed a workout today.

He'd burned four condoms with her last night. Make that very early this morning.

Then she'd told him he had to leave before daylight.

Hadn't taken a rocket scientist to figure out why. So no one saw him. CeCe rarely left her house before late morning.

He sighed and hung his head. He should be used to that by now—having an attractive woman fawn all over him, share an intimate night, then shuffle him out the door before daylight like a dirty secret.

Jeremy lifted a screwdriver and started removing a metal panel on the cooler. He should be thankful CeCe wanted to keep things casual between them, but he'd been angry since stalking home this morning and his mood hadn't improved all day.

Maintaining the playboy image at thirty was getting old.

He'd thought CeCe was different, but she'd made clear what she wanted from him last night and this morning.

Why should he be surprised? She probably wanted an everyday Joe with a regular job who kept regular hours, which Jeremy had never done.

He'd never be a nine-to-fiver who could be expected to come home every night. Not when he left town on short notice to work undercover, and to make matters worse he couldn't tell her what he did for the BAD Agency or when he'd be back. Impossible situation. Which was why he should accept whatever came his way and not complain.

"Um, Jeremy, are you . . . "

He snapped around at the softly spoken words and found CeCe close to him. He took in the whole gym with a sweeping glance, checking to see if anyone was paying attention to where they stood. He avoided getting caught alone anywhere in the gym with a woman for so many reasons, the main one being that it sent the wrong message to the string of females on the hunt that paraded through this environment daily.

He dropped his screwdriver back into his toolbox and wiped his hands on the shop rag hooked to his belt.

"Am I what?" He crossed his arms and stood there, waiting to see where this was going.

"Busy tonight?" she said quietly.

"Maybe."

She folded her arms and looked away.

Jeremy hadn't meant for his words to come out with a bite, but he was starting to figure out what last night was all about and didn't like his assessment. CeCe had been jumpy when her brother showed up yesterday. Her brother had been flying out this morning and was probably the reason she'd kept her distance from Jeremy until now.

CeCe told him during refreshments on her patio that she had three overprotective older brothers. He'd caught her point that someone she dated had to pass their approval.

Her conclusion based on being shuffled off this morning? She thought he wouldn't measure up.

"Why do you want to know if I'm busy?" he pressed.

CeCe lifted her head, hope shining bright in her eyes. "I thought I'd cook dinner . . . if you'd like to come over . . . tonight." She'd pulled on a pair of black warm-up pants and a baggy gray sweatshirt that hung off one smooth shoulder. She fidgeted with the oversized sleeve. The wavy ponytail pulled high on her head flopped to one side.

She'd refused to join him for lunch today when he'd called her earlier, but meeting after dark in her house was acceptable, huh?

He had no self-control around her. If dinner went anything like what happened last night she'd be the main course.

Dessert would be her in that twisted yoga position. In the middle of the bed or on the sofa or kitchen table.

But where would that leave him tomorrow morning? Skulking away in the dark again?

When he didn't answer right away, she glanced around and fiddled with the cuff of her sleeve then lowered her voice. "I know you're leaving town, but I thought we could have some fun . . . while you were here."

Well, that cleared up any confusion he had over where he stood with her. Just his luck the minute he convinced himself he was through playing loose with women that he'd meet one who wanted no strings. At least, not from him.

He'd never stepped completely over the line from casual to caring, but he'd scuffed it somewhere with CeCe, which meant getting dumped later on was going to feel like shit.

So why make being cut loose later any worse by spending more time together?

"I don't think so," he told her.

"Why not? I haven't cooked a full meal since moving in and I'm not a half bad cook," she joked, but her eyes were tinged with worry.

Jeremy paused as one of the personal trainers walked past chatting on a cell phone. Then he speared CeCe with a no-bullshit gaze. "Your brother coming by tonight?"

"No, he couldn't make it back until tomorrow," she said excitedly then stopped talking and cocked her head to one side. She frowned as if she didn't understand why they were talking about her brother.

"I see." Jeremy hesitated to say more with so many people walking around behind CeCe to access the equipment in this area.

Her mouth gaped open. "Is something wrong? I mean, I thought last night was, like . . . "

The vulnerable look in her eyes and her pleading tone stabbed him to the core.

". . . really nice," he finished for her. That was a lie.

Last night had been spectacular, had sucked him right in to thinking how much he'd like to wake up next to her every day.

She raked a hand over her hair, knocking the ponytail further askew, and hissed a sigh. "Then I don't understand why you won't have dinner with me tonight."

Now she was hurt.

Jeremy knew better than to change his mind about seeing her again, alone, but this was not the place to pursue their discussion. He'd handle it tonight.

"In that case, I accept," he finally conceded. "No reason we can't have dinner . . . as friends." No reason other than the idea of only being friends and not touching CeCe grated on him. After tonight they would just be neighbors. Not even that since he planned to put in for BAD to move his residence while he was gone. He checked his watch. "I won't get out of here until after eight."

"Friends, right," she muttered. Her smile faltered a little then she offered a conciliatory smile. "Come over whenever you get in. Late is fine." She turned to walk away.

Jeremy remembered something he had for her. "CeCe?"

"Yes?" She spun around, her gaze lit with interest that stroked a warm place inside him.

He cursed silently over how deep she had burrowed under his skin. In three weeks, she'd come to matter to him in spite of having spent most of that time in a platonic mode.

Last night had drawn him under her spell so far he would not walk away unscathed.

"Got a copy of today's paper for you." Jeremy reached over to where the newspaper lay next to his toolbox and lifted it. "Your picture is front page in the living section."

Her eyes rounded, then she frowned. "You're kidding."

What was wrong? "No. It's a nice shot of you. Nice write-up." He lifted the folded papers and handed her the section he'd pulled out.

She took the paper. Her forehead creased in a deeper frown. She finally mumbled her thanks and hurried off.

What the hell was that all about?

Jeremy rubbed his forehead. Women. The man who figured them out would rule the world. All *he* had to do was figure out one female and what it would take to get her *out* of his system.

———————

STARFACE PAUSED IN wiping the oil from the barrel of his Smith & Wesson .357 Magnum and used his little finger to press the button on his Bluetooth headset. "You find the woman in the newspaper?"

"No problem," Dorvan answered, then chuckled. "Didn't have to threaten the first chump. Receptionist at Double Take took one look at my phony detective badge and coughed up everything I needed. She showed me a picture of the statue from Sunday. That's our girl."

"Sweet." Starface snapped the gun parts together. "Go get that memory card and meet me back here." He'd paid a man to secretly film and videotape a meeting between an ambitious Chicago family and a Russian organization planning to partner up then wipe out all the midsize crime family competition in North America. That memory card was worth a small fortune to Ziggy Gambino. The Chicago family had tricked Ziggy's people into a trap then tipped the feds to a major drug operation that cost the backbone of his organization. Ziggy had offered Starface a premium contract for evidence that would take down the Chicago leader. A sweet deal all around since Starface had been burned in the same sting.

Everything had fallen into place until Sam the Man interfered.

Starface had promised Ziggy delivery this week and Ziggy had no patience for hiccups.

Sam the Man had put his nuts in a vice by snatching the photo card. Sam paid the price for screwing with the wrong bastard.

Starface wouldn't be so kind to the next person who interfered.

CLUTCHING TWO ARMLOADS of groceries, CeCe stormed from her car into the house that had been the perfect place to live until Jeremy Sunn started driving her crazy.

What was all that at the gym about her brother?

Vinny called earlier to let her know he'd hit a snag and wouldn't get in until tomorrow morning. Which left her the whole evening with Jeremy again.

Great news. Right?

So why wasn't Jeremy excited about another night together? She'd told him how her brothers were an overprotective bunch. Didn't he realize she was trying to make it easy for them to spend some time alone?

Or did he think that she hadn't enjoyed the evening?

Or had he not enjoyed last night?

Juggling bags all the way to the kitchen, she thought back on how Jeremy had acted when she'd asked him to leave before daylight this morning. He'd been a little cranky, but she'd attributed that to his not being a morning person. He seemed to accept her explanation that her brother might stop by on the way to the airport and how it might be uncomfortable for everyone.

Mainly her.

Jeremy had dressed, kissed her, and left quietly.

So what was bugging him? Why had he withdrawn? Did he think she would make assumptions based on last night? She'd made a point at the gym of letting him know she wasn't trying to push him to the altar after sleeping together.

To be honest, she'd never push any man to the altar, but last night with Jeremy produced a revelation.

She wanted a man like him in her life.

No, she wanted Jeremy in her life.

And with a little patience from him she could be creative enough to make this work, but he'd have to agree to keep their relationship quiet for a while. At least until she could get settled here and figure out how to introduce him to her family.

She'd planned to explain her situation over dinner tonight, but now she was reconsidering after Jeremy's about-face in the gym. Guys had the strangest way of thinking. What had happened since this morning for him now to want to be only *friends* all of a sudden?

Was he backpedaling, worried she was going to cling?

CeCe shook her head and yawned. With Vinny out of the way, she had twelve hours to show Jeremy that he was more than a neighbor to her, but she'd have to rethink her original plan of laying it on the line with him. If she approached tonight wrong, Jeremy might back away big time at the first sign of anything that sounded too serious.

Opening cabinets, she started shoving cans onto shelves, getting more ticked off by the minute.

At everyone, including herself.

Her brothers meant well and had been her rocks of support since her mother died when she was in high school, but the men in her family expressed that love by smothering her.

Her fault for letting them.

CeCe finished shuffling everything into place then raced into the bathroom to shower, shave her legs again, and groom any other wild hair on her body. She attempted to tame her wavy locks as they dried and finally gave up.

Jeremy hadn't seemed to notice her uncivilized morning hair.

But then Jeremy hadn't even noticed the new outfit she'd picked up today just to do her stretches at the gym. He'd been more interested in that damn cooler.

When the familiar sound of a vehicle next door reached her, CeCe ran over to peek out between the slats of her blinds. Night had taken over the city. Jeremy drove his sport utility into his garage, then the lights went dark. She felt like she was sixteen again, watching for the cute guy in the neighborhood to walk by her yard.

But back in high school she'd been warned against acting on a primal urge to go out and flirt with a boy.

Tonight she intended to act on a primal urge that went way beyond flirting with Jeremy. She didn't have experience in holding the attention of a man like him, but she had one chance to pull out all the stops and find out if she could.

Spinning around, she strode over to her antique bureau that had one drawer filled with fabulous lingerie she'd been buying for a night like tonight. CeCe glanced at the pink robe lying across her bed.

That had *friends* written all over it.

Digging through the drawer, she shook her head at the pastel colors and paused when her fingers touched lacy red and black selections she'd purchased from an online store. Lifting two sinfully sexy pieces into view, she chewed on her lip.

If Jeremy saw her in this and still wanted to be just friends she had no chance of keeping him.

JEREMY SHOWERED, THEN pulled on a pair of jeans and shoved the wallet and cash he'd tossed on the bathroom vanity into his pockets. He'd finger combed his damp hair back off his face and strolled into the bedroom when a light blinked twice over the doorframe to the bathroom. Someone had tripped the silent alarm for his backyard, which meant he'd jumped the chain-link fence since his gate was locked.

It could be an animal but he doubted it since there was nothing to draw a dog or cat to his yard. In his line of work he took any intruder seriously.

Yanking on a shirt, he palmed his weapon off the night-stand. He opened a drawer where he found a pair of night-vision binoculars and moved silently through the dark house.

Years of living on the edge had taught him to leave the lights off anytime he didn't absolutely need them on.

He checked his security panel hidden in a kitchen cabinet, which showed additional sensors being tripped. Someone was moving through his backyard. Jeremy shuffled over and barely lifted the curtain aside where he could scan the pitch-black area filled with just two trees and patio furniture.

A stocky figure that might top out near six feet and moved through the shadows in a decidedly male way crossed his yard and climbed the fence into CeCe's yard.

Lucky for this guy neither he nor CeCe had dogs.

But the intruder's luck ran out at that point.

Jeremy checked for any additional threats before easing out the sliding glass door that opened to his patio. He vaulted over the fence into CeCe's yard and crouched all the way to where he found the sliding glass door open just enough to let a person pass through.

She'd probably left it unlocked for him.

He entered silently and paused in the kitchen. A deep voice rumbled low in the living room.

Much as he wanted to race in there and slam a head, Jeremy couldn't make a mistake that would put CeCe in further danger.

A rough male voice said, "You're Cecelia Caprice. Pretended to be a statue at the festival this weekend, right?"

"Y-yes, but I don't understand," CeCe answered as Jeremy crept forward. "What do you want from me?" Her voice went up an octave every couple words. She was closing in on hysteria.

Jeremy covered the last fifteen feet to the short hallway leading to the living room and paused again, peeking around the corner.

The bulked-up intruder held a weapon to CeCe's head. "Calm down. If you scream, I swear I'll blow your brains out."

Rage sheared through Jeremy like a honed razor. He lifted his weapon and stepped into the room.

Five

The intruder stood to the side of CeCe, who sat shivering on the couch. Wearing a red silk kimono might not be the warmest clothing, but she was shaking from terror of having a weapon shoved against her head.

If this was a mission for BAD, Jeremy would take the clear shot he had. There were plenty of reasons not to, but the only one that mattered was the danger of the weapon at CeCe's head discharging.

Jeremy pulled a penny from his pants pocket and tossed it down the hallway where the coin bounced against a baseboard.

"What was that?" the intruder said, eyes turning toward the sound.

"I don't know," CeCe whispered. "I live alone."

Indecision played through the perp's hardened face until he backed a step away from CeCe, pulling his weapon off her head.

Just what Jeremy had hoped for. He let the guy take a second step toward the hallway that brought him closer to Jeremy, who rushed him.

The perp's eyes flashed surprise. He hesitated in raising his gun hand just a second, long enough for Jeremy to reach him in time to knock the weapon away.

But that left Jeremy open for the left hook that felt like a sledgehammer when it clipped his jaw. He took the hit then came back with a right cross of his own, using his gun to slam the guy in his temple.

The intruder fell back against her front door and dropped down between the door and the end of her couch.

"Jeremy." CeCe had barely said his name as if she couldn't breathe for hyperventilating.

"Are you okay?" He gave her a quick glance while he bent to pick up the intruder's Glock and shoved it inside the waistband of his jeans. She wasn't screaming and her eyes hadn't glazed over with shock yet in spite of being terrified.

CeCe nodded from where she sat frozen. Her eyes zeroed in on the weapon in Jeremy's hand and widened. If her face lost any more color he worried she might pass out.

Taking a look to ensure the guy was still out cold, Jeremy stepped over to where CeCe sat frozen in place on her sofa, hands gripping the cushion on each side of her legs.

He leaned down and put his palm against her face. "Are you okay?"

She nodded, fighting to hold back tears.

He kissed her, just enough to give her some comfort. When Jeremy lifted his head he was heartened to see her shock fading. Giving her a task would take her mind off the fear she'd just endured. "Have you got duct tape?"

She blinked, clearing her gaze. "Yes."

"Walk around the far end of the coffee table and go get it."

The minute she exited the room Jeremy went back to the guy, whose fingers were moving. He'd come to in a minute. The intruder packed an easy two hundred and twenty-five pounds of corded muscle into black pants and a tight-fitting T-shirt. Thick ruddy brown–colored hair an inch long covered his blockhead and deep lines carved into his ugly mug. A scar made up of X's ran from elbow to wrist on his left arm. Prison cuts?

The guy shook his head and opened eyes that narrowed with hate.

In that instant, Jeremy saw something familiar in his face, but he couldn't place him. "Who are you?"

"Someone you shouldn't be pissing off," the thug answered.

"Hard not to do when that's my specialty."

The guy's arrogant gaze flattened. "You're fucking with the wrong person."

"I could say the same thing." Jeremy listened for CeCe who was digging through drawers in the kitchen, followed by slamming a drawer and cursing. His gaze stayed on this guy, who was too calm for being caught breaking and entering. "How do you know CeCe?"

Dull gray eyes stared then he shrugged. "Picture was in the paper."

"What do you want with her?"

"What do you think?" The perp grinned.

Jeremy drew on all his discipline not to shove that smile down to the guy's boots.

"Wait a minute," the intruder whispered. His eyebrows

lowered over soulless eyes that pondered on something. "I know you."

Shit. He hated to be right some days. "No you don't."

When CeCe slammed a drawer this time it was followed by her footsteps rushing back to the living room.

The guy's face shifted from trying to place Jeremy to problem solved. "I *do* know you."

Jeremy would have liked another minute to find out how this guy knew him, but he didn't want that conversation in front of CeCe or the police. Just before she entered the living room, Jeremy slammed his weapon against the perp's head hard enough to knock him out for a long while.

"What happened?" CeCe hurried over to him.

"He lunged at me. When I get him rolled over, tape his hands," Jeremy instructed her.

When he had the perp on his face and hands behind his back, Jeremy nodded. CeCe tore off a strip of tape she slipped under the man's wrists and wrapped the length around and around with shaking hands.

"Tape his ankles too." Jeremy waited until she finished to send her to the kitchen. "Call the police and tell them someone broke into your home, but that he's contained."

She hesitated for a second, then rushed away and called. After turning the guy around and dragging him over to prop against the couch so they could get the front door open, Jeremy stepped into the kitchen.

CeCe hung up her wall phone. "They're on the way."

Jeremy walked over to her but kept his body where he could watch the intruder for movement. "Have any idea what he wants?"

She shook her head. "He asked me if I was a statue at the park Sunday."

That damn photo in the newspaper. "Someone in your office must have given out your address."

"They're not supposed to and why would he go to that trouble? I mean, I don't drive a fancy car or live in an expensive home and—" She paused in the middle of arguing. Her thought process ended with the realization of why a stalker would track down her home address. What color she'd regained flushed from her face again. "Do you think he came here to . . . attack me."

"I don't know." The guy didn't hit Jeremy as a stalker or petty thief. He was too professional feeling.

Jeremy ignored the disconcerting sensation that something was odd here and pulled CeCe into his arms before her knees folded. "It's okay. He's going to jail as soon as the police get here."

She hooked her arms around his neck and held on as if he was her only lifeline.

Jeremy hugged her and rubbed her back to calm her, but he had to do something with his weapon before the police arrived. He eased her over to sit at the kitchen table then crossed to the cabinets where he slipped his weapon onto a high shelf inside. During missions for BAD, he carried every conceivable weapon known to man, but when in civilian mode Jeremy was subject to the laws of this country that stated a prior convicted felon could not carry a weapon. Since BAD technically did not exist, he couldn't claim his felonies were part of his job and committed while in the service of his country.

He turned back to CeCe to find her gazing intently

between him and the cabinet. "What are you doing?"

Jeremy considered what he could tell her on the way back to where she sat. He dropped down in front of her. "The gun belongs to a friend of mine who asked me to keep it for him while he was out of the country. I grabbed it when I saw the guy climb into your yard. I don't have a permit to carry. No point in complicating things."

She was still too pale and the skin on her arm beneath his fingers had chilled. Part of the problem was the skimpy outfit she had on.

"Sit tight." He got a lap blanket out of the living room, checked their prisoner, who hadn't made a sound, and came back to the kitchen. Wrapping the soft blanket around her shoulders, he leaned down and kissed her forehead.

"I'll get you some water." On the way to the sink, Jeremy glanced at the perp again. The more he studied her unwanted visitor, the more he thought he knew him. Not an encouraging sign considering what Jeremy did for BAD.

He'd like to go through the intruder's pockets to look for anything that would explain why he had broken into CeCe's house, but CeCe might wonder why he'd do that.

Plus, if this guy was some sort of professional he wouldn't be carrying identification.

Jeremy had just handed the water to CeCe when flashing lights pierced the sheer drapes covering her living room windows. Uniformed officers showed up at the front door by the time Jeremy reached it to let them in. He handed the Glock to the police, gave both officers a quick rundown of what happened, and told them he had defense training and got the jump on the guy.

The police replaced the duct tape with handcuffs and carried their perp out to the cruiser.

This guy's lack of ability to speak saved Jeremy from finding out if CeCe would have backed up his lie about having a weapon. He hated to put her in that position, but the only other option would have been to explain why he had a criminal record.

Couldn't do that unless he wanted BAD to come looking for his head.

The police took CeCe's statement. She hesitated once when they mentioned her having to testify in court. That was easy to understand. She was afraid to see the thug again, but Jeremy would pull strings to be with her when that day came.

An hour later, Jeremy closed the door after the last officer left. The intruder was on his way to the Marietta City lockup and bail wouldn't be set before tomorrow morning.

Jeremy walked to the kitchen where CeCe sat at the table, silent as a trapped mouse.

He didn't think the company she contracted from would just willingly hand over her address to anyone, but he couldn't find out more until tomorrow when Double Take was open. Right now, CeCe needed comfort more than questions.

Jeremy asked, "Do you want to call your brother?"

"No." She glanced up, eyes widening with fear, then must have realized how that sounded—like she was afraid of her brother. "He would pack me up and have me moved before daylight."

Jeremy couldn't fault her brother for that since the idea of bundling her off somewhere safe had crossed his mind more than once tonight.

"I-I don't want to stay here tonight," she whispered.

As if he'd let her stay alone tonight. "You can stay with me."

"What about dinner?" She gave him a shaky smile that teetered close to tears. "I'm never going to pay all my debts to you at the rate I'm going."

"You don't owe me a thing." He walked over to pull her up out of the chair. "But I won't turn down dinner together." He kissed her gently. "We'll order in at my house."

She wrapped her arms around his back, hugging fiercely. He hated that she was still so shaken by the encounter.

When she pulled away to look up at him, he saw hope warming her eyes. Hope that he'd go along with the idea of an affair behind locked doors?

If she asked him right now, he would deny her nothing. Seeing her in danger had vanished any thoughts of his earlier decision to break things off now before it was too late.

In fact, when he'd heard her life being threatened Jeremy realized it was too late to walk away clean. He'd have died a thousand deaths tonight if anything had happened to her.

Letting her go would be the final death of his soul.

She chewed on her lip, indecision warring again in her gaze. "I'm really glad you were here tonight and I don't want you to take this wrong, but I have to ask you something." Her voice shook nervously.

"Ask." He had an idea what she was going to say. She hadn't liked it one bit when he'd told her they'd have dinner as friends. He considered jumping in first to let her know she meant much more than anyone he'd ever considered a friend, but she didn't give him a chance.

"Is there a *legal* reason you can't get a gun permit, Jeremy?"

"WHAT DO YOU mean you couldn't get Dorvan sprung?" Starface adjusted the listening volume on his Bluetooth headset, not believing his ears. "It's nine in the fucking morning! They've had him twelve hours." He stomped around his apartment in midtown Atlanta. He'd been up all night trying to find out what had happened to Dorvan.

Now he wanted to know why one of the best defense attorneys in the Southeast couldn't get bail set.

"Marietta hasn't set bail"—his asthmatic legal counsel spoke in short phrases and a voice too soft to belong to the barracuda this man could be in a courtroom—"because the FBI showed up . . . early this morning." He wheezed softly. "They took Dorvan before the courts opened."

"When are they going to let him see his attorney?" Starface growled.

"Soon as he's processed. No telling how long . . . that will take." The attorney took a long pause then asked, "Why does the FBI want him?"

Starface wasn't sharing that information with anyone. "I don't know. Just get him out of there."

Dorvan was of no use and Starface needed that photo card now before Ziggy sent someone for his ass. He hung up and dialed another resource. When the connection was made, he picked up the notes he'd given Dorvan yesterday and told his new tracker, "Easy contract to locate a woman.

She works for a group called Double Take. Find her today and I'll double your standard fee."

And pay him a bonus to take care of another loose end if Dorvan spilled his guts.

JEREMY WALKED FROM the bathroom into his bedroom wearing his jeans and toweling his hair dry. Early morning daylight bled through cracks in the blinds, adding to the soft glow from a lamp on the nightstand.

He stopped dead in his tracks.

CeCe lay sprawled across his bed on her stomach facing away from him, propped up on her elbows and engrossed in a magazine. That sweet bottom of hers peeked out from under the tail of one of his shirts. No underwear.

Have mercy.

Once he'd gotten her relaxed at his house last night, he'd joked with her about having dessert in bed only to take her mind off what had happened at her house. The last thing he'd wanted to do was make an overt move toward making love that might scare her worse after a man had threatened her at gunpoint.

But she'd wanted to make love with an almost desperate need he understood. To know she wasn't vulnerable. He'd let her take the lead, giving her what she needed to feel in control.

None of that would have happened if he hadn't figured his way out of her question about the gun permit. He told her he'd gone to jail as a teenager for boosting cars, had done his time and paid the price for his crimes, which he had.

Then he'd waited for her judgment and hoped she

didn't ask more since the crimes *he'd* committed were the least damning entry on his current rap sheet.

She'd accepted his explanation and come over to his house, where they'd ordered pizza and watched movies until late.

Like a normal couple.

And now she should be fully dressed since she'd showered first, but no, she was stretched out on her stomach on his bed facing away from him. She casually kicked one foot up and down, preoccupied with the magazine she was reading.

He had to get her off that bed and completely covered up for any hope of leaving here without using another condom. "What time does your brother land today?"

"Vinny gets in late this morning," she answered over her shoulder.

That hadn't gotten her attention like it had last night when he'd pressed her about calling her brother.

She'd finally explained how her three older brothers would all show up on Jeremy's doorstep looking for blood if they knew she was here. Vinny had been designated to oversee her adjustment to living away from home for the first six months, but they would all take turns checking on her.

Now Jeremy understood why she'd run him out of her house so early yesterday. Not simply because she thought it would be awkward for him and Vinny. She thought if her brother had caught Jeremy in her bed Vinny might have harmed him.

He smiled to himself. He could deal with a couple of posturing brothers any day. "Aren't you worried about Vinny showing up unexpectedly?"

"No. He wouldn't give me the wrong flight information just to catch me off guard." CeCe rolled over on her back and that view almost sent him to his knees.

"You need to get dressed."

"I'm as dressed as you are, just that my top half is covered where you've got jeans on." She smiled, enjoying her defiance.

"It's not the same when your bottom half is uncovered. I've got a meeting in an hour." In total conflict with his words, his feet started moving toward the bed. He tossed the towel to the floor and dropped down over her, his knees on each side of her legs. He used one arm to brace his weight.

She reached up and hooked her fingers around his neck to tug him closer, then smoothed his damp hair from his face. Warmth curled through his chest at the impish smile she gave him.

"What are you smiling about?"

"How nice it is to be here with you." Her eyes glittered with so much happiness the room should be sparkling. "But if you're really in a rush to get me out of your bed . . ." Her words drifted off in a whisper. She shrugged.

Jeremy leaned down and kissed her. As if on autopilot, his free hand slid beneath the shirt—his shirt—covering her. He needed to feel her to know she was still here and real. That this woman wasn't dashing out the door with no plans of coming back.

That she wanted him as much as he wanted her.

When his fingers closed around her breast, she moaned. He caressed the suddenly hard nipple, drawing his thumb slowly across the tip. She arched each time as though all the nerves in her body were attached to that tight little bud.

Taking the kiss deeper, lost in her taste, he lowered his body until they were hip to hip. She rubbed up against the rigid cock inside his pants and he clenched his teeth.

No, he sure as hell didn't want to push her out of his bed, but he was worried about last night.

He didn't really have a meeting in an hour. But he had to wait for CeCe to leave so he could contact BAD to ask for a couple more days off, then have someone in BAD's tech department research criminals with a scar like the intruder's and crosscheck hits with Jeremy's incarceration history.

He had a sneaking feeling about where he'd met that guy before.

CeCe nipped at his lip, tempting him to forget about threats and research. Testing his control against spending every free minute exploring her body until her brother returned. But her safety was too important, so as much as Jeremy would love to use up another condom right now there was no time. He'd have to move this moment along quicker.

But not until he had her satisfied.

Like that would take long? He grinned against her soft lips, looking forward to watching her hit that high again.

Unbuttoning her shirt, he kissed her neck and along her shoulders. She sighed and smiled, running her fingers through his hair playfully. Her hips twisted slowly from side to side driving him crazy with each stroke over his erection.

When he moved his hand down her abdomen to slip his fingers between her thighs she made a desperate sound and opened for him. He kissed the creamy skin surrounding two pert nipples then suckled one plump breast.

CeCe arched up, a guttural groan vibrating her chest.

Jeremy plunged a finger inside her and she tightened around him. Her thighs clenched. When he pistoned his finger in and out, in and out, her breaths came faster. Teething her nipple lightly, he pulled his finger completely out and stroked across the one spot that would send her reeling.

Three strokes and . . . liftoff.

She cried out and gripped his head, clutching him to her taut body.

Sweat broke out across his skin. He'd never get over how fast this woman climaxed.

When the last shudder passed through her she flopped back down on the bed, spent and panting. He ached, seriously ached, to continue, but after the past two nights he knew continuing could go on for a long time with her.

His mouth sought hers. Kissing her had become as natural as breathing, and just as essential to his survival. He wrapped her in his arms and rolled until she lay on top of him. She broke the kiss, lowering her head to his chest. Soft waves of brunette hair blanketed his chest.

"We'll get to you . . . as soon as I catch my breath," she mumbled.

"That'll have to wait until later." He rubbed her bare bottom with his hand, then thought better of that and moved his fingers up her back before he instigated another round.

She huffed out a deep breath, reached up to place her hand on his chest, and shoved up. Her eyes tilted with a curious look. "Will I see you later?"

He pushed a handful of hair off her face and cupped her cheek. "Depends."

"On what?"

"Your brother, from what you said. If I had a sister that looked like you, I'd keep her away from someone like me too," he teased.

She leaned down and kissed his chest, raising her gaze to his. "But I don't want to be kept away from you. I've been letting my family coddle me for too long. I came here to build a new life on my terms, but I've let them control what I do or don't do. I need to make them understand that I'm capable of making my own decisions and that they'll have to live with my choices."

He feathered her hair between his fingers. "What sort of decisions . . . and choices?"

"Like choosing what kind of man I want to be with, regardless of my family's opinion."

"What kind of man do you want?" He doubted he fit her criteria and definitely not her family's, but he had to know just what he was up against if he wanted to keep her close.

"Someone honest and considerate. A man who looks at me like I'm his world." She cupped his face. "Someone like you."

He'd never had a woman look at him the way CeCe was gazing at him with adoration right now. Like he was *her* world.

"A man who could make me feel safe even after facing a gun pointed at my face," she whispered right before her lips settled on his. Her kiss was sweet and endearing.

Different than any he'd shared before. The warmth and caring in this kiss rocked him to the soles of his feet.

His chest tightened with a feral need to keep her in his arms and safe. He'd never spent so much time getting to know one woman. CeCe had become his friend first since moving in next door. That was new all in itself.

Yes, she'd become his friend first and lover next.

He didn't want another in his bed. Ever.

CeCe lifted her head, staring at him with her heart in her eyes. Everything about this woman was right up front and honest. No games or lies.

Jeremy didn't care how many brothers he had to face.

He was not letting this one go.

First, he'd have to explain what he really did for a living, which would be tough since he couldn't actually tell her about BAD. She thought he owned a gym.

The front doorbell rang.

She tensed, eyes rounded. "What if Vinny caught an earlier flight and that's him?"

"I'll deal with it. You get dressed." Jeremy kissed her on the forehead, lifted her to her feet, and sent her to the bathroom before he walked to the front door.

The person outside had abandoned the doorbell and was now knocking. Pounding.

Jeremy opened the door to what had to be two feds. He could spot them a mile away. "Can I help you?"

One guy with a thin line for a mouth and receding hairline reminded Jeremy of the Joe Friday character from old *Dragnet* reruns he watched on television as a kid. His sidekick was a little taller at six feet with his black curly hair buzz cut, his skin the color of charred wood. One lazy eye gave him a half-interested look.

Both men flipped their badges. Joe Friday's actual name

was Special Agent Al Denton and his sidekick was Special Agent A. J. Quincy.

Denton asked, "You Jeremy Sunn?"

Jeremy nodded.

"You know a Cecelia Caprice?"

He nodded again.

Denton's eyes narrowed to slits showing no patience. "Do you know where she is?"

"Depends. Why do you want to know?" Jeremy wasn't handing her over without finding out what the FBI wanted.

"That's none of your business."

Jeremy crossed his arms. "Then I can't be of any help."

"Maybe you'll be more helpful when we haul you downtown and book you for obstructing an investigation." Quincy glanced past Jeremy, searching.

Jeremy would go with them and make one call to Retter, BAD's lead agent, who would hopefully find a creative way to spring him. "Hopefully" because getting busted by law enforcement for BAD was part of Jeremy's job description in most missions. This was a bit outside the parameters, but he'd gladly do it to keep CeCe out of the picture until he could figure out what the hell was going on.

Jeremy maintained a bored stance. "What investigation?"

"You're just begging to spend time in jail today, aren't you?" Denton threatened.

"I'm right here," CeCe said from behind Jeremy. "What do you want?"

Jeremy sighed. He had no doubt what the next words out of Denton's mouth would be and the agent didn't disappoint him.

"I'm with the FBI, Miss Caprice. We have a search warrant for your house."

"Why?" Jeremy asked since CeCe had gone rigid.

"Because she's a Canadian citizen and doesn't have a gun permit."

Hell, Jeremy had no choice. Besides he took the dive under the bus for everyone else, he might as well take it for CeCe. "She doesn't have a gun. I had the gun last night."

"But he didn't shoot it so is that a big deal?" she asked.

Denton smiled. "That's something we'll discuss downtown."

Jeremy turned to her. "Go home and wait until you hear from me."

"Actually," Denton interjected. "She's coming with us to answer questions about the man found in her house last night."

Six

So this was what an interrogation room looked like? The movies got the blank off-white walls and sterile feel right.

CeCe took a deep breath and wished she hadn't. A lingering odor of despair and fear clung to everything in the room.

Or maybe the fear was all hers.

She continued to sit with her hands folded in front of her, glancing from time to time at the two-way glass.

When the door finally opened, in came Special Agent Al Denton, the wiry man with no personality. His dark suit was stereotypical of what she'd imagine FBI agents wore, but that was only a guess on her part. The FBI was a U.S. agency and her family had always been in Ontario, except Vinny who moved to D.C. after receiving his law degree several years back. But he swore his work here was all completely legal so she hoped this didn't create any problems for him.

How could it since she hadn't done anything wrong?

"Can I get you anything, Miss Caprice?" Denton's

hair had been black at one time, but the short tufts were peppered with gray. Nicotine clung to his clothes, wafting through the room when he closed the door and leaned against it.

She shook her head. "No thanks. Why am I here when someone broke into my home?"

"What do you know about Sam the Man?"

She frowned, wondering where this was going. "Never heard of him."

"What about Dorvan or Starface?"

"Nope." Her family had always said less was more. She wanted to ask who these men were, but Vinny said never show an interest in anything. The minute he got back to Atlanta and found out about this he'd want her packed and moved to Ontario before the end of the week.

No more. She was getting through this and staying put. Jeremy hadn't said it in so many words, but she could tell he cared about her. More than as a friend or neighbor. She wasn't letting her family run off the man she wanted to see every morning she woke up.

"So you're claiming Dorvan was just breaking and entering?" Denton pressed.

"Is that the name of the guy who threatened to kill me in my living room last night?" She'd asked that in as sarcastic a voice as she could muster but clenched her hands together in her lap to hide her nervousness. She'd learned how to verbally fence with the best of them after listening to Vinny over the years. But Denton's insinuation that Dorvan might know her raised the hair along her arms. Was he suggesting that Dorvan might be more than a sicko who had entered her home only to attack her?

As if that wasn't terrifying enough.

"Yes, that was the man arrested." Denton stood away from the door and crossed his arms. "And you didn't have any photos or videotapes he wanted?"

Photos and videotapes? "What are you insinuating?" She sat forward in the chair, hands balled into fists. "That I do some kind of porn work?"

Denton's eyebrows snapped down over a confused look, then he relaxed and shook his head. "Don't get cute with me."

"I'm not. What kind of photos?"

He studied her with a flat gaze before his mouth curved in a wry smile. "Okay, let's pretend you don't know. A memory card with photos and a video of two men talking, making a deal to join forces for a criminal . . . operation."

CeCe leaned back. Please don't let her family be connected to any of this. The DeMitris were no longer a major underworld operation since her brothers had started shifting into legal ventures years back, but dear old dad still had contacts and operated illegal gambling venues in Ontario.

She asked in a calmer voice, "Why do you think I have anything to do with this Dorvan character other than his breaking into my house?"

"Because of your consorting with a prior felon, for one reason."

"What? Who?" Her throat closed up. But she guessed where he was going with this.

"Your boyfriend, Jeremy Sunn." The federal agent lifted away from where he'd been leaning and took a step toward the table between them.

CeCe said silent thanks that Jeremy had shared his past

with her. His honesty outweighed having a record as a teen and it was in that moment when he told her the truth that she realized how much she cared for him.

Her first thought upon waking up in his arms this morning was to rush home before Vinny came back.

But her second thought squelched that urge.

She was in love with Jeremy and she didn't love halfway. He'd stepped between her and danger last night. She'd protect him just as fiercely, even if it meant going up against her family she'd started explaining about this morning. As soon as she had a chance to talk to Vinny, CeCe intended to tell Jeremy everything. He deserved honesty too.

Giving the FBI agent what she hoped was a stony stare, CeCe said, "I know about Jeremy. He told me he boosted cars as a teenager and that he did his time. Don't turn him into some bad guy just because of that."

"Boosting cars?" Denton's eyebrows shot up. He belly laughed for a minute then stopped chuckling and stared at her. His eyebrows lowered in a sober glance. "You're serious?"

"Of course I am." Her stomach flipped over at the incredulous look in his eyes.

"Jeremy Sunn has a rap sheet as long as my leg." Denton was clearly not joking now.

"Jeremy has a record, like an adult criminal record?"

"Hell, yes. Not a secret since it's public record."

What? She couldn't catch her breath. Had Jeremy lied to her the same way her stepfather had lied to her mother when he omitted a few simple facts, such as that he ran illegal operations? Sure, her stepfather turned out to be a wonderful man who had adored her mother, but he still married her mother without telling her what he did for a living.

CeCe's mother had loved her stepfather but warned CeCe to not make the same mistake. She apologized for exposing a child to this life even if the DeMitri men had always taken good care of them. Her mother had made her promise to start fresh in a new place. Away from illegal operations.

I fell in love with a criminal? Pain squeezed her heart. CeCe wanted to pitch a screaming fit, but now was not the time.

She had to talk to Vinny and find out if he knew anything about all of this. For now, her brother's tutorials on law enforcement kicked in. "Are you charging me with anything?"

"Not yet."

"What about . . ." She had to consider the implication of asking about Jeremy.

Denton's gaze sharpened, but he said nothing, playing the silent bit, which was supposed to make her blather everything she knew. He had a long wait coming.

She shouldn't care what happened to Jeremy, but he wouldn't have been in this spot if she hadn't invited him over to dinner and he hadn't protected her. He'd stepped into danger without a second thought last night, which had made her wonder for just a moment if he'd had law enforcement experience.

Actually, he had. From the wrong side of the badge.

And, blast it all, she had to find out what they were going to do with Jeremy because she loved him and couldn't just turn off her feelings. He was the man she'd wanted to spend the rest of her life with up until a few minutes ago.

She'd deal with this new revelation once they got out of here. Jeremy had questions to answer.

"What about Jeremy?" she finally asked.

After a slow rise and fall of a deep breath, Denton answered her. "We're booking Sunn on felony possession of a firearm."

She stood up. "You can't do that. He didn't do anything wrong." Other than get involved with her and crush her dreams.

"Oh, yes, I can. This conviction could send him back to prison. And if we don't get that memory card with the photos, not even your stepfather and his sons in Canada will be safe from the underworld genocide planned by two powerful mob families, Miss Cecelia Caprice DeMitri."

JEREMY SLOUCHED IN the interrogation room's metal chair, giving the feds on the other side of the two-way mirror his usual don't-give-a-shit expression.

The feds had come after CeCe for the firearm permit when they knew Jeremy had been the one with the weapon. That had been an excuse to bring her down here until he admitted having the gun. Why bring her down once they got what they wanted?

Something didn't make sense, but Jeremy couldn't put his finger on it.

Denton had surprised him when he told Jeremy the guy who broke into CeCe's home was Dorvan, a bone breaker. That's when Jeremy realized he *did* know Dorvan, an enforcer who had teamed up with Starface several years ago. *I'll keep that little discovery to myself.*

Starface and Jeremy had been in the same penitentiary four years back when Jeremy had gone undercover to find the person inside who was behind a string of witness deaths on the outside. He should have recognized Dorvan last night, but he'd seen the brute only once during the six weeks he'd spent locked up.

Why had Dorvan broken into CeCe's house?

Denton tried to feed Jeremy some crap about CeCe knowing about photos on a memory card. What photos? Some pile of bullshit Dorvan was shoveling at the FBI?

Jeremy had a bad feeling Dorvan was trying to pull him into this mess, but he couldn't figure out why. The feds were playing a game, acting as though CeCe had some secret identity and was hiding information the FBI needed. That was crap. She'd been living in Canada before she moved here. How could she possibly be involved in this mess? Dorvan had to be pissed Jeremy had busted him and was trying to use Jeremy's prison record against him, claim some criminal association.

The FBI probably believed Dorvan and now they were trying to convince Jeremy that CeCe was involved to put pressure on him. But for what reason?

He refused to play their game. He stuck with what he knew, that CeCe worked for Double Take and practiced yoga at his gym.

Even if she was involved, which was impossible, Jeremy would never pass judgment without giving her a chance to explain first.

Too many people had done that to him over the years.

One of those who hadn't was the director of BAD, Joe Q. Public. The minute Jeremy landed in jail for this, Joe would have him moved to another facility and Retter would spring Jeremy during the transfer. As long as Joe and Retter believed he had only been in the wrong place at the wrong time. Plus, the rap sheet BAD had created over the past nine years was as much at fault as anything for sending him away.

Jeremy would give the feds enough to draw their attention away from CeCe to buy her time to get in touch with her brother.

He'd fall on the blade for her as an apology for what she hadn't known about him. Everyone he'd been arrested with had thrown him to the wolves at one time or another so he was used to being the scapegoat. He wouldn't blame her for turning her back on him and agreeing to anything that would get her out of here since he knew full well Special Agent Denton had told CeCe about his prison record by now.

That this trumped-up charge might land him back in prison.

But she'd give him a chance to explain, right?

He had more problems to deal with first. He thought he'd planned ahead for a worst-case scenario by keeping several text messages in his cell phone draft file. When he'd walked to the bedroom to get a shirt while the agents had waited in his living room, he'd sent a text to Blade to come down and bond him out as soon as he got booked to avoid contacting BAD.

That was before Denton made it clear Jeremy would have a better chance of winning the lottery than being turned loose. Once Jeremy could get a new message to Blade, he'd tell him to forget the bond, to pick up CeCe's fiberglass base out of Jeremy's garage, repair it, and return the base to her.

The more he thought on it, CeCe probably wouldn't want to see his face again. The picture of her disgust would gut him worse than mere anger. He couldn't dwell on that right now with no idea what they were going to throw at him.

Denton entered, flipping the door wide with a bang. "You're free to go." He wasn't happy about it.

Jeremy sat up. "What?"

"Your hearing bad?"

"Who sprung me?"

Denton scowled. "Your girlfriend's attorney. Guess it pays to be connected."

"Connected?" Jeremy didn't want to blow a chance to walk out free without having to involve BAD, but this just did not happen to him. "What are you talking about?"

The look Denton gave him was ripe with impatience. "Vincent DeMitri of the Ontario DeMitris. Cecelia's step-brother, your squeeze's family? Any of that ring a bell?"

Slamming Jeremy in his solar plexus with a baseball bat would have been an easier blow to take. He'd heard of the DeMitris.

CeCe was part of a criminal organization?

"One more thing, Sunn," Denton said. "If I find out she does have the photo memory card we're looking for, you'll both be facing an indictment."

What memory card? Jeremy would ask, but Denton had dropped that little bomb for a reason, so he gave the FBI agent no response.

CeCe hadn't thrown him to the feds. She'd used her contacts to free him, but she was related to a racketeering family that had been entrenched in Ontario for decades. Jeremy knew a few things about the DeMitri bunch that had surfaced on a couple of investigations over five years ago.

He needed some time to figure out what the hell was going on before he contacted BAD. Joe and his codirector, Tee, took care of their agents and would send help if he called, but Jeremy didn't want to pull them into his personal problems and he wanted answers before he faced anyone from BAD.

BAD would eventually hear about this and that the FBI had found a member of the DeMitri family at Jeremy's house half dressed early in the morning.

CeCe wasn't going anywhere until he got answers.

ALL CECE COULD do was put one foot in front of the other and keep pace with Vinny's long stride toward the exit. Anger boiled off him like an invisible steam. She understood. More than being angry about the mess she was in, Vinny felt as though he'd failed her. He'd been all business the minute he walked into the interrogation room. She'd had to admit he was damn good at what he did.

She'd just never expected to need his services.

Vinny stepped ahead of her and opened the glass doors. She followed him into a gloomy overcast day that matched her mood.

Ten paces down the walkway she heard, "CeCe, wait up."

Vinny stiffened next to her, but she'd made a decision

last night to stop letting everyone tell her how to live. Her family was going to have to accept her decisions, just as Jeremy would have to.

And she had to take responsibility for anything she did.

CeCe put a hand on Vinny's arm. "I need to talk to him." She turned around to find Jeremy closing in on her. She'd expected anger, but the disappointment ringing his gaze struck her harder than anger ever could have.

A strong breeze lifted the hem of her jacket, which she smoothed back in place. She'd run home and changed to a conservative pants suit before leaving with the FBI agents. Squaring her shoulders, she walked away from Vinny to meet Jeremy halfway.

"We need to talk," Jeremy started.

"No, I need to go pack up my house and move." She stood her ground, struggling not to give credit to the pain in his eyes. She'd changed her mind about asking Jeremy anything after walking out of the interrogation room. There was nothing he could say that would magically fix all this. Instead, she pointed out, "I asked you about your past."

Jeremy shook his head and released a snort of disbelief. "You're condemning *me* for having a record when *you're* a member of the DeMitri family?"

At that barked reply, Vinny pounded up next to CeCe who glared at him. "As her attorney, I'm advising her not to talk to you."

"As her attorney or her brother?" Jeremy snapped right back, anger boosting his sarcastic tone.

Before she could speak, Vinny added in a low and controlled voice, "As her brother, I'm advising you to walk away and never speak to her again if you like the way your face looks."

"Bring it on."

Vinny's chest expanded with a breath of fury. "Back down, asshole."

"I'll back down if and when CeCe tells me to. Not for you or a hundred brothers just like you."

CeCe realized in that moment that Jeremy would not let anything or anyone stop him from getting to her when he was determined. That was the man she wanted. How could she love him so much when the same heart felt like it was tearing down the middle?

"Vinny, give me a minute, would you?" she asked. Wind batted loose hair around her face. She swiped a handful behind her ear and waited for her brother to move back, then she swung around to Jeremy. Before she could vent, Jeremy got in the first shot.

"You said you were all about honesty, but *you* didn't say a word about being part of the DeMitri organization."

CeCe jerked back at the accusation in his voice. "I'm not part of the organization. My mother married into the DeMitri family and I'm not going to apologize for that because they've always loved me like a sister and daughter. They understood when I moved here that it wasn't because I didn't love them. I just didn't love what they did. As for honesty, you didn't tell me you had an adult record and I asked you point blank."

"I told you—"

"—about a boosting conviction as a teenager." She fisted her hands at her hips. "Do you or do you not have a string of convictions that you've spent time in prison for?"

Jeremy locked his jaw shut to keep from trying to explain. He couldn't tell her how he'd amassed a criminal track record just for BAD or that since signing on with the agency he hadn't gotten a traffic ticket unless BAD had orchestrated the offense for a mission.

"Yes, and I *can* explain, but not right now," Jeremy admitted softly.

CeCe's throat muscles moved when she swallowed. Her bottom lip trembled until she clenched her jaw. "I moved here to get away from a life built on lies. And for your information the DeMitri men are good citizens, changing things in the organization—"

"That's enough, CeCe," Vinny interjected.

She nodded and glanced back up at Jeremy. "How can you expect me to understand any of this if you can't tell me the truth now? I didn't want to be around cr—" She stopped short before the next word came rolling out.

"Criminals," Jeremy finished for her. "I did my time and continue to pay my dues every day. You believe the men in your family are decent upstanding citizens but not me?"

"I'm not saying that . . ."

"But you're leaving . . . me."

"I don't want to live around . . . someone who can't tell me the truth." She lowered her eyes to her hands, unable to take any more of his tortured gaze.

"I never lied to you." Technically. He'd withheld some things, but he'd intended to explain more to her once he figured out how to do it and not expose BAD.

"Keeping something important from me is lying by omission."

"I can make the same accusation."

She nodded. "For what it's worth, I planned to explain everything . . . if . . ."

"If we stayed together." Jeremy checked to see that Vinny was still ten feet back then lowered his voice so that only CeCe heard his words. "You're right. I did keep something from you just like you kept things from me. But the difference is that *I* understand why you did and am willing to give you a chance to explain."

When she sucked her bottom lip in and didn't answer he took a fist to the heart. "I did withhold some things, but I need you to know one very important detail. I care about you, CeCe, and would never involve you in anything criminal or let anyone hurt you. I can explain everything on my record but, like I said, not right now."

Silence spun between them with a swirling wind that tossed her hair back and forth around her delicate shoulders.

He held his breath, begging for a break. Just once.

Tears clung to her eyelashes but not a one fell. "It's probably best that we don't speak again."

Her dismissal smashed that flickering hope he'd been clinging to. Hurt clawed up his chest and churned into anger, but he wouldn't unleash that on CeCe. He could never hurt her.

And she was still at risk until he figured out what was going on with Dorvan and Starface. Jeremy shoved his emotions into that dark hole they should have stayed in and dropped his professional mask into place.

"What do you know about the photo card the FBI is looking for?" he asked.

"Nothing."

He glanced over her shoulder at Vinny. CeCe followed his gaze then snapped her head back to face Jeremy.

She lifted her clenched fists and her chin, ready for battle. "My family is *not* involved in this. Vinny told me so."

What Jeremy wouldn't give for a woman who would stand up as confidently in support of him. He placed his hands gently over hers and said, "I believe you."

All the bluster dissipated at his easy acceptance. She opened her mouth as though she wanted to say something, but her brother's patience had expired.

"Let's go, CeCe." Vinny walked up and gently took her arm, tossing a brotherly warning glare at Jeremy.

CeCe glanced over her shoulder at Jeremy, telling him with one look how disappointed she was . . . in him. He couldn't get a word past the lump in his throat so he said nothing as she moved away with Vinny.

"Ready to go, J?" Blade strolled up.

"Sure." Jeremy swung around and followed Blade, sorting through all the facts and the unknown as he walked. He wanted to figure out what was going on with the feds before he left town to rejoin BAD. Blade might be able to help. "You know anything about a guy called Dorvan?"

Blade scratched his chin and stopped at the driver's side of his customized silver-blue Corvette that had started out as a 1972 model. "Not really."

Jeremy climbed in and waited to continue until Blade had cranked the engine and exited from the parking lot, just ahead of Vinny's dark sedan.

"You in a jam with this Dorvan, J?"

"I don't know," Jeremy admitted. "What about a guy

named Starface? Has a birthmark shaped something like a star on the left side of his face."

"Funny you should mention him. Heard something on that one just yesterday." Blade leaned back, his long arms easily reaching the steering wheel. "He's in town for a score of some sort."

"Drugs?"

"Naw." Blade merged into Atlanta traffic heading north of Clairmont Road on Interstate 85. "Nobody knows. Just happened to hear about him because of word that Ziggy Gambino has men here ahead of his arriving sometime this week. Speculation is he and Starface got something cooking, but no money moving yet."

Jeremy turned that around in his mind. Starface had been sent to prison for getting caught in a net that snagged some of Ziggy Gambino's men. Jeremy hadn't been involved in that case. He'd ended up in the same cellblock as Starface for another mission, but he'd learned that Ziggy wanted the family that had sold his operation to the feds. His little empire had taken a beating since then.

Ziggy was after payback, but when he hadn't retaliated in the first two years everyone assumed he wouldn't.

Was Starface helping Ziggy go after retribution?

How did photos fit into all of this?

Jeremy looked over at his driver. "I need a favor."

Blade just nodded. "Told you back in the pen when you stopped a guy from shoving a knife in my gut you never had to ask. Just tell me what you need."

Jeremy had contacts all over the country he could call on but had never expected to tap one so close to home. Blade's resources were in a limited geographic area, but he could find out anything on anyone in his circle. His body shop was totally legit and making money, but he still had close ties to those working under the radar of law enforcement.

"Starface is looking for a photo card of some sort," Jeremy explained. "Find out what's on it."

"You got it." Blade parked in Jeremy's driveway and left the car running.

"One more thing," Jeremy added before climbing out of the Corvette. "I need you to fix CeCe's fiberglass base, but I'll pay for that. I'll have it ready for you to pick up tonight."

"You got it. Call you as soon as I have something."

"Thanks." Jeremy got out and glanced at CeCe's empty driveway. Was she already gone?

He unlocked his front door, went through the house and out to his garage. Might as well clean CeCe's base to get it ready while he killed time waiting to hear from Blade. He pressed the button to open his garage door.

Vinny was pulling a dark sedan into CeCe's driveway.

Jeremy couldn't make his feet move to back out of sight. This might be the last time he saw her.

CeCe stepped out of the car and her gaze shot straight to Jeremy as if she, too, wanted a last look. Then she lowered her head and walked to her front door.

Vinny, on the other hand, headed for Jeremy's garage.

Jeremy snatched up a shop rag and grabbed a can of acetone off a shelf and squatted down to clean her base.

"You're not going to try to find CeCe once she's gone, right?" Vinny said more as a statement than a question when he stepped inside the garage. Big brother issuing warnings.

"Get out of my garage."

"I want to talk to you." Vinny said that in the most reasonable, let's-just-talk voice.

"What the fuck do you want?" Jeremy wasn't in a reasonable, let's-just-talk mood. He soaked the rag then rubbed the top of the fiberglass. Acetone fumes burned his throat on each clenched-jaw breath.

"To clear up something. I'm not her keeper. My family loves CeCe and we're all trying to give her what she wants."

When Jeremy didn't comment Vinny went on. "None of us were happy about her moving away from the family where we couldn't easily protect her, but she's had her mind set to do this for a long time."

"Why are you telling me this?" Jeremy paused in his cleaning.

"To let you know we *will* do whatever it takes to make her happy and keep her safe, even from bad choices."

"You worried about her hanging around a criminal?" Jeremy shot a sarcastic eyebrow up at her brother. "Considering how she grew up that ought to make her feel warm and fuzzy, right?"

"You don't get it, do you?"

"Guess not." Returning to the cleaning job, Jeremy said, "Why don't you explain it to me?"

"You've hurt her like no one ever has had a chance to before."

Jeremy put the rag down, fury ripping through him when he stood to face her brother. "I'm not a fucking criminal, regardless of what the FBI told her. She's choosing to walk away, not me. So how do you figure *I* hurt *her?*"

"Because you let her fall for you without telling her the truth. Since you *do* have a criminal record and can't level with her, she's never going to change her mind and stay even if she's hurting. That's why I need to know you won't come after her once this is over."

Jeremy wondered if Vinny was guessing or reading his mind, because, hell yes, he'd intended to go after her as soon as he could. Once he found out what Starface, Ziggy Gambino, and the FBI were after.

And once he determined it had nothing to do with the DeMitris as CeCe proclaimed. Because he believed her.

And he loved her. He just hadn't realized that until he watched her walk away. How could anyone expect him not to go after the woman he loved?

He'd take on the entire DeMitri organization to find CeCe and get her back.

Vinny sighed and shook his head. "You can't do this to her. She'll never settle down with someone she thinks is hiding anything from her and our father won't clear you as acceptable for her. If you really care about CeCe, you won't make me and my brothers ensure you stay away."

"Don't threaten me." Jeremy turned his back on Vinny to dismiss him and hoisted the base up on its side.

A plastic box smaller than a matchbook fell out and landed between his feet.

"That wasn't a threat, just notification," the attorney brother clarified.

Jeremy's phone rang. He ignored Vinny and pushed the base back down flat. Then he flipped the phone open and bent over to pick up the plastic case.

"Got some news," Blade reported before Jeremy could say hello.

Jeremy's heart skipped a beat at what he held in his hand—a plastic case covering what appeared to be a photo memory card.

"What?" he finally said to Blade and glanced at Vinny, whose eyes were locked on the plastic case in his hand.

"Starface is after a photo card with pictures and a video of a meeting between the heads of two major families. One out of Russia and one from Chicago."

"What was the meeting about?" Jeremy kept his voice down but Vinny was tuned in to every word.

"If my source isn't off the mark, and he's a good one, two powerful families are teaming up to wipe out the upper to middle operations in North America so they can split the continent."

"No way." Jeremy stared at the card in his hand. His heart started thumping at the realization of what this meant. "Thanks. I'll call you back." He flipped the phone shut and started for CeCe's house only to have Vinny step in his path.

"We don't have time to screw around," Jeremy said. "Go get CeCe. I think the FBI turned her loose as bait."

Vinny cursed and spun around, moving fast for a wide-body man.

Jeremy ran inside his house to the computer in his office and shoved the card into a slot. He punched up the keys and played fifteen seconds of the video. Enough to realize Blade's sources were dead on the mark.

The two families teaming up had the money and power to wipe out anyone who wouldn't immediately fall into line behind them.

The Chicago family was the one who had thrown Ziggy Gambino's operation to the feds. Ziggy would pay anything, and kill anyone, for this card that he could use to screw over the Chicago group.

Either way, the end result would be a mob war if the card went anywhere but to the FBI.

"Sunn!" Vinny yelled from the kitchen, then his feet pounded toward him.

Jeremy ejected the card and had it back in the plastic case in his pocket by the time he turned to CeCe's brother.

Vinny's natural deep olive skin tone had paled three shades lighter. He heaved a breath from running. "She's gone."

Jeremy's phone rang. CeCe's number popped up on the caller ID. He lifted his finger to his lips for Vinny to stay quiet then answered. "Sunn."

"Everything made sense when my tracker found out you were involved," Starface said. "Can't really blame Dorvan for not anticipating you, but my new guy took the extra time to find out who had helped your girl here last night at her house. Now it all makes sense. Sam the Man was taking the card to you so who are you dealing with?"

Jeremy's whole body clenched at the reference to CeCe. He'd play along since Starface assumed he was involved. He slid into his criminal persona, hoping for his best performance yet since CeCe's life depended on it.

Seven

"When have you ever gotten information for free?" Jeremy countered to Starface in a cool voice that said more than words. His hands clutching the cell phone were damp, though. He'd faced crazed killers in prison, whacked-out druggies in a bust, and terrorists with automatic weapons.

Nothing had ever scared him the way he feared for CeCe's life right now.

"Always a first time," Starface crooned, chuckling. "I've got something you want and you have my merchandise."

Jeremy had one choice. "Where do you want to meet?"

"Be in Buckhead by five, have your phone handy, and don't screw with me or you'll get her back in pieces." The phone line died with a sudden click.

"I'm calling the FBI." Vinny reached for his cell phone.

"Wait!"

Vinny closed the phone. "I'm listening."

Jeremy nodded, thankful Vinny understood they were both after the same thing. Getting CeCe back alive. "She's only in this spot because the FBI used her so I don't trust them not to put her in further danger."

"You got an idea?" Vinny's professional attorney veneer faded away, leaving the hardened eyes of a brother willing to do whatever it took to protect his sister.

That was nothing compared to what Jeremy would do. He nodded. "I'm going to make a swap with Starface for the card."

Vinny's eyes narrowed in thought for a moment before his shoulders settled with resignation. "My skills are in the courtroom, not in the field. I don't want to take any chances with CeCe's life. I'll call in backup," he said, clearly indicating his family in Ontario.

"No time. We have four hours. That's it. I *am* trained in the field so we do this my way." Jeremy waited for an argument.

If he didn't know better he'd swear the new shift in Vinny's eyes was respect, and just maybe a little trust. That would be funny if not for the fact that what Jeremy had in mind was going to prove to CeCe he was as much a felon as Starface.

And if that animal touched her, Jeremy would kill Starface with his own hands.

Vinny spoke in his attorney voice again, as if advising a client. "You do realize if the FBI finds out you gave the memory card to Starface, you'll fry, and I can't help you."

"Already figured all of that out. All I need you to do is your part while I do mine." Jeremy expected Vinny to want to come with him, but her brother would only get in his way.

"Agreed."

JEREMY TAPPED HIS fingers on the steering wheel. He'd parked his Tahoe half an hour ago at the IHOP restaurant in the triangle made by the Peachtree Street and Roswell Road intersection. Most central spot he could think of in the tony Buckhead area. Five o'clock rush hour through the middle of Atlanta had settled in for the afternoon and nasty weather tripled the road rage factor for the packed interstates.

Rain poured over his windshield and thunder rocked the heavens.

His cell phone rang. He answered, "Sunn."

"Ready to deal?" Starface chuckled.

"Where?" Jeremy ignored the chuckle. He believed in the old saying that "he who laughs last laughs best."

Starface gave him directions to a closed nightclub three miles away. Jeremy spun across the intersection at the entrance and cut through side streets. When he reached the nightclub, he drove around to the parking lot in the rear where empty beer cans floated in a low spot filling with water. The jersey jacket he pulled on had been made with fine aircraft cable running along the inside from the top to carry weight without pulling down on the material. He shoved his Walther P99 into the right-hand pocket reinforced with the cable to carry the barrel level without broadcasting the weapon's position.

Other than that, he always carried a knife in his boot. The habit was a holdover from being a teenager when staying alive counted more than worry over breaking the law.

Jeremy keyed up a text message on his cell phone ready to send to Vinny and slipped the phone carefully into his right front jeans pocket. He threw the keys under the seat and climbed out. Fat raindrops battered his face and lightning speared the dark skies.

Before he reached the back door of the out-of-business nightclub, Jeremy eased his hand into his left jacket pocket shielding a pair of pliers and the photo card. He slipped his right hand in his jeans pocket in a casual pose as if waiting for someone.

The back door opened on its own, as he'd expected.

Jeremy folded his left hand around the handles of the heavy pliers and gently closed the teeth snug, then withdrew his hand with the photo card pinned into view.

"Tell Starface I have the card." Jeremy waited for a response. They could shoot him, but anyone with half a brain wouldn't risk the chance that one simple squeeze could ruin the card or that he might not have the real one.

"I told him," a voice called out. The door yawned all the way open.

Jeremy entered, thankful the weather outside had turned the sky dark so that his eyes could adjust faster. Stale smoke and body odor ghosted through the air as he followed a rangy guy close to his height and build. Starface's backup was late forties and carried a 9mm Browning with the ease of man who rarely made a move without it.

When they reached the bar area, Jeremy called out, "Where is she?"

Across the dingy room, Starface stepped into view from around the corner. Smiling, he tugged on a rope attached to something out of view.

CeCe appeared at the end of the rope, which was tied

around her waist. Sheet-white terrified and stumbling, she stopped next to Starface.

Fury roared through Jeremy but he couldn't get her out of here if he lost his focus. And he would get her out of here. He only wished he had one minute to tell her that he loved her.

He gently fingered the key on his cell phone in his pocket to text a message and prayed it went through.

"Okay, let's trade," Starface demanded, holding up the end of the rope to make his point.

"Send her over here then I'll hand your man the card."

"No. Put the card on the bar and I'll let her go."

Jeremy laughed as though he and Starface were cutting up with each other. "Like you really expect me to do that. You know my word is solid."

"It was in the pen, but I haven't seen you in a few years so . . ." Starface shrugged, indicating his lack of faith.

"You owe me," Jeremy threw out.

Starface frowned, twisting the birthmark into a hideous shape. "How you figure that?"

Jeremy couldn't look at CeCe when he said, "Sam the Man was going to the feds. If I hadn't cut him a better deal someone else would have and we wouldn't be standing here." He didn't have to see CeCe to know she understood what he'd said. He heard her sob at his admission of being involved.

Of all the things he'd endured, breaking her heart would be the hardest to live with.

"How'd you find out about all this?" Starface wanted to know.

"Ziggy covering his bases," Jeremy said, sticking with

his story. He had to get her free now. "You're late delivering. He's got money out all over town looking for this card." Blade had come up with that little tidbit when Jeremy was on his way down to Buckhead.

Starface cursed something low and vile.

CeCe flinched back, drawing Jeremy's attention to her. She looked through him as if he were dead, which he had to be to her by now.

Time to move this along or things were going to get dicey. "We dealing or not?" Jeremy snapped.

The room tensed with all four of them waiting on someone to make a move. Starface finally untied CeCe and waved his arm toward Jeremy telling her to go.

CeCe couldn't decide if she wanted to cry with relief or out of rage. She was too terrified to do either at the moment with both her and Jeremy's life in danger.

This Starface guy would not let Jeremy just walk out of here.

She moved across the room on shaky legs, her eyes on the backup man pointing the second gun she'd faced in two days. She swallowed and turned her attention to Jeremy, who didn't look anything like the man she'd spent the last three weeks falling in love with.

Gone was the easygoing charmer.

Danger radiated from Jeremy, his rigid stance threatening anyone who twitched the wrong way and that look on his face more feral than anything she'd ever witnessed.

Regardless of how deep he was in this mess, she knew without a doubt in that moment that he could, and would, kill anyone in this room who hurt her.

That might be comforting if he was law enforcement,

but not after admitting he was involved in this whole scheme. Had known Starface in the pen. She'd berated herself for hours over judging Jeremy by a double standard. If she could just stop time and tell him she was sorry, that she owed him as much of a chance to explain as he'd offered her.

But he'd just admitted his part in all this.

When she walked up to Jeremy, she searched for something to say. He gave a brief shake of his head, without looking at her. The deadly glint in his eyes remained focused on the threat at her back.

Jeremy took her by the arm and gently pulled her behind him. She glanced around at their potential escape route through the rear door. The narrow walkway went fifteen feet then took a hard right turn to the exit.

Did Jeremy intend to back them out of here?

"Get out of here," Jeremy said softly without turning around. He was talking to her.

"They'll kill you the minute I leave."

"For once, it'll be worth it." He swallowed. "You're worth any cost."

She didn't like the sound of that. "No, Jeremy—"

"Nobody moves," Starface snapped. "Not until I get my card."

"*I'm* staying. She's leaving," Jeremy said in an unyielding tone. "Once she's gone you get the card." He paused, then ordered, "Now, CeCe."

How could she leave him? They'd kill Jeremy the minute he handed over the card. "But—"

"You're putting us both in more danger if you stay," he said, ending any argument she could come up with.

Jeremy had a plan and she might get him killed by not knowing what it was. In spite of everything that had happened, she trusted him so she had to trust what he told her right now.

CeCe backed slowly to the rear exit while the three men stood silently facing off. When she reached the door and stepped outside backward she was slammed by a driving rain. As the door was closing all the lights inside the bar went dark.

Shots boomed through the room.

Jeremy. She reached for the door but hands grabbed her, wrenching her back. FBI agents surrounded her.

She struggled to free herself, yelling at them to get inside and help Jeremy.

Vinny rushed up, ordering, "We had a deal. Give her to me."

Sirens screamed between booms of thunder exploding overhead. More gunshots cracked inside the building.

"Jeremy's in there," she yelled at her brother and anyone who would listen. "Somebody help him. Let me go!"

"They know," Vinny told her and held her firm in his grasp while she struggled and beat at his hands like a wild woman.

The gunshots stopped.

She held her breath, afraid to think of what had happened to Jeremy. Vinny wrapped a coat around her.

FBI and a SWAT team poured in from everywhere, swarming the building from all sides. New shots were fired inside but the battle was over in seconds.

An ambulance tore into the lot, spraying water off the tires.

Vinny tried to guide her away.

"*No!* I want to see Jeremy." Her heart had shattered at Jeremy's admission, but she had to know if he was alive. She gripped her hands together, praying for a miracle.

The EMTs stood ready. What the hell was taking the FBI so long? Jeremy could be bleeding to death if he'd been hit.

Special Agent Denton emerged from the back door. She hadn't realized he was here. Denton waved the EMTs forward. "Interior is secured. We got one alive."

She weaved on her feet as the EMTs disappeared into the building. Vinny wrapped his arm around her for support.

The rain subsided into a drizzle. Water mixed with tears that ran down her face.

When the EMTs rushed out with the gurney, her knees almost buckled at the site of an oxygen mask over Jeremy's face. Blood spread across his chest from where he'd been shot in the shoulder.

She broke free of Vinny and ran to catch up with the gurney. Jeremy's eyes were shut, his skin a blanched gray, but he was alive.

"I want to go with him," she told the EMTs when they started to load him.

"You can't, ma'am."

"Why not?" She'd take on the whole lot of them, including the FBI and her brother, if she had to so she could stay with Jeremy.

Vinny was pulling her back again. "You can't, sis." He gave up when she wouldn't move and said, "He's under arrest."

That's when CeCe saw Jeremy's wrist handcuffed to the rail on the gurney.

Vinny added, "But you're free to go. I made a deal with the FBI."

The EMTs loaded the gurney and closed the doors.

CeCe turned on Vinny, all the misery and hurt she'd kept bottled up today gushing out. She yelled, "He risked his life to save me. How could you throw him to them?"

Vinny sighed and leaned close to her, whispering, "It was Jeremy's idea. He gave me the real photo card to trade for your freedom."

Oh, dear God. Her brothers didn't think any man was good enough for her, but she'd finally found a man she loved . . . and didn't deserve.

And now she'd never see him again.

Eight

Jeremy pressed the button on his Bluetooth to engage the cell call while he drove along Dallas Highway, headed to his gym in Marietta. "What?"

"You're a surly bastard this time in the morning," Retter replied. "Get up on the wrong side of the bed?"

If he'd been in bed at all last night, Jeremy might have gotten up on the wrong side. But after being gone for over two weeks, he'd spent the first night at home rambling around like an abandoned dog dumped on the highway.

"I'll be ready to work by the end of the week," Jeremy told him rather than address Retter's question.

"Joe wants you to put in some time in your gym for a couple weeks before you come back to active duty. Get that shoulder in shape. Besides, we're not sure what we're going to do with you now that the president personally cleared you from any trouble with the FBI. Not sure you're of much value undercover in a prison. Too big a risk that someone inside a federal agency might slip and blow your cover."

"I still have the best rap sheet on the team," Jeremy argued, though his heart wasn't in it. He'd done such an outstanding job for BAD he was their number one ex-con.

"Not any more."

"What do you mean?"

"Joe got your entire rap sheet expunged in exchange for heading off an apocalypse in North America. We're looking at moving you into coordinating short-term missions. Tee was actually the one who said you had enough holes in your body. She figured your warranty would run out with one more."

"Tee?" Jeremy said, incredulous. Hard to imagine any sympathy from Joe's codirector, who had ice in her veins and loved only her furry little mutt, Petey.

"Don't take that to heart," Retter cautioned. "She said at the cost of training new recruits she was just thinking of saving money."

"That sounds more like her." Jeremy couldn't believe the irony in all this. *Now* he had no criminal record. Too bad it had come two weeks late.

As if CeCe hearing him admit that he knew Starface and had cut a deal with Sam the Man hadn't been damning enough. From what Jeremy had been told later, CeCe had watched in horror as EMTs carried him off in handcuffs.

BAD had taken him to one of the agency's safe houses in northern Georgia to heal once Jeremy was stable enough to be moved from Piedmont Hospital. He'd assumed Joe and Retter had worked some magic to free him but never expected to have a clean record. They'd sent a medical team to oversee his recuperation from then until he'd been released to come home yesterday.

Clean bill of health. No criminal record. Just an average guy for once and unable to have the only woman he wanted. Vinny had made it clear that his family would protect CeCe from danger, even her own bad decisions.

Jeremy would top that list of bad decisions in her family's view.

"I'll be in touch." He hung up and tossed the phone into his cup holder. He unhooked the Bluetooth. At least tonight he could burn off his stored-up energy in the gym.

Blade had a couple guys with remodeling experience who needed some work so Jeremy figured the weight room and aerobic area could stand a new look.

He'd instructed Tim, his evening manager, to close the gym early so Jeremy could survey it without having to talk to everyone. He enjoyed his customers, but his heart wasn't up for making happy talk.

Or for seeing the gym without CeCe stretching and smiling.

Jeremy parked in the lot and frowned. Blade's Corvette was the only car out there. Where was his manager's car?

When Jeremy pushed his car door open his shoulder ached, but not so severely today. He stretched that arm on his way into the gym.

Blade opened the glass door and broke out a high-powered smile. "Heard you were coming in tonight."

"Where's Tim?" Jeremy stepped inside. Instead of the ghostly quiet he'd expected, soft rock music spilled from the overhead speakers. But the gym always seemed abandoned when it was empty like this.

Would forever be empty without CeCe.

"Tim had a hot date, so me being the incredibly generous person that I am—"

"And humble," Jeremy added, finding his first smile in a while.

"That too." Blade nodded. "I offered to keep an eye on the place until you showed up."

Jeremy walked over and leaned his good arm against the check-in counter. Blade always had an angle. He probably expected Jeremy to do a quick scope of the area to be remodeled then pick up the tab for some cold brews so they could chase skirts.

He owed Blade that, and more. Blade had come through when he needed someone. He'd tapped contacts who were known felons and put his freedom at risk to get the information Jeremy had needed to save CeCe.

He'd been a true friend.

"Thanks for letting Tim go early." Jeremy glanced in the direction of the aerobic room. "We'll do a walk-through for your guys then get some beers." He'd go with Blade, but the idea of taking anyone home after having had CeCe in his bed just didn't seem right. Didn't excite him in the least.

"No can do." Blade fished his keys from his pocket. "Gotta roll. I'll take a rain check on those beers."

"You're kidding. So what are you doing here?"

"Dropped off CeCe's fiberglass base. Didn't know what you wanted to do with it."

Jeremy's breath caught at hearing her name. He'd have

to get used to it since she'd been well liked in the gym and he was bound to hear someone ask about her not being around.

"Guess she's gone for good," Jeremy muttered.

"Mm-hmm." Blade shrugged with understanding. That was as close as they ever came to discussing something personal. "I stuck the base in your aerobic room. Figure you wouldn't forget it that way since I understand you got another problem in there."

Standing away from the counter, Jeremy hooked his thumbs in the pockets of his jeans. "What problem?"

Blade held up his hands. "Forget I said anything." He looked at his watch and grinned. "Got to run. Call me tomorrow."

When Blade reached for the door, Jeremy said, "By the way, thanks for everything you did."

Blade flashed that wicked smile of his. "Oh, I plan to collect big time . . . soon as you can hang with me again."

Some things never changed. Jeremy waved him off and locked the door as Blade fired up his land rocket.

He turned toward the aerobic room. Locating Vinny's address wouldn't take long. The urge to deliver the base personally for a chance to see CeCe again chewed at Jeremy, but he wouldn't do that.

Besides, Vinny had her tucked away somewhere safe by now.

Jeremy strode across the gym. Once he had an address for DeMitri he'd ship the base. Even if Vinny and his squad of brothers would stand aside for Jeremy to visit CeCe again, he doubted she'd even answer her door to him.

She wouldn't want to speak to him again after all that had gone down.

As he neared the aerobic room he heard a noise and went on alert.

Jeremy approached the room cautiously, wondering why the lights around the base of the room were still on. One of his yoga instructors liked to use them instead of overhead lights for a softer mood.

When he stepped through the door, he was sure his heart skipped a beat.

CeCe lay on a blue foam mat in front of the wall of mirrors, stretching her amazing body with liquid movements. She hummed quietly along with the music playing.

The fiberglass base Blade had repaired sat in the corner.

She looked into the mirror and met his gaze, then stopped moving. "Hi."

Her shy greeting kicked his heart into beating again.

"Hi." Jeremy moved slowly toward her, not wanting her to vanish if she was only a figment of his imagination.

She sat up, still staring into the mirror, their reflected gazes locked in a timeless moment.

When he stood behind her, looking down, Jeremy waited for a painful breath to flow out of his lungs so he could speak. "Good to see you."

"You too. How's your shoulder?" Her words came out fragile, as if they might break if she spoke too loud.

"Healing. Why are you here?"

"I got a call from Blade about the base and . . ."

"Oh." He would have said more but the words backed up in his tight throat.

"That's not what I meant." Her eyes shied away from his. She took a breath and raised her beautiful gaze to meet his in the mirror. "When Blade called, I talked to him for a while. He wouldn't really share anything about you and didn't know where you were, but he said you'd come back eventually. I've been visiting my family in Ontario so I asked him to let me know when he knew you were back. That I wanted to come see you."

"Why?"

"To tell you I'm sorry." The words rushed out in a strained whisper.

That threw him. He really looked at her. She'd lost weight. It showed in her face, which was turned up staring at his reflection.

"For what?" he asked. Why was *she* apologizing?

"For judging you by one set of standards and others, like my family, by another set."

His pulse jumped at the hope her words offered. "What do you mean?"

She shifted up on her knees, never breaking eye contact. "Took me a while to sort things out, but I think I finally got my head straight. I was willing to accept that the men in my family were decent men, in spite of their heritage. Their grandfather and father—my stepdad—ran illegal gambling operations, but when their grandfather was killed in a bust, my three stepbrothers made a pact before they graduated high school to change the family business. They started legitimate businesses over four years ago and have slowly moved the family enterprise away from illegal numbers games."

Jeremy knew she waited for some comment, but he wanted to see where this was going.

Hope had been an evil mistress over the past month.

CeCe drew a deep breath. "I went home to see my dad

and brothers after . . . everything happened. I told them about you and that I couldn't hold you to a double set of standards. If I could accept them with the DeMitri past then they had to accept that I cared for you."

His heart was beating so fast he could feel his chest move. "What *exactly* are you saying?"

She stood up and turned around, facing him with her heart in her eyes. "That I should have been willing to let you explain whenever you were ready, to give you a chance to tell your side of what happened in your past. That if you tell me you're not involved in criminal activity I believe you. I know how you found the photo card in my statue base and that you gave the real one to Vinny to use in a deal for my freedom. Then you walked into that . . ."

Her lip trembled and a tear streaked down her face. "You walked into that death trap knowing you had no way out. I thought you'd died when all those shots were fired. Then they took you away and wouldn't let me go with you and you were bleeding and no one would tell me where you were and . . ." Tears poured down her face.

Jeremy took her into his arms and hugged her. Holding her was a gift he never expected to experience again. Her arms went around him and she sobbed against his chest.

"It's okay." He shushed her, rubbing his hand up and down her back. "I made it."

"No it's not okay." She lifted red eyes full of regret to his. "I'm sorry you didn't know how much I loved you before you walked into that building prepared to die for me."

She loved him? Jeremy couldn't move as hope flooded him from head to toe.

CeCe had come back and she loved him.

He laid his palm along her cheek. "I'm sorry too, that I couldn't tell you about so many things. I don't have a criminal record anymore . . ."

Her forehead wrinkled with confusion. "What do you mean?"

"My entire record has been expunged. With the exception of boosting cars when I was a teenager, everything else on my rap sheet was created as a cover for my . . . job."

She sniffled. "You don't own a gym?" Her lips puckered in concern. Then her tongue slipped along her bottom lip.

All he'd thought about for the past sixteen days was CeCe.

Jeremy gave up waiting to kiss her. When he dipped his head, she cupped her hands on his face and opened her lips to his invasion. His world tilted back into place and started spinning forward again.

He kissed her over and over again, wanting to hold her like this forever. But to do that he'd have to tell her everything.

Slowly ending the kiss, he said, "Time for all the truth."

She looked as though she prepared herself for the worst, then nodded. "I'm ready to listen."

Using his thumbs, he wiped away the last of her tears. "In addition to owning this gym, I do contract work for an agency that protects national security."

"Oh, crud. I had the thought that you might be law enforcement, then I blew it off when everything happened. I can't believe what I put you through and . . ." She paused, blinking. "What kind of law enforcement?"

He smiled, then turned serious when he told her, "I

work undercover for a group that has no public identity. I used to insert into prisons for intel, but the powers that be have decided not to use me that way anymore. I can't share details about my work with you, so there will be times when I'm technically lying by omission, but I'll never lie to you about anything between us. I love you too, and never want to lose you again."

Tears started fresh again. She kissed him hard and passionately for what seemed like forever and not long enough, then pulled back with a worried look. "What about my family? Every one of my brothers is an honest businessman, but you of all people know how the past can cause problems. Will they be on your agency's radar, because I don't want to put my brothers or dad at risk . . . by me being with you."

Trust was a bridge between them that could go crashing down or bind them together depending on if they could build it.

Jeremy trusted her so it came down to whether she could trust him. "I'm glad you have brothers who watch over you for when I'm not at home to protect you myself. As long as your family doesn't threaten U.S. national security they won't be on our radar. And I swear I won't be watching them like an agent when I'm around your family, which is bound to happen. That is, if you stay with me."

She didn't hesitate this time. "I'm not going anywhere, because I trust you and love you. And I don't want to ever lose you again either. You belong with *me*."

She wanted to *keep* him.

Relief whipped across his skin, freeing the tension in his body. Jeremy lifted her off the floor, swinging her around and around in his arms, ignoring the pain throbbing in his shoulder. He could endure anything with her at his side.

CeCe's laugh was music to his soul. He intended to hear that song played over and over. When he stopped spinning and settled her to her feet, CeCe's eyes twinkled with a mischievous smile.

He kissed her forehead. "What?"

"Holidays with you and my family are going to be interesting."

Leave No Trace

Cindy Gerard

It is not power that corrupts, but fear. Fear of losing power corrupts those who wield it and fear of the scourge of power corrupts those who are subject to it.

—*Aung San Suu Kyi, 1990*

One

It had become too much about the scotch, Cav admitted with brutal honesty. Too much about relying on it to make it through the nights. Too much about craving it to help him deal with a life where the shots called him, instead of him calling the shots.

With a heavy breath, he leaned back in the mahogany and leather desk chair in the Jakarta mansion that had been his base of operations for the past six years. He slowly swiveled until he faced his office window, then rocked back and held the heavy-bottomed glass aloft, watching the sunlight play over the amber oblivion before indulging in another sip.

Yeah. Way too much about the scotch.

That was all about to change.

Everything was about to change.

Tomorrow morning he was going to give notice via his handler. After a decade and a half of being a good little spook, David Cavanaugh and the CIA were finally going to part ways.

It was past time.

He watched the ebb and flow of traffic shooting by the window and wondered why he didn't feel relief. Instead, ever since he'd made his decision, he'd been overrun with recurrent flashes of guilt. And, yeah, panic. What now? What next? Where did he go from here? What did he have left to give?

The sound of light footsteps on the polished teak floor brought his head around. He'd dismissed the two bodyguards that were a part of his cover earlier, but Dira, his *aman*, stood in the towering office doorway, the wide strap of her woven straw purse slung over her shoulder. The twelve-foot ceilings dwarfed the quiet Indonesian woman's five-foot stature.

"Is there anything else I can do for you, Mr. Windle?"

Frank Windle had been Cav's CIA cover for the past six years. Windle's expat, unprincipled venture capitalist persona came with this fully staffed luxury mansion, the personal bodyguards, a force of *jangas*—armed guards with dogs who patrolled the high cement wall surrounding the compound—and an expense account that would make the Prince of Wales weep with envy.

He'd come a long way since his initial CIA assignment in Ouagadougou, Africa, working undercover as a lowly U.S. embassy staffer and sharing a three-room tenement flat with fellow rookies Wyatt Savage and Joe Green. He lived in luxury in Jakarta now, and he regularly rubbed elbows with the scum of the earth.

"I'm good, Dira, thanks." He dismissed his longtime housekeeper with a soft smile. "Enjoy your evening."

He planned to enjoy his. Alone. With a farewell toast

to both the Company and his love affair with Glenlivet.

With grim determination, he looked around the polished opulence of the wood-paneled room. He wouldn't miss the subterfuge, but he'd sure as hell miss this place. The spacious office was one of twenty luxurious rooms in a mansion that personified the historical Dutch East Indies architecture with its steeply pitched gables, large airy rooms, and soaring finials. The house was a jewel. Cool, airy, and regal . . . and living here had choked the life out of him.

He downed the last of the fine single malt and wondered how the Company would explain it when *Windle*, who'd made a name for himself as an unscrupulous player in not only the Indonesian but the international black market by being open to any number of illicit business transactions, made a sudden departure from Jakarta and cut off its intel pipeline.

The Company's problem, not mine.

Right. So why did a knot of anxiety tighten inside his chest like a fist? And, *Jesus*, why the guilt? He'd been a good Company man. He'd had plenty of incentives to flip and go over to the dark side. Lucrative incentives. And while he wasn't as naive about the international spy game as he had been when he'd first signed on to play, he was still a patriot. He didn't need to feel guilty about anything—not about his work, not about leaving. And yet . . .

"Screw it," he muttered. Screw the guilt. It was someone else's turn to run the gauntlet. He'd be thirty-five next month, and some days he felt as old as fucking Methuselah. It was the weight of those dead bodies and repeat adrenaline burns. He'd carried both as long as both his body and his soul could bear.

He rubbed at a scar on his right thigh, a memento from an AK-47 round in Beirut in '99. And whenever it rained his collarbone ached like hell from when he'd broken it escaping an op gone wrong in Mogadishu in '05.

His cell phone rang, *Private Number* showing on the readout. He'd personally fitted the security screens on his cell—*this* phone, even the CIA didn't know about—but just in case he answered with his cover. "Windle."

"Cav, it's Wyatt."

The chair creaked as Cav sank back. It had been months since he'd heard Wyatt Savage's soft southern drawl, yet his old friend was one of the few constants in Cav's history. He hoped that would be true in his future as well. In the spook world, where black and white too often bled into shades of gray, there had never been a question that Wyatt was also one of the good guys.

That didn't mean he couldn't give his old partner a hard time.

"Why is it that every time the phone rings and I hear your voice, I feel a knee-jerk reaction to say 'wrong number' and hang the hell up?"

"I need your help."

"Ah. *That* would be the reason." The last time Wyatt had enlisted Cav's help it had involved infiltrating a human trafficking ring, the takedown of a rat-bastard Chinese crime boss, and several blown-up buildings near the Jakarta wharfs.

"Look, Cav. I don't have a lot of time. So here's the quick and dirty."

"It's always quick and dirty with you, Savage." Just like Cav was always going to say yes to whatever Wyatt asked of him.

Over a decade and several dead bodies had stacked up since he, Wyatt, and Joe Green had guarded one another's backs in service to Uncle. While Wyatt and Joe had said *hasta luego* to the CIA several years ago and teamed up with Nate Black's private security and military contract firm, Black Ops, Inc., Cav had stuck with the Company. Until now.

"Cav . . . you still there?"

"Yeah. Yeah, I'm here," he said when he realized he'd lapsed into silence. He glanced toward the liquor cabinet. "What's going on?"

"Two days ago an American woman stepped off a plane in Mandalay, Myanmar, hired a taxi that let her off near her hotel downtown, and she hasn't been heard from since."

Cav reached absently for a pen, then flipped it back and forth between his fingers. "One of yours?" Black Ops, Inc. specialized in immobilizing bad guys on the international front.

"No. She's not with BOI. Carrie's a friend. And she's as green as the damn grass."

"What kind of friend?" Wyatt had gotten married last spring, yet he sounded damn rattled over this *friend*. Cav had missed the wedding. Like he'd missed many important events over the years, because he'd been embroiled in some covert op to gum up the works in a would-be tyrant's attempted coup to overthrow a U.S.-sanctioned government, or an op to intercept an arms shipment bound for a terrorist training camp, or a score of other missions that had kept him on the razor's edge of life or death. A lot of lives. A lot of deaths.

A lot of post-op scotch to blur the memories that hovered like ghosts around a crypt.

"Just a friend," Wyatt said, snapping Cav back. "I grew up with her. Our families go way back. She's a small-town hospital administrator. She wasn't prepared for Myanmar. She's never even been out of the States. Hell, for all I know, she's never been out of Georgia."

Cav could hear the desperation in Wyatt's voice.

"Her family begged me to talk her out of going, and I tried. Believe me. I tried to scare her smart. But there was no stopping her.

"Look"—he paused, and Cav could visualize his friend rubbing his brow with his index finger—"she's important to me, Cav. I'd be there in a heartbeat but Sophie . . . she's pregnant and . . . Christ, Cav." His voice broke and Cav sensed that what came next wouldn't be good.

"There are complications. We . . . we might lose the baby." His voice was thick with strain. "I can't leave her right now. The doctors say it's going to be touch and go for the next forty-eight to seventy-two hours."

"I'm sorry, man." Cav knew all about Sophie. One drunk midnight, shortly after the Company had paired them up as partners all those years ago, Wyatt had told him about the one who'd gotten away. Cav had been happy as hell when they'd finally found their way back to each other this past year. Now this tough break. One that was clearly tearing Wyatt apart.

Now he understood the reason for Wyatt's call. *He* couldn't go to Myanmar. *Cav* could. And he could get there a helluva lot faster from Jakarta than Wyatt could from Georgia.

"What's the word from our embassy?" he asked.

"They've got nothing. It's like she fell off the face of the earth. They've got calls in to both local and government officials, but so far it's clam city."

Cav listened intently while Wyatt gave him Carrie Granger's physical description.

"Let me make some calls. See what I can find out. I'll be back in touch."

"Thanks, man."

"Don't insult me." They'd been too much to each other to ever have to say those words.

"Right. Love you, too."

A quick smile curved Cav's lips as a glimpse of the Savage he knew finally surfaced. He disconnected, then started looking up old contacts who might have connections in Myanmar.

TWO HOURS AND several calls later, Cav still had nothing. In a city peopled with Asians, a slim, pretty, blue-eyed blonde, five foot seven or eight, should stick out like a square peg in a round hole. But he'd butted up against dozens of brick walls. No one had seen or heard anything about an American woman. This wasn't good.

Myanmar was a country where human rights—especially women's rights—were basically nonexistent, and this was starting to stink like a government cover-up. Which meant two things. One: Carrie Granger of Nowhere, Georgia, was in big, bad trouble. Two: Cav couldn't hang up his spy shoes just yet.

It was a full forty-eight long hours later before he finally managed to rattle the right chains and come up with some answers. He flipped open his phone and called Wyatt's number.

"I found her," he said without preamble when Wyatt picked up. "As far as I know, she's still alive."

"And the bad news?" Wyatt asked, too savvy to feel relief.

Cav glanced toward the window.

"You don't want hear the bad news."

TWO

Until last week, the closest Carrie Granger had come to a monsoon had been in the comfort of her living room, watching news footage on CNN. Detention camps where people were held with no shelter, their food tossed in through the bars of a crude wooden cage, were the stuff of documentaries exposing the horrors of third world injustice.

Until last week, she hadn't truly understood the term "living nightmare."

This week, after being herded into the back of a truck like cattle with several other prisoners, then traveling for hours over mountainous roads to this hellhole, it was far too clear.

She huddled into the corner of the make-shift outdoor cage that was her jail cell and new living quarters. She and a dozen captives—all of whom appeared to be Burmese and none of whom spoke English—had been forced to build the cage themselves at gunpoint when they'd arrived at the labor camp.

Their cage was identical to ten others, also filled with slave laborers, crowded along the mountainside. The bars were made of roughly cut wood that her jailers had hastily chopped from a stand of small trees. Her hands were still raw from the wood and hemp rope slivers she'd gotten lashing the poles together. The reward for their labor? Each night after they'd worked in the mud and the rock and the ruby mine for twelve or sometimes fourteen hours, they were shoved inside the seven by seven-foot cell like animals.

No roof. No shelter from the elements or the creepy crawlies that slithered out of the jungle edging the mining site.

Wet to the bone, Carrie dragged the sodden hem of her coarse work pants out of the mud and shivered against the unrelenting downpour. Even the vicious dogs that patrolled the site had better quarters.

She stared at the guard who took particular pleasure in shoving and hitting and prodding with the nose of his rifle. The one who had been watching her in a way that made her nauseous in anticipation of the day he decided he wanted more from her than endless days of hard labor.

Watch your back, you slimeball, she thought, before cutting her gaze away from where he stood under the shelter of a tree in the fading daylight, his back to her, his rifle slung over his bony shoulder. If he and his buddies force-marched them up the steep mountainside path into the mine tomorrow and he came within shoving distance, the little sadist was going to find himself on a fast ride to the bottom of the deep, rocky ravine.

Once, she would have felt guilty for having such horrible thoughts about another human being. That was before she'd experienced the depth of man's inhumanity to man.

Her belly growled with hunger. She tried not to think about it, or about the cuts and bruises on her body and her feet and the utter, consuming hopelessness that clogged her throat like a rock. Instead she thought of ruby slippers, a magic lantern, a get-out-of-jail-free card. Anything to keep her from dwelling on the dull, lifeless eyes of the others who shared this prison with her.

She'd settle for a rabbit hole in Wonderland. A frickin' time continuum. Please, God, anything to take her back in time to before she'd flown halfway across the world, wide-eyed and ready to embrace the first big adventure of her life—a humanitarian mission to help set up a dialysis unit in a rural Myanmar hospital.

Something to take her back to a time before she'd stepped out of a taxi onto a bustling, vital, wildly exotic city street, only to gasp in horror when she'd seen a young girl being beaten with the butt of a gun. She'd run to the girl's defense and been promptly arrested for "interference" in a police matter.

"You have been charged as an enemy of the state of Myanmar."

Verdict: *guilty*.

Sentence: *ten years of hard labor*.

She closed her eyes and dug deep to keep from giving in to burning tears as rain streaked down her face. Panic knotted in her chest, tight as a clenched fist.

Surely someone was looking for her. They *had* to be looking for her, right? Only how would they ever find her?

She clutched her hands together between her breasts, wishing she hadn't been so thorough in her research. Wishing she didn't know that this country formerly known as Burma was the largest country in mainland Southeast Asia—260,000 square miles, much of it the dense, mountainous rain forest surrounding these mines. Wishing with all her heart that she'd listened to her family and Wyatt when they'd begged her not to go to this fascinating yet frightening place, where military rule was often arbitrary and brutal.

260,000 square miles.

She bit back a sob.

How could anyone possibly find her?

The sound of a struggle and angry voices jarred her head up just as the cell door swung open and her captors shoved a Burmese man inside. A dozen faces—their eyes dull, their hope gone—glanced up, then away from the new captive, who landed in a sodden heap on the muddy ground.

Only a week into this "adventure" and she got it. They didn't see the old man as one of them. They saw him as one more invasion of precious little space, one more belly in need of precious little food, one more soul doomed to suffer and eventually die in this godforsaken work camp.

As she stared at the pathetic lump of humanity curled into a ball at her feet and reached out a tentative hand—an offer of comfort, of human kindness—she finally accepted the brutal truth.

She could die here.

A bone-wrenching shudder ripped through her. For certain, they were going to make her *wish* she was dead, long before starvation or the elements or some virulent infection finished her off.

Suddenly her father's voice echoed in her mind.

"You're a scrapper, sugar doll. That's what's gonna see you through this ol' life."

She'd heard those words all through her life whenever she'd run up against seemingly unbeatable odds.

She drew a deep breath, finding a new well of resolve. Her father was right. She had a choice. She could lie down like a lamb and die here or she could stand like a lion and fight. It was up to her—only her. No one else was going to save her. Her fellow captives had their hands full keeping themselves alive.

That was the operative word. She was still alive, and as long as she had breath she was going to stay that way.

Tomorrow or the next day, no matter what, she had to attempt an escape. While she still had the strength to run.

HOT, MUGGY AIR, pungent with the scents and sounds of the bustling streets of Mandalay, blew through the open driver's-side rear window. The black sedan that the Tatmadaw military commander had arranged to transport Cav to the ruby mines near Mogok shot recklessly through heavy traffic. Though Yangon was the country's capital, Mandalay, a city of more than a million people, was the last royal capital of Burma, the capital of the Mandalay Division, and Upper Myanmar's main commercial city.

Cav had arrived on a charter flight from Jakarta for an early morning appointment with the commerce minister, who had been the key to setting his plan in motion. Once he'd been wheels down on the tarmac at Mandalay International, there was no turning back.

He was proceeding on blind faith now, counting on Wyatt to put everything into play from Georgia to ensure that Cav could get Carrie out of the country once he rescued her from her abductors. *If* he managed to rescue her.

Cav watched the action fly by outside the car window. Men on small bicycles and motorcycles wove through streets glutted with battered taxies and city buses, while women on foot carried big bucket baskets filled with produce on the ends of long poles balanced on their shoulders. Colorful umbrellas covered merchandise lining the crowded throughways. City police wearing blue uniforms and carrying assault rifles stood on every corner.

If their presence alone hadn't announced absolute military rule, the huge murals painted on the sides of buildings, depicting soldiers in front of a backdrop of the red, white, and blue Myanmar flag, would have.

Cav let it all pass by in silence, his relaxed bearing as bogus as his cover story. As far as the CIA was concerned, he had a family emergency and was on personal leave. As far as the Junta government of Myanmar was concerned, Frank Windle was here, representing the interests of Horizons, International.

Windle's false but well-known reputation as an unscrupulous player, willing to do business with oppressive military regimes, had placed him and HI on the International Dirty List—and, consequently, high on trade-agreement lists with corrupt military regimes.

Would the CIA be happy to find out Cav was freelancing

using his CIA cover? Not so much. Uncle would never sanction an official op to find one lost American. But by the time his handler discovered he'd gone off the grid it would be too late to stop him.

Cav had counted on the Windle name to open back doors in the dirty underbelly of unethical international commerce. And since the military government backed all the unethical commerce in these parts, he had figured the trail would lead to Carrie Granger.

He'd figured right. Carrie Granger, it seemed, was the victim of a bungled arrest, and the Myanmar government hoped to cover up its blunder simply by making her "go away."

No evidence, no crime, no complicity.

And no chance in hell was he going to let them get away with it.

He glanced at the driver, who wore an olive drab uniform with a red patch on the upper sleeve. His matching helmet was standard military issue. Another soldier with an assault rifle rode shotgun. Cav's personal "security guard," who had been assigned as "protection" by General Maung Aye, the commerce minister, sat on the far side of the back-seat, eyes forward.

While Maung Aye had granted Cav access to the ruby mines, it was no surprise that he had not agreed to let Cav bring his own security detail for the overnighter up in the mountains. Cav had expected as much, and the driver and a couple of heavies he'd hired locally had been mostly for show. A fat cat American investor would be expected to travel with a protection detail, so he'd come equipped with all the bells and whistles.

The fact that Cav was the only one in the vehicle without a gun spoke to the commerce minister's distrust. Smart man, Maung Aye.

Cav was still holding his breath over the small backpack between his feet. He'd hidden a KA-Bar Warthog folding knife, an area map, a GPS locator, and his cell phone in a secret compartment in the specially designed metal frame. So far, the compartment had gotten by the quick, cursory search by the military—most likely because he'd been carrying a decoy cell and GPS that had been taken away from him despite his very vocal protest. He'd learned a long time ago that a little acting went a long way to deflect attention from what he really wanted to hide.

It had been almost three days since Wyatt had called Cav. Seventy-two hours, and the promise of several hundred thousand kyat to grease palms, loosen lips, and open doors, to finally find out what had happened to Carrie Granger. Cav figured it was going to take roughly seventy-two acts of God to pull this off and get her out of the deep, deep trouble she was in.

He settled in for a minimum five-hour ride, noting landmarks as they traveled. When the driver stopped a couple of hours out of the city and Cav's "security guard" gave him the option of placing a hood over his head himself or having one of them do it for him, it got even longer.

Three

The guard dogs—six mangy mixed-breed rottweiler types, all big, half starved, and trained to be mean—barked maniacally and tugged on their chains as the car approached the mining camp.

Head down, her hands busy sifting through dirt and rock and debris, Carrie squinted against the late-afternoon sun as the vehicle snaked up the narrow road cut into the mountainside. Military vehicles came and went on a daily basis, hauling out the day's precious mineral finds and delivering supplies, so it wasn't unusual to see traffic.

What *was* unusual was that when the car pulled into the main base and stopped by the commanding general's tent, a tall, dark-haired Caucasian man stepped out of the backseat.

Oh, God.

Her heart jumped when he stood and, hands on his hips, surveyed the mining site from behind his aviator sunglasses.

Maybe he was American! Maybe the American embassy

had found out what had happened to her and sent him to take her home!

She took a step in his direction and opened her mouth to call out to him—and a long whipping stick promptly cracked across her shoulders. Gasping at the stinging pain, she fell to her hands and knees.

"Work!" the guard ordered in Burmese. "Work!"

Fire lanced across her shoulders, so sharp she could barely breathe, but if she didn't get to her feet soon there would be another blow. The throbbing wound on her ribs from when she'd tried to escape two days ago was a constant, painful reminder. She'd been lucky they hadn't let the dogs loose on her.

Biting back a cry, she struggled to her feet, her gaze darting back to the man as she slowly resumed her work.

He stood twenty yards away from her work station at the mouth of the mine. From that distance, even though she was taller than everyone else around her, she would look the same as the rest of the laborers. They all wore filthy, oversized gray shirts and pants and pointy straw hats. All were bent over their tasks, heads down, backs bowed.

If he saw her he didn't give any indication. If he cared, he gave even less as the general emerged from the tent. The general extended his hand, offering a warm, hearty greeting, which the newcomer returned.

Excitement zipped through every cell in her body as the two men exchanged a few words. Carrie sneaked furtive glances his way so she wouldn't draw the attention of the guard again. Even if the dogs' incessant barking hadn't interfered, the distance was too far for her to make out each word. Still, she heard enough to pick up a mix of Burmese and English. That knowledge set her heart rate on a crash course, then sent it plummeting when the general lifted a hand toward the tent, indicating they should go inside out of the heat.

She had to get his attention. She had to get him to notice her.

Desperate, she stared at his back and willed him to turn and look at her. Miraculously, he paused at the opening of the tent, turned, pulled off his dark glasses . . . and looked straight at her.

Her heart nearly exploded.

Their eyes connected.

And she could have sworn he mouthed her name, just before he turned back to the tent. Then he disappeared, leaving her cursing the desperation of a mind that had just played a cruel trick on her.

CAV REMOVED HIS shoes, as was the custom, before stepping inside the tent. Even though he felt physically ill at what he'd seen, he smiled his best shyster smile and accepted the shot of whiskey the general's aide offered on a sterling silver tray.

Forgoing his pact with himself to swear off the booze, he downed the shot in one toss, not giving a damn that it wasn't scotch. He needed it. *Gawddamn*, he needed it. Not because he was tired and thirsty after the long ride over winding mountain roads. Not because he'd had a few moments of panic under the black hood that had been removed only a few minutes before they'd driven into the camp. Not even because he was now deeply embroiled in a rescue mission that had less than a snowball's chance in hell of success.

He needed the booze after getting a glimpse of the horrific conditions of the slave laborers forced to work the ruby mine. He needed it because when he'd spotted the slim figure hunched over a crude flume and she'd lifted her head and met his gaze, beneath the rickshaw hat he had seen misery and hope and blue, blue eyes.

He'd found Carrie Granger.

And with one look he'd felt the full weight of her future on his shoulders.

"Yeah." Cav nodded when the general offered him another shot. "Absolutely."

He wrapped his fingers around the glass and smiled again for the general, who had clearly been given advance notice of his arrival by Maung Aye.

Cav's Burmese was spotty, and given there were about a hundred different dialects in Myanmar, what he *did* know wasn't going to help him out very much. The general wasn't much better equipped to speak English, but it didn't matter. Their common language was greed and money. The promise of a *lot* of money.

He extended the letter Maung Aye had provided, then stood in silence, arms folded over his chest, while the general read it. The amount of money that had exchanged hands between Windle and the commerce minister, plus the promise of under-the-table kickbacks, had bought his passage to the Mogok mines. By the time Maung Aye discovered the account on which he'd written a check was bogus, he and Carrie Granger would be well away from here. Or dead.

In the meantime, greed and Windle's reputation—which the commerce minister had no doubt researched even before meeting with him—had given him carte blanche to explore the mines. The letter instructed the general to allow an up-close-and-personal inspection of the operation, because HI was supposedly contemplating infusing it with millions in investment capital.

Love of money. The root of all evil. And the means to save Carrie Granger from rotting in this hell on earth.

When the general handed the letter back with a nod, Cav breathed a silent sigh of relief. Another hurdle jumped.

The general turned to his attendant, who promptly presented a serving tray filled with an assortment of food.

"Hatamin sa pi bi la?" *Have you eaten?*

"Mâhou' pabù." *No,* Cav said, getting the gist of the offer and knowing enough Burmese to decline. "But later. First, business," he added in English and gestured, indicating he wished to leave the tent and tour the operation.

His host nodded and said something to the aide, who quickly produced a hard hat and handed it to Cav.

"Chèzùbè." Cav added a nod to his thanks. After settling the battered gray hard hat on his head and slipping on his shoes and shades, he followed the general out into the sweltering heat.

Even though he was prepared for what he would see, it was all he could do to keep from knocking the heads of the guards and inciting an insurrection. But the guards and the guns and the dogs numbered too many. Even though the slave laborers outnumbered their captors ten to one, in their poor physical condition they were no match for the Junta.

Young men, old men, women, and children, all emaciated and covered in grime, hauled dirt and rocks in rickety wheelbarrows over steep, narrow paths. Others disappeared into the narrow mine opening carved into the mountain, hauling buckets hanging from poles balanced on their stooped shoulders.

Metal clinked against stone as twenty or so people worked the flumes along the edge of an open pit. Carrie was among them, laboring to lift heavy, screen-bottomed trays out of murky water, then balance them on the edge of the flume in order to roll the stones trapped on the screen with their bare hands and search for the precious bloodred rubies.

Even as she worked, head down, Cav knew she was watching him. He felt the desperation of her gaze on the back of his head like a tractor beam from twenty yards away. He wished he could give her some assurance that he was here to help her, but he couldn't risk blowing his plan sky high. He'd taken enough of a chance mouthing her name just before he'd ducked into the tent.

He played the part of the cold, calculating investor, nodding in approval when the general explained the operation in a surprisingly understandable dialogue made up of Burmese, broken English, hand signals, and a little Indonesian thrown in for good measure. They spent two hours tromping along the edge of the open pits, into the mouth of the cave, and along the assembly line of workers and the dozen or so cages that acted as their sleeping quarters.

The tour served three purposes. It put the general at ease with Cav's presence in the camp, and it gave Cav an opportunity to do a complete recon. It also left Cav's scent all over the place, which would slow down the dogs if they used them to track them when they blew this place.

At the end of the second hour the sun was starting to set and Cav had seen what he needed to see. One road leading in. Same road leading out. A lot of thick, mountainous jungle in between.

It was time to put phase two into play and hope to hell he could keep on his timetable. Everything hinged on timing.

"Thirsty." He tipped his hand up to his mouth to mimic taking a drink. "Hungry," he added, patting his stomach. "We can finish the tour tomorrow morning."

The general nodded that he understood and turned back toward his tent.

Cav stopped him with a hand on his arm, then grinned a man-to-man grin, propped his sunglasses on top of his head, and cupped his crotch. His request was unmistakable. He wanted sex.

The general's smile was lascivious. This man was no stranger to depravity.

"Belao'lè?" Cav asked. *How much?*

The general shrugged and swept out a hand that encompassed the entire workforce, indicating that for the right price Cav could have his pick. A woman. A man. A child.

Cav controlled the urge to shoot the twisted bastard with his own gun.

"Woman." He pressed open palms to his chest.

When the general shared a lewd smile and dispatched his aide to select a woman, Cav stopped him again. This was the tricky part.

"Anglo?" he asked.

The general's congenial smile turned to a frown.

Don't want me anywhere near the American woman, do you, you slimy bastard? Carrie Granger's arrest and sentencing had been a mistake, one the government honchos had found out about too late to fix. Now all they wanted was to hide any evidence that it had ever happened, to avoid an international incident. And, of course, to get some work out of her while they kept her alive, just in case she might be of future use as a diplomatic pawn.

"Belao'lè?" Cav repeated, pulled his wallet out, and peeled off several bills.

When the general showed wary interest, Cav added to the stack and kept adding until the general's greed took priority over his fear of possible reprisal. After all, his commanding officers weren't here. They didn't need to know.

Cav drew a breath of relief when, with a crisp nod, the general pocketed the bills and nodded to his aide, who trotted toward the woman whose life wouldn't be worth a plug nickel if this op unraveled.

Four

All of Carrie's senses jumped into overdrive.

Something was happening.

The American—after hearing more snippets of conversation she'd decided he was *definitely* American—had been touring the labor camp and mine site for the better part of the afternoon. Blood pounding with adrenaline and fear, she'd made two unsuccessful attempts to get his attention, pulling back each time for fear of being caught. And now the general's aide was heading toward her.

Her heart went haywire as she glanced at the American. His gaze was intent on her the entire time, almost like he was warning her. To what? Stay silent? Stay put? To do as she was told? *What* was he trying to tell her? Or, in her desperation, was she merely imagining it?

He didn't make any gestures. His lips didn't move. He just stood by the general's side, quietly watching her. When the aide reached her and motioned with the barrel of his rifle that she was to move, she glanced his way again.

He gave a slight, almost imperceptible nod.

Hope spiked to new levels of desperation.

Head down, eyes on the ground, she struggled for balance as the aide shoved her roughly down the path.

Her knees felt like rubber as she stumbled toward them barefoot over bruising rocks and blistering hot dust. Her breath was rapid and shallow. And her heart went absolutely over the top crazy when she stopped in front of him. Not daring to meet his eyes, she prayed every prayer she knew that he was here to help her, and that she wouldn't do anything to screw it up.

The general barked an order to his aide. Her pulse thundered through her ears and she didn't understand a word . . . until a harsh hand grabbed the neck of her shirt and, with a hard tug, ripped it off her shoulders.

She recoiled in shock, fighting back a scream as she instinctively crossed her arms over her bare breasts.

Someone yelled and she realized it was the aide, barking at her to uncover herself. Eyes wide in a plea for compassion, she shook her head and backed several steps away. Two guards immediately flanked her. They each grabbed a wrist, then jerked her arms away from her body, forcing her to stand there completely exposed, humiliated, vulnerable, and terrified.

"Adequate," the American said in a flat voice.

The cold assessment in his voice chilled her, as did his eyes. His gaze raked her body like she was a piece of meat, lingering on her breasts before rising to her face. Then the bastard stepped forward, gripped her jaw, and turned her head from side to side.

"Yes. She'll do."

Beyond humiliated, beyond caution, and unable to fight

the gathering tears, she met his dark eyes. "Help me," she whispered. "Please . . . please help me."

She received a cold glare for her efforts. "Clean her up," he said to the general. "Then bring her to me."

He smiled then. A calculating, predatory smile laced with an ugly carnal heat, and he shared a laugh with the general.

Revulsion gagged her as rough hands dragged her toward the outdoor shower area reserved for the guards. There she was forced to strip off her pants and, completely naked, was shoved under the solar shower with a block of coarse soap.

She was beyond mortified as the guard watched her, beyond resigned to her fate as she scrubbed her body like an automaton, then rubbed the soap over her matted hair to work up a lather. When she had finally succeeded in removing over a week's worth of dirt, sweat, and grime, the guard shoved a blanket that felt like burlap into her hands.

Grateful, she wrapped the rough cloth around her body sarong style and secured the ends between her breasts.

As she'd stood under the spray, she had tried to prepare herself for what would come next. The thought sickened her, but she could do it. She could prostitute herself to this man and maybe buy her freedom. It wasn't as if she had a choice. She was weak from lack of food, exhausted and sapped of her strength. He was going to do what he wanted anyway; she had to try to work it to her advantage.

She swallowed hard as she was marched back across the compound and past the block of tents set up on the perimeter. One was reserved for the general. She'd gotten glimpses of communication equipment in another. There was the cook tent where the general's meals were prepared. The fourth was a barracks for the guards. The fifth was reserved for important visitors. Since she'd been here, she'd seen two other Asian men—both businessmen, judging by their clothes—come and go. One had spent the night in the tent she was being taken to now.

"It's about damn time," the American grumbled when the guard shoved her inside. "Sit. I've ordered food. It should arrive any moment."

Her stomach growled involuntarily, and hope rose out of the ashes of her degradation. He was going to feed her. That had to be good, right?

Seconds later, the general announced himself outside the tent flap and entered, followed by his aide, who set a tray heavy with covered dishes on a small, low, wooden table.

"Excellent. For stamina," the American said, giving her a predatory wink. "Can't have you passing out when things get a little rough."

Nausea roiled in her stomach. She hated the police who had arrested her. Hated the judge who had sentenced her, and the guard who'd delighted in beating her. But this man was the vilest of all. His arrival had raised her hopes of rescue, but he'd turned out to be one more insult to her safety and her sanity. For that, she felt more contempt for him than she did for her captors.

With their big whips and bigger guns, they at least looked the part of villains. This tall, unreasonably handsome American with the perfectly styled dark hair, deep brown eyes, and easy smile was evil and deception incarnate. Pretty on the outside but, inside, nothing but ugliness and depravity.

"Well," the American said, digging into his backpack, then tossing a string of foil packets onto the table, "let's get this party started."

He moved toward the tent flap, all long limbs and athletic grace, then indicated with a lift of his hand that the general could leave now. His smile said he had an agenda that didn't include spectators.

The general hesitated, then with a glare at Carrie that clearly said, "Please him or else," he and his aide left.

CAV WATCHED CARRIE Granger's face as she stood awaiting her fate. Whoever had said that eyes were a window to the soul could have been talking about hers. Those blue eyes said volumes about her opinion of him. They also told him that despite the horror she'd gone through, she hadn't given up. She still had some fight left in her. Clearly, she would like to gut him, skin him, then burn him alive. *After* she cut off his balls.

But she was smarter than that. Even though she saw him as a bastard who had bought her for sex, she understood that he was still her best chance for a ticket out of hell.

Much as he wanted to reassure her, he needed to keep her in the dark until he was certain she wouldn't give him away. The general had left guards outside the tent and they could potentially hear everything that happened inside.

"Eat." He pointed toward the table.

Her gaze cut to the food. He could see how badly she wanted and needed it, and how desperately she fought the hunger.

Her control broke and she turned venom-filled eyes back to his face. "I'd rather eat dirt."

She might be half starved, beaten down by exhaustion and fear, but she still had grit to spare. Good. She was going to need it.

Keeping her in sight, for fear she might attack him if he turned his back on her, he walked over to the table that held the food and his backpack. He fished around inside the pack and came up with a notebook and pen.

"You're American," she said letting go of her animosity long enough to appeal to him. "Please. You have to help me." The slight hint of a Georgia drawl colored her words. "If you can't take me with you when you leave, please, *please* get a message to my family. Or to the U.S. embassy—"

"I'm not your good Samaritan, sweetheart, so save your breath," he snapped for the benefit of any ears outside the thin tent walls.

If she'd wanted his balls before, she wanted his heart now. On a stake.

He quickly wrote in the notebook, then held it out to her.

"Go ahead, take it," he said, knowing that anyone who might be listening would assume he was offering food. "Take it," he demanded harshly.

Eyes wary, she slowly reached out a hand and, after shooting another distrustful glance his way, lowered her head and read his note.

Don't react. Wyatt sent me. I'm here to get you home.

Her head flew up. Her eyes widened with hope and disbelief as she frantically searched his face for confirmation that it was true.

Cav pressed his finger to his lips in warning. One wrong word, one careless action, and this whole thing could blow like a block of C-4.

He reached for the note, tugged it out of her frozen grip, and added, *Play along, Carrie. It's going to be okay.*

After she read it, she just sort of crumpled. He caught her as her shoulders sagged and her knees buckled.

"Easy," he whispered, wrapping his arms around her and pressing her face into his shoulder to muffle her sob. "Keep it together. You've made it this far. We're going to get you out of here."

Small hands pressed against his chest, and her fingers tightened in a death grip on his shirt. "Don't . . . don't leave me . . . here."

Aw, God.

He'd always been a sucker for a damsel in distress. Always had a great appreciation for the softness and the strengths and the surprises inherent to women. But never had he been so utterly and unexpectedly moved as he was by the collapse of this strong woman's guard and the raw desperation that caused it.

Careful of the bruise he'd seen on her ribs, he drew her tighter against him because it felt as though she were coming apart in his arms.

"When I leave, you leave," he promised against her damp hair, and then he felt a subtle shift back to strength in the fragile body pressed against his.

If her momentary collapse had shaken him, her valiant effort to regroup humbled him. Though her body felt delicate and slight, she possessed rock-solid core strength.

Every protective instinct in him roared to life like an

enraged lion. No woman should ever have to go through this hell. He fought the knee-jerk burn to make the bastards pay for what they'd done to her. Pay with their blood. Make them sorry they'd ever laid a hand on her. He wanted it with a fervor that had him shaking.

He needed to get a grip. He'd let things get way too personal, way too touchy-feely way too fast. Not his MO. So why?

He swallowed hard, recognizing with brutal honesty that this wasn't just about her. It was also about turning his back on the CIA when this was over, about dealing with the demons that constantly baited him with the promise of oblivion in scotch.

And it was about Carrie Granger not being the only American on this mountain in need of rescue.

He drew a deep breath and made himself disengage. Now was not the time to indulge in the mind fuck of self-pity. And until he could get a handle on what was happening with his head he needed to be very careful around this woman.

"It's going to be okay," he promised her, surprised at the gruffness in his voice. Surprised again when he lifted a hand and gently brushed a fall of blond hair out of her eyes. "Take it to the bank, Carrie. You're going to be okay now."

"Thank you." A world of gratitude, relief, and trust shimmered in her eyes.

Eyes so brave and true, he found himself praying he deserved that trust.

Praying? Hell, he didn't pray. And even if he did, prayer wasn't going to get them out of this. Keeping his head in the game was. Starting now.

"Eat," he said forcefully for the benefit of the guards. "We need to get some protein in you."

This time she didn't hesitate. With one hand latched in a death grip on the blanket between her breasts, she rushed to the table and sat down on the woven matting that covered the dirt floor. Then she tore into the soup, white rice, and chicken curry.

He'd been hungry himself before, but he'd never understood the term *ravenous* until he watched her eat.

"Easy," he cautioned. Ignoring the warning alarms telling him not to, he reached for the whiskey bottle the general had left. He poured a tall shot and downed it in one swallow. "Slow down or you're going to make yourself sick."

He watched her get control again. Couldn't help but notice that despite the brutality of her captivity, there was no disguising how astonishingly beautiful she was. The bones always told, and hers were amazing. She had high cheekbones, perfectly arched brows, and a cupid's bow upper lip that just begged for attention.

Christ.

He thought about hitting that bottle one more time . . . but he knew where that road led and the last thing he wanted to do was let this woman down.

Five

Daylight had faded, and the inside of the tent was cast in shadows by the time she'd eaten her fill, savoring every bite. Cav understood. It was as much about nourishment for the soul as it was for her body.

Her body.

She was naked beneath the blanket. He did his damnedest not to think about it. Or to remember the generous perfection of the breasts the guards had brutally forced her to bare.

What he needed to think about were the bruises crisscrossing her shoulders and back. The angry welt on her rib cage, just below her left breast. The cuts on her feet, the blisters on her hands.

A motor roared to life in the distance, and a bare bulb flickered to dim life overhead. He'd noticed the gas-powered generator on the other side of the camp earlier. Its noise would provide partial cover for their conversation.

"How are you, physically?" he asked, still cautious, leaning in close so they wouldn't be overheard.

"Much better now."

"Infections? Fever? Anything broken?"

She shook her head, and the ends of the blanket picked that moment to slip and fall away from her breasts. She reached up and caught it, but not before he got a glimpse of a dusky rose nipple.

"I need to check your ribs."

Her face flushed pink in the pale light. "It's just a bruise."

"The skin is broken."

Her eyes met his, beseeching.

He got it. She was humiliated over the way they'd stripped her, then held her there for everyone to see her naked from the waist up.

Yeah, he got it, but he couldn't give her a pass. Besides, he had to start acting the part of the paying customer. Daylight had actually provided more anonymity inside the tent than the night did. The overhead light, anemic as it was, cast their shadows against the tent walls for inquisitive eyes to see.

"Trust me," he mouthed and sat down cross-legged beside her. "On my lap."

Her eyes widened, suspicion rampant on her face as she glanced at the strip of condoms he'd dropped on the table earlier.

"They're props," he assured her quickly. "If you talk the talk, you gotta walk the walk to convince the bad guys. Trust me," he whispered again, and nodded toward the tent wall.

He saw the moment she understood. Just like the condoms, this was for show. Whoever was out there would see their shadows and assume they were watching a man having his way with a woman.

Very gingerly, she moved toward him and settled herself sideways on his lap, her right side pressing against his chest.

She was tall and lean, and while she'd doubtless dropped some weight during her captivity he was very much aware that she still had plenty of curves.

"That's more like it, baby." Even if the guards didn't understand English, they'd recognize his lewd tone. "How about a little gratitude for getting you out of your cage for the night?"

She stiffened but let him pull her against him.

"Easy," he whispered, pressing his mouth against her ear and trying not to think about her firm ass nestled up tight against his groin. "Once we make our break, we have to head through some rough territory. In this climate, in this terrain, even a small cut is ripe for infection."

She turned her face toward him, her mouth very near his. Anyone outside watching their shadows would think she was letting him kiss her. "When? When are we leaving?"

The anxious edge in her voice made it clear she wanted him to say "now."

"When I say it's time." He ran his hand over her hair to enhance the visual, then stroked her shoulder and reached down to her thigh. "Now I need to look at those ribs."

She stiffened involuntarily and he made himself slow down.

"You trust Wyatt, right?"

She swallowed, then nodded.

"And he trusts me to get you out of here. You need to follow his lead. Let's just get this over with so we can move on."

She closed her eyes and, in what must have taken formidable effort, lifted her right arm and wrapped it around his shoulders.

Progress. Only he was the one shaken now. He'd asked for her trust and now that he had it, it felt like a Mack truck had just parked on his shoulders.

"What about the others?" she asked tentatively. "When we go, we can't just leave them here."

Cav had already thought about releasing the workers, creating a little pandemonium to buy them some time, and then he'd thought better of it.

"If we release them when we make our break, it will wake up the entire camp. The guards will come out shooting and a lot of people will get gunned down. We'll do more harm than good." He saw the compassion in her eyes and felt regret in his gut.

"But—"

"No discussion, Carrie. We go out alone tonight. But I promise you this: I'll be back." He had made that decision the moment he'd set foot on the mining site. When the time was right he would get these poor souls out of here. Until then, he'd be haunted by the dead eyes that had looked right through him.

"Take it to the bank," he assured her. "I'll be back with a team to get them out."

The regret in her eyes slowly transitioned to grim acceptance.

After a long, quiet moment, she finally relaxed enough

to lean against him. Like a lover. Like a woman who knew what the action would do to a man.

The tent was warm. Her skin was hot. Flickering light played along the slender line of her throat and the gentle slope of her shoulder. Her thigh was warm beneath his hand, and her weight was all woman and enticing on his lap. In the moment, the idea that she'd been summoned to his tent as a sexual diversion felt a little too close for comfort.

He still didn't understand why he was having such a strong reaction to her. She was just another woman in a long line of them.

"How do you know Wyatt?" she asked quietly.

"Long story. We can talk about it later," he said, then warned her so she could prepare herself. "I'm going to pull the blanket away now."

Louder, he said, "Okay, doll. Let's have another look at the merchandise . . . Nice," he said when the blanket pooled around her hips.

She closed her eyes and covered her breasts with her free arm, a small concession to her modesty and an action that would appear seductive from the outside looking in.

Hell, it *was* seductive. And it was very . . . southern. Like her voice. And very sweet.

Yet she was very, very tough, he conceded as he probed her bruises and she barely flinched.

"Give me a groan," he whispered. "A loud one. And make it sexy." If nothing else, it would give her a cover for the pain he knew he was inflicting.

She hesitated but then gave it her all.

"Oh, God," she whispered, lowering her head. "That sounded ridiculous."

He smiled against her hair. "Trust me. They're panting out there."

"Then they're sick."

He chuckled softly. "Tell me what you can about the camp routine. When do the guards change shifts?"

Her breath was warm against his throat as she leaned farther into him to enhance the show. "They change around eleven and again around seven. Maybe also around four in the afternoon. That's as close as I can figure, judging by the position of the sun."

"Good observations. I counted around twenty guards."

"Twenty-four," she corrected.

"All with automatic weapons," Cav muttered absently as he lowered his mouth to the curve of her throat and traced her ribs with his fingertips in search of more injuries. "And there are what . . . a hundred and forty, maybe a hundred fifty workers?"

"Something like that."

"I saw five vehicles. Two trucks, two old jeeps, and the sedan that brought me here. That sum it up?"

She nodded. "They use the trucks to transport supplies, fresh troops, and new batches of workers. The general makes use of the two jeeps to move around the mine site."

He traced the welt that ran from just below her left breast, under her arm, and around her back, where it stopped under her shoulder blade. Her skin was very soft. Her bones extremely fine. And damn . . .

She sucked in a quick, pained breath when he pressed at the swelling.

"Bad?" He studied her profile with concern.

She bit her lower lip, shook her head in denial of the pain.

"You're not much of a liar," he whispered, then said in a louder voice, "It's okay, baby. You can scream if you like it. Turns me on."

What came out was more of a growl but she stuck to her guns about the pain. "It's better than it was."

Yeah, he was right about the tough part. And she was very sexy, too.

He backed away from that thought in double time. Wrong time, wrong place, and *Jesus*, wrong thinking. Damn, he wanted another drink.

"I don't think anything's broken," he said gruffly, and he quickly applied the salve from his backpack. "Now we need to move this to the cot, before the natives start questioning my motives."

And before the swelling action in his pants embarrassed her even further.

CARRIE ROSE SLOWLY from his lap, placing a hand on his shoulder for balance. She was anxious to get some distance from his probing, yet she was reluctant to move even a few inches away from him. *What if she'd gone off the deep end and this was all some cruel fantasy, and the minute she broke contact he disappeared?*

But he'd felt real enough, she thought, walking the few steps to the cot. His body had been hard and hot beneath hers. His hands had felt strong and rough even as he'd taken care not to hurt her.

When she'd leaned into him his heart had beat like thunder against her breast. His breath had been warm and scented of whiskey when he'd whispered in her ear. And while she knew he hadn't intended for it to happen, she'd felt him grow hard against her hip.

She flushed hot, thinking about it as she sank down on the cot'sthin mattress. After a deep breath, she made herself look at him when he sat beside her. Big. Imposing. Strong. If he wanted to, he could overpower her in a heartbeat.

Thank God this seduction scene was just for show.

And thank God he was real. Real and here and . . . "I don't even know your name."

He turned the most intense dark eyes on her. "Sorry. It's David. David Cavanaugh." He smiled then, and all she could do was stare as it transformed his face.

Wyatt sent one of People *magazine's hundred sexiest men alive to save me.*

She almost laughed at her absurdity, but it was true. With that dark hair falling over his forehead and the smile that was a little bit reckless and a lot rogue, she couldn't shake the image of Johnny Depp with a little Hugh Jackman thrown in for good measure.

And he'd just seen her naked. Just touched her bare skin.

"My friends call me Cav," he added. "Now lie back and let the sex fiend indulge in his twisted foot fetish, while *I* take a look at those poor battered tootsies of yours."

She smiled, as he'd no doubt intended, and her opinion of him rose even higher.

She tried to remain covered as she lay back and he lifted her calves over his thighs. Her best efforts, however, couldn't keep the coarse blanket from parting at mid-thigh and separating slowly by degrees. Seeing her problem, he reached for the ends of the blanket, folded it over her legs, then tucked it tight beneath the outside of her thighs. Seen from outside, the action could have been misinterpreted as an unwrapping.

She felt like a mummy, a little bit pampered yet a lot intrigued. She watched his face as he administered to her foot with gentle, sensual hands. So sensual that anyone seeing their shadows would have assumed he was caressing her in sexual foreplay.

She gasped in pain and surprise when he probed an open sore on the bottom of her heel.

"Sorry," she apologized, her voice tight, then let loose of another yelp when he probed deeper into the cut.

Cav hated that he'd hurt her but couldn't let it sidetrack him. He didn't like the look of that cut.

"Make all the noise you want." He notched his chin toward the tent wall. "The louder the better. Convince 'em we're having a party in here. It'll be good for my image."

She went so still he realized he'd embarrassed her again.

"You *do* have very tender southern sensibilities, don't you?" he teased, charmed by the flush on her cheeks.

"I passed tender about five days ago."

He hadn't meant to sound like he was discounting all she'd been through. Then she smiled, and damn if he didn't feel a whole new level of respect for her.

"Yeah. I imagine you did." He reached into his backpack, powerfully tempted to reach for her. "I need to do some deep cleaning on this cut."

He came up with a plastic packet of antiseptic wipes, then made a big production of running his hands up the length of her calf and caressing her foot. "This is going to sting like blazes."

"Man of your word," she said through clenched teeth as he squeezed antiseptic liquid directly into the cut, then held the wipe against the wound before cleaning it.

"Sorry. I'll dress it with ointment, bandage it, and hope it'll see you through."

"I'll be okay."

He finally looked at her. Ever since she'd lain down on the cot he'd had a damn hard time *not* looking at her.

"I know you will," he said. "I know you're going to be just fine."

Six

Carrie's heart kicked up.

"I know you will. I know you're going to be just fine."

She heard more than simple conviction in those few words. She heard a world of respect. Felt it in the way he gave her foot an affectionate squeeze before he dug in his pack for the bandages.

She swallowed back a lump of gratitude along with the sudden threat of tears as he finished with the dressing. For the past several days she'd been treated like a mongrel dog. No dignity. No hope. Above all, no respect.

He'd just given it all back to her. And as she watched his amazing face in profile, his head lowered over her feet, she realized that he'd also made her feel something like a woman again.

It was a feeling she'd lost even before she'd been arrested. Yes, she'd had altruistic reasons for coming to Myanmar. She had a good life and she wanted to give back. But she'd also left her mundane routine because, frankly, she'd always had a thing for Wyatt Savage. When he'd come home for a visit a year ago, she'd made that clear to him.

Only Wyatt didn't love her. He'd made *that* clear to *her*. He'd been very kind, but the truth was he loved someone else. Loved her so much he'd married her last spring.

That had broken her heart a little, just enough that she'd needed to shake things up.

Well, she'd shaken them up, all right.

She forked her hair out of her eyes and glanced at David Cavanaugh, wondering at her lack of disappointment that Wyatt himself hadn't come.

She still couldn't believe that *this* man—this stranger—was actually here to save her. She was *really* getting out of here.

And that's what she thought about when he lowered her foot, then planted his hands on either side of her ribs and leaned in close.

"You need to get some rest," he whispered, lowering his mouth to the corner of hers, "but we probably ought to make this look good."

Her reaction was instant and knee-jerk and embarrassing. She reached between them for the blanket and tightened it over her breasts like a schoolgirl. "How much longer do we play out this charade? When can we leave?"

He brushed his lips along her jaw line. "Patience, Miss Granger."

She was out of patience. And all this pretend love play was driving her out of her mind.

"So are we going to steal one of the vehicles? Is that how we're getting away?" She needed a distraction from the physical contact as much as she wanted to know what he had planned.

He shook his head. "We'd never get past the checkpoints. I was blindfolded but I could tell they were heavily fortified."

"They're all manned by at least a dozen armed guards." When they'd trucked her up here with the others who had been "convicted" at trials, there had been several roadblocks. "All barricaded by trucks that don't move unless they get a chain-of-command clearance to proceed."

"They've got a lot to protect. Wouldn't do for the wrong eyes to see the rubies or the slaves."

"What *is* the plan?" What if they couldn't get out? What if they were caught trying to escape?

"You *do* have a plan, right?" she pressed when he didn't say anything.

"Sweetheart." He leveled her a smile that, if she hadn't already been lying down, would have put her right on her back. "I *always* have a plan."

He saw her frustration.

"Look, Carrie. Let's revisit that trust issue one last time, okay?" he suggested gently. "I know you're scared, but you have to trust me to know what needs to happen, and when it needs to happen.

"And what needs to happen now is that you rest. *Then* we'll talk about whether you're up for making a run for it."

She nodded. "I'll run barefoot over broken glass to get out of here but I can't run very fast wrapped in this blanket."

"I've got it covered. There's a T-shirt and a pair of cargo pants in my backpack. I guessed on the size but they'll have to do."

Another worry undercut her relief. "What about shoes?"

He thought of her poor bruised and cut feet, thought of the guard. The one who had been so happy to hit her with the whipping stick and prod her down the rough trail without any regard for how difficult and painful it was to walk across the jagged rocks.

"You will by the time we leave," he promised her. The bastard's sandals would fit her just fine.

CARRIE WAS TRYING to interpret the sudden dark look that crossed his face when she heard movement outside the tent. Suddenly Cavanaugh was lying flat on top of her, covering her mouth with his and grinding his hips into hers.

She'd been riding the razor's edge of flight or fight for days and both kicked in with a vengeance, rocket-fueled by panic.

She bucked, she rolled, she pulled his hair and rammed her knee up hard into his groin.

"Whoa. Whoa now," he said around a mean laugh, like he was enjoying the fight as he easily grabbed her wrists and pinned them above her head with one hand.

She finally came to her senses. Came back to the fact that he was not the enemy and that there was method in his actions.

He turned his head and looked over his shoulder as he worked his shirt buttons with his free hand. "She's a wild cat," he said, and she realized the general had arrived unannounced.

"I'm always up for a party, but I prefer to handle this on my own." He shrugged his shirt off one shoulder and, fumbling for his belt buckle, lowered himself over her again in a clear indication for the general to leave.

"My apology," the general said, and he walked back outside.

Her heart beat like thunder as Cavanaugh pressed her into the mattress. Broad chest. Thick biceps. Intense brown eyes. Eyes that were regretful and something else. Something that kicked her heart rate even higher.

"Sorry," he whispered against her mouth. "The pervert wanted to make this a threesome."

Oh, God. She was suddenly aware of the hard rise and fall of her breasts, which had been bared by her wild struggle. By the pounding of his heart against hers. And by the irrational thrill of the thick erection against her belly.

CAV NEEDED TO get up and off of her. He never let anything distract him from an op. Never. Yet it would be damned easy to get sidetracked by her. Practically naked, frightened, and alive like fire was alive.

He *damn* sure needed to get up.

Only he couldn't—not yet.

First, the general was clearly distrustful, and Cav was certain he'd left someone nearby. There would be . . . expectations.

Second. Carrie Granger had knobby knees and they'd connected with her target. The *boys* were not happy, and he wasn't certain he could walk just yet.

"Sorry," he gritted out again and tried to shift some of his weight off her while reaching between them and making a careful adjustment to his package.

Bad move.

Very bad move.

The warm, naked flesh of her belly pressed against the back of his forearm. The heat of her mons and the sweet cleft between her parted thighs cradled the back of his hand. With only the most minor of adjustment he could be there. Right there. Inside her. And his stupid dick was totally on board with the idea.

Fuck.

Screw caution. Screw pain. With Herculean effort, he shot up off the cot and turned his back to her, giving her a chance to cover herself.

Giving himself a chance to get it the hell together.

He reached for the lone lightbulb and yanked the damn string. The tent went dark, providing anonymity from spying eyes. Only then did he shrug back into his shirt and start working the buttons, his fingers shaking.

Jesus.

He walked to the table and reached for the whiskey bottle, then poured a shot glass full with an unsteady hand.

He didn't get it. Didn't get why he felt not only responsible for her but also inexplicably drawn to her.

He'd known a lot of women. Seen them at their best. Seen them at their worst. Never, though, had he seen one this vulnerable—and never had he felt such an intense and visceral reaction to a woman because of that vulnerability and her utter determination not to give in to it.

He slammed back the whiskey. Savored the burn.

He couldn't explain a thing about his reactions to her. They'd barely exchanged words. She was in a state of shock. Her responses were propelled by desperation and fear, and her actions spoke less about who she was than about what had happened to her.

But there was something in those eyes . . . those all-American-girl blue eyes when she'd stared up at him . . . something that touched places inside him he'd never let anyone have access to before.

So why is she getting to me?

Because Carrie Granger was a woman of substance, that's why. Her courage, as she had endured yet one more humiliation, told him just how much strength she really had.

He wiped the back of his hand across his mouth. That didn't mean he could afford to let this escalate. And for damn sure it didn't mean he could break his own rules.

Never get involved.

Never let things get personal.

Just do the job.

Rules he lived by. Rules that had kept him alive in the past, and rules that would get them both out of this alive now.

"I'm going outside," he said without further explanation.

Just like he didn't have an explanation for what had almost happened on that cot.

Seven

If there was a God, Cav thought twenty minutes later as he headed back for the tent, the distracting, delicious, and distressed Miss Granger would be dressed when he stepped back inside. The olive T-shirt and camo cargo pants ought to go a long way toward drabbing her down.

He nodded cordially to the guard who stood near the tent with an AK-47 slung over his shoulder. Then he tipped a finger to his forehead in an amiable good night to the other guard who had shadowed every step of his stroll around the dimly lit perimeter of the camp.

For all they knew, he'd just stepped out to relieve himself, get a little recovery time, and was heading back in for another round. Security was very present . . . but it was also very slipshod. These guys weren't the best trained soldiers; discipline was on the low side. He liked that.

It was still a long way from midnight, but the heavy cloud cover made for a nice, dark night. Only a haphazardly strung set of lights illuminated the mining area, and the shadows outnumbered the lighted areas.

The dark night, the feeble electrical generator, and the loose security were three very high marks on the plus side for their escape attempt.

The tent was still dark when he ducked back inside. He stood still for a moment, letting his eyes acclimate. The generator hummed in the background, making it difficult for him to pick up any sounds inside the tent. Difficult for Carrie to discern that it was him, too.

He decided to risk it and groped above his head for the light string. With a soft *snick* the bulb flicked on—and there she was.

Dressed—*Thank you, God*—but crouched in a corner, eyes wild and wary, ready to defend herself.

Both hands were wrapped around a three-foot length of wood that was cocked over her shoulder like a baseball bat, and she was ready to swing.

He grinned, only then noticing that the table that had held their food and his whiskey lay on its side, missing a leg. *God bless the woman for her resourcefulness.*

Guilt quickly undercut his amusement. Damn his stupid hide for leaving her alone and undefended, all because he hadn't been able to deal with his physical reaction to her.

"Fuck," he muttered and went to her. "I'm sorry." He crouched down in front of her. "I'm sorry I left you alone and afraid."

"I . . . I wasn't sure you'd . . . come back."

Aw, God.

He was a clueless bastard to have forgotten the desperation he'd seen the first time he'd looked into those blue, blue eyes.

"I'm sorry," he whispered again as he reached out and very deliberately pried her fingers off the table leg.

Her white-fingered grip relaxed by slow degrees until he finally relieved her of her weapon. Still as tense as a piano wire, she rocked forward to her knees, lowered her head, and propped her open palms on her thighs. She was shaking hard and working even harder to pull herself back together.

Disgusted by his stupidity, he tossed the table leg aside and drew her against him in apology. In reassurance. In near desperate need for forgiveness.

Her body was ramrod straight and unbending as he folded his arms around her.

Then her breath rushed out on a sigh and she melted into him, wrapped her arms around his neck, and clung.

And there they stayed. On their knees on the straw mats covering the hard dirt floor.

Overhead the lone bulb flicked. Hot, humid air surrounded them. Misery and pain permeated the tent, the entire camp.

But all Cav was aware of was the softness of her body pressed against his, the amazing silk of her hair beneath his hand, and the undeniable forging of a bond he no longer wanted to question or analyze.

He lowered his face into the curve of her neck. Inhaled her warmth and her courage and the essence of this very soft yet formidable woman.

"Try to rest now." He made himself pull away from her. "Just for a little while."

"I couldn't sleep if you drugged me."

"Humor me." He helped her to her feet, led her to the cot. "Give it a shot."

Because she was a good southern girl she lay down.

Because his mother had raised him right he didn't.

At least not next to her. He found a spot on the floor and sat down. Then he tried like hell not to think about the way she looked in the cargo pants that fit her fine butt like a glove and the T-shirt that was a size too small. Could *not* think about the gentle sway of her full, unbound breasts or the tight buds of her nipples pressing against the stretchy cotton.

Drab her down? No such fucking luck.

He checked his watch. They needed to wait a short while before checking out of Hotel Hell. On a determined breath, he stretched out on the floor, folded his hands behind his head, and made himself a promise: *she was hands off until he got her safely gone from here.* But when they got out of this fix he was going to find out a helluva lot more about Carrie Granger before he let her walk away.

If he let her walk away.

"IT'S TIME."

Carrie's eyes flew open with a start. With consciousness came instant terror. The same terror she'd awakened to for more days than she could count.

Then she realized she was not in the cage. A dozen exhausted, ragged slaves were not sharing the same squalid misery with her.

She struggled to get her bearings. She was in a tent. It was dark. And hot.

"It's time," a man's voice whispered again, closer this time as a gentle hand touched her shoulder.

Cavanaugh.

Real.

Helping her.

Relief was instant.

"I fell asleep?" she whispered into the dark silence. She no longer heard the generator running.

"Exhaustion and starvation will do that to a person."

She sat up straight, stretched out the kinks, and let her eyes adjust to the darkness. Cavanaugh's shadow loomed along the tent walls before he returned to her side.

He squatted down in front of her. "Awake now?"

She nodded, then whispered, "Yes," when she realized he probably couldn't see her.

A big hand squeezed her knee. "Good girl. Can you carry this?" A bulky weight landed on her thighs.

His backpack.

"I pilfered some of the bottled water stocked in this tent, so it's heavy."

"I can do it." She figured that he needed her to carry the pack because he would need his hands free for other things. Things she didn't want to think about but knew would be necessary to get them out of here.

"Let's get the straps fitted."

She stood and slipped the pack onto her back. His big hands were deft and steady as he stood behind her and helped her adjust them.

Helped her.

An overwhelming flood of gratitude swept her right to the edge of control, and she had to fight to keep her knees from buckling.

"Hey." Strong hands gripped her shoulders, steadying

her. "Hey," he repeated gently and turned her around to face him. "What's happening?"

She blinked back a damning rush of tears. "It's . . . it's just . . . I thought I was going to die here."

She swallowed hard, made herself meet his eyes. Even in the dark she could see the compassion and the strength and the promises there. "Thank you."

He squeezed her shoulders, then leaned forward and pressed a kiss to her forehead. "Don't thank me yet, sweetheart. We're a long way from gone."

And she was a long way from grasping exactly what it was about this man that had her wanting to throw herself into his arms one instant and back away the next. Both of their lives were on the line here, and she *so* did not have it together.

"What's the plan?" she asked abruptly. If she didn't inject something concrete into this very tense, very intimate situation, she was going to do something very, very stupid. Like fall into his arms again.

"Stealth," he said simply.

She blinked. "That's it?"

"That's what you need to know," he said evasively. "For now."

"Fine. What about the dogs?" Even more than the guns, those dogs terrified her.

"They're more for intimidation than for tracking."

"Yeah, well, the intimidation part is definitely working."

"Even if they're trackers," he assured her, "both of us have left our scents all over this place. It'll take them forever to figure out where to start looking. In the meantime, we're steering way clear of them on the way out."

She shivered involuntarily, remembering one day when the dogs had mauled a man who had attempted to escape.

"The generator shut off two hours ago," he went on, "so unfortunately we don't have that noise to help provide cover. On the plus side, at this time of night the guards are fighting sleep, if they aren't sleeping already. No perimeter fences, either, which tells me they're not too worried about anyone trying to slip away."

"It's a little difficult to run when you don't have the strength to put one foot in front of the other," she whispered in agreement.

"This isn't going to be pretty." His voice was hard, all business. "I'm going to have to take out your favorite guard first. He drew watch outside the tent."

She swallowed, understanding that "take out" had nothing to do with dating or Chinese food, and was most likely a permanent resolution. *Oh, God.* For the first time in her life she *truly* understood gallows humor. She'd wished the guard dead a hundred times since she'd been brought here at gunpoint. Faced with the probability of it actually happening, however, she felt a fissure of regret. She had dedicated her career to saving lives. The thought of someone dying because of her . . .

"Don't think about it," Cavanaugh said softly.

He not only rescued women, he read minds. And he was right. She needed to remember only one thing: this was life or death. Better the guard's death than hers.

"I'm okay." If she said it often enough, maybe that would make it true.

"Yes. You are." It was as much an order as a statement. "Don't move. I'll be right back."

She nodded and he ducked under the tent flap.

She stared at the spot where he'd been, heart pounding, adrenaline rushing.

Before she could reconcile herself to the fact that the sound she'd just heard was most likely the sound of a neck being snapped he was back.

She couldn't make out his expression, but she could smell the adrenaline on him. Could feel violence crackle around him like electricity.

He handed her a pair of sandals, the soles still warm to the touch.

Oh, God.

She put them on.

When she straightened, she realized he was carrying a rifle. Of course. He'd taken it from the guard.

"You stay on my six." He reached for her hand and dragged it to his belt. "Hang on, you got it? From this point on, we are officially connected at the hip. It's all about running now. No questions. Just follow me and keep as quiet as you possibly can."

She could run. She could be quiet. She could do anything he told her. What she *couldn't* do was keep herself from stopping him when he turned to lead her out into the night.

His eyes were full of questions as she moved in close against him.

And then he got it.

"Carrie." His breath was warm against her lips as she lifted her face to his. "You don't want to do this."

"What I don't want to do," she whispered, standing on her tiptoes and wrapping both arms around his neck, "is regret that I didn't."

Her heartbeat was already wild from the fear and the danger and the risk. But when her lips touched his, wild didn't even begin to cover the sensations that bolted through her blood and apparently slammed through his just as hard, just as fast, because there wasn't an ounce of caution in his kiss. He wrapped his free arm tightly around her waist and lifted her flush against him, his body hot and responsive, his mouth hungry and fully, carnally engaged.

He was a big, hard man. Yet all she could think about was the softness of his lips, the sleekness of his tongue, the profound restraint with which he held her that both excited her and reminded her of the danger he was in because of her.

She wanted the kiss to go on forever. Wanted this intense exploration of mouths and tongues and sensations, which *she'd* initiated but that *he'd* taken to an entirely different level, to obliterate the harsh reality that once they set foot outside this tent their lives could very well end in an explosion of gunfire.

And in this moment she wanted him almost more than she wanted her freedom, because she was desperately afraid that freedom would come at the cost of his life.

Fortunately, there was a cooler head in this tent than hers. There was a man who would not allow her to give up the promise of a future for the price of one moment in time. No matter how amazing that moment promised to be.

He lifted his head on a groan, pressed her face into his chest, and held her against a heart that beat like thunder.

"If I were to pick a cliché," he murmured against her hair, "*wrong time, wrong place* pretty much sums it up."

She swallowed hard, willed her heart rate to settle. He was right. "I'm sorry."

"That makes two of us," he said gruffly.

Shouldering the rifle sling, he cupped her chin in his hand and lifted her face so she could see his eyes. "So be warned, Carrie Granger. The next time I kiss you, you're going to end up naked and flat on your back, and it's going to take an army to keep me from making certain you never feel the need to say you're sorry again."

It was all she could do to keep her legs under her, let alone assemble a coherent thought.

"Nothing to say to that?"

"I . . . um . . . *gulp*?" She finally managed to answer his smile with one of her own.

He pressed another kiss on her forehead. "Well said."

When he pulled back and searched her eyes he was all business again. "Ready to do this now?"

"Yeah." She drew a bracing breath. "I'm ready."

He squeezed her arm. "Like glue," he reminded her.

Then he turned toward the tent flap and led her into the night, either to freedom or to death.

Eight

Gripping the rifle in his left hand, Cav crouched low to minimize his profile. He thanked God and good fortune that the sky was still cloud heavy and the night dark. He chanced a glance over his shoulder and motioned for Carrie to follow his lead.

She instantly mimicked his movements and, as promised, stuck like a tick as they skittered across twenty yards of open ground, then ducked down behind the relative cover of the five vehicles parked in a tight row in front of the silent cook tent.

Even though he'd clicked into combat mode, a small part of Cav's body and brain—as well as a big part of his libido—was still engaged in that kiss she'd laid on him. The proper southern belle just kept surprising him. He had every intention of relishing that kiss for a long, long time . . . later.

Right now, he had more pressing issues. Like the sleeping dogs on the far side of the camp. And the two guards on foot patrol who, if he'd timed this right, would be walking down the path any moment and filing right past the jeep they were hiding behind.

He slipped the safety off the AK as quietly as possible, then touched Carrie lightly on her arm. When he had her attention, he pressed a finger to his lips, signaling her to be quiet. Then he dropped to his haunches behind the front wheel well, urging her down behind him.

Less than twenty seconds later the sound of voices and the muffled crunch of sandals drifted too close for comfort. The pair of guards walked toward them, AKs slung over their shoulders, their footsteps unhurried.

The guards walked directly in front of the jeep. Some six feet and the width of an engine block separated them. And then they stopped.

Cav barely breathed. While Carrie was still sleeping, he'd retrieved the KA-Bar Warthog from his backpack frame. Very slowly, he lifted his pant leg and pulled the knife out of his boot. Behind him, Carrie was statue still in the shadows. The gentle warmth of her breath against his back, where she huddled against him, told him she was doing fine.

Come on, come on, he willed the guards silently. *Move on, you lazy bastards. Finish your rounds.*

Just when he was certain they would be on their way, a match flared in the dark.

They were taking a smoke break.

Carrie's hand tightened on his belt loop but she didn't make a sound. Several more minutes passed. Sweat ran down Cav's face and trickled down the middle of his back as they waited it out.

She had to be miserable. Even in the middle of the night

the heat was killer, depleting their bodies of fluids and salt. His calf muscles started to cramp from the awkward way he was crouched. He was betting Carrie was struggling with muscle issues as well.

He could tough out the pain. But she was already in a weakened physical and mental state, and he was worried about how much more she could take.

If the guards didn't move on soon he was going to have to do something. The last thing he wanted to do was shoot them. The gunfire would wake up the entire camp, and dodging bullets on the run was a surefire way to get her killed. He could take one guard out with his knife, but the other would be yelling bloody murder before he could shut him up.

Move, move, move!

And still they stood, leaning against the jeep, passing the cigarette back and forth, talking about women. Carrie pressed her forehead harder into his back, a sign that she was struggling.

He had to do something before she gave them away.

He felt around on the ground until he found a Ping-Pong ball–sized stone. After hefting it to get a feel for the weight, he looked around for overhead obstacles, then gave it a hard fling in the opposite direction from their flight path.

Both guards stopped their chatter and came to attention. So did the damn dogs. Six deep-throated barks rang across the mountainside. He couldn't pick up the guards' new conversation, but when they took off at a fast walk toward the spot where the stone had landed Cav didn't waste any time.

He helped Carrie to her feet and knew by the slow way she rose that she was cramping up.

"Foot or calf?" he whispered close to her ear as the dogs wound down with a few halfhearted yelps and finally fell silent after a shouted order from the guards.

"Calf," she ground out between clenched teeth.

He handed her the rifle, quickly dropped back to his knees, and felt along the backs of both of her calves. He found the knot—rock hard and the size of a marble—in her left calf and started working it out with his fingers.

Her quick intake of breath and her fingers digging into his shoulders spoke of the pain, but she toughed it out.

"I'm sorry," he whispered but was relentless until he was satisfied he'd worked out the knot and the muscle wouldn't seize up again, at least not immediately.

"Can you walk?" He stood and dug into his pack for the salt tabs he'd brought with him.

"Yes," she answered without hesitation and downed the pills with some water. He did the same, then recapped the water bottle and stowed it in the pack.

"Hold on a sec." He opened up the KA-Bar, dropped to his back, and shimmied under the first jeep in line. If he remembered right, the fuel line ran along the driver's side of the frame.

He felt around. *Bingo.* He then felt around for the rubber fittings leading to the fuel filter and cut them. The gas wouldn't leak out immediately, but when they started her up the fuel pump would spray gas all over, and the engine would run for a bit but then die of fuel starvation.

He slid out from underneath the vehicle, motioned for Carrie to follow, and took the thirty seconds he needed to repeat the process with the middle and the rear vehicles. As tightly as they were parked, the other two weren't going anywhere anyway.

"Okay," he whispered, "let's boogie before they decide to come back."

He crouched low and, with Carrie close behind, he sprinted toward the far side of the encampment, keeping to the shadows, ducking between the mining equipment and steep wall cut into the mountainside. She stopped him with a hand on his arm before they'd traveled twenty feet.

"Are you sure we can't free them now?" she asked looking back toward the caged slaves they were leaving behind.

"Trust me on this, Carrie. I'm not going to forget about them. I'll be back with enough resources to get them out of here. Right now, we've got to worry about getting our own asses the hell gone."

KEEPING HIS PROFILE low, Cavanaugh alternately sprinted and crept along the upper perimeter of the camp, leading them farther from the center of operations and higher up the mountainside. Carrie wanted to ask where they were headed, but she kept her mouth shut and her feet moving, and she made herself think past the painful cut on her foot and the exhaustion and her sore calf muscles.

She was physically depleted. Neither her muscle mass nor her motor control were what they should be, but adrenaline was a wonder drug. She just prayed the rush lasted long enough to get her past the worst of it, because when she crashed she was going to drop like a stone.

In the meantime she followed Cavanaugh's lead, even

though she wondered why he was taking them farther up the mountain instead of down.

"When they wise up to the fact that we're AWOL," he whispered as he tugged her down behind a boulder to catch their breath, "they're going to figure we went down, not up."

That was at least the second time he'd read her mind. She wasn't going to question it, just like she wasn't going to think about the guard whose sandals she wore or the way his body had looked, slumped and lifeless where Cavanaugh had propped him in a sitting position outside the tent.

Except she hadn't been able to stop thinking about it.

"Drink," Cavanaugh prodded, gripping her hand and shoving a bottle of water into it. "We need to keep hydrated."

She drank, then handed back the bottle. The generator kicked on just then, flooding the mining site with dim light. A shout rang out. Then another.

"The jig is up," Cav said, helping her to her feet. "Now we run like rabbits."

She glanced over her shoulder as he took her hand and pulled her along behind him. Less than fifty yards away the camp came alive with soldiers scrambling, rifles at the ready, as the general yelled orders that needed no translation.

It was an all-out manhunt.

"Don't look back," Cavanaugh ordered as the dogs started baying and snarling. "It'll only slow us down."

He was right, so she forced herself to forget about the guns and the dogs. She concentrated on putting one foot in front of the other as Cavanaugh led her away from the mining road and into the thickness of the jungle.

"THE BAYING IS getting farther away, don't you think?"

Cav leaned back against a thick tree trunk, boots braced on the ground against the steep downhill slope, and tried to listen past the blood pounding in his ears and his heavy breaths. They'd been on the run for at least an hour. The sound of the baying dogs was a powerful incentive to keep moving. This was only the second time he'd allowed them to stop and rest.

"I think so. Yeah. At the risk of another cliché, it sounds like they're barking up the wrong tree."

She smiled. It felt damn good. What felt even better was that the guards were searching down the mountain. As he'd also hoped, it appeared the dogs hadn't been able to pick up their exit scent. When they tried to start the vehicles and gasoline sprayed all over the place, it would be even more difficult for the dogs, whose highly sensitive sense of smell would be bombarded.

"Once they figure out the dogs don't have a trail, they'll realize that we went up, not down." He accepted the water bottle from her, drained it, then wiped his mouth with the back of his hand. "But we bought at least an hour. Maybe two."

Now all they had to do was get off this frickin' mountain, meet up with the contact Wyatt was supposed to have arranged for them, then lay low until the extraction team—also arranged by Wyatt—showed up at the designated landing zone.

Yeah. That's all.

"Let's move." He folded up his map and consulted the GPS. He hadn't bothered with his cell phone because his research had told him they weren't anywhere near a cell tower.

"There's a village about ten miles southwest of here, and that's where we're headed."

"Because?"

"Because we're expected."

"You really *did* have a plan."

Yeah. He had a plan. Normally he'd have taken weeks to plot out a rescue op of this scope. He and Wyatt had had only hours to pull this together and hold it together with kite string and duct tape.

"You're going to start trusting me one of these days." He grinned back at her as he pushed away from the tree, relieved her of the backpack, and adjusted the straps to fit his shoulders.

When he reached for her hand again, she didn't hesitate or complain. She just hopped to. Cav's admiration for her kept rising.

The jungle was dense and dangerous underfoot, so he'd risked using the miner's flashlights from his backpack. He'd figured correctly that the general wouldn't question the lights, since the supposed purpose of his visit was to tour the dark mines. The fact that he'd had an extra in his pack hadn't raised any eyebrows, either because batteries died or bulbs got broken.

This far away from the mining camp, the risk of using the headlights strapped around their foreheads outweighed the risk of falling and breaking a limb in this rough terrain. Cav might be able to carry Carrie out if she sprained or broke something, but she sure as hell couldn't carry him— although, knowing her, she'd damn well try.

"Watch your step," he warned. Every step over gnarled roots, tangled vines, and deadfall was a step toward life, just as every misstep could be tantamount to death.

They had ten grueling miles ahead of them. Ten miles that, in a perfect world, they would cover before sunrise. But this world wasn't perfect. And this woman couldn't possibly last until sunrise, as weak as she was.

It was inevitable that her body was going to fail her.

He just hoped to hell that he didn't.

Nine

Carrie felt the shift before she understood what was happening. Like the pulse thrumming through her body, she could feel the mountain jungle transition from the deep, breeding gloom of night to a darkness fostered by shadows and shade.

The sun had risen. She couldn't see it but she sensed that dawn had broken, even though daylight would never reach the floor of this dense, loamy forest.

She'd been moving on autopilot for hours, had lost feeling in her legs long ago. She made herself move because, if she stopped, she died. And she couldn't die. Not after all she'd been through.

"Stay with me, Carrie."

Cav's voice was filled with concern and encouragement. She'd clung to the steady strength of it through the grueling trek down the mountain. Just as she'd clung to him to keep her balance, to keep her here in the moment, to keep her moving.

It would be so easy to just stop walking. Stop thinking.

Stop wanting the pain to ease, just enough to make it bearable.

One more step. One more after that. Just . . . one . . . more.

A brilliant light hit her full in the face, as blinding as a fireball. The piercing blast would have sent her to her knees if Cav hadn't grabbed her.

Suddenly he was laughing and lifting her off her feet. "You did it! You amazing, astonishing woman, I don't know how you did it, but we made it!"

His words registered in a haze of pain as she buried her face against his shoulder to block the burning brightness.

The sun, she realized finally. She lifted her head and squinted against the glare. They had broken through the jungle and stumbled onto a road. Narrow, filled with potholes, nothing but dirt. But it *was* a road.

"Drink," Cav ordered after setting her back on her feet and handing her a water bottle.

The water was warm but wet. And the protein bar he handed her would go a long way toward making her feel attached to her limbs again.

"Whoa." Just as she felt herself sway again, Cav grabbed her arm and steadied her. "Come on. Let's sit you down for a bit." He eased her to the ground.

"You may never get me on my feet again," she said, peeling the wrapper off the energy bar.

He checked his watch, his GPS, then gave her arm an encouraging squeeze. "Hold on. If all goes as planned, you may not have to. Be right back."

Before she could ask him what he meant he was gone, jogging down the road and disappearing around a bend.

She was too weary to be concerned. She just sat there, drinking water and eating the protein bar. She'd just finished both and was starting to feel marginally human again when she heard voices coming from the direction Cav had disappeared.

Moving as quickly as she could she scuttled back up the embankment and into the forest, then hunkered down and hid behind a tree surrounded by heavy foliage.

"Carrie, it's okay. Come on out."

Wary, she popped her head up and spotted Cav and a Burmese boy who looked about twelve or thirteen, driving a two-wheel cart harnessed to a team of horned oxen.

"Your chariot, awaits, m'lady," Cav said with a grin as he climbed up the embankment to help her back to the road and the grinning boy.

"Nanda." She repeated the boy's name when he introduced himself and returned his handshake.

"English means river," he announced proudly.

Carrie looked from the boy to Cav.

Cav gave her a wink. "Come on. We're hitching a ride."

He lifted her into the back of the cart filled with bolts of cotton fabric.

As he hitched himself up beside her, Cav explained, "from what I've gathered, Nanda's father is a merchant in the village. Nanda is on his way home with a delivery."

"He wasn't afraid of the gun?" she asked as the oxen started lumbering down the curving mountain road. Then she got it. "Oh wait. *We're* the delivery? He was expecting us?"

"Thanks to Wyatt. He's been putting things in play at

his end," he told her. "Lie down and take advantage of the ride. We've got a ways to go."

He didn't have to tell her twice. She laid back on the bolts of cotton that were hard yet so much softer and cleaner than the ground she'd tried to sleep on at the camp. Immediately, she was gone.

SHE'D CRASHED LIKE a shooting star, as he'd known she would. Cav watched as Carrie slept on a pallet of blankets in the corner of the small bedroom in the tiny house where Nanda lived with his mother, father, and three younger sisters.

She hadn't even awakened when Cav had picked her up and carried her into the cool interior of the house in a village whose name he still hadn't figured out how to pronounce. Just like he still hadn't figured out how to deal with his feelings for this woman. Feelings that just kept getting stronger.

Nanda's mother had met them at the door. Thura was a lovely Burmese woman somewhere in the neighborhood of thirty-five. Three darling little dark-eyed girls peeked out at him from behind their mother's legs, and Cav had felt guilty for taking advantage of the family's willingness to help.

Their presence here was placing the family in danger. If it were up to him, they'd eat, rest for an hour, and be on their way. But it wasn't up to him. Time remained the enemy, but now it was too much time instead of too little. They had no choice but to hold out here until the extraction team could get into place at the prearranged time he and Wyatt had decided on forty-eight hours ago.

He'd worked this end of the equation too many times to worry that Wyatt wouldn't come through. And given that they had no options but to impose on Thura and her family, all he could do was wait it out.

Earlier, Thura's husband, Tun, had joined them, making certain they were settled. When Cav had expressed his gratitude, the young father had shown Cav into the living area, then pointed to a framed photograph on the wall.

It was a picture of Aung San Suu Kyi, the democratically elected prime minister of Burma, who had never been allowed to govern. Instead, the Nobel Peace Prize recipient had been placed under house arrest by the Junta military regime. Twenty-five years later she was still a virtual prisoner.

"You fight Junta. You are friend," Tun had stated solemnly.

And since the Junta military government ran the slave labor camps that worked the mines, it was apparent that Tun and Thura considered Cav and Carrie their friends. It was a measure of the oppression the people of Burma felt, ruled by a brutal military regime that had even taken away their country's name, renaming it Myanmar.

"We will help," Tun had added with a respectful bow. "I have car. When it is time, I drive you to meet your friends."

That had been three hours ago. Carrie had been sleeping for five, as the ride on the oxcart had taken the better part of two hours. Since she needed to recover physically, and it was still too early on the timetable to move on, Cav let her sleep.

When a soft tap sounded on the door, he shot across the

room and opened it up to Thura. She was carrying a tray loaded with a teapot, two cups, and a plate of cheese and fruit.

"She is well?" she asked with a concerned glance toward Carrie, who didn't stir even when Thura set the tray on a small table.

Like her son, Thura was delighted with the opportunity to practice her English.

"She'll be fine," Cav assured her. "Thank you again, Thura, for your help."

After Thura left them, Cav watched the rise of Carrie's breasts beneath her T-shirt, was captivated by the gentle curve of her hip, the sleek muscles of her thigh. Even found himself smiling at the utter serenity of her deep breaths, the thick lashes that were an intriguing mix of golden blond and honey.

He should take the opportunity for a quick combat nap himself before they set out again. He eased down onto the bed of blankets on the floor beside her, careful not to wake her. Dog tired, he closed his eyes. And after a few moments of just listening to her breathe he drifted into sleep.

AWARENESS CAME LIKE light, easy, unannounced. He was asleep, then he wasn't.

Awareness. That the shadows had shifted, that the day had grown shorter. The room had warmed under the noon sun; a soft breeze drifted in through the open window.

Awareness. Of soft eyes open and watching him.

He slowly turned his head and encountered blue as perfect as a New England summer day.

"Hi," he whispered.

She blinked once, slumberous and slow, as she rolled to her side facing him. "Where are we?"

He checked his watch; barely half an hour had passed since he'd lain down. He shifted to his side, facing her. "We're someplace safe," he assured her.

Her smile was soft, secure. "I already had that figured out, or you wouldn't have been sleeping."

He tried not to read too much into her trust in him. Tried not to feel protective and possessive and . . . *Christ*. This was so insane.

He barely knew her. And yet . . . he *knew* her. Knew her strength and her heart and her remarkable, resilient spirit.

His heart rumbled hard in his chest when those blue eyes full of questions and longing searched his. When she reached out, touched his face with the very tips of her fingers, he knew he should pull away. Just like he knew he couldn't.

Didn't want to. Didn't intend to.

He covered her hand with his—sandpaper against silk—and brought it to his mouth.

"You've been through a lot," he whispered a warning against her fingertips.

"Doesn't mean I don't know what I want." Sky blue transitioned to smoky cobalt as she brushed an index finger along the seam of his lips. "Doesn't mean I don't know what I need."

He groaned and gave a Hail Mary thought to playing the saint, but he didn't have it in him.

"Sometimes," she whispered, moving in until her face was just inches from his, "it's just got to be about the moment."

He was humbled by the entreaty in her eyes and by her

lack of expectation beyond the here and now. She'd just told him not to feel any responsibility, any obligation or guilt. She'd given him a pass in the accountability department.

He wasn't feeling quite as cavalier. Possibly a first for him.

"I've had a lot of bad moments lately," she went on. "I need a good one. I want it to be with you."

He sucked her fingertip into his mouth, bit it lightly, then drew her flush against him. "Just promise me you won't be sorry."

She brushed her mouth against his, then skimmed her tongue along his lips. "I think you worry too much."

"Occupational hazard," he agreed, and finally kissed her.

She was turning to him in desperation. He knew that and felt guilty about it. Just not guilty enough, he thought as he deepened the kiss and slipped his hand under her clingy T-shirt to feel skin on skin.

She arched into his touch, letting him know she was totally on board, totally involved, and wonderfully responsive.

Silk, he thought, as he skimmed his palm up her rib cage and cupped a full breast in his palm. She made a soft sound that was a mix of pleasure, impatience, and a lot of encouragement. Following his lead, she slid her hands up and under his shirt. And damn near blew the top of his head off.

The touch of her hand was so sensual and seductive he had to remind himself that no matter how eager she was he needed to go easy with her. She was bruised both physically and emotionally. He was not going to charge in like a bull and overwhelm her with his own need. He didn't want to add to her problem. He wanted to fix it.

So he took his time with his hands, leisurely drank his fill of her mouth, enticing her unhurriedly to that place where pleasure outdistanced any possibility of pain, where satisfaction became the prize in a lazy and lengthy seduction that took him to a place he'd never been before with a woman: complete commitment to her needs.

He'd never been selfish, but he'd never desired to be selfless either. Until now.

With her help, he lifted her shirt over her head, gave himself a moment to look and indulge and appreciate before he lowered his head to her bare breast.

Pillow soft. Woman sweet.

And her sighs. The fluid way she moved against him, inviting him to take what he wanted, do as he pleased . . . she stole his breath. Despite his best intentions she turned him into a pulsing mass of sexual hunger by stoking a craving that needed to be assuaged more than he needed to breathe.

He was on fire for her. Five-alarm, fully involved, on fire. He buried his hands in her hair, shifted to his back, and pulled her over on top of him. Her weight was slight and hot nestled against him as he fumbled to drag a condom out of his backpack and put it on. Her breasts were heavy and full as he reclaimed them with his mouth, and he wished to God that he could keep wanting only to please her.

But she did things to him. Turned selfless into selfish, and suddenly it became about tasting. And stroking. And

sucking his fill as she writhed against him, pressing her pel-
vis against the erection that raged beneath his zipper.

He couldn't believe he was with her like this, couldn't
believe that she was all but ripping his shirt off, then turning frantic fingers to his buckle before going to work on his
zipper. Caught up, caught in, and caught by the storm of
desire she had whipped into a frenzy, he made quick work
of her cargo pants.

He knew she was commando beneath them. Still, he
growled when he felt nothing but skin against his palms.
For as long as he lived, he would never forget the quiver-
ing silk of her belly and buttocks as he brushed his hands
against her, then lifted and settled her over his straining
cock.

"No," he ground out when she would have taken him
inside. "Too soon. I want you ready."

She actually laughed, as much in frustration as amusement, as she took him in her hand and guided him to her
opening. "Trust me on this. I'm ready."

And Jesus, oh, Jesus, was she. Her slick heat enfolded
the tip of his engorged penis like a warm, wet kiss, wel-
coming him deep, demanding complete penetration and
obliterating caution.

She was like a vessel waiting to be filled. He gripped
her hips, fully engaged and selfishly locked in what was
supposed to have been her moment but had become his
as well.

He lifted his hips to meet her, to impale and immerse
himself in the sweetest friction, the most electric heat . . .
and the absolute, incomparable sense of coming home.

She gasped his name, braced her palms on his chest, and

rode with him in a rhythm that called to the ages and with an abandon that called to him like a siren's song.

He couldn't take his eyes off her as she straddled him. Her back was arched, her eyes were closed, and the expression on her face was pure, uninhibited bliss. Endless longing and forgotten pleasure. When she suddenly stiffened and her head dropped to her chest to ride out the wave of her climax, he knew he'd witnessed something important.

Something more than sex, more even than an emotional healing. He'd just witnessed the liberation of a spirit that had been held captive by abuse, degradation, and shame.

He was already shooting over the top when she clenched around him, shivered, and collapsed across his chest.

And later, as his hand drifted lazily over the silk of her hair, he wondered when he had started thinking, *So this is the woman I've been waiting for.*

Ten

"And this one?"

Cav shivered when Carrie traced a fingertip over the scar on his right thigh. When he didn't answer, she reached for a piece of fruit.

He'd retrieved the food and tea Thura had brought earlier, setting the tray on the floor at the head of their makeshift bed.

Though he was on the road to recovery physically he hadn't recovered from the rush of emotions, or from the sight of Carrie, gloriously, unself-consciously naked and stretched out on the blankets beside him. She'd propped herself up on an elbow and was nibbling at the fruit and cheese, studying him with a mix of concern and curiosity and the prettiest lingering sexual glow.

Those eyes. They saw too much. Said too much. The way she looked at him was as disarming as her hand was pleasing, as it drifted back to the tense muscles of his thigh.

This is the woman I've been waiting for . . .

He kept coming back to that. What was the point?

Where was the logic? Besides, she'd made it clear that all she'd needed was a moment in time. Well, they'd had it.

And it had been astounding.

"Cav?" she pressed softly. "How did you get this scar?"

"The scar's not a big deal." He needed to follow her lead and enjoy the moment. They still had over an hour before they could leave to meet up with the extraction team. He reached for her hand and lifted it to his lips.

"Hum." She sounded as skeptical as she looked. "Yet it looks like a big deal."

She didn't need to know how he'd gotten it or the scar on his biceps or any of the dozen or so others that seemed to intrigue and worry her. When this was over she'd go back to her life in Georgia, and he'd . . . Well, he didn't know where he would go.

"When I told you that you worry too much, you said it was an occupational hazard." She offered him a grape. He sucked it off of her fingertips. "So what exactly do you do? Or does that fall into the 'if you tell me you'll have to kill me' category?"

He plucked some fruit off the plate. "Have another grape," he said evasively, then grinned at her put-out look.

"I still don't know how you know Wyatt," she said, respecting his privacy on the occupation question. "Or is that off-limits, too?"

For the life of him, he didn't understand how he could feel so content in the midst of a life-or-death situation, but he did. Carrie's "good moment in time" philosophy had apparently rubbed off on him.

He stretched back, folded his arms behind his head, and closed his eyes. "You first."

"This is just an observation . . ."

He could hear the smile in her soft southern voice.

"But it occurs to me that you practice avoidance better than anyone I've ever known."

He smiled, too, because she was not only beautiful and sexy but smart and funny. "It's that occupational-hazard thing again."

She made a sound that was something between a snort and acceptance. "We grew up together," she said, giving him his way. "Stayed friends."

He opened one eye. "Define friends." That issue had been working on him since Wyatt had called him in Jakarta.

She cocked her head and considered. "More than friends once. In high school we were an *item*."

"And he walked away from *you*?"

She leisurely traced a fingertip from his left collarbone to his right and back again. Her touch made him shiver and burn at the same time.

"Not so much away from me, as from Adel, Georgia." She lifted a shoulder. "Lotta people do. Not much excitin' goin' on around there."

He loved how her drawl had intensified as she relaxed. "Were you heartbroken?"

She was quiet long enough that he opened his eyes again. And by the time she said, "For a while, yeah, but not anymore," he was pretty certain he didn't believe her.

She still had a thing for Wyatt.

Which probably answered his next question. "Why did you come to Myanmar, Carrie?"

Another hesitation. Another *Ah ha* moment when she had to think about it a bit too long.

The truthful answer probably went something like: Not long ago, Wyatt had come home to Adel with a new wife. It had stung. So Carrie Granger had gone looking for adventure. Something to help her douse the old flame and soften the blow.

He understood. Savage was a great guy. Carrie-worthy. Something he wasn't.

"I might have been a little disenfranchised," she said, breaking into his thoughts.

It occurred to him that these were the kind of moments he'd been missing for a long time. Quiet, intimate moments with a woman who mattered. Moments where barriers fell and truths came out. Dangerous moments for a CIA asset. Moments he'd had to avoid at all costs, for more years than he wanted to count.

The same years that had brought him to the place he was today: a man who could not possibly be someone good for someone like her.

"Maybe I was a little hurt that Wyatt was once and for all off-limits," she admitted.

Her soft words drew his gaze back to her face.

Her smile was whimsical. "A girl never forgets her first love, you know."

Her candor didn't surprise him; it was who she was.

"But that was then. I'm over it."

Didn't change a thing where he was concerned. He was still no good for her.

If he was honest, he had to admit that he was teetering very close to alcoholic status. He couldn't count the number of times he'd wished he had a drink in the past twelve hours.

He was burned out and just plain tapped out of good-will toward man. He didn't know if he had enough left to pull himself away from the abyss, let alone be the man that a woman like Carrie needed.

"Why did you come for me?" she asked.

At last, an easy question. "Because Wyatt asked."

"And he knew you'd do it."

He closed his eyes again. "Yeah. He knew."

Her hand lay flat on his bare chest now. Warm and light and the most sensual presence he'd ever known.

If she had thoughts or questions about why Wyatt hadn't come himself, she didn't voice them. She lay down close to him instead and rested her head on his shoulder as if she needed the contact to keep her grounded.

"How did you find me?"

He touched a hand to her hair, pulled her closer, and thought, *Fuck it*. He was going to enjoy the moment. "Wasn't easy. Do you know why you were arrested?"

She made a sound of frustration. "No idea. I got out of the cab, saw a girl in trouble, and I tried to help her."

He knew the rest of the story. Had spent a lot of money and a lot of hours ferreting out the facts.

"That girl was a prostitute who had stolen from a customer, who had sent a hired enforcer to punish her. As it turns out, that same customer was also a high-ranking military official—the judge presiding over your trial."

"Oh my God," she whispered.

"And since the girl was a known prostitute, when the police saw you aiding and abetting a criminal, they assumed you were a working girl, too, and hauled you off to court."

"Some court." She shivered and snuggled even closer. "How did you find all of this out?"

"I have . . . sources," he said evasively, then laughed when she punched him. "My contacts checked out all the taxi companies in Mandalay, found a driver who remembered a fare for a blond English-speaking woman. He filled us in on what happened and that it was the military, not the city police, who made the arrest. After that, it was just a question of finding the judge."

A greenback still talked louder than the Myanmar kyat. A little grease on the palm had helped a court clerk remember the trial of a blond woman, possibly American, who had been sentenced and shipped off to the ruby mines.

"Did they really think they would get away with it?"

"They did," he said soberly. "You weren't going to get out of here through any diplomatic channels. The Junta military regime would never have acknowledged that you went through their system. We're talking international incident of epic proportions here.

"So once the top brass figured out what the judge had done, they went into full cover-up mode. Their intent was to leave no trace that you ever set foot on Burma soil. I'm betting some heads rolled over this, but they were in too deep to let you go."

She was quiet for a long moment. "The entire military must be looking for us by now."

He nodded. "That they are."

"How are we going to get out of the country?" She

rose up on an elbow, her eyes intent on his. "My purse with my passport and all my luggage were in the taxi when the driver saw the MP and took off. I don't have a shred of ID."

"You don't need ID," he promised her. "You've got me."

He didn't want her worrying; that was for him to do. So he pulled her down and kissed her. Not because she looked like she needed kissing but because *he* needed it. Because he needed to feel her soft and giving beneath him one more time. Because he needed to feel the pulse of her body take him inside and remind him of the good things life had to offer.

And because he needed, even more, to have one final memory of what it felt like to make love to her in this incredible moment in time.

Eleven

Cav was pulling on his pants and making plans to get going when he heard an increase of activity outside the window.

He touched a hand to Carrie's shoulder to wake her.

She sat up abruptly. "What?"

"Something's happening. Get dressed."

An urgent knock sounded on the door. He opened it up a crack. "Soldiers have arrived," Tun said, sounding panicked. "They search the village."

"How many?"

"Two trucks. Two jeeps."

Cav swore under his breath. They hadn't skimped on the manpower. This was an all-out manhunt.

"We must go now," Tun said.

"No," Cave said adamantly. "You take the children and Thura to a safe place. I don't want you implicated in helping us." God only knew what the Junta would do to Tun and his family if they discovered they'd helped criminals.

"But—"

Cav laid a hand on Tun's shoulder, cutting him off.

"We'll be fine." He checked his watch. The extraction team would already be in flight, so he had to come up with alternate transpo fast.

"Go take care of your family."

Tun hesitated. "You can find the way? You are certain?"

While Carrie was sleeping, Tun and Cav had gone over the map and he'd plugged the coordinates into his GPS. "I'll get there."

Tun finally gave in with a sober nod. "Be safe, my friend."

"You, too."

He shut the door and turned back to see Carrie had already pulled on her T-shirt and was zipping up her pants and toeing into her sandals.

"I take it we just lost our ride to wherever we were supposed to go, to meet whoever was supposed to get us out of here?"

"That pretty well sums it up." And since there were no cell phone towers for a hundred miles around, he had no way to contact the team to change the rendezvous point.

"I'll figure something out," he said, as he quickly tugged on his boots, then stuffed any shred of evidence that they'd been there into his backpack. "Ever fired a rifle?"

She paled.

Fuck. "I'll take that as a no. Okay, let's give you a crash course. This'll be fast and dirty."

He set the AK's selector switch to semiautomatic so she wouldn't dump the entire magazine on a five-second blast. Then he showed her how to work the safety and warned her to keep it on until she knew she was going to fire.

"Put the front site on the target," he said, helping her position the butt at her shoulder, "and squeeze the trigger. Thats it. Don't fight the recoil but be aware that it's gonna have some kick."

If she actually fired she was going to have a helluva bruise on her shoulder, but the adrenaline would be pumping so hard that she'd never feel it.

"You're going to miss more than you hit and that's okay. Just keep your head and avoid yanking on the trigger, or you'll dump your ammo too fast. Like my old DI used to tell me, squeezing a trigger is like touching a woman's nipple. A caress is appreciated but a yank will get you slapped."

"Well, we can't have that," she said in a tone that told him she was way out of her comfort zone.

"You'll be fine." He wished he had a set of earplugs. If she ended up firing that puppy her ears were going to ring for a week.

He policed the room one last time relieved her of the rifle, and headed for the door.

"Got one more hide-and-seek game left in you, sweetheart?" He wanted to get a read on her frame of mind.

She gave him a brave smile. She was rock solid and steady. "Monopoly's more my style. But I suppose I'll let you choose the game, being you've got the gun and all."

He didn't know many women who could keep their sense of humor over a broken nail, let alone keep their head in a life-or-death situation. He was damn proud of her.

"You're a pretty good time, you know that, Carrie Granger?"

"Oh, honey, wait till you see me when I'm not scared half out of my mind. I'll show you a *real* good time then."

"It's a date."

He hoped to hell he could keep it, because he needed to get them to the extraction point in less than half an hour.

THE SUN BURNED like a brand. Sweat trickled between Cav's shoulder blades as he hunkered down behind a small wagon hitched to a donkey and watched the military jeep parked across the street.

The wagon was filled with vegetables and fruit, and the owner was currently relieving himself in an alley. For the most part, the street was as quiet as the rest of the village. Most of the residents were either napping out of the sun or loafing and shooting the breeze with friends. The only ripple in the pool was the military presence. Four Junta soldiers had just pulled up in the jeep, jumped out, and started working their way down the line of shops.

Cav gauged the distance to the jeep, the distance of the soldiers from the jeep, and the probability of reaching it without being seen. Doable. It wasn't as if they had a lot of choice. Of the dozen dilapidated vehicles he'd spotted in town, Cav didn't think he could count on a single one to transport them across a street, let alone over twenty miles of winding mountain roads.

But a sure thing sat just ten yards away, provided they could get to it. And provided he could start it once they did. He figured it for a 1988, maybe '90 model. No roof, no doors, just a roll bar and sprung seats. Strictly a bare-bones imported civilian model, which meant it would need a key that was most likely with the driver.

He drew the Warthog out of his leg sheath. There was more than one way to skin a cat.

"On my go, we head for that jeep," he told Carrie, who was mouse quiet beside him. "You dive for the floor in the back. Keep your head down and pray like hell that I can get that sucker started before the nice men with guns come back for their ride."

"I can do that," she assured him.

He shoved the AK into her hands and hoped his lesson had stuck. "On my word, you point at the bad guys and squeeze the trigger, okay?"

She gave him a quick nod.

"One major point: even with the safety on, keep your finger off the trigger when we're running. Then neither of us has to worry about you shooting me in the back."

All the blood drained from her face. "Oh, God."

"You can do this. Ready?"

She drew a bracing breath and gave him another nod.

"Atta girl."

He did another visual recon of the street, saw the soldiers disappear inside a building, and shot to his feet. "Go."

He sprinted across the dusty street, peripherally aware of Carrie keeping pace beside him. The few seconds it took them to cover the ground felt like an eternity, but they made it without being spotted.

Carrie followed orders like a good soldier and scrambled onto the floor in the back. He dove for the floor in the front, then checked around for a key. No such luck.

Keeping low, he smashed the hilt of the Warthog against the steering column until he broke the plastic molding around the ignition and exposed the lock. Then he held his breath, unfolded the blade, stuck its tip into the hole, and turned it.

Nothing.

Cursing and sweating, he fiddled with the blade, reached down and depressed the clutch, and tried again. *Bingo!* The engine grumbled to life with a hiccup and a whine. He shot up off the floor before the motor fell into a rumbling purr, slid behind the wheel, and shifted into first gear.

"Keep your head down," he reminded her and peeled rubber, sending a rooster tail of fine dust flying in their wake. They'd made it! Almost.

The unmistakable *pop pop pop* of an AK-47 shattered the passenger-side windshield. So much for getting out of here unnoticed.

He glanced over his shoulder. Four Junta soldiers were squared up in the street behind them. All four had shouldered their rifles and were firing on full auto.

"Need some cover fire, sweetheart!" he yelled over his shoulder. "Just aim and squeeze. And keep your head down!"

Less than five seconds later he heard the AK shucking out rounds from the backseat.

The return fire stopped immediately.

He laughed out loud. *Jesus.* What a woman.

"Nice going, deadeye!" he yelled over the whine of the motor as he lead-footed the accelerator and they roared out of town.

Twelve

"Still clear," Carrie told Cav from the passenger seat.

She'd climbed into the front shortly after they'd cleared the village.

That had been a good ten miles ago and if his GPS coordinates and crash map lesson were correct, this narrow, serpentine road would lead them to the designated landing zone where the extraction team would be waiting for them in—he checked his watch again—less than five minutes.

Providing the team was waiting for them.

And providing they could limp their way there with one flat tire. One of the Juntas had scored a hit. The flat had slowed then down, but there was no way in hell Cav could stop and change it.

Blind faith was a powerful thing. It had to be, because right now that's all they had going for them.

Cav kept both hands on the wheel and one eye on the rearview mirror as they topped the rise of yet another steep grade, then rolled down a thirty-degree decline toward a long metal expansion bridge.

Straight out of an old erector set, it spanned a wide river basin flanked by deep ravines and lush grass. Small green islands floated like clouds on water the color of café au lait. A herd of brown horned cattle grazed placidly along the banks. Tall, jagged mountain peaks towered in the distance. And directly ahead of them hung the blazing ball of the sun, guiding their path down the road like a beacon.

The scenery was beautiful, idyllic and serene, and all Cav could think about was how in the hell a chopper was going to manage the wind currents that were bound to be prevalent at this altitude.

"How much farther?" Carrie yelled over the wind and the motor and *thump thump thump* of the deflated tire.

Cav glanced at her. She looked like a Rambo wet dream with the AK balanced across her lap, her unbound breasts straining against her tight olive T-shirt, and her long legs encased in green camo pants.

And she looked like a woman he did not want to let down. Ever.

"Getting tired of my company?" He was only half joking.

"Getting worried about that dust trail that just topped the hill behind us!"

His gaze shot to the rearview mirror and he saw Junta jeep.

"Fuck!"

He'd hoped they'd had a big-enough head start to meet up with their ride before the soldiers arrived.

If they met with their ride.

He searched the road ahead of them, scanned the sky for a chopper. Except for the sun and a flock of birds *nada*.

He slammed down on the accelerator to spread the distance between them and the Junta, who were no more than a quarter mile away.

"Hold on!" he yelled and charged toward a pothole the size of a small ox.

Carrie clamped one hand around the roll bar, dug her fingers into his thigh, and let out a scream as the jeep hit hard, then went airborne. They crashed back down with a bone-rattling bang.

Miraculously the chassis held together.

"Hold on!" he repeated as they began to climb a forty-degree incline, the flat tire giving him ten kinds of grief as he struggled to keep the jeep on the road.

The sun was completely hidden by the hill rising in front of them; all he could see was road and sky. The motor whined and complained but he never backed off the gas. He was practically lying back in the seat as they struggled toward the peak, fishtailing and clawing for purchase.

Just when he thought they were going to stall out they crested the rise—and there, silhouetted against the burning sun, was a big, bad Huey hovering above the road like the Goodyear blimp.

The big bird was gray and gorgeous, with the *thwump thwump thwump* of the main rotor drowning out everything but his rebel yell. It was the most welcome sight he'd ever seen.

"*Oh my God!*" Carrie ducked, a knee-jerk reaction to the low-hanging Huey.

"It's the cavalry!" Wyatt had promised a Huey and damn if he hadn't delivered.

The pilot was good. The Huey banked hard left, made

a full one-eighty, then flew straight down the center of the road toward them.

"Thank you, Wyatt!" Cav pounded the flat of his palm on the steering wheel.

"Are they going to land?" Carrie yelled, casting a nervous glance over her shoulder as the Junta vehicles—a truck had joined the jeep—showed no sign of backing off.

"That was the plan," Cav yelled back, straining to be heard as the decibel level reached new heights. But when one of the chopper's crew appeared in the open doorway and kicked out a coil of rope he knew the plan had changed.

"Oh, God!" Carrie went pale. "Does that mean what I think it means?"

Cav studied the terrain ahead of them, which allowed no spot for the chopper to land. He glanced at the Junta behind them. The truck had gained ground and a gunner had gotten into position behind the big gun mounted on a tripod on the truck's roof.

Not just a big gun. Ma Duce. A Browning .50-caliber heavy-barreled belt-fed machine gun. *Christ.* Each projectile weighed an ounce and a half, and if one of them hit either the Huey or their jeep, there'd be nothing left but fireballs, fumes, and red mist.

Fire flashed from the big gun's muzzle and a series of roaring *boom*s reverberated through the air.

When the road exploded ahead of them, Cav swerved hard right. The jeep skidded, fishtailed, and nearly slipped off the side of the eroding shoulder before he regained control.

Shit! If the bastard got any closer they were done for. "Switch places with me!" he yelled.

Shifting his left foot from the clutch to the accelerator to maintain speed, he scooted toward the middle of the bench seat. "Take over driving so I can catch the rig."

Her wild gaze flew to his face. "What rig?"

He hitched his chin skyward.

She looked up, saw the rope, and gasped. "You're serious?"

"You can do this! Now move!"

She gave herself a nanosecond to come to terms, then, God love her, flew into action.

He'd never switched drivers in an open vehicle racing fifty mph down the road while being chased by men with guns, but they somehow managed to shift and shimmy and change seats with barely any loss of speed or control.

A second volley from Ma Duce kicked up dirt just behind them. Another narrow miss. Third time, someone was bound to get lucky.

But then the unmistakable *chuck chuck chuck* of an M-60 gave Cav a reason to believe they might just get out of this.

He glanced skyward and, sure enough, the barrel of an M-60 mini-gun poked out of the belly of the Huey. The gunner was peppering the Junta truck with 7.62 x 54 NATO rounds like he was seasoning a steak.

Cav let out a war whoop. These boys knew how to throw a party!

He stood up, one hand gripping the windshield frame, the other grabbing for the tail end of the hundred-plus feet of rope that dangled from the Huey. The rotor wash whipped the rope and the attached harness back and forth like a pendulum on a wide, arching swing.

"Can we really do this?" Carrie yelled.

"Piece of cake!" he promised as the Huey pilot timed its speed perfectly to theirs, then tucked in directly overhead just low enough for Cav to finally grab the spinning harness when it swung by.

Behind them, the Junta truck and jeep had gained ground. Ma Duce kept firing. The M-60 kept answering. Cav paid no attention. He unhooked the SPIES—Special Patrol Insertion/Extraction System—harness from the dangling rope, then concentrated on getting himself buckled in.

Now came the leap of faith. There was only one harness. They needed two. He improvised by quickly making a loop out of an extra length of webbing.

"Under your arms!" he ordered Carrie as he tugged the looped strap over her head, then under her armpits in a dizzying dance of coordination and caution while her hair flew around her face and she managed to maintain control of the fast-moving jeep.

"I don't want to know what's going to happen next, do I?" Her eyes were dead ahead on the road as Cav hooked a carabiner attached to the front of his SPIES rig to the strap he'd made snug around her chest.

"One more act of faith!" he told her as he quickly hooked his SPIES harness back up to the rope, looked skyward, and gave the Huey crew a thumbs-up.

"Let go of the wheel!" He pulled Carrie out from beneath the steering column and, just that fast, they were airborne.

"Arms and legs out!" he yelled when they'd cleared the jeep and the Huey lifted them fifty feet in a split second. "Spread-eagle it or we're going to spin like a top, and then I'm going to embarrass myself and make you very unhappy!"

"I'm already unhappy!" She buried her face against his chest as the ground fell away beneath them and the *chuck chuck chuck* of the M-60 sang like music above them.

As they flew through the air and cleared the tree line, Cav looked down to see the jeep roar off the road. It bounced several yards, then rolled end over end down a steep ravine and exploded in a ball of fire. Even more spectacular was the sight of the M-60 lighting up the Junta truck in a blazing fireball when the Huey's gunner scored a direct hit.

Prettiest sight he'd ever seen. Well, almost.

He glanced down at the woman in his arms as they continued to climb, dangling from the end of that long rope at a dizzying two hundred feet above the ground and a heart-racing seventy or eighty mph.

She was the prettiest sight he'd ever seen as she lifted her face to his. Through her fear and her shock, she met his eyes with a smile so dazzling it lit a fire inside him that made the flame-engulfed Junta truck pale in comparison.

"MAN, YOU GUYS are a sight for sore eyes!" Cav yelled above the Huey's engine roar.

They'd set down in a field a safe mile away from the extraction site so Cav and Carrie could climb on board.

"Just like old home week." Luke—Doc Holliday—Colter grinned as he held out a hand and pulled Carrie up into the chopper bay.

He had that right, Cav thought as he scrambled up behind her, shook hands all around, and saw the men who'd enlisted his help to blow up half of Jakarta's waterfront over a year ago in their rescue mission of Crystal Debrowski.

"Glad we could return the favor." Johnny Reed sat at the bird's controls with none other than Nate Black riding in the copilot seat.

"Thanks, man." Cav returned a quick embrace and back slap from Joe Green, his old CIA buddy. "When Wyatt said he'd send a team, I didn't know he was going to call out the big guns. Appreciate it."

"Like Reed said"—Nate turned in the seat—"one good turn needs another."

"I'd say this more than makes us even." Cav glanced at Carrie, who was still wide-eyed and a little shocky. "Carrie," he yelled to be heard above the Huey's big engine, "meet Reed, Doc, Joe, and Nate. Friends of Wyatt's. Friends of mine," he added as he strapped in while Doc made sure Carrie was secure.

As soon as they were buckled up, the Huey lifted off and they tore through the skies.

"It's over," Cav said, leaning in close to Carrie. "It's finally over."

Not until then did she finally break down and cry.

Thirteen

Her life had gone from colorless to vivid Technicolor, then back to shades of gray again.

Rain streaked down the tall glass panes as Carrie stood alone, staring out the window of the waiting area outside the consulate's office at the U.S. embassy in Jakarta.

She still couldn't believe she was in Indonesia. Or that Cav was in conference with the consulate, arranging her passage back home.

Home. The concept was abstract to the max, even though she'd spoken to her parents a short while ago, fighting tears as they'd wept openly with relief.

She didn't feel relief yet. She still felt numb disbelief. Less than twelve hours ago she'd been outrunning soldiers with big guns, flying through the air at the end of a very long rope before being set carefully back on the ground, then hustled into a helicopter by men she'd never met but now owed her life to.

Reed. Black. Green. Colter. Friends of Cav's. Friends of Wyatt, who had orchestrated their action-adventure-movie rescue from thousands of miles away in the United States.

Life in living color.

She folded her arms beneath her breasts and sighed deeply. It was what she'd wanted: a little excitement, a little color. Well. She'd gotten way more than she'd bargained for.

Her memories were so out of focus that she couldn't accurately reconstruct what happened after the chopper had touched down. A fast, loud flight. Landing somewhere in Bangladesh. Boarding a waiting jet for a charter flight to Jakarta.

Shock, she supposed. Shock and confusion and a sense that life as she'd known it was never going to be the same again.

How could it be, after David Cavanaugh?

She flashed on a vivid, visceral memory of him naked and needing her. Of the dark eyes that had burned into her soul when he'd made love to her. The connection had been intimate and meaningful, and now . . . Well, now, apparently, it was over.

It had become acutely clear that with the transition from peril to peace, the only part David Cavanaugh intended to play in her future was that of a memory.

She jumped when she heard a sound behind her, spun around, and there he stood: the reason her life had changed forever.

Her savior. Her lover. And very soon part of her history, if the emotional distance he'd erected between them was any indication.

She watched him walk toward her, swallowed back the

pain. He was larger than life, twice as imposing, a vibrant light as moving as a sunrise . . . but for the veiled look in his eyes when they met hers.

"It's a go," he said, holding up a handful of legal-looking documents. He gripped her elbow and steered her briskly toward the exit. "But we've got to move fast, before they change their minds and we end up hamstrung by paperwork that could keep you here until the next millennium."

She didn't ask him how he'd managed to unsnarl the paperwork; he wouldn't answer her anyway. He never answered anything.

It didn't matter. She'd already figured out by the deference he was shown at the embassy that David Cavanaugh was an important man. She'd already known he was extraordinary. And even though he had to know she was confused and hurt, he remained as distant as her freedom from the labor camp had once seemed to be.

Rain poured down in a deluge as they sprinted to a waiting car. She was soaked to the bone as they ducked into the backseat, then a driver took them through the clogged city streets to the airport, where a chartered jet waited to fly her back to the States.

Silent, she watched the city speed by through rain-blurred windows. What was the point in talking? Idle conversation would be both painful and insulting.

"You doing okay?" Cav finally asked from across the very far distance to his side of the backseat.

She nodded, unable to look at him. If she looked at him, she'd just see that carefully imposed distance that meant heartbreak, regret, and good-bye.

Could she really just let this happen without saying a word? Without at least making it a little easier for him? Didn't she owe him that much?

She glanced at him, saw his dark eyes watching her with regret and maybe even a little longing. But she couldn't go there. If he wanted more, he'd had ample opportunity to say so. Plenty of chances to reach for her, to pull her into his arms and tell her . . .

No. There was a bottom line here that she couldn't ignore. He'd done none of those things. He was letting her go. It was the end of this particular love story, and she had to let him know it was okay.

"Look." She drew a steadying breath to settle herself. "I get it, okay?" She forced a smile. "I understand that saying good-bye isn't easy for you either."

"Carrie—"

She held up a hand, stopping him. She didn't want to hear that he was sorry. She didn't want to make him tell her what she already knew. He deserved to walk away with a clear conscience.

After all, he hadn't known she was going to fall in love with him. And as outrageous and illogical as it was she had. She'd fallen hard.

He leaned forward, pushed a button, and raised the glass partition between the front and back seat so they could speak in private.

"It's okay," she said forcing herself to hold his gaze. Forcing a smile despite the pain, when his expression told her how uncomfortable he was. "We got a little lost in the moment out there. Desperate times, desperate measures and all that." She lifted a shoulder. "People get caught up in a life-or-death situation and it's human nature to say things, do things . . . things they meant at the time but don't translate to the real world."

He looked away, ducked his head as if he was struggling to form the right words. When he finally spoke, his voice was thick with regret. "You're an amazing woman, Carrie Granger. Another life . . . another time—"

"Don't." She let herself touch his arm, just one last touch. "You don't need to explain anything. And you don't owe me anything. But I owe you. I owe my life. More, even. You gave me the adventure of a lifetime," she added, desperate to make him think she wasn't dying a little inside. "To steal a line from my all-time favorite movie, 'You're the best time I've ever had.'

She made herself smile for him. "What matters is that I asked you for a moment back there. You gave it to me. And it was wonderful. But now it's time for both of us to move on with our lives."

She averted her gaze to the window then, willing back the tears that threatened to expose her for the liar that she was.

If he realized how close she was to coming unglued, he wisely chose to pretend right along with her that everything was fine.

Black and white and gray and fine.

CAV WATCHED THE G-550 Gulfstream business jet taxi down the tarmac, wait for clearance, then fire its powerful engines and roll down the runway.

For a full minute after the sleek silver bird disappeared he stood there in the rain, soaking wet and numb to the bone.

Carrie was on her way home to Georgia. Exactly where she should be, safe and sound, doing good things, having good things happen to her.

He was right to let her go. Like she'd said, what they'd had was a moment in time. And it was over.

He turned and climbed back into the waiting limo. Made a decision.

He was going to find himself a big bottle of scotch. He shoved his wet hair back with both hands, closed his eyes, and leaned his head back against the seat. A *huge* fucking bottle. Then he was going to do his damnedest to drink her out of his life.

Fourteen

"Hey, sugar. Got a cup of coffee for a thirsty man?"

Carrie looked around her computer monitor to see Wyatt Savage standing in her office doorway. During the past two weeks she'd gotten used to his impromptu visits. Since Sophie was a patient here, Wyatt spent most of every day at the hospital with her, but he often popped in to say hello.

"Pot's on. Help yourself."

She'd been home from Jakarta for fourteen days now, and life had remained as gray and dismal as the weather. As fate would have it, the rain had followed her from Jakarta to Georgia and hadn't let up yet. She hadn't seen the sunshine since she'd been back.

"How's Sophie doing today?" she asked as Wyatt helped himself to coffee from the fresh pot she kept on the credenza beside her desk.

Carrie had been shocked to learn that Sophie had been admitted to the hospital the same day she'd left for Myanmar. While it had been touch and go for a while, as of yesterday both Sophie and the baby were in stable condition.

"She's doing great." Wyatt sat on the leather easy chair across from her desk. "So's the baby. The doctors are thinking she'll make it to full term now. They may even release her by the end of the week."

"Oh, Wyatt, that's wonderful news." Carrie smiled at her friend. Between worrying about Sophie and the baby and concern over her, he'd been a wreck when she'd returned. It had taken him a couple of days to tune in to her somber mood, and he'd chalked it up to her harrowing ordeal. But it hadn't taken long for him to put two and two together and realize there was something more going on.

"So how are *you* doing?" he asked over the steam rising from the cup.

"I'm good," she said meaningfully. "And I don't want to talk about it." Her face flushed with embarrassment as she thought about the way she'd fallen apart yesterday.

She'd had a long, grueling day, a "poor me" moment, and Wyatt had caught her with her defenses down. She'd sniveled all over his shoulder about her heartbreak over David Cavanaugh. It had not been her finest hour.

"I'm *good*," she repeated when he gave her a look that telegraphed concern, skepticism, and pity. Then she glanced out the window. "I'd be a lot better if the sun would come back out."

He didn't say anything for a moment. "He's a complicated man."

"Yes," she agreed. "Who's half a world away with a life to live. I've got a life, too. A good one, so stop looking at me like my dog died. Go back to your wife and give her a hug for me. I've got to tie up this report, then I'm heading home. It's been a long day."

"Fine. I get it. I'll butt out." He rose, his kind eyes assessing. "But if you ever want to talk . . ."

"I did enough of that yesterday. Now go. I'm fine."

She was still trying to convince herself of that when she pulled into her driveway an hour later. The drizzle had transitioned to a steady rain, so she gathered her purse and laptop and sprinted for the door.

"Come on, come on," she muttered as she dug into the bowels of her purse for her house keys, trying to keep from dropping her laptop.

"Can I help you with that?"

Her head flew up.

And there he was.

The man who had haunted her days and kept her awake at night.

She simply stared incapable of speech as he relieved her of the laptop.

"I don't know about you" he said with a trademark David Cavanaugh smile, "but I'm getting a little wet."

Yeah. He was. So was she. She didn't care. "What . . . what are you doing here?"

He smiled. "Getting wet. But we already covered that."

"Oh. Right. Sorry. Hold on." Her hands were shaking as she dug back into her purse and finally came up with the elusive keys.

"Damn it!" she swore, almost dropping them when she couldn't make her fingers work.

A big hand covered hers. "Let me help."

She let him take the keys. Then she just stood there,

staring at his beautiful, hard, amazing face, trying to come to grips with the fact that he was here, in Georgia, on her porch.

He calmly inserted the key in the lock, turned it, and swung the door open.

"Carrie?"

She blinked. Lifted a hand. "Go on in."

He motioned for her to lead the way.

Her legs felt wooden as she stepped into the small foyer. Her heart beat like crazy. And though it was a muggy eighty degrees outside, she shivered in her wet clothes as the door closed behind her.

"Pretty dress," he said from behind her.

"I . . . um . . . thanks." It *was* a pretty dress. It was a sleeveless, summery yellow linen, and why they were talking about it was beyond her.

Apparently *any* semblance of rational thought was beyond her, because she couldn't come up with a single thing to say to him that didn't start and end with her begging him to stay. Only pride kept her from doing that.

"How are you, Carrie?"

She walked across the foyer, set her purse on a small table, and after drawing a steadying breath, turned back to him. He looked so big standing there in her little house. Big and imposing and uncomfortable as he held out her laptop. And wet. His hair was wet. His shirt was wet and plastered to his skin. And why, oh why, was he here?

"I'm okay." She took the laptop, then set it down beside her purse. "You . . . you look good."

He looked fantastic in dark dress pants and a pale blue silk shirt that was open at the throat. She could see his pulse beating there, and suddenly she was swamped by a memory of her lips pressed there, where he'd been hot and salty and vital.

"Let me get you a towel." She took off like a shot, because if she stood there one moment longer she was going to do something stupid. Like fly into his arms. Like kiss him until they were both senseless and show him exactly how desperate she was to keep him here. Right here, where he couldn't possibly want to stay.

In the hallway that separated the living area from the bedrooms, she flattened her palms against the wall and leaned back against it. She closed her eyes, made herself draw a deep breath, willed herself to get it the hell together.

"Carrie."

Her eyes flew open. He stood right in front of her, his dark eyes steady and unblinking on her face. His big body close and moving closer. "I don't need a towel."

His mouth was a shallow breath away. Heat pulsed off of him like a heartbeat.

"N-no towel?"

He shook his head, brushed his nose against hers. "No. What I need is you."

"Oh, God," she sobbed and flew into his arms.

She didn't care anymore that she should exercise caution. And when his mouth slammed over hers in a kiss of desperation and desire, she knew he felt the same way.

He lifted his head long enough to murmur, "Bedroom," against her lips before taking her under again with a blistering kiss that stole what was left of her breath.

They managed to stumble down the hall, fumbling with buttons and zippers before falling onto her bed. Naked.

Hungry. Beyond greedy for the feel of skin on skin, his mouth on her breast, his hands in her hair, his body pressing hers into the bed.

"I'm sorry," he whispered against her breast, his breath hot and damp on her nipple. "I'm sorry I let you go. I'm sorry I hurt you."

She choked out a sob, a memory of the pain of losing him, and embraced the reality of now. He was here now. He was hers now. And there wasn't any pain. Only deep, penetrating pleasure.

She arched against him, reveling in his weight and his heat and his passion as he parted her thighs and entered her on a long, deep stroke.

She cried out with wonder as he led her to a rich orgasm that shot through her like a fire that an entire year of rain could never douse.

Trembling, clinging, crying, she rode the stunning wave while he pumped into her one last time, then collapsed as his own release ripped through him.

It was dark by the time Cav roused himself enough to realize he was alone in the bed. A dim light glowed from the top of a chest of drawers across the room.

He rolled over to his back, willed the fatigue away, and indulged himself in his surroundings. Soft greens, pale, pale blues. Cloud whites. The woman knew how to create a serene, peaceful haven.

Ultimately, that's what he'd come here searching for. A safe haven in the arms of this woman he loved.

"You're awake."

He glanced toward the doorway and felt both arousal

and gratitude when he saw her standing there. Her pretty blond hair was a mess and he felt a swell of pride that he'd been the one to mess it up. To mess *her* up. Her lips were swollen. Her eyes were slumberous and dark.

She was wearing his shirt. One button buttoned, falling off her left shoulder. It had never looked better.

He held out a hand. She crossed the room, took it, and sat on the mattress by his hip. He lifted their linked hands and studied the fit of their entwined fingers before shifting his gaze and searching her face.

Her beautiful, open face.

She was uncertain about what would happen next. And she was edgy with it.

"I'm not going anywhere," he said, because she needed to hear it, he needed to say it, and because it was true.

She closed her eyes and lowered her head, but not before he saw a tear trail down her cheek.

"Come 'ere," he whispered and tugged her down beside him.

He wrapped her in his arms and held her while she cried.

"I'm sorry," he murmured against the silk of her hair.

"I don't know why I'm doing this." She sounded embarrassed and angry at herself.

He knew why. And it broke his heart.

"I'm not usually such a weenie."

"Sweetheart." He squeezed her hard. "I know what you're made of. You don't have to apologize for anything. But I do."

She sat up and wiped her eyes. He scooted over so she could sit cross-legged beside him, the tails of his shirt tucked between her legs.

"I didn't think I was ever going to see you again." She looked down at the cuff of his shirt, which hung well past her fingertips.

"That was the original plan." He reached for an extra pillow and propped it behind his head.

"But you changed your mind."

Hands crossed behind his head, he stared at the ceiling. "I'm not sure I'm going to be any good at this," he admitted. "At being the man you need. At being the man I need to be. For you. And for me."

"Cav—"

He cut her off with a shake of his head. "You need to know up front what you're getting into, Carrie."

More than that, he needed to tell her.

"My old man was career military," he said after the long moment it took for him to decide to just tell it like it was. "Loved the army, his booze, and his family, in that order. He was a good man. Just didn't always have his priorities straight, you know? He always figured he'd die in action, but in the end it was the booze that got him."

He glanced at her, then away, and went on before he lost his nerve.

"Look, I don't want this to come out like the ramblings of a poor, neglected army-brat son of an alcoholic. It wasn't that way. I admired him. Even though I knew where I stood on his food chain. And it was okay. It set my career course."

He glanced at her again, half expecting her to ask, but she didn't. Another measure of her intelligence and sensitivity. She knew instinctively that he had to tell this in his own time, his own way.

"I was CIA," he said, knowing those three little letters were right now painting a picture in her mind of shadowy warriors pushing the envelope of diplomacy and international law.

"We're not everything the novelists and journalists would have you believe we are. We don't do all the things you might have been led to believe we've done."

"You save lives," she said simply. "You serve your country."

He swallowed, humbled by her absolute, unquestioning belief in his motives and integrity.

"Yeah," he said. "All that."

He looked at her then. "It . . . it takes a toll after a while."

"How could it not?"

He firmed his lips, looked away. This was the hard part. "Service to country isn't all I inherited from the old man," he finally admitted.

She was quiet for a while. "You said he was an alcoholic."

"Yeah." He looked back at her. She watched him with quiet eyes, no judgment. "And I don't want to be."

Her gaze held his, steady and unwavering in the face of what he hadn't said. That he had a problem. That he wanted to fix it.

"That's why I resigned," he clarified, and even now he felt the weight of that decision and the shock wave that had rippled through the chain of command. "I've developed an unhealthy relationship with scotch over the years."

"To help you cope."

And to help him forget. "I don't want to use that crutch anymore. I *can't* use that crutch anymore."

"Then you won't," she said simply.

He smiled, feeling cynical and weary. "You don't know me well enough to know that. And I don't deserve that much credit."

"This is what I know." She reached for his hand and folded it between both of hers. "I know that I love you. I know that for you to open up to me this way, you love me, too."

"I do." He reached for her and pulled her down until her mouth was a breath away from his. "I do love you. More than life."

"Damn," she whispered against his mouth. "I'm going to cry again."

And he was going to spend the rest of his life making sure she didn't ever have a reason to cry again.

"So what took you so long?" Carrie teased as she wiped her hands on a napkin.

They were naked in the middle of her bed. Still working on slaking their desire for each other, refortifying their energy with a bucket of take-out chicken.

"To come for you? The guys and I had a little unfinished business to tend to." Cav set the bucket aside.

She settled into his arms like he'd had a place for her there forever. "The guys?"

"Reed, Green, Colter, and Black."

Her eyes went all soft and adoring. "You went back to the mines."

"I told you I wouldn't forget about those people."

He couldn't save the world. He'd thought he could once, but he knew better now. He *could* save those starving, abused souls who'd been enslaved at the Myanmar ruby mine, though.

And thanks to this woman, he might even be able to save himself.

"Thank you," she whispered, pressing soft kisses along his jaw line.

"The pleasure"—he rolled her beneath him, thanking good fortune that she'd come into his life—"is all mine."

When she fell asleep a little while later, he simply laid there and watched her. She was smiling. At peace.

So was he. He'd made the right decision to come to her.

He still had no idea what his future held. After years of service, that should have been unnerving. But now he had Carrie by his side.

Haven. Yeah. It was right here, he thought, drifting off to sleep. Right by this woman's side.

Unstoppable

Laura Griffin

One

Sometimes they went in with a flash and crash, but Lieutenant Gage Brewer always preferred stealth. And tonight, because the team's mission was to outsmart a band of Taliban insurgents, stealth was the operative word.

The night smelled like smoldering garbage and rot as Gage crept through the darkened alley in an industrial neighborhood on the outskirts of the city. They were in a hot zone, a place where anyone they encountered would like nothing better than to use them for target practice.

As the SEAL team's point man, Gage moved silently, every sense attuned to the shadows around him. Particularly alert at this moment was Gage's sixth sense—that vague, indefinable thing his teammates liked to call his frog vision. Gage didn't know what to call it; he only knew it has saved his ass a time or two.

In the distance, the muted drone of an electric generator

in this city still prone to blackouts. And, closer still, foot-steps. The slow clomp of boots on gravel, moving steadily nearer, then pausing, pivoting, and fading away.

Wait, Gage signaled his team. Lieutenant Junior Grade Derek Vaughn melted into the shadows, followed a heart-beat later by Petty Officers Mike Dietz and Adam Mays. Gage approached the corner of the building, an unimpos-ing brick structure that was supposedly a textile factory. Crouching down, he slipped a tiny mirror from the pocket of his tactical vest and held it at an angle in order to see around the corner.

A solitary shadow ambled north toward the front of the building, an AK-47 slung casually across his body. The shadow told Gage three things: the intel they'd been given was good, this building *was* under armed guard, and what was going down tonight at this factory had nothing to do with textiles.

Gage eased back into the alley.

"Sixty seconds," Vaughn whispered.

Gage had known Vaughn since BUD/S training. Besides being a demolitions expert, the Texan had the best sense of time and direction of any man in Alpha squad, and tonight he was in charge of keeping everyone on schedule.

Soundlessly, they waited.

Then, like clockwork, a distant *rat-tat-tat* as the rest of Alpha squad exchanged carefully staged, nonlethal gunfire in an alley much like this one.

Beside Gage, the building came alive. Footsteps thun-dered in a stairwell. Excited voices carried through the walls. A door banged open and more shouts filled the night as men poured from the building. A truck engine roared to life. Gage and his teammates watched from the shadows as a pickup loaded with heavily armed insurgents peeled off, no doubt to help wipe out the American commandos gullible enough to walk into a trap.

Twenty more seconds and Vaughn gave the signal. Gage peered around the corner. The guard now stood in a pool of light spilling down from a second-story window. The sour expression on his bearded face told Gage he wasn't too happy about being stuck guarding hostages while his comrades got to slaughter American soldiers. His lips moved, and Gage guessed he was cursing his prisoners— two Afghani teachers whose heinous crime had been taking a job at a newly opened school for girls.

Their boss, the school's principal, had been beheaded on live Webcam two days ago.

Watching the footage had made Gage's blood boil. But his anger was tempered now, a tightly controlled force he would use to carry out his mission.

In addition to rescuing the Afghanis, the SEALs were tasked with finding and retrieving forty-two-year-old Elizabeth Bauer, an American reporter who had been working on a story for the Associated Press when the Taliban stormed the school. She was thought to be next in line for execution, if she wasn't dead already.

Gage chose to believe she was still alive—at least, pictures of her beheading weren't yet bouncing around cyberspace. The picture Gage *had* seen—the one provided during the briefing—reminded him of his aunt back in Chicago. The minute he'd seen it, Gage had felt an emotional connection that went beyond his usual hundred-and-ten-percent commitment to an op.

The guard turned the corner. Vaughn and Dietz fell back, circling around to the building's other side.

Follow me, Gage signaled Mays. The kid was young, green. He'd grown up in Tennessee and spoke with the thickest accent Gage had ever heard. But he could shoot like nobody's business.

A quiet *thud* as they rounded the corner told Gage that Vaughn and Dietz had neutralized the guard about ten seconds ahead of schedule. Gage stepped over the lifeless body and entered the building with his finger on the trigger of his M4. He glanced around. The space was dim and cavernous, empty except for a few junked-out trucks and some tires piled in corners. A band of light shone onto the dirt floor from some sort of upstairs office. Given the satellite dish they'd seen mounted outside, Gage figured it was used as a media room. According to their intel, the hostages were being kept in the basement.

Vaughn went up to take out any hostiles who might have stayed behind. Gage scanned the room's perimeter and quickly located an open doorway leading down to a lower level.

The earthen steps were steep and Gage took them silently. Clearing out the bulk of the tangos with a diversion had been a good plan, but one that relied on a fair amount of luck. Gage was a gambling man, and the first rule of gambling was that luck eventually ran out. He expected an armed guard at the foot of the stairs and that's exactly what he found.

Gage delivered a well-placed blow with the butt of his rifle, rendering the man unconscious before his weapon even clattered to the floor. A collective gasp went up from across the room as Gage knelt down to collect the Kalash-nikov. He slung it over his shoulder while Mays zip-cuffed the guard. Their orders were to keep at least one of them alive, if possible, in case they needed him for information.

The hostages stumbled to their feet and Gage turned his flashlight on them. The beam illuminated two slightly built Afghani men and a fortyish woman.

"Lieutenant Gage Brewer, U.S. Navy." He zeroed in on the woman. "Ma'am, are you—"

"Betsy Bauer." She reached out and touched his arm, as if to make sure he was real. "And I've never been so glad to see anyone in my life."

Vaughn tromped down the steps to join them. "All clear up there." He held up a black piece of cloth. It was a flag with a skull and a sword painted on it, and Gage recognized it from the video footage.

He'd found the beheading room.

"Anyone injured?" This from Dietz, the team corps-man. "Anything that might prevent you from—"

"We're fine." Betsy Bauer cast a worried look at the door. "Let's just get out of here."

Gage's thoughts exactly. He led everyone up the stairs. Mays and Dietz guarded their flanks and Vaughn watched their six.

"Five minutes," Vaughn said from the back.

They were ahead of schedule. Another stroke of luck. More than four minutes until their helo would drop down in a nearby field. The other half of their squad would already be on it, after having spent a few minutes pretend-ing to be ambushed by Taliban fighters before vanishing into the night.

Gage started to get anxious as he neared the door. That damned sixth sense again . . .

His gaze landed on something long and black sticking out from the back of one of the trucks. He jogged over to investigate.

"Holy shit."

"What is it?" Mays asked.

Gage blinked down at the truck bed. "I'm looking at a shit-ton of weapons. RPGs, AKs, a couple of Carl Gs." He glanced up at Vaughn and a flash of understanding passed between them.

"Let's hit the extraction point," Gage said, jogging back to the group. He checked the surrounding area before hustling the hostages to a nearby clearing. Gage watched the reporter, relieved that she seemed to be moving okay. No telling what hell she'd endured these past forty-eight hours.

A familiar *whump whump* grew louder as their helo approached. Gage scanned the area, ready to eliminate anything that might try to botch their extraction. Dust and trash kicked up as the Seahawk dropped down onto the landing zone. Gage loaded in the hostages, then counted the heads inside. Every man in Alpha squad accounted for. They were good to go.

Another glance at Vaughn. He was a demo man, as was Gage, and they were thinking the same thing.

"Two minutes," Gage yelled at his commanding officer.

Dirt tornadoed around them as Gage squinted into the Seahawk. It was too loud—and time was too short—for him to explain what he wanted to do. It was a critical moment. Did his CO trust him or not? The officer gave a brief nod.

Gage and Vaughn took off at a dead run. In under ninety seconds they had the two truck beds rigged with enough C-4 to blow up a tank. No way were they going to leave a fuckload of ordnance around for the enemy to use against U.S. troops.

"Ten seconds," Vaughn said.

Gage's heart pounded as he added more C-4, just to be sure. Then they got the hell out.

Less than a minute later, an earsplitting blast ripped the night. Gage's face hit the dirt. The earth shook beneath him as the building fireballed and then fireballed again. Debris rained down around him—concrete, mud, chunks of brick.

Burning embers pelted him as he tried to move, but his body seemed cemented to the ground. Vaughn grabbed his flak vest and hauled him to his feet just as a truck careened around a corner and barreled straight for them.

"Go, go, go!"

They leaped for the helo as a dozen arms reached out to pull them aboard. And then Gage was inside, his heart hammering, his face pressed flat against the metal floor as the Seahawk lifted into the air. Machine-gun fire sputtered below, and Gage sat up, shocked. He gazed down at the inferno. He glanced at Vaughn.

A little too much boom, his friend's look seemed to say, and Gage smiled. He couldn't believe they'd made it out of there unscathed.

A bullet whizzed past his cheek. Gage whirled around. He wouldn't smile again for a very long time.

LOWER PECOS RIVER VALLEY, TEXAS
Three months later

KELSEY QUINN CROUCHED at the bottom of the damp grave, her heart pounding against her sternum.

It couldn't be. She'd shot this sector with the radar herself. And yet as she dragged the trowel ever so gently across the earth, she felt it again—that barely perceptible resistance.

"Kelsey?"

Reaching for the sable hair brush tucked into the back pocket of her shorts, she bent closer to the patch of dirt. She dusted away a layer of silt, blew, then dusted again. Sweat trickled between her shoulder blades. She held her breath as the smooth slope of a cranium began to emerge.

"Kelsey?"

Her brush moved swiftly now, in time with her pulse. Cranial sutures not yet fused. It was a child.

"Dr. Quinn?"

Everything went dark. Kelsey's gaze snapped to the person who'd stepped in front of the lamp. She recognized her field assistant's gangly silhouette instantly.

"Yes, Aaron?"

"There's a message for you. From your mother."

She stared at him, taking a moment to comprehend the words.

A message from her *mother*? Besides a few e-mails, she hadn't heard from her mom in weeks. For her to call in the middle of a field school must mean something important.

Aaron stepped out of the light and Kelsey squinted at

the glare. She glanced down again at her discovery, then sat back on her haunches.

"We have another one." She couldn't suppress the excitement in her voice. "Tell Dr. Robles I've got a cranium."

Kelsey got to her feet and pulled off her baseball cap. Another burial. And in their last week, too. She didn't know why, but for some reason the best finds always came at the end of a dig.

Kelsey mopped the sweat from her brow and hiked up the four rough-hewn stairs to the top of the pit. Situated at the mouth of the cave, this particular sector had been worked first and was declared finished weeks ago. Kelsey had spent her first three weeks in this pit, sifting through dirt and lifting ancient bones from the soil. Her last week on the dig, and she'd returned here why? Nostalgia, maybe? Instinct? The nagging hunch that there was something more to find?

Kelsey stepped from the dimness of the cave into the blinding sunlight. The sky was a rich, cerulean blue. This morning's mist had been vaporized hours ago, and several wilted anthropology and archaeology students were standing beneath a tarp, trying to catch some shade as they swilled Evian water.

You can take the kids out of the city. . . .

She put her cap on again, pulling her ponytail through the hole in the back. She glanced down at the smudged slip of paper Aaron had handed her. *Call your uncle Joe. Love, Mom,* followed by a phone number. The area code was San Diego, where her uncle lived and where Kelsey had spent a huge chunk of her hugely chunky childhood.

Her mother had tracked her down in the west Texas

desert because Joe needed to talk to her? Kelsey sensed a trap, but she didn't have the first clue as to what it could be.

She scoured the cluttered campsite until she found the satellite phone beneath a table crammed with plastic containers. It took ten minutes and three attempts before she reached her uncle at the naval base. He was stateside for a change, not off fighting bad guys with his team of SEALs.

"Quinn here."

Despite the heat and the mystery and her annoyance at being pulled away from an important find, Kelsey smiled. "You needed to talk to me?"

"Kelsey. How's it going?" His voice was brisk, but she heard the fondness in it, and her smile widened. Whatever this was, it wasn't some horrible emergency.

"Pretty good," she said, "considering it's a hundred and ten degrees out and I haven't had a shower in two days. How's it going with you?"

"Listen, your mom called last night. She's worried about you."

"Oh my God, she didn't. Is this about that girl from Del Rio?"

Pause. Kelsey's anger bubbled up as she put it all together.

"She tells me you're alone out there digging up bones—"

"Amazing. This is amazing." She fisted her hand on her hip in frustration. "I told her when she e-mailed me that article that she's *way* overreacting."

"You're telling me some woman didn't get dragged from her car and shot, not twenty miles from where you are?"

"People get shot all the time! You live in San Diego, for Christ's sake. It happens every day!"

Another pause, and she could picture her father's brother frowning down at the phone. She was being disrespectful, and if there was one thing Lieutenant Commander Joseph Quinn had harped on her entire life it was respect.

"Joe, really. I'm fine. And I'm definitely not alone. I'm out here with dozens of people—"

"Camping by yourself at night, though, right? Just you and that seventy-two-year-old professor?"

"We're in *campers*," she said, hoping he picked up on the plural. Did he really think she was shacked up with Dr. Robles? Eew.

Kelsey glanced around impatiently. A trio of students stood at one of the tables, their heads bowed over various labeling tasks while they pretended not to eavesdrop. Kelsey needed to wrap this up. At twenty-eight, she was considered a mere toddler in academic circles, and she already had enough trouble getting students to take her seriously. Her kick-ass job at a world-renowned forensics lab, which set her apart from the rest of the university faculty, was her saving grace. But even her job at the Delphi Center couldn't salvage her reputation if word got out that her mommy had been calling her at a dig to fret over safety.

"Listen, Joe, I appreciate the call. I really do—"

"I'm sending someone out there," he bowled right over her. "He should be there today, about sixteen hundred."

Four heads turned as a car rumbled up the dirt road leading to the dig site.

Sixteen hundred. Kelsey's mind reeled. She clutched the phone to her ear and stared, stupefied, as the car-that-turned-out-to-be-a-pickup-truck rolled to a stop beside the row of SUVs. Dust coated the truck's sides and tires. Smashed bugs dotted the windshield, hinting at a lengthy trip. The door pushed open and a man climbed out.

But he wasn't a man, really—he was a giant. He stood well over six feet tall, with wide shoulders and muscular arms that screamed *warrior*. His olive-drab T-shirt stretched taut over his pecs, and he leaned an elbow on the roof of the truck while he scanned the area.

His gaze landed on Kelsey and her throat went dry.

"Kelsey? You there?"

"You sent me a SEAL?" she choked.

"His name's Lieutenant Gage Brewer, Team Nine, Alpha squad. Like I said, he should be there by sixteen hundred. He's got two weeks' leave, so it worked out perfectly."

"You *hired* someone to . . . to—"

"He owes me a favor. It's no big deal, really. This'll be a silver-bullet assignment for him. He's looking forward to it."

Lieutenant Whoever-He-Was reached up and peeled off his sunglasses to reveal a pair of laser-blue eyes as hard and unyielding as the rest of him. *Looking forward to it.* Yeah, right. This guy was *so* not happy to be here.

He slammed the door of his truck and strode toward her.

Two

"Kelsey Quinn?"

Her ability to speak evaporated as she stared up at him.

"Gage Brewer," he said. "I'm here to sign up for your dig."

Sign up for your dig. Right now. Today. The field school had only a week remaining, and every last person here had been toiling in the sun all summer.

His gaze bored into hers, daring her to challenge him. Damn right she'd challenge him. As soon as she could talk.

She glanced around.

And as soon as she could get away from all the prying eyes of her students.

"Glad you made it." She forced a smile. "Right this way, please."

She started for her camper, then realized it would look strange, disappearing into a private room with a man she'd only just met. She changed course, heading for a rocky outcropping about a hundred yards away. The petroglyphs. They'd be within plain view but well out of earshot.

"So you're thinking of joining us. Why don't I give you a tour of the site and you can make up your mind?"

He followed silently, his gaze scanning the horizon looking for . . . what? Rapists? Mountain lions? Serial killers?

"Where, exactly, did you come from?" she asked when they'd reached a safe distance.

"California."

"You drove here from *San Diego*? At my uncle's request?"

He said nothing to this, just followed her strides across the rocky terrain.

"Listen, Lieutenant—" She suddenly blanked on his name.

"Brewer," he supplied. "And you can call me Gage."

"All right. Gage. I'm not sure what my uncle told you, but your being here, it really isn't necessary. My colleagues and I are—"

"He told me his niece needed protection. I told him I'd come. When you're safely packed up and headed back home, I'll return to San Diego, mission accomplished."

Kelsey picked her way over the stony creek bed, fighting back tears of frustration as she listened to him talk. He was just like Joe, just like the stubborn, mule-headed man who had been a father to her most of her life. Good God, she'd never get rid of this guy. He considered her his *mission*.

Kelsey scaled the side of the creek, grabbing a branch to heft herself up. It snapped free and she fell backward. A pair of enormous hands caught her shoulders.

"Easy there."

Her pulse skipped as the feel of him, the *smell* of him permeated her brain. A jolt of raw sexual awareness zinged through her, and she scrambled away.

Was *that* what this was about? Was her mother matchmaking with one of her uncle's SEALs? The idea was unbearable. Mortifying. She felt color flooding her already pink cheeks.

And it suddenly hit her. She must look like roadkill. She was grimy, sunburned, and her last encounter with a mascara wand had been before Memorial Day.

Kelsey scurried up the hillside to the limestone escarpment that looked out over the valley and into Mexico. She ducked under the shade of an overhang and stopped beside a wall of rock decorated with ancient engravings. She turned to face the lieutenant, waiting until her eyes adjusted to the dimness so that she could read his expression.

He stopped, maintaining a respectful distance from her as he folded his arms over his chest.

Kelsey tried to sound composed. "My uncle is your commanding officer, is that correct?"

"Yes, ma'am."

"And your commanding officer asked you—as some sort of favor—to come protect me for the duration of my job here, is that it?"

"That's correct, ma'am."

She closed her eyes. "Please don't call me 'ma'am' again, okay? I mean, you're probably older than I am."

He didn't comment, even though she felt certain he knew precisely how old she was. Her uncle had probably given him her bio, for heaven's sake. That's how Joe worked. Every mission came with a file, a set of facts to be committed to memory. Kelsey remembered the Abe Lincoln project from fifth grade, the one that—according to Joe—couldn't be undertaken until she'd memorized the Gettysburg Address.

She shook off the memory. "So your being here, it's not really a direct order, is that right? I mean, you're not going to get fired if you don't—"

"Joe Quinn asked me to come, so I came. It's that simple." Something sparked in his eyes, and she sensed that whatever had brought him here wasn't simple at all.

"This may be simple for you but it's not for me," she said. "I'm the field supervisor here. I'm in charge of eighteen graduate students and six undergrads. I have research to conduct, reports to write, grades to submit, and a professional reputation to uphold. How do you think it looks when my uncle sends out some hired hunk of muscle to protect me from the bogeyman?"

He eyed her coolly, not even flinching at her "hired hunk of muscle" comment, which had been intended to piss him off. Kelsey knew the SEAL code. And she knew whatever debt this man owed Joe it had nothing to do with money.

He nodded slightly. "That Ruger you got strapped to your belt, what's that for?"

Kelsey's gaze snapped to her holster. She'd become so accustomed to it that she didn't even notice it anymore.

She looked up and cleared her throat. "This isn't Disneyland. We get mountain lions and rattlesnakes around here."

He lifted an eyebrow. "Coyotes, mules, maybe even a few border bandits?"

Her gaze narrowed.

"Don't get me wrong. It's a nice weapon." He paused. "You know how to use it?"

"Of course."

"And when'd you get the holster?"

She didn't answer.

"I'm guessing back home in San Marcos, you usually carry it in your purse, right?"

So Joe had told him about her. At least where she lived. What else had Joe told him? Had he mentioned how her boyfriend had dumped her six months ago?

"When'd you get the holster, Kelsey?"

She squared her shoulders. "Five weeks ago."

He nodded. "After the second break-in. That was *your* camper, right? The first was Dr. Robles."

She bit her lip.

"And then when that woman was dragged from her car and murdered last week, not ten minutes from here, I bet that made you think twice, right?"

She didn't say anything.

"Your uncle cares about you. He told me you're a smart woman." He stepped closer until he was towering over her. "He also told me to provide protection for you while you finish your work here, and I agreed." He unfolded his arms and planted his hands on his hips. "I'm not here to get in your way or get in your business. You want to keep this between you and your uncle? Fine by me. Call me a graduate student and hand me a shovel. But I made a promise to Joe and I intend to keep it."

Kelsey recognized defeat when it was staring her in the face.

And anyway he was right. She hadn't had a decent night's sleep in nearly a week, not since the sheriff had visited the dig site to inform them of the nearby murder and ask if they'd seen or heard anything suspicious.

Kelsey hadn't. But she'd been in a state of anxious hyperawareness ever since. Just hiking out to this cliff was the farthest she'd ventured away from the group in days.

"Okay, you win." She crossed her arms. "Now what do you want me to do?"

Heat flickered in his eyes at the question. Or maybe she'd imagined it.

"You don't need to do anything," he told her. "Just pretend I'm not here."

KELSEY QUINN'S ARCHAEOLOGY project was bigger than Gage had anticipated. It encompassed four separate areas, two out in the open and two more inside the cave. Including the work tents—which were really just tarps supported by metal poles—and the campers where Kelsey and her boss stayed, the site included almost three acres of privately owned land that was being cleared of ancient artifacts to make room for a mining project. The area wasn't large from a security standpoint, but it had its challenges.

The main issue was the unpaved road that skirted their setup. It provided a direct—if bumpy—route from the town of Madrone almost straight to the dig site. Just a short detour off the road and you were right there. Problem was, the road also provided a direct route between the U.S.–Mexico border and Interstate 10—and a predictable array of security risks associated with one of the most rugged and least governable tracts of land in the entire Southwest.

Kelsey and her college kids, parked out here with all their SUVs and computer equipment, were sitting ducks. Gage found it amazing they hadn't had more than a few break-ins. Of course, the fact that the students headed into town each night, back to the relative comfort of the lodge they'd taken over for the summer, made the dig site less of a target for thieves. But the setup left Kelsey and the geriatric Dr. Robles alone with a crapload of computers and equipment.

For a woman who worked at one of the world's top crime labs, Kelsey showed a remarkable lack of street smarts.

Gage hauled his zillionth bucket of dirt and emptied it onto a large wire screen for sifting. Kelsey's beanpole assistant Aaron gave him another one of his sullen looks.

"Thirty minutes, people." Kelsey's voice rang out across the site. "Then we'll call it a wrap."

Gage cut a glance at his principal. She was sweaty and sunburned and her skinny legs were dotted with scrapes and old bruises. A lock of that fiery red hair had come loose, and she stuffed it back inside her Padres cap as she meted out instructions to one of her underlings. Gage watched her work. She was bossy and annoying and promised to be a royal pain in his ass for the next seven days.

And yet there was something about her that made his blood hum. He had no idea what it was—she was the polar opposite of his usual type. And yet he felt it, just beneath the surface, the steady thrum of lust coursing through his veins.

Gage needed a woman. Soon. Didn't it figure that the one woman to stir his interest after months and months of celibacy would be the niece of his CO, a woman completely off-limits for some quick-and-dirty fun?

But "fun" hadn't been part of Gage's vocabulary in months. And that wasn't going to change anytime soon. He'd come here to work, not play, and the last thing he needed was to get tangled up with a woman guaranteed to make his life an even bigger mess than it already was.

Gage trudged back into the cave for another bucketful of dirt.

KELSEY FOUND AARON working on the ossuary at the back of the cave, where a battery-powered lamp illuminated a jumble of prehistoric bones. Besides being a brilliant scholar, her field assistant was one of the most meticulous diggers she'd ever known, and she watched with admiration as he worked his roped-off patch of earth. He lay flat against a fence slat that spanned the pit. The makeshift brace enabled him to reach down and remove soil without causing unnecessary disturbance to the burial site.

"Only two centimeters to go on that skull," she said.

Aaron glanced up at her and lifted an eyebrow. She'd made major progress this afternoon.

"Where'd you get the beefcake?" he asked.

She cocked her head to the side. She hadn't expected such open hostility.

"Mr. Brewer is a law enforcement colleague visiting from California." *Liar, liar, pants on fire.* "He's interested in our dig, and I told him he was welcome to lend a hand."

Aaron got to his feet and wiped his hands on his jeans. He glanced over Kelsey's shoulder, where at the mouth of the cave Gage had been making himself useful hauling dirt.

He'd been at it two hours, and by Kelsey's estimation he equaled about six of her anemic grad students.

Aaron crouched down and began dropping tools into a canvas bag.

"If it's not too much trouble," she said, "I thought you might give him a brief tour before you pack up for the day."

Aaron snorted. "No trouble at all. Although I'm not sure 'tour guide' falls within my job description."

"Fine, I'll do it. You can type up the notes for Dr. Robles."

"I didn't say I wouldn't do it. Just don't expect me to teach him Archaeology 101. He can crack a book like the rest of us."

Kelsey swallowed a bitchy comment. She didn't really want to bicker. She'd had enough aggravation convincing Dr. Robles to allow a newcomer on the project at this late date. Maybe he would have been more cooperative if she'd told him the truth about Gage's purpose here, but Robles was a lifelong pacifist and she didn't want to risk a negative reaction if he found out Gage was a Navy SEAL. So she'd come up with the law-enforcement-colleague spiel, which vaguely resembled the truth. It was the only way she could think of to explain Gage's obvious cluelessness about archaeology and the SIG Sauer plastered to his hip.

"Thank you," Kelsey said. "I'm going to type up my notes. If I don't see you before you leave—"

"Dr. Quinn!"

Kelsey whirled around to see a pair of students picking their way around the cave's stalagmites. They stepped into the lamplight and she saw that it was Dylan and Jeannie, a couple who'd hooked up over the course of the summer.

"What is it?" Kelsey asked.

"We found something," Jeannie gushed. "Something you need to come see. It's a mandible."

"Human," Dylan added. "We found it in the creek bed just south of the mine shaft."

"What were you doing at the mine shaft?" The old mercury mine was almost a mile south, along the same stretch of roadway where that woman had been shot.

And the sudden flush of Jeannie's cheeks told her exactly what they'd been doing at the mine shaft.

Kelsey huffed out a breath. "You guys, come on. Did you listen to anything at all I've said about safety? That area's not even part of our dig."

"It's not part of anyone's dig," Dylan told her. "You're the expert, but I'd say this bone looks fresh."

Three

The sun had dipped below the horizon but the stones lining the creek bed still retained the day's heat. Kelsey lay flat against them, blinking sweat from her eyes as she positioned her Nikon camera. She heard the police cruiser pull up. She heard the heavy crunch of boots. She took one last shot of the mandible, collected the ruler she'd used for scale, and walked over to greet the sheriff she'd met the other day.

"Word is you found us a jawbone," Sheriff Sattler said.

"Actually, two of my students found it." She glanced up at the line of onlookers who had gathered on the edge of the dried creek. Gage wasn't among them, and Kelsey wondered where he'd disappeared to.

She led Sattler to the bone and he knelt down for a closer look.

"You think it's one of your Indians?" he asked.

"At a glance, I couldn't tell you the ethnicity. But it's definitely modern, not ancient." She crouched beside him and pointed to the molars. "For one thing, there are the

fillings. Also, traces of dried soft tissue, in this case liga-
ments. The scratches suggest animal activity, probably car-
rion birds, but it looks like they missed a few spots."

Sattler stood up now and surveyed the surrounding
area. The lawman was tall and bulky, and his thick silver
hair contrasted sharply with his leathery brown skin. If
not for the badge pinned to his chest, Kelsey would have
guessed him for a cattle rancher.

"Just a jawbone, huh? Anything else?"

Kelsey stood, too. "Nothing readily apparent, but of
course you'll have to conduct a thorough search. A cadaver
dog would be a huge help. Does the county have a canine
unit?"

"Just the drug-sniffing kind."

"Well, that won't work for this." She brushed her hair
out of her eyes and glanced around, hoping to see some
evidence she'd missed earlier. It was that strange time of
day, lightwise. Everything looked flat and gray and a bone
would be easy to overlook among all these rocks.

Sattler pulled a toothpick from his breast pocket and
popped it in his mouth. He didn't say anything, so Kelsey
continued.

"Given the animal activity, I'd say there's a good
chance the skeleton could be scattered over a wide area."
She paused and waited for a reaction. Nothing.

"Another possibility is that the remains were buried
and an animal dug them up. You might find the rest of
the skeleton, except for the skull, obviously, in a shallow
grave nearby. You could rope off this area and use ground-
penetrating radar—"

"Who could?" Sattler asked around the toothpick.

"You. Your deputies. And your medical examiner will want to—"

"Seco County doesn't have a medical examiner. Not big enough. Our justice of the peace serves as coroner around here."

"Your JP, then."

He nodded. "Fella by the name of Sam Niederhauser, 'bout seventy years old. Not much on death investigating."

Kelsey stared at him, pretty sure she knew where this was going.

"Fact, that shooting we had last week pretty much wore him out." Sattler plucked the toothpick out and looked her in the eye. "I hear when you're not digging up old skeletons, you work at that crime lab in San Marcos. The Delphi Center."

"That's right. I'm scheduled to go back there in less than a week, in fact."

"You're a forensic anthropologist. An expert on bones." He nodded in the direction of the campsite. "You're already out here with all your equipment, why don't you take a crack at it? See what you come up with."

"I've got a field school to run. And I don't have jurisdiction."

"I'm giving you jurisdiction. Thing like this, we have to get outside help anyway. You're here already, I'd just as soon get it from you."

She gritted her teeth, irritated at being steamrolled yet again today. And the look on Sattler's face told her he knew he'd won.

Actually, he'd won even before he pitched her. Kelsey had never turned down a request for help, and she wasn't about to start now, in front of her students. Some of them could be headed for jobs like hers, and the reality was when a call came you went. Police work didn't always adhere to a convenient schedule. In Kelsey's experience, it never did.

"We sure appreciate it." Sattler nodded. "Tomorrow I'll send out one of my deputies to give you a hand with the search."

"I'd rather have a cadaver dog."

He smiled slightly. "I'll see what I can do."

IT WAS AFTER dusk when Gage returned from town, and he wasn't happy to see the sheriff had already left. Speedy investigation. Gage pulled up to the campsite just as Kelsey stepped out of her door, keys in hand.

He parked his truck and climbed out. "Where you headed?"

"Nowhere."

He walked over to the steps of the camper, and they stood there, staring at each other.

She'd cleaned up while he'd been gone. Her damp hair hung loose around her shoulders, and she wore a snug-fitting black T-shirt and brown cargo pants that hit her mid-calf. Something black and bulky stuck out of her pocket.

"You got a minute?" he asked. "I need to show you something."

She darted a glance over his shoulder, clearly worried about Robles seeing him go into her place. Evidently satisfied that the guy had turned in for the night, she opened the door behind her.

"I'm making dinner," she said without enthusiasm. "You're welcome to have some."

"I'm good, thanks." Gage ducked his head and walked through the door, then instantly regretted his words as the spicy aroma of whatever she had cooking hit him full force. He hadn't eaten all day, and the dinner he had waiting for him tonight was a cold MRE.

"It's a mess," she said, squeezing around him.

Mess was an understatement. The camper was small and chock-full of clutter. Beside him was an eating alcove with a Formica table that had a notebook computer on top and books stacked beneath. Gage put his plastic shopping bag on the table as his gaze skimmed over the minuscule kitchen and a door that probably led to a bathroom. Beyond the kitchen, he caught sight of what looked like a fold-out bed with a sleeping bag on top. Something red and lacy was strewn across it.

Holy God.

"What's in the bag?"

His attention snapped back to Kelsey. "Huh?"

"The bag?"

"It's for you," he said. "Your com setup here sucks."

She peeked inside. Then she gazed up at him with those big brown eyes, and he had a flash of her in that red bra. "My com?"

"Communications. You've got one sat phone for the entire group."

"We're in the middle of nowhere," she said defensively. "The cell service is extremely patchy. That's why we have the sat phone."

"You need something for you. On your person. I need to be able to reach you at all times." He took out one of the radios and turned it on to demonstrate. "See? Just press this button here when you want to talk. It's got a long-life battery and a range of about five miles, which should be plenty." He paused and waited for her to look up at him. "Were you going to wait for me to go with you?"

"Go where?" She was doe-eyed now, innocent as hell.

"Wherever you were going when I pulled up."

She hesitated. "I need to check something at the recovery site."

He stepped closer until he was invading her personal space. "Lemme explain how this works, Kelsey. You set foot off this dig site, I'm coming with you. That's a dangerous highway and I don't want you driving around alone, especially at night."

She crossed her arms. "What happened to 'hand me a shovel and pretend I'm not here'?"

"That was before I knew you were camped out within spitting distance of a homicide scene."

She rolled her eyes. "You're jumping to conclusions. I've hardly had a chance to examine the bone, much less determine the manner of death."

"Oh, yeah? What do you think your uncle would say if I called him and told him about your little find today? I bet you a thousand dollars he'd say 'tell her to pack up camp and hightail it home.' "

"That's ridiculous. I have a job to do here."

"Yeah, and although this might come as a surprise to you, I get that. Which is why we aren't packing. But I don't plan to go back to my CO and tell him I let his niece get carjacked or killed or so much as breathed on wrong under my watch. So until your work's done here I'm your shadow. Get used to it. Now, where are we going?"

She gazed up at him, and he could see the frustration simmering in her eyes. He could understand it, too. She had a job to do, and she wasn't used to people standing in her way. But Gage had a job to do also, and this was one job he didn't plan to fuck up.

"All right, fine," she said. "Let's get going. You can help."

She took the black thing out of her pocket and handed it to him. It was lightweight and slender and looked like some sort of high-tech Maglite.

He glanced up at her. "Help with what?"

"The search," she said. "I want the rest of those bones."

KELSEY WAVED HER UV lamp over a pile of rocks. She took a few more paces and did another scan. Another few paces until she was at the very edge of the area she'd mapped out for tonight.

She shoved her orange-tinted glasses up on top of her head and glanced around at the blackness. "You finding anything?"

"No," came Gage's faraway response.

Kelsey sighed and switched off the blue light. They'd been out here nearly two hours and had netted nothing more than a few pieces of trash, a broken eggshell, and some miscellaneous long bones, all easily identifiable as belonging to small mammals. Each time she'd spotted the faint bluish glow, she'd felt a surge of excitement, only to be disappointed by an up-close inspection.

"This what you do back in San Marcos? Tromp around crime scenes looking for skeletons in the dark?"

"No," she admitted. "We work by day, usually, and

usually with cadaver dogs. But you never know what you might see with an alternative light source. Teeth. Clothing. Lots of dyes contain chemicals that fluoresce. I was hoping we'd find something out here that could lead us to the rest of him."

She let her gaze scan the area again, without any luck. She glanced at her watch and saw that it was nearly midnight.

Kelsey tipped her head back to look at the stars. It was amazing how many you could see out here. It was something she forgot during the rest of the year, then reminded herself of every summer.

"You hear that?"

She jumped and whirled around. "Omigod, you scared me!"

Gage was a giant shadow right beside her—so close, she now felt his body heat. And yet she hadn't heard a sound.

"Hear what?" she asked.

"Just listen."

She listened, but all she heard was the whisper of wind through the scrub brush and the quiet hum of crickets.

"I don't hear—"

"Shh."

And then she *did* hear it, a faint engine noise, growing nearer by the second.

"It's coming this way." Gage scaled the side of the creek bed with one big step, then turned and gazed north. The engine noise grew louder.

He dropped back down into the dried creek. "Come on," he said, taking her arm.

"Where are we going?"

"The mine shaft. It's this way." His hand was firm on her arm as he pulled her toward the entrance to the mine, which she couldn't even see in this darkness.

"Why are we hiding?"

No answer. He helped her out of the creek, practically lifting her off her feet when she missed a step. He was in a hurry.

"Gage?"

"They're driving blind."

"Blind?"

"No lights." He towed her into the even darker shadows of the mine shaft that was carved into the hillside. He seemed to know precisely where he was going without the aid of a flashlight.

She jerked her arm loose and halted. "I still don't see why—"

"You know any law-abiding citizens who drive around the border zone at night with their lights off? Either they're up to no good or they're looking for people up to no good. Either way, I bet they're armed, and I don't want to surprise them." He took her by the elbow and pulled her into the inky darkness of the mine where the air felt cool and damp. "You got your Ruger?" he asked.

"Yes, but—"

"Good. Now stay here." He reached down and switched on the radio clipped to her belt. "And keep this on. I'll be right back. Try not to shoot me."

Then he disappeared.

Kelsey huffed out a breath of annoyance. But she stayed put.

The engine noise drew closer and closer until it was almost on top of them. It sounded like a truck, and it was moving fast. She heard the skid of tires on gravel as it took the bend in the road.

The noise faded and Kelsey waited for Gage to reappear. Something fluttered behind her. Bats? Oh God, she hated bats. Spiders, snakes, bugs, no problems, but *bats* she could not abide. She closed her eyes and tried to push away the fear. Whatever bats lived here were probably out feeding. She'd probably just heard a bird. She took a deep, calming breath, which didn't work because she recognized the pungent smell of guano. And then a high-pitched squeak, like fingernails on a blackboard. She squeezed her eyes shut as she imagined millions of bats lurking behind her in the dark.

Her radio squawked to life and she snatched it off her belt. "Where are you?" she demanded.

"I'm almost there. Holster your weapon."

She'd never unholstered it. "Hurry. I'm starving and I want to get home."

"Yes, ma'am."

She detected the sarcasm in his voice. Maybe he thought she was a pain in the butt. It was late, and Joe Quinn's spoiled niece was getting cranky without her dinner.

Kelsey didn't care what he thought. She just wanted out of this damn mine shaft and away from these bats.

"Hi."

His warm, low voice brought a wave of relief.

"What was it?" she asked.

"I'm not sure."

He took her by the arm and led her into the open air

again. It felt dry and warm and smelled like mesquite trees instead of bat droppings.

"So you didn't see it?"

"It was a truck," he said, releasing her arm. "I saw it and then it disappeared."

"What do you mean it disappeared?"

"One second it was there. Then a cloud passed in front of the moon and *poof*, nothing."

"*Poof?* You mean like Harry Potter *poof* or is this some SEAL term I don't know about?"

"It was just gone," he said, and she heard the wonder in his voice. "It was the damnedest thing."

He got quiet then, and for a few moments all she could hear was his breathing. It had been a long time since she'd been this close to a man in the dark. And then it was back again, the question that had been dogging her since this afternoon. The same question that had been in the back of her mind as she'd directed students and talked to Sattler and sat alone in her camper, hunched over the mandible with a magnifying glass. The question of the decade, or at least of the summer.

Just where, exactly, was Gage Brewer planning to sleep?

Four

Gage awoke with a crick in his neck and a rumble in his gut. He squinted at the light streaming through the windshield and checked his watch. 0640. He looked at Kelsey's camper. If he guessed right, she'd be up shortly, getting ready to crack the whip on her soon-to-arrive students.

As if on cue the door swung open. She stepped out and scanned the campsite, and her gaze met his across the hood of his truck.

He pushed open the door and got out. His stomach growled again, reminding him of the bowl of homemade chili he'd refused last night, not just once but twice. He'd needed something to eat, yeah. But what he hadn't needed was another minute alone with Kelsey Quinn and her strawberry-scented shampoo. He needed that torture like he needed a hole in his head.

She walked over and planted her hands on her hips. "You slept in your *pickup*?"

He shook out his stiff legs and stretched his arms over his head.

"Don't you at least have a tent or something? You weren't even lying down!"

Gage didn't bother to explain. He was a SEAL. He could sleep anywhere.

He nodded at the purse slung over her shoulder. "Where're we going?"

"I've got some errands in town."

"Okay. Mind if I borrow your shower?" He glanced over her shoulder at the camper. He could have sworn he smelled coffee, and his nose was usually pretty accurate.

"Help yourself," she said. "There's coffee in there, too. I won't be long. I just have to meet with Sattler and get this bone sent off to the Delphi Center for testing."

He reached into the truck and grabbed his seabag off the floor. "Gimme five minutes."

"You really don't need to come. Why don't you just take your time showering and help out around the dig until I get back?"

He gazed down at her and for the first time he noticed the freckles dotting her nose. They'd been hidden yesterday underneath all the dust. Besides the same khaki shorts she'd worn yesterday, she had on a thin white T-shirt that was definitely going to mess with his head all day.

"I'm not here to guard the dig," he said. "I'm here to guard you."

"It's broad daylight, and I'm going to a police station, for heaven's sake. What could possibly happen?"

"Nothing," he said. "Because I'm coming with you."

Gage double-timed it in the shower, and they made the forty-mile journey into Madrone in half an hour. Kelsey wanted to get there bright and early for some reason, and he was happy to oblige her. But once in town his morning turned into an endless wait in the parking lot of the Seco County sheriff's office. Gage wasn't patient by nature and got especially antsy waiting around for women to do things. He minimized the boredom by people watching and adding to the intel he had on the area.

Madrone occupied a semiarid patch of land about a hundred miles west of the Pecos River. This was cattle country—hard, dry, rugged—and the people he saw in town seemed to mirror the land they worked. Despite being the county seat, Madrone was barely a spec on the map. It had three stoplights, two gas stations, and one bar, and the only motel looked to be a run-down hunting lodge on the south end of Main Street. The entire place had a parched feel to it, as if the blazing west Texas sun had sucked out all its energy.

Whatever Kelsey had wanted at this cow town sheriff's office, Gage doubted she was going to get it.

Finally, she exited the little building, looking frustrated. It seemed to be her default expression, and he wondered if she was always this way or if it had been a rough summer.

She yanked open the passenger door and slid in.

"Where to?" he asked, firing up the engine. Hot air shot from the vents as he pulled onto Main. He glanced at the woman beside him. "Kelsey?"

She blinked at him, as if surprised by the question. "What?"

"Where to?"

Her eyes searched his, and he got the impression she still hadn't processed his words. "Does it seem reasonable to you that in all of west Texas there isn't *one* available cadaver dog?"

He gave up on getting any direction.

"I mean, how can that be possible?"

"I don't know," he said.

"It isn't possible. It's crap. Sattler's just too lazy or too stubborn to get me someone, even after I showed him evidence we're probably dealing with a murder here. I get a deputy. That's it. A few hours of unskilled labor from one of his rednecks, then I'm done."

Gage pulled into a space in front of the town's only restaurant, and Kelsey's brow furrowed as she looked around.

"What are we doing?"

"Getting some lunch." He pushed open his door.

"But I need to get back. Dr. Robles—"

"Can manage fine without you. Come on, I'm starved."

She joined him on the sidewalk and glanced at the sign in front of them, then shot him a look. "You know this place is a grease pit, right? I think everything on the menu comes with a side of eggs."

"Sounds perfect." He pulled open the door to the diner and enjoyed the rush of cool air.

A waitress with big blond hair seated them at a booth near the window and handed them some menus. Kelsey tucked hers behind the napkin dispenser without looking at it, then proceeded to order the tuna melt. Gage scanned the menu and ordered the Cowboy Breakfast Platter.

When the waitress was gone, Gage settled his attention on Kelsey. She'd been in here before, obviously, probably grabbing a bite to eat with some of her students. Or was there one student in particular? That guy Aaron was very

territorial. Gage could feel the man watching him whenever he got within ten feet of Kelsey, which was pretty
much all the time. Aaron's preoccupation seemed to go
beyond professional interest, but from what Gage could
tell it was a one-way street. At the dig site, Kelsey was
completely wrapped up in her work, much like right now.

"Okay, spill it." Gage rested his arm on the back of the
seat. "What's the problem?"

She blew out a sigh. "Sattler's the problem. He's not
taking this seriously."

"What's to take seriously?"

"I think we're dealing with a homicide. He should be
all over this. The rest of the remains need to be recovered,
and he needs to launch a murder investigation. Instead, you
know what he's doing today?"

"What?"

"Speed traps between here and I-10."

"He told you that?"

"I overheard one of his deputies talking while I was
waiting to meet with him."

Their drinks came and they both downed half the glass
in one gulp.

"How can you be sure this is a murder case?" Gage
asked.

"I can't, especially not until I have the other bones, but
I definitely found signs."

Gage lifted his eyebrows and waited.

"Tiny flecks of metal embedded in the mandible," she
said. "Probably the result of a bullet fired through the
skull."

"And you showed Sattler?"

"Whipped out my magnifying glass and everything. He wasn't convinced."

"So forget the cadaver dog. Why don't you get a metal detector out there, see if you can find the bullet? If he was shot on site you might even get a shell casing."

She leaned back against the booth and blinked at him.

"What?"

"You ever thought of becoming a cop?" she asked.

Gage glanced away. Life beyond the navy wasn't something he talked about. But Spec Ops was a young man's game, and he'd just turned thirty-two. He'd been doing a lot of soul-searching lately, especially since Kandahar.

Kelsey stirred her drink with a straw. "I sent the jaw off to the lab for testing. Before they run the metal, I'm going to have my friend Mia take a look at it. She's a DNA tracer, and I'm hoping she can get something useful from the tooth pulp."

"Don't you need something to compare it to so you can get an ID?" Gage asked.

"There could be something already in the Missing Persons index. If there is, we'll get his remains turned over to his family. If there isn't, we'll enter the DNA profile in case someone comes looking for him someday."

Gage watched her, intrigued by the way she talked with so much emotion about a little chunk of bone. Obviously, to her, it represented a lot more than that.

Their food came and she immediately dug into her sandwich. She had an appetite, which didn't surprise him given the amount of time she spent working outdoors. Gage had never cared much for skinny girls, but this one actually had some meat on her—in all the right places.

She caught him staring. "What?" she asked and took a slurp of Diet Coke.

"You keep saying 'him.' You're sure it's a man?"

She shrugged. "Mia can tell me for sure, but it looks that way, given the shape of the mental protuberance."

"The who?"

She motioned him closer. He hesitated a second before resting his elbows on the table and leaning in.

"The mental protuberance." She rubbed her index finger over his chin. "It tends to have a square edge and be thicker for males." Her finger moved to the side of his jaw. "And the gonial angle here? In males it's usually more flared."

She dropped her hand away and picked up a french fry. "Anyway, we'll know the sex for sure when Mia runs the DNA. I also found some interesting dental work."

"Oh, yeah?" Not that he gave a damn whatsoever. Gage forked up a bite of eggs and tried to shut out the thoughts racing through his head.

"Two porcelain fillings. It goes a long way toward disproving Sattler's theory."

"And what's Sattler's theory?"

"That we're dealing with an illegal immigrant, maybe a drug runner who got himself into trouble down near the river. It would be surprising for someone like that to have this sort of dental work."

Kelsey checked her watch and signaled the waitress. "Do you mind if we go soon? I really want to get back before that deputy shows up." She smiled slightly. "Robles hates idle hands. If he sees him just sitting there, he's liable to put him on bucket duty."

"I know all about bucket duty."

The waitress reappeared and Gage took the check. He reached for his wallet but Kelsey deftly snatched away the bill.

"Don't even think about it," she said. "You slept in your truck last night. The least I can do is feed you."

SATTLER'S DEPUTY HADN'T shown up by the time they made it back to camp, so Kelsey went ahead without him.

She cherry-picked a team of her most capable students and started them at the highway. Their skeptical expressions told her they thought she was off base, that the search should have focused on the place where the mandible had been found. But when she'd mapped the area last night, she'd decided to start with a swath of land about a hundred yards north, her logic being that whoever had brought the victim here—dead or alive—had probably come via the highway and wouldn't have wanted to stray too far off course. Scavengers could have moved the bones, whether they'd been left in the open or buried in a shallow grave.

And so it began, the painstaking process of combing the ground, inch by inch, beneath the blistering Texas sun. At the outset energy was high. The students seemed to welcome a break in their routine, and Kelsey was counting on their enthusiasm to make up for their lack of formal training. This wasn't a search and recovery squad, but she'd worked with volunteers before, and she knew what to expect.

And as expected walking at a snail's pace, head down, in the scorching heat eventually lost its appeal. Muscles ached.

Eyes burned. Minds began to wander. After four hours of fruitless searching, she could tell everyone was ready to get back to the relative comfort of the caves and tarps.

Everyone but Gage. He worked doggedly, without complaint, looking totally undaunted by both the climate and the task.

For the millionth time this afternoon, Kelsey checked her watch. Still no deputy. Her temper festered. What could be keeping him? And why hadn't Sattler so much as put in an appearance today? Kelsey didn't understand how he could be so blasé about a potential murder within his jurisdiction.

"Whoa, check it out!"

Kelsey's head snapped up at the gleeful words. Rohit, a PhD candidate in cultural anthropology, had dropped to his knees beside a prickly pear cactus.

"I think it's a femur."

Kelsey and the rest of the team rushed over. It was, indeed, a femur. But was it animal or human? She would need to examine a cortex sample under a microscope to be sure. But the size looked good, as did the joint surfaces.

A shadow fell over her and she glanced up to see Gage.

"You look excited," he said.

"This is good. A femur will tell us a lot. Stature, sex, probably PMI."

"PMI?"

"Postmortem interval. The time since death. I can look at a cross section and get an idea." She turned to Rohit. "Could you get my camera bag?"

He sprinted off, and the rest of the team wandered away to find shade and break out their canteens.

Gage crouched down beside her, shielding her from the sun with his body. "You sure it's not from a cow or something?"

"We'll find out. But my hunch says it's our guy. Now we just need the rest of him." She glanced around. They'd crossed over to the west side of the road, but they weren't far from it, maybe sixty yards. She was gaining more confidence in her roadside execution theory.

Gage stood up and shrugged out of his backpack. "Nice work, Dr. Quinn." He unzipped the pack and handed her a bottle of water. "Now, drink up. You look like you're about to pass out."

She stood up and swigged, then passed back the bottle. He took a long gulp, and her stomach fluttered as she watched his throat move.

"Thanks for helping," she said. "You don't have to do this, you know."

He screwed the cap back on. "Now you tell me."

She felt a pang of guilt. "You could knock off for the day. If you're tired—"

"Who says I'm tired?" The side of his mouth curled up.

"You're sweating."

"It's hot."

"Yeah, well, I'd think you'd be more into water sports." He gave her a quizzical look.

"You're a SEAL. We're in the desert."

"Sea-Air-Land, SEAL." He smiled fully now. "Didn't your uncle teach you anything?"

His eyes twinkled with amusement as he gazed down at her. It was the first time he'd smiled at her, and for a moment she couldn't breathe.

Don't do it, Kelsey. Don't you dare fall for this beautiful man who has to leave in a few days.

She looked away—at the ground, the road, the cactus. Anything but Gage.

And that's when she spotted him.

"Sattler's guy showed," Gage said.

Kelsey set off toward him. "It's about goddamned time."

Five

It was the perfect night. Clear. Breezy. The temperature had even dipped below ninety. It was an ideal time to be out with friends, sitting at one of the riverfront bars, laughing and drinking margaritas.

Instead, Mia Voss was headed home to an empty apartment, and the computer bag slung over her shoulder was stuffed with unfinished reports.

She reached for her keys just as her purse started to glow and sing. She checked the number on her phone. Darn it, she'd forgotten to call Kelsey.

"I'm *so* sorry," Mia said, juggling computer, purse, and phone as she slid behind the wheel of her Jeep. "Yes, I got your message. And yes, he brought the bone."

Silence on the other end.

"Kelsey?"

"*Who* brought the bone?"

"The sheriff's guy." Mia backed out of her space and nestled the phone in her lap so she could shift gears. "He had a ten-gallon hat and everything. Very *Lonesome Dove*."

"You're telling me Sheriff Sattler had someone personally deliver my package to the Delphi Center?"

"You sound surprised," Mia said.

"I am. So far, he hasn't had the slightest interest in this case. At least, I thought he hadn't."

"Well, evidently someone's interested, because this guy was under strict orders *not* to simply leave the package with the evidence clerk. He had me paged down to the lobby to make sure I knew that his item had arrived and it was top priority."

"I'm shocked," Kelsey said. "Did you have the heart to tell him the true meaning of top priority around there? And why am I on speaker phone?"

"I'm in the Jeep," Mia said. "Stick shift and cell phones don't mix."

"It's after ten. Don't tell me you're just leaving work."

"Okay, I won't. Actually, I'm glad you called. There's a chance your case could get bumped to the front of my line. What's your estimate of the postmortem interval on this thing?"

Kelsey paused. "I'd say six months to a year."

"Hmm . . ."

"That's a loaded *hmm*. What's going on?"

The Delphi Center's electronic gates parted. Mia waved at the guard and rolled through, then turned onto the two-lane highway that would take her into San Marcos.

"It's *possible* your case could be related to an ongoing federal investigation," Mia said.

"You're kidding."

"It's a missing person case. About three months ago I got a bone sample in from Del Rio, which isn't far from you. I was asked to use mitochondrial DNA and get a pro-file for comparison with a known sample. It was all very urgent. The agent who brought me the sample—"

"Wait a second. Are we talking FBI?"

Mia didn't say anything, knowing her silence would be confirmation enough.

"Why wouldn't they send it to Quantico?"

"I'm not sure," Mia said. "But from what I gather, this investigator had an in at the Delphi Center and knew he could get a quick turnaround. I was ordered to analyze it ASAP, and that's just what I did."

"And?"

"And the results weren't what they had hoped. Who-ever their missing person is, the bone isn't his."

"His?"

"The missing person is male. Have you determined the sex on these bones yet?"

"I think so," Kelsey said. "We found the femur this afternoon and I've been working on it all night. I can tell you it's human, large in stature, probably male. And defi-nitely an adult."

"If the bone has been there six months to a year that would fit with my case, too."

"Do the feds have dental records on this missing per-son?" Kelsey asked.

"I'm not sure. Why?"

"He's got some distinctive dental work. Expensive. You should get our forensic odontologist to take a look."

"I'll do that."

"Are you going to fill me in on what this is about?"

Mia heard the annoyance in her friend's voice. They

didn't normally keep secrets but, in this case, it wasn't Mia's decision.

"I wish I could," she said. "I'll let you know what develops. Probably by late tomorrow."

"*Tomorrow*? Mia, come on. What in the world is this about?"

"I don't know yet," she lied. "But I'll tell you more as soon as I can."

KELSEY HUNG UP the satellite phone, baffled. She walked over to the stove and stirred her pot of soup as she tried to decipher Mia's words.

The Delphi Center was known for its rapid turnaround time. It was one of the things that set the lab apart from publicly funded crime labs around the country. But in her three years as a tracer, Kelsey had never once had one of her cases get bumped to the front of the line. And she'd worked on some high-profile investigations.

What had she stumbled into?

A light tap sounded at the door and her pulse jumped. Maybe it was Gage. He'd been standoffish earlier, and she'd been feeling snubbed.

She opened the door to find Dr. Robles standing in the drizzle. He wore a yellow rain slicker, and with his gray beard he looked like the fisherman from those seafood commercials.

"I've finished my examination of your femur," he said, pushing his glasses higher on the bridge of his nose. "I concur with most of your findings, but I think your height estimate is a bit high. I would say five-eleven."

"Thanks for the second opinion." Kelsey opened the

door wider and waved a hand at the stove. "Would you like a bowl of soup? I was just about to eat."

"Thank you, no. I should get to bed." He glanced uneasily over his left shoulder. "But you might offer the same hospitality to your friend."

"What?"

"Your police detective." The professor's look turned disapproving. "He shouldn't have to sleep in the rain."

Kelsey poked her head outside and spotted the long dark lump beneath one of the nearby shade tarps.

"Oh my God." She stalked over to him. "Gage! What are you doing?"

He opened one eye and peered up at her in the dimness. "Trying to get some sleep."

"You can't sleep out here!"

"Not with you yelling at me."

"But . . . I thought you were in your truck."

"Decided to stretch out tonight."

"Get up. This is ridiculous. You don't even have a sleeping bag." He was using his duffel for a pillow, for crying out loud.

"Kelsey, I'm fine. Go back to bed."

"I'm not *in* bed. And there's no way I can sleep tonight knowing you're out in this rain. Come inside."

He sighed heavily and dropped his arm over his face. "Kelsey, come on. I can't sleep with you. Jesus. If Joe finds out—"

"I didn't ask you to *sleep with me*. You can sleep on my floor. *In*side."

He gazed up at her and she crossed her arms, adamant.

Finally, he got to his feet. He wore the same jeans and

T-shirt he'd had on earlier, and he'd gone to bed with his gun on. Was he really that worried about her safety?

He shoved his feet into the boots parked beneath one of the worktables. "You're trying my patience, Quinn. I was almost asleep."

She turned her back on him and went inside the camper. She moved a few stacks of books, then retrieved the sleeping bag from her fold-out bed and spread it out on the floor. She'd settle for a blanket tonight.

Gage stood in the doorway, watching her. His gaze shifted to the stove.

She tossed him a dish towel. "You told me you ate already."

"I did."

She watched him dry off, trying to imagine what he'd put together for his dinner while she'd been in here buried in work.

"I've got chicken tortilla soup," she said.

"Really, I'm okay." He glanced at the stove again.

Kelsey took a clean bowl from the milk crate where she stored her dishes. It was one of her few indulgences. She didn't mind cold showers, and Laundromats, and no phones all summer. But she despised eating with paper plates and plastic utensils, so she brought dishes from home. She filled a bowl with steamy soup and put it on the table.

Gage stepped onto the camper, finally, and looked around for a place to stash his duffel.

"Under the table's fine," she said. "You can move those books."

Gage stowed his bag and slid onto the bench seat. His long legs stuck out into the middle of the room.

"Sorry about the clutter." Kelsey put two spoons on the table, then filled another bowl with soup and slid onto the seat beside him.

Gage rubbed his eyes and sighed.

"You weren't really asleep, were you?"

His gaze met hers. "No."

She sampled her soup. It was hot and spicy and the chicken chucks were tender. Kelsey wasn't much of a cook, but Gage took a bite and didn't leap up from the table in disgust, so she took that as a good sign.

"You know," she said, "I *do* know a few things about SEALs. I'm pretty close to my uncle."

He watched her as he scooped up another bite.

"I know about BUD/S training, and Hell Week, and all those practice missions on San Clemente Island and up in Alaska."

"What's your point?"

"My point is, you don't have to act like Superman all the time. I'm already impressed."

Their gazes locked. She'd told him she was impressed. And she was. She had an incredible amount of admiration for these talented men who dedicated themselves to training and practicing and honing their skills in order to be part of one of the most elite fighting forces in the world. She felt the same admiration for her uncle.

But along with her admiration for Gage—and every other man in his profession—was something more. Something that had nothing to do with his job and everything to do with the way her pulse raced whenever he came near her. She'd never responded to a stranger this way, and she wasn't sure exactly what to do about it. He'd be gone in a few days. She needed to remember that.

Maybe this was just about sex. And maybe, as Mia had so often suggested, Kelsey needed a rebound man. Her ex-boyfriend Blake lived in suits and went through life with a BlackBerry attached to his ear. He hated camping and kept hand sanitizer stashed in his glove compartment for emergencies. A hardened warrior he was not.

Kelsey eyed Gage's T-shirt. Today's was desert-brown instead of olive drab, and the collar was slightly frayed. It would be tough to imagine a man less like Blake, and maybe that explained her fascination. Ever since Gage had shown up she'd felt edgy.

But it was a good edgy. A warm-feeling-low-in-the-belly kind of edgy.

Gage tipped his bowl to get the very last spoonful. He glanced up at her with those impossibly blue eyes. "What?"

"Nothing."

Nothing was right. He was leaving soon, and this was going nowhere.

Kelsey got up and felt his gaze on her as she retrieved a couple of beers from the minifridge.

Gage raised an eyebrow. "Drinking on the job?"

"I'm done for the night." She used the cuff of her sweatshirt to twist the cap off her bottle. "Here's to silver-bullet assignments."

He gave her a look she couldn't read. Then he twisted his cap off and clinked bottles with her.

KELSEY MADE A mean bowl of soup and she liked Miller Genuine Draft. All the more reason for him to get his butt back out there in the rain.

And he would. Eventually. He planned to do some reconnaissance tonight while she was asleep. But for now sitting inside her messy camper and watching her put away dinner felt just a little too good.

And so he stayed. And watched her. She'd changed into boxer shorts and a sweatshirt and he tried not to notice how good her legs looked without any shoes on. Gage forced himself to look away and wondered, again, what the hell Joe had been thinking sending him out here. Did he realize what he was asking? It was like sending a man across the desert and then asking him to guard a glass of water.

Gage cleared his throat. "Guess we needed this rain, huh?"

She gave him an amused look over her shoulder. Shit, had he really just teed up a conversation about the weather?

"It's okay, I guess." She got them two more brews and joined him back at the table. "Not a problem for the dig, but I doubt it will help our search-and-recovery effort."

It was a good point. A very obvious one, too. And when he got back to San Diego, Gage really needed to hit the bars with his buddies and brush up on some of his conversation skills.

She was sitting beside him now, looking at him. The only light in the place came from a battery-powered lantern across the room, and she was half in shadow.

"Are you ever planning to tell me about this favor you owe my uncle?"

He untwisted the cap from her bottle and slid it to her. Then he twisted the cap off his. "What favor's that?"

She tucked a lock of that auburn hair behind her ear

and smiled. "The one that gives him the right to put you on seven days of babysitting detail?"

Gage took a sip, stalling. He rested the bottle on the table. "He can put me on any detail he wants. He's my CO."

She rolled her eyes. "Yes, but you're off duty. You said you were on leave."

Gage shrugged. "Once a SEAL, always a SEAL." It was a lame answer, but that's all she was going to get. He wasn't about to sit here and rehash the worst night of his life. He wasn't going to sit here and tell her how he'd spent the past three months fighting depression and how he could easily be out of a job right now if her uncle hadn't intervened.

"O-kay. I guess it's off-limits." She looked away, obviously stung by the brush-off, and he felt mean. She checked her watch. "It's getting late, anyway. I should get to bed." She started to stand up and he caught her arm.

"Joe Quinn's the best Texas hold 'em player I ever met. You play?"

She looked at him as if he'd just asked her if she was terrorist insurgent. "Are you kidding?"

"No."

"He taught me when I was, like, seven or something. I'll kick your butt."

"Doubtful." He reached under the table and retrieved a deck of cards from his seabag.

"Oh, sure. Like I'm going to let *you* provide the cards."

He made a show of peeling off the cellophane, relieved that the awkwardness had disappeared. "It just so happens I picked up these cards a week ago."

"Where?" she asked.

"You always this suspicious?"

"Joe taught me to gamble, so yes."

"O'Hare Airport." He removed the jokers and shuffled the deck. When he was finished he let her cut the cards.

"What are we betting?" she asked. "I don't keep cash around ever since the break-in. Oh, wait." She popped up and disappeared into the back of the camper. He heard her shuffling around, and then she returned with four rolls of quarters. "Laundry money," she said, dropping the rolls on the tables.

Gage dug a twenty-dollar bill out of his bag and traded it for two of the rolls.

He dealt. She picked up her cards, and a wicked smile spread across her face, as if he'd just given her a pair of aces. But he saw straight through her bluff.

He checked his cards. He'd play five or six hands with her. Ten, tops. He glanced across the table. Her tongue swept over her upper lip as she contemplated her cards.

Gage's gut tightened. This was a bad idea. He should be doing recon right now, not playing poker with his CO's niece.

He looked at Kelsey. He looked at his cards. And he knew, with certainty, that this wasn't going to be his lucky night.

Six

The bones were buried in a shallow grave about thirty yards west of the highway. It wasn't ground-penetrating radar or a metal detector or any other gadget that led to their discovery, but rather the eagle-eyed gaze of a seventy-two-year-old anthropologist.

"Nature doesn't like straight lines," Dr. Robles had said, after calling Kelsey over to have a look at the rectangular pile of rocks. They hardly stood out against the stony creek bed but Robles was right—on close inspection the arrangement looked man-made.

After it became clear what he'd found, Robles returned to the shade of the caves, taking most of the students with him. A few stragglers loitered behind, clearly more interested in recent bones than ancient ones.

Kelsey shut out all distractions now as she worked within the string boundaries she'd staked out around the site. After thoroughly photographing the area, she'd removed dozens of rocks, examining each for any sign of trace evidence before laying it aside. After just the first layer she'd begun to find scraps of rotten clothing and human bones: an ulna, a radius, several metacarpals. When the full arm took shape, she stood up and photographed it from multiple angles before moving on to the thoracic cage.

The sun blazed down. The minutes crawled by. She was at the digging stage now, and with every scoop of her trowel and swipe of her brush her sense of alarm grew. A leather belt. A scrap of rope. The tattered remnants of a pair of blue jeans.

A shadow fell over her, and she glanced up, expecting to see Aaron. Instead it was Gage, who'd spent the better part of the day on the hillside, watching God only knew what through his binoculars.

Kelsey returned her attention to the form emerging from the dirt. She carefully dusted a humerus with her boar's hair brush, knowing that any marks left behind by a metal tool could be mistaken later for signs of violence.

"Still no sheriff," she muttered.

"A deputy's on his way," Gage said. "Sattler just called the phone at the dig site."

Kelsey gritted her teeth. It was late afternoon. She could have used the sheriff's help this morning.

Gage knelt beside her, respecting the string boundary she'd erected around the grave. He watched her for a moment.

"You all right?" he asked in a low voice.

"Fine."

"You're shaking."

"Adrenaline," she said. "It always happens to me."

"Anything I can help with?"

"Not unless you want to be subpoenaed to testify at a murder trial."

Gage glanced down at the remains as she brushed away another clump of dirt. It was the rope. Seeing this man's wrists still trapped in their bindings made her feel . . . not anger, exactly, but a consuming sense of injustice.

Gage put a hand on her shoulder. "You need some water?"

"I just need to concentrate." She glanced up. His blue eyes were filled with compassion, and she realized she was being brusque.

She sat back on her haunches and sighed. "I'm fine, thank you."

He leaned over and kissed her. Just a soft brush of his lips against hers.

A few seconds ticked by before she could speak.

"What was that for?"

"I don't know." His hand dropped away. "You looked sad."

For a moment, they stared at each other. Then he stood up, and she realized there was a car coming. She got to her feet and recovered her composure as a sheriff's cruiser pulled off the road. The deputy parked and got out, then retrieved something from the backseat.

To her acute disappointment, it wasn't a cadaver dog.

"Dr. Quinn?"

Both Kelsey and Gage turned around to see Aaron trekking across the creek bed. Everything about her field assistant, from his tone of voice to his expression, telegraphed disapproval, and Kelsey knew he'd seen the kiss.

She snapped off her surgical gloves and stuffed them in her pocket. "What is it, Aaron?"

"We've got a problem. Dylan is missing."

"He's on the escarpment, photographing the petroglyphs." She looked around for her water bottle. Where had she left it?

"That was after lunch. No one's seen him since two."

"Where's Jeannie?" Gage asked. "Maybe they're taking a little break at the mine shaft."

Kelsey looked at Gage, surprised how clued in he was.

"Yes, ask Jeannie," Kelsey said. "She probably knows."

"She's the one who told me he's missing," Aaron said. "Apparently they had an argument, and no one's seen or heard from him in two hours."

"I have." This from Rohit, who'd just walked over from the other side of the creek bed. "I saw him back at camp. He asked me to go get a beer with him, said he was knocking off early today."

"He's supposed to be working the ossuary," Aaron complained.

"*This* is why we have a sign-out sheet." Kelsey checked her watch, annoyed. It was nearly four and Sattler's deputy was just now arriving. He trudged toward them with a sour look on his face and a metal detector in his hand.

She turned to Aaron. "See if you can reach him by sat phone. If he's in town, maybe his cell is working. In the meantime, I've got to get these bones out of the ground before nightfall."

Aaron walked off in a huff, but Kelsey didn't much care. She didn't have time to track down truant grad students.

The forecast called for rain tonight, which meant the clock was ticking on this excavation.

"If you're good here—"

"I am," she told Gage.

"In that case, I'll help the deputy. Maybe we can locate a shell casing."

"Start here first." Kelsey glanced around, looking for any unnatural rock patterns. "I think there's another grave."

"You're saying we've got two victims?"

She stared down at the remains protruding from the soil. "At least."

"How do you know?"

She lifted her gaze to his. "Because this one isn't missing a femur."

GAGE STOOD IN Kelsey's camper and practiced the SEAL art of making himself invisible. He didn't contribute to the debate. Not because he lacked an opinion, but because no matter what Kelsey and Robles concluded Gage had already decided on a battle plan.

"I don't see how much more secure it could be," Kelsey was saying. "We've got a sheriff's deputy patrolling the area and a"—she turned to Gage and seemed to bite her tongue on the word "SEAL"—"an armed law enforcement officer right here in camp."

Robles nodded. "And their presence is appreciated. But I can no longer overlook the situation. Our dig is located near a dangerous highway. Two fresh graves are ample evidence—"

"Those crimes occurred months ago." Kelsey turned to

the stove and stirred the soup she was making. "And what about the students? Some of them are conducting research for their dissertations. They paid good money to attend this field school, and we haven't finished what we came here to do."

Robles shot Gage a look that seemed to say, "Help me out here." When Gage didn't throw him a lifeline the old man stood up from the table.

"Dissertations don't matter in the scheme of things, Dr. Quinn." He picked up his gray fishing hat and arranged it on his head. "Given the way you spend most of your professional time, I would think you'd know that by now."

Kelsey stood silently, her expression a mixture of frustration and acceptance. She knew she'd lost.

"When the students arrive in the morning we'll start packing. I want all the equipment loaded by ten." Robles nodded at Gage. "Good night, sir. I thank you for keeping an eye on my field supervisor this evening."

The incensed look on Kelsey's face as he left the camper was comical, but Gage didn't dare laugh. He kept his expression carefully neutral as she slammed around the kitchen.

"This is bullshit," she muttered. "If I were a man, this wouldn't even be up for discussion."

"Yeah, but you're not a man," Gage felt compelled to point out. "And he's right. This isn't a safe place to be right now. Ultimately, Robles is responsible for everyone here, and you can't expect him to take risks with their safety."

"*I'm* responsible for my safety." Kelsey waved her wooden spoon at him. "I've got my own private security detail. How much safer could I get? And I still haven't finished my work here."

Gage pulled two soup bowls from the crate where she kept her dishes. He was starving, and he was pretty sure she was in no mood to wait on him. "You were too busy getting mad to listen. Robles didn't say anything about *you* leaving. He was talking about the field school."

Kelsey rested a hand on her hip and watched him ladle soup. "You're saying I should continue helping Sattler?"

He put the bowls on the table and sat down. "Eat," he ordered. "And no, I'm not saying you *should* do anything. But I know you're going to. I know you're invested in this thing, and you're not going to leave until you've finished. I plan to stick around until that happens."

She watched him warily, then joined him at the table. "You'll really stay?"

"I said I would." He scooped up a bite of beef stew. It tasted incredible, and he knew he'd never be able to look at the MRE version with quite the same gusto.

"Thank you," she said quietly.

"I've got some rules, though."

"I knew it."

"We're moving you into town, starting tonight. You can get a room at the lodge. And you're only going to work during daylight hours. And no driving alone. You can pack after dinner."

He held her gaze as anger flashed in her eyes. This woman didn't like taking orders. Too damn bad. He wanted her in town, in an actual building, behind an actual door, not camped out in this piece of shit RV.

Gage needed a break from this place, too. If he had to spend another night in that sleeping bag that smelled like her, all the while knowing she was curled up, soft and warm in that bed just a few feet away, he was going to start howling at the moon.

Gage considered himself a disciplined man, but he didn't have nearly the willpower he needed to spend another night alone in Kelsey Quinn's sleeping bag. He'd already slipped up once today by kissing her at the creek bed. It had been pure impulse, a gut reaction to something he'd seen in her eyes. It had also been a mistake.

"What?" Gage asked, as she gave him a peevish look.

"I'm just thinking it's no wonder you're a lieutenant. You're very comfortable giving orders. Reminds me of Joe."

Gage watched her get up and take a pair of beers from the minifridge. He realized he knew very little about her background besides the fact that she was his CO's niece.

As she sat down, he twisted the caps off both beers and slid one to her. "I take it you're from San Diego?" he asked.

"Not originally, why?"

"You said you were close to Joe, so I just assumed."

"We moved down from Seattle when I was nine. After my dad died." She eyed him over the rim of her beer and seemed to read his mind. "Car accident," she added.

Shit. "That must have been . . ." He shook his head. "Sorry. I shouldn't have brought it up."

"No, it's okay." She turned her bottle on the table. She didn't look upset to be talking about it, just . . . resigned, as if the pain had been processed a long time ago. "It was my birthday. He'd driven up to Bellingham to pick up my present." She glanced up at him and rolled her eyes. "It was a puppy. I'd been begging my parents for months. My dad found a litter of Weimaraner puppies for sale, so he was on his way to get one when a logging truck hit him."

Gage didn't say anything. But as he looked at her he knew he'd been wrong. The pain was still very real, she'd just learned to mask it.

"That must have been rough," he said, knowing exactly how inadequate that sounded.

"We got through it. But I've always felt guilty, you know? Like I caused it." She looked up at him and her expression was thoughtful. "Do you ever wonder how your life might be different if you could go back and change just one thing?"

Gage stared at her. It was like she'd reached out and slapped him. Had Joe told her about Adam Mays? Or was his paranoid imagination screwing with him again?

"Sorry. Too much information, right?" She gave him a phony smile. "When you asked about San Diego, you probably wanted to talk about the Padres, huh?"

The sat phone rang and she jumped up to answer it, saving him from a response. It was the DNA woman, Mia, and Gage distracted himself by listening in on their conversation.

"That's right, two," Kelsey said. "We discovered the second grave late this afternoon, but I didn't want to start in case we got rain tonight . . . Yes . . . Uh-huh. It's been disturbed by animals." She moved to the window. "Say that again? It's raining here and my reception's bad."

Gage watched her talk to her friend. She rested her hand on her hip and tipped her head to the side, as if considering something. She wore shorts again tonight, and he couldn't stop looking at her legs. That first day, he'd thought they were skinny, but now he knew there was nothing skinny about her. She had the perfect body—all long, slender limbs and squeezable curves.

She caught him staring and he looked away.

"Gage found it, using a metal detector. It was near some spent shell casings. When we excavate tomorrow, I won't be surprised if we find a slug mixed in with the bones." She turned her back on him and parted the blinds to peer out the window. "Oh. Yeah, he's . . . he's new on the dig."

Gage let his gaze roam around her camper as she exchanged shop talk with Mia. Her computer was stowed in the corner, atop a pile of files. Towers of books lined the walls. The sleeping bag he'd used last night had been rolled up neatly and tossed beside a stack of archaeology journals. Gage sighed. This had never happened before. Most of the women he dated tended toward the vapid, cheerleader type, groupies who hung around Coronado for the express purpose of picking up SEALs.

Kelsey was about the least vapid woman he'd ever met, and she in no way resembled a cheerleader. Gage would be willing to bet she'd spent all of high school with her nose in a book.

He looked at her legs again. For the first time in his life he'd fallen in lust with a nerd.

"I'm getting that advice from all sides now," Kelsey told her friend. "I'm moving tonight. I'm sure I'll be safe and sound at the lodge, so you can quit worrying."

She turned to face him when she got off the phone. "That was Mia. She wants that second set of bones as soon as I get them excavated. The FBI's been calling her."

"The FBI?"

"Something about a missing-person's case. Mia thinks

the missing person could be one of their agents. They're really pressuring her for an ID."

The sat phone rang again and she picked it up.

"Hello?" She listened neutrally for a moment, and then her face clouded with worry. "Are you sure? Rohit said—" She paused, then crossed the trailer and jerked the door open. Rain pelted it as she peered outside. "Well, he's not here. Have you tried the lodge?" She closed the door and shot Gage an anxious look. "Okay, call me if you find him."

"Dylan's still AWOL?" he said after she hung up.

"He's not at the bar, the diner, or the lodge."

"Car trouble, maybe?"

"No one spotted him on the way into town."

Gage's gaze settled on the camera that was sitting on a chair beside Kelsey's baseball cap, and something he'd wondered about this afternoon was back in his head.

"Maybe he never went to town," he said.

"Where else would he go? There aren't a lot of options around here."

"I'm not sure." He stood up and grabbed his keys off the table. "But I've got an idea."

IN THE FADING light the petroglyphs looked oddly modern, like some strange graffiti made by pre-Columbian teenagers. Kelsey stepped back from the rocks, trying to imagine where Dylan would have stood to capture the most impressive angle.

"Are we sure he was up here earlier?" she asked Gage.

"You said that, not me. I haven't seen the guy today."

She surveyed the area for clues. "He *said* he was coming up here. His research includes these engravings."

"Well, his footprints are here."

She turned to Gage.

"Two sets of tracks, one coming in, one going out. Keen hiking boots, size ten."

She gaped at him. "You know his shoe size?"

He shrugged. "It's an estimate. But the boots, I know. I noticed them the other day because I used to have a pair." Gage pointed to a footprint in the dust. The limestone overhang had kept the rain from obliterating it. "See that? The logo's part of the tread."

She looked at him with a renewed sense of appreciation. Her "hired hunk of muscle" comment had been way off base, and she felt a twinge of remorse. How would she have felt if he referred to her as a piece of meat? But he'd treated her with nothing but respect since his arrival. He was firm, yes, but always respectful.

Gage was looking out over the valley now. He glanced at her over his shoulder. "Come here for a sec."

"What?"

He took her arm and tugged her over, then turned her until she was facing due south. He left his hands on her shoulders and she pretended to be relaxed.

"What am I looking at?"

"Same thing Dylan was probably looking at when he was up here with his zoom lens."

"Okay." She took a deep breath and tried to concentrate on the landscape. It was twilight and everything was washed with periwinkle. No shadows. Just endless desert dotted with scrub brush and the distant vegetation line that marked the Rio Grande.

"I still don't know what I'm looking at."

Gage sighed, clearly disappointed with her powers of observation.

"Hey, I was never an Eagle Scout," she said. "You're going to have to spell it out for me."

His hands dropped away. "This is the same view we had from on top of that mercury mine the other night. Remember with the night-vision goggles?" He pointed at something straight in front of them. "I was looking right at that mesa. At that same stand of mesquite trees, in fact."

She turned around. "I was stuck in the cave with all the *bats*. You were the one traipsing around with the high-tech toys."

"Okay, point is, what if Dylan was out here taking pictures and he saw the same thing I saw? Maybe he got curious later and decided to drive out there and take a look."

"You're talking about the vanishing SUV?"

"Or whatever it was." Gage's attention was fixed on the horizon now. He shrugged out of the backpack he always carried and unzipped it, then pulled out a pair of binoculars. "You see his black Explorer down there?"

"I can hardly see anything. It's getting dark."

"I'm thinking maybe he left the dig site to go get a beer, like he told Rohit, then decided to take a little detour first to do some exploring."

The idea made Kelsey's stomach knot. She envisioned one of her students down in that valley, near where that girl had been dragged from her car and shot. She scanned the horizon, desperate now for any sign of the SUV. Would Dylan really have driven down there?

Gage passed her the binoculars. "I don't see jack."

"What about the night goggles?"

"Not dark enough yet."

Kelsey peered through the binoculars. The light was terrible. If his car *was* out there, would she even be able to spot it? She saw a clump of mesquite trees. A twisted oak. A dip in the landscape. More mesquite.

And then she spied something. Black. Rectangular. Poking out from behind a clump of scrub brush.

"Oh, God."

"What is it?" Gage asked.

"I'm not sure. Probably nothing." But the knot in her stomach tightened because she knew she was wrong. It *was* something. Something that didn't belong down there.

Nature doesn't like straight lines.

"Oh God, Gage." She looked up at him. "I think I might have found his Explorer."

"MAYBE IT'S JUST a stalled car."

Gage turned to look at her as the pickup bumped over ruts in the primitive highway. He didn't say anything. He couldn't. He didn't want to encourage her to get her hopes up.

"Or maybe he had a flat." Kelsey stared straight ahead through the windshield as the headlights lit up the muddy road. "He'd stay with his vehicle, right? I mean, if he couldn't get a cell signal. That's what they say. If you're stranded in the desert, *don't* leave your car."

Her voice was firm, confident. As if saying it with enough conviction would make it reality.

Gage was pretty sure he knew the kind of reality they were going to find when they drove up on Dylan's Explorer. It wasn't going to be pretty. And no matter how many skeletons Kelsey had pulled from the ground, it was going to hurt her. It was different when it was someone you knew.

"Try my cell again." Gage fished his phone from the cup holder and handed it to her, mainly as a distraction. "Maybe we'll luck out, get a signal. Sattler can't be doing anything tonight, right?"

Like a robot, Kelsey dialed the numbers. Again, no dice. She let the phone drop into her lap and just stared out the window.

She felt responsible, and Gage ached for her. He knew that feeling well, and it sucked. And to make things worse, he knew this was a bad idea. What they should have done was double back for the sat phone and call the sheriff out here. But Gage had seen the look on Kelsey's face after she'd spotted the SUV. No amount of persuasion would have kept her away. If Dylan was out here alive, he probably needed help, and Sattler wasn't known for his quick response time.

Gage tore his gaze away from Kelsey and focused on driving. This was a crappy road under normal conditions, but with the rain earlier it had become a mud pit. The highway jogged east and Gage slowed as he pulled off. The headlight beams bounced along the pitted terrain, lighting up cacti and rocks and scraggly bushes. He tried to drive by feel, letting his tires find the natural path that had been carved out by repeated use. This was the most basic kind of road—no pavement, not even gravel, just a strip of land made bald as people sought out the shortest distance between point A and point B.

The headlights flashed over a clump of mesquite trees.

He spotted an odd-shaped boulder that looked familiar. This was the spot.

But no black Ford Explorer.

Gage rolled to a stop beneath a gnarled oak tree and parked. He reached into the back of the cab and retrieved his rucksack, which contained a collection of weaponry, including his backup gun. He tucked the pistol into the waistband of his jeans as Kelsey watched him, wide-eyed.

"When I get out, scoot into the driver's seat," he said. She had her radio clipped to her belt alongside her gun, and he reached over her to switch it on. "Keep the engine running. If anyone approaches you, take off."

"But what about you?"

"Get your Ruger ready. And don't be afraid to use it if you feel threatened. You got that?"

"No. I'm coming with you."

"I need you to stay in the truck," he said. "It's not safe for you to——" She pushed open the door and got out. "Goddamn it, Kelsey!"

She stalked right over to the stand of mesquite. She did a complete turn and gestured at the trees. "It was just here a minute ago. I *saw* it. How could it disappear like that?"

Gage scanned the area for threats as he joined her beside the trees. He'd never met a woman who was so bullheaded.

"I need you back in the truck while I look around."

She turned to face him. "It was *here*. Right near this weird boulder. I *saw* a black SUV sticking out from these trees. You saw it, too." Her eyes looked slightly wild now as she glanced around in the dimness. "Am I going crazy here? Is this the Bermuda Triangle?"

"No." Gage wasn't sure what it was. But he had a hunch the explanation was frighteningly simple.

Giving up on getting her back in the pickup, he pulled her closer to the big rock. "Stay here. And be quiet a second."

She fell silent, and Gage took a full minute to absorb his surroundings. To their west was a low mesa. Less than a mile south, the river. The valley rose gently to their north until it butted up against the limestone cliffs that marked the southwest boundary of the dig site.

Gage looked west, where the sun had disappeared behind the mesa. Night was falling faster than usual because of the cloud cover, and in ten minutes it would be nearly impossible to see.

"Stay here," he repeated, squeezing Kelsey's shoulder to reinforce the command. Then he moved off toward the boulder.

The rain had stopped, but the air felt saturated, and he knew it was going to be one of those on-again off-again storm nights. Thunder rumbled low to the north, as if echoing his thoughts. Wind rustled through the scrub brush. An animal snarled in the distance, but he heard not a single sound that resembled a motor.

His eyes had adjusted, and he could still see somewhat, despite the coming darkness. He walked all the way around the rock, looking for any sign of Dylan or his SUV, half expecting to stumble over the guy's bullet-riddled body. He circled the clump of trees. He even pulled out a penlight and combed the ground around them.

Fresh tire tracks, leading back toward the highway. But no Dylan.

Gage stood there, running through scenarios. Dylan could have been out here changing a tire, then left, just as they'd been coming to his rescue. But, if so, why hadn't they passed him on his way back to camp?

The kid could have heard them coming and been afraid for some reason and driven away. Maybe he'd been injured by someone or something and had just now made it back to his vehicle.

He could be dead, and someone could have taken his SUV.

Gage made his way back to Kelsey, letting his flashlight beam trail over the ground.

"Gage," she hissed. "Come look at this."

And that's when he spotted it.

Camouflage netting tossed carelessly over some bushes. Only it wasn't careless at all. And suddenly everything fit together—the traffic, the shootings, the disappearing vehicles. He crouched down and lifted a corner of the netting, revealing a small metal grate.

"Gage, you have to—*oh!*"

He whirled around. "Kelsey?"

She didn't answer.

Seven

Kelsey blinked up at the blackness. She couldn't see. She couldn't breathe. She tried to sit up but it felt like sandbags were piled on top of her chest.

"Kelsey, answer me, damn it! Where are you?"

She opened her mouth to talk but all that came out was a strangled cough.

"Kelsey?"

His voice was moving farther away, and she summoned every ounce of strength to turn onto her side and push herself up on an elbow. "Here," she wheezed.

He was beside her in a heartbeat. His hands were all over her—her arms, her legs, her face.

"Are you okay? Did you break anything?"

"I hit my . . . solar plexus . . . knocked the wind out." She was getting her breath back but she still couldn't see, and she clung to Gage's arms. A flashlight blinked on.

"Is anything broken?" He shined the light in her face and she squinted. "You fell about ten feet."

"I'm fine." She experimented, moving her legs, her arms. "My coccyx hurts a little, but—"

"Your what?"

"My tailbone. I'm fine otherwise."

The light blinked off, and his quiet laughter surrounded her. At some point he'd put his arms around her, and she leaned into him now, absorbing his heat as she tried to catch her breath.

"Guess you're all right if you still know your anatomy." He eased her away. "Can you stand up, you think?"

He helped her to her feet. She felt unsteady so she held onto his arm.

She glanced around. The air felt cool and damp, but she still couldn't see anything. "What is this hole?"

"Not a hole. A tunnel."

She blinked into the darkness and turned around. There seemed to be more light behind her, a very faint glow.

"A tunnel," she repeated. "You mean like a mine shaft? I saw an opening. It's probably a mercury mine."

"It's not. Maybe it was at one time but that's not what it is now. It's a border tunnel." The light flashed on again, and he directed it over the walls around them.

"Oh, my gosh," she murmured.

The passageway was wide and tall. They both could have stretched their arms out and not touched the sides. And unlike the mine shaft near the dig site, these walls were made of cinder blocks.

"They have these between San Diego and Tijuana," Gage said. "But I've never heard of any in the middle of nowhere like this. And I've never heard of any this big."

He switched off the light and began guiding her toward the dimly lit end, which must be the way out. She'd thought it was dark outside, but this was an entirely different level of blackness.

"This is huge," she said. "Big enough to drive a truck through."

"From the smell of it someone has."

She sniffed the air and realized how else this place was different from the mine shaft. Instead of guano, she smelled gasoline fumes.

Gage halted.

"What?"

"Someone's coming."

She heard it then, the faint rumble of a truck. It was coming from the direction of the glow. From outside.

"Where do we go?" she yelped.

"Don't panic." And then he was towing her into the blackness, deeper into the tunnel.

She resisted. "But we don't know what's in there."

He pulled her against the wall and moved faster. "I'm feeling for a door. A turn. Anything where we can duck out of sight."

The rumble grew louder until it was nearly a roar. They were running now, and her foot caught on something as she struggled to keep up.

"Come *on*."

"I'm coming." Her heart galloped. Her legs burned. She moved as fast as she could but the noise was closing in. He hooked an arm around her waist and practically lifted her off her feet as they surged forward. The noise was like a freight train bearing down on them.

"Gage!"

Lights illuminated the far side of the tunnel as the truck rounded a bend. In an instant, they'd be lit up by headlights and mowed down. Suddenly her arm jerked sideways and she was smashed against a wall, Gage's body pressed against her.

"Don't move," he yelled into her ear.

He'd found some kind of nook, and she was flattened against the back of it as the engine noise reverberated all around, making even the walls shake. Kelsey held her breath as the tunnel brightened and the noise became deafening.

And then it receded. Just like that, it was fading away, along with the light.

Gage eased back a fraction and Kelsey let out a breath. She was still clinging to him, gripping his T-shirt in her fists. Something hard dug into her neck and her back.

"You okay?"

"Uh-huh." She managed to let go of him.

"That was close," he said, and the utter calm in his voice sounded unnatural. Her feet were frozen in place. Her heart hammered.

"Come on," He took her hand and tugged. "Let's get out of here before it happens again."

Numbly, she took a step forward and pushed off the wall. She paused for a second and turned around but it was too dark to see what she'd felt.

"There could be more, Kels. We need to move it."

"Wait." She curled her fingers around something straight and wooden. She pulled her other hand free and groped around. "I think I found a ladder."

GAGE PUSHED UP the grate and moved it aside, then swiped away the camo netting. He climbed out of the hole and reached a hand down for Kelsey.

"Careful. That last rung is a bigger stretch."

She hoisted herself up onto the ground and brushed the hair from her eyes.

Gage glanced around, on alert for even the slightest noise. Whatever traffic was moving through here, he didn't want Kelsey anywhere near it.

He stood up and pulled her to her feet. It was dark out but not as dark as in the tunnel, and he was able to get his bearings from the shadow of the ridge to the west of them. They were southeast of the big boulder. He still hadn't laid eyes on the supposed "mine" entrance, but he guessed it was tucked into the nearby canyon wall.

"What is this, some sort of ventilation hole?"

Gage replaced the grate and the netting. "Air. People. Guess anything can move through it."

He took her arm and led her toward the spot where he'd parked the pickup. He chose his steps carefully, wanting to avoid another uncovered hole. Beside him, she was limping slightly, and he knew her fall had been worse than she'd admitted.

"You think Dylan found this place?"

He heard the dread in her voice. But as much as he wanted to, he couldn't candy coat it for her. "Yes."

The word hung over them as they trekked back to the boulder. "I found something interesting, too, while I was looking for you. There was a big delivery truck parked near the entrance to the tunnel."

"Did anyone see you?"

"Don't know. The truck was empty but there might have been a security cam."

"How do you know it was empty?"

"Cargo door was up. No one in the cab." Gage stopped and looked around. A few more paces and he stopped again. He studied the shadows. He consulted the compass on his watch. He pulled out his penlight and beamed it around uselessly.

"Well, fuck me."

Kelsey moved closer. "What now?"

"They stole my truck."

She halted beside him. "You can't be serious."

"I'm completely serious."

Gage did a three-sixty but it was no use. He knew where he'd parked the damn thing. They'd fucking boosted his pickup.

He took a few steps toward the boulder and the hair on the back of his neck stood up.

"This has to be a mistake. Maybe—"

"Shh!" He jerked her down beside him as he pulled out his SIG.

"What?"

"Quiet." He eased close to her, until his mouth was nearly touching her ear. "Two men, about fifty yards east of us. Walking this way."

Rat-tat-tat-tat!

He hauled Kelsey behind the nearest boulder, then whirled in the direction of the gunfire. A muzzle flashed, maybe eighty yards south.

Two shooters directly south. And two men approaching from the east, probably armed.

Another staccato of bullets, and Kelsey yelped beside him.

"Oh, my God, *Gage!*" She crouched in a tight little ball against the rock.

He rested his arms on top of the boulder and peered over it. Another muzzle flash, about fifty yards out.

"Why don't you shoot *back*?"

"That'll give away our location," he said. "Their aim's all over the place. I don't think they know where we are."

Another *rat-tat-tat-tat*.

Gage cursed. He needed to get her out of here before these assholes got them pinned down. If it were just him or him with his teammates, they'd wait these guys out and pick them off, one by one. But he wasn't willing to put Kelsey in the middle of a firefight.

"Get your—"

"I got it."

He glanced down and saw that she was, indeed, clutching her weapon. Good girl. He took her arm with his left hand. "There's a ravine just west of us. On three, we're going to sprint for it. Try not to make a lot of noise, okay?"

She made a little squeak of agreement.

"One . . . two . . ."

Ping! A shot ricocheted off the rock near his head.

"*Three!*" he said and they made a dash.

Eight

Kelsey stumbled over the rocks, not knowing if her next breath would be her last. Her right hand hurt from gripping her pistol. Her left hand hurt from gripping Gage's belt. And her ankle was pretty much on fire.

"Where are we going?" she asked and heard the quiver in her voice. They'd hiked a long time without a word. It had seemed like hours, but maybe it had been only minutes. That last burst of machine-gun fire—so close it had made her ears ring—had wiped out even the slightest capacity to think.

Gage halted and gripped her arm.

"What?" she whispered.

"Listen," he said in a voice she could barely hear.

She listened. She heard nothing. Just like she saw nothing. She had no inkling of anything around her, with the exception of Gage. He was a giant, rock-hard presence beside her. And somehow, miraculously, he seemed to have an unerring sense of where they were going.

"What do you hear?" she whispered.

"Nothing. That's good." He pressed her hand against his waist, making sure her fingers were still hooked around his belt. "Let's keep going. I'm pretty sure we've lost them."

They moved forward again, and Kelsey tried to breathe. She willed her heart to slow down.

The ground beneath her feet grew steeper. The air felt lighter. A breeze stirred. She still couldn't see but she knew somehow that they were coming out of the ravine.

"Where are we going?"

"West, around the mesa."

"But isn't the camp north*east*?"

"I don't want to go back the way we came. We'll skirt the mesa, then go straight north, then cut east as soon as I'm sure our tail's clear."

Kelsey's mind reeled. Walking around the mesa could take hours, and that was in daylight. The thought of hiking so far in the pitch dark, over this treacherous landscape, seemed impossible.

But Gage said they needed to do it, so they'd do it. He was the SEAL. She was the lab rat who'd gotten caught up in some horrible game of cat and mouse, and she was by no means confident she was going to make it out alive. At least not without help.

"How's the ankle?"

"Fine." How had he known about that? She hadn't uttered a word of complaint.

"You need me to carry you?"

Yeah, right. "It's fine," she said. "I don't think you could, anyway. I'm not exactly a featherweight."

"Doesn't matter. If it starts to hurt I'll carry you."

"It's *fine*," she said. They were running for their lives

from armed thugs, and yet that tiny insult made her eyes sting with tears.

She was definitely losing it. She needed to get a grip on her emotions. With every painful step, she told herself to just keep moving, to just keep up with him. Forget about everything else and just get back to safety.

"Interesting place for a tunnel," Gage said. "Not a major urban area within a hundred miles."

"Maybe that's the point."

"Interesting tunnel, too."

"How do you mean?"

He glanced back at her over his shoulder. "It's clean."

She scoffed at him. It had smelled like car exhaust. And if her knees and palms were any indication, the place was filthy. "By what standard?"

"By illegal border tunnel standards. I've done some ridealongs with Border Protection in San Diego. The tunnels there are tagged up with graffiti, littered with trash, crowded with warring gang factions."

She waited for him to make his point.

"This one was different. Quiet, clean, hidden. Almost like it's privately controlled, probably even guarded. I don't think it's any accident those guys walked up on us."

"You think they heard us pull up?"

"That or they could have a surveillance system. Anyway, it explains some of the violence going on around here. This route is probably controlled by a cartel that doesn't want outsiders around."

Gage stopped and stood still for a few moments. She'd learned to get quiet when he did this. "I'm pretty sure we've lost them."

"Okay." She wanted to feel relieved, yet she sensed a "but" coming.

"But we can assume they have night-vision goggles," he added. "So it's possible they could spot us, even if we don't see them."

Her blood chilled at the thought. "Why do you think they have night-vision goggles?"

"I heard a vehicle, earlier, but there weren't any headlights, which means they were driving blind again. That's how you do it."

"And you know this because . . . ?"

"I've done it, running desert patrol. You mark the roof of your vehicle with glint tape so friendly planes don't mistake you for the enemy. Then you kill the lights and go."

Of course. Simple as a trip to the minimart.

Kelsey glanced around at the inky blackness, then edged closer to Gage. The warmth of his body was the only comforting thing in her universe right now. That and her Ruger. But the gun wasn't really that comforting because she couldn't see worth a damn and her hands were shaking. She tucked it back into her holster, where at least she wouldn't accidentally shoot herself or Gage.

They trudged on through the darkness. He moved with confidence, as if he knew exactly which way to go, even though it was black as tar. Kelsey didn't talk. She didn't complain. She didn't say one word about the terror swamping her, but she knew Gage sensed it. He kept touching her hand, as if to reassure her, while he guided her every step.

She wouldn't think about it.

She wouldn't think about Dylan, her student. A young man she should have been responsible for.

She wouldn't think about Gage, who'd been shot at and had his truck stolen while trying to protect her.

And she wouldn't think about the memories those gunshots had triggered, memories she worked hard to keep locked away. She wouldn't think about the panic churning inside her, and how even now—probably an hour since the last sputter of gunfire—she still couldn't stop shaking.

Gage would understand, probably. He'd been in a war zone. But her nerves were raw, and her fear was choking. She couldn't talk about it now. All she could do was walk and hold on to him and hope that they'd make it out of this.

A brief flash, then a rumble of thunder. Kelsey glanced up at the sky. Not a star in sight. No moon either. At sunset, the clouds had been thick and ominous. She knew if their current luck held, at any moment the sky would open up.

Another flash of lightning, and then it did.

KELSEY WAS SOAKED to the skin and limping, and Gage's last offer to carry her had been met with a snarl. The woman was stubborn, and two hours of hiking through the rain on an injured ankle hadn't dampened her resolve.

He stopped to look around and she bumped into him. He checked his watch and, in the dim green glow of the dial, he glimpsed her face. She looked wet and ragged and in dire need of a hot shower. Plus, she was shivering, probably less from the rain than the still fresh fear of being chased by men with machine guns.

"I'm going to carry you now. No arguments."

Without waiting for a response, he gripped her waist and scooped her over his shoulder in a fireman's carry.

As expected she went ballistic.

"Stop it!" She pounded on his back. "Stop it right now! I can *walk*, damn it!"

"We're going up a hill," he said, carefully balancing his load as he made his way up the steep terrain.

"Put me *down*!"

"Quit squirming unless you want both of us to fall off this mountain."

She went still, thank God, and Gage adjusted her weight. He felt the backs of her knees under his hands, and her breasts pressing into his back was making it seriously hard for him to concentrate.

Finally they reached the top of the steep incline. A few more steps and they were under the protective shelter of a rock overhang.

Gage set her on her feet and her shoulders quivered.

"You okay?" he asked.

A shudder moved through her and he heard her teeth rattle.

"Here, you're freezing." He wrapped his arms around her and pulled her against his chest. Even soggy and cold, she felt incredible, and he tried not to focus on her body as he shared his heat with her.

"This is so stupid," she muttered. "It's probably seventy degrees out." Her arms went around his waist.

"We're wet. And you're in shock. Getting shot at can do that to you."

"Does it happen to you?" She tilted her head back and he could feel her breath on his neck.

"I'm used to it."

"I thought I was used to it, too, but maybe I need more practice."

He took her by the shoulders and eased her away from him. "When have you ever been shot at before tonight?"

A quiet sigh. "In northern Iraq."

"That's one of the most dangerous places on the planet. What the hell were you doing there?"

She drifted closer and her arms went back around him. "Excavating mass graves. Not everyone was glad for us to be there. We ended up needing an armed guard just to get our work done." She rested her forehead against his chest. "I still have nightmares."

She shuddered again and his grip tightened instinctively. His few objective brain cells were screaming for him to let go of her, but she felt too good. And she smelled too good. And the realization that she *wanted* this kind of comfort from him was a perverse turn-on. This was the one woman he could *not* have, and yet he'd never wanted anyone more. What the hell was wrong with him?

She tipped her head back. "Where are we?" she whispered.

"At the petroglyphs."

She pulled away and glanced around. "I didn't realize we were so close to camp. Why'd we stop? Let's just go."

He pulled her behind a rock before switching on his flashlight. No sense broadcasting their whereabouts with a lantern. "I want to look at this ankle." He shrugged out of his rucksack and crouched at her feet. "What'd you do, sprain it?"

"Cut it, going through that hole. Then landed on it wrong."

He shined his flashlight on her leg and pushed her sock down.

"Ouch!"

"Sorry." The swelling wasn't bad. The sock was saturated with blood, though, and he gently pulled it away from her skin. He reached into his pack for a water bottle and doused the cut. It was about three inches long but not too deep.

"We need to get this cleaned up back at the lodge," he said.

"Do you have any alcohol in your pack? Maybe some hand sanitizer?"

"I've got some Super Glue for emergencies," he said. "But a butterfly bandage should do it for something this shallow. You had a tetanus shot recently?"

She didn't answer. He shined the flashlight up at her and he saw she was gazing down at him with the strangest expression.

"What's wrong?"

"Nothing," she whispered. "Nothing, I just . . ." She lifted her hand and combed her fingers into his hair and the jolt of lust nearly knocked him over. He switched off the flashlight and rose to his feet. Another hand in his hair, then his heart gave a kick as her cool fingers curled against his scalp.

"Kelsey—"

She pulled his head down and kissed him.

SHE FELT HIM hesitate for maybe a half a second. And then his arms wrapped around her and he melded her body against him as his tongue swept into her mouth. For days, she'd had romantic fantasies about kissing him, but she'd been wrong. There was no romance here, just a fierce hunger that thrilled her right down to her toes.

An ache spread through her and she pressed against him, loving the taste of his tongue and the hardness of his body and the surprising softness of his hair between her fingers. He eased her back against a rock, protecting her head with his hand as he held her in place and continued to kiss her as if he'd never get enough, as if he couldn't stop. Something had snapped in him. And she realized that cool disinterest he'd shown her these past few days had been an act. He'd been burning, just like she had. She wished she'd known. She wished she could see his face. She wanted to see the fire in his eyes as he finally let her in on this secret he'd been hiding.

She slipped her hands into the pockets of his jeans and pulled him closer, as close as she could get him. She ground her hips against him and heard the low groan deep in his chest.

He pulled back. "Kelsey——"

She rose up and kissed him again, just in case he was crazy enough to put the brakes on. Something about her uncle. Or her honor. Or some other such bullshit that she didn't want to hear right now.

He pulled back again. "Kelsey, we can't." His voice sounded strained.

"Why can't we?"

He slipped her hands out of his pockets and eased back. "Look . . . I like you."

Her blood went cold. "Don't say it." She turned away. God, if he used the word "friend" she was going to scream.

"If circumstances were different——"

"Let's just go."

He took her arm and she shook him off. Then she walked away from him, as far as she felt comfortable. It would be just her luck to take a wrong step and tumble off the cliff. She felt mortified. *Look, I like you.* Who was he trying to convince?

"Can we get back, please?" she asked. "I'm freezing here."

In the darkness, he muttered a curse. He walked over to her, hooked her hand onto his belt as it had been before, and set out for camp.

KELSEY WAS STILL shaking when she whipped her battered Chevy Suburban into the parking lot of the Madrone Hunting Lodge. Fear, embarrassment, anxiety—plus a major dose of adrenaline—were knocking around in her system, making it nearly impossible for her to focus on the task at hand. After enduring an extremely awkward car ride, she now had to relay tonight's discoveries to the sheriff. What had she been thinking? She couldn't have come up with a worse, more inappropriate time to throw herself at a man.

"Aw, shit," Gage said—his first words in half an hour.

The night manager was just switching off the light above the reception desk as Kelsey pulled into a space. Before she'd even parked Gage jumped out of the Suburban and rushed for the door.

Kelsey collected her overnight bag from the backseat and cast a worried look around the full parking lot. Dr. Robles had left a note saying he'd be staying here, and she hoped to hell he hadn't gotten the last room.

A black Explorer on the far end of the lot caught her

eye. In the back window was a university parking sticker. Kelsey slammed her door and walked toward the vehicle, a dizzying combination of relief and anger flooding through her. She stopped in front of room 109 and pounded on the door.

A light went on. Shuffling. A curse as someone stumbled over something. Then the blinds parted and Jeannie peered through the gap. She unlatched the door.

"Dr. Quinn." Her eyes widened as they took in Kelsey's sodden clothes. "Oh my God you're bleeding."

Kelsey nodded at the man sprawled out on the bed amid the rumpled sheets. Dylan didn't even stir. "Where's he been all night?" Kelsey demanded.

"Here with me. And everyone." Jeannie looked sheepish. "See, after our fight? He drove into Marathon to shoot some pool. He came back, though." She smiled apologetically. "We tried to call you but you didn't pick up, so—"

"The next person to leave the dig site without signing out will receive an F for the summer. Do you understand?"

She nodded silently.

"Tell your boyfriend."

Kelsey turned and strode back to the lobby, practically vibrating with fury. If anyone so much as looked at her crosswise she was going to explode.

Gage stepped through the front door of the motel and spotted her. Then his gaze shifted over her shoulder and he no doubt spotted the black Explorer.

"Dylan's back," she said crisply. "Guess it was someone else's SUV I saw earlier."

He handed her a room key and frowned. "You okay?"

"Fine."

"Mind if I borrow your car? I need to run an errand."

"Knock yourself out. Good night." She tossed the car keys at him. He caught them one-handed and she stormed off. The clunky wooden key chain was shaped like a deer and had the number 102 painted on it. Terrific. Right by the lobby, where she'd be sure to get plenty of traffic noise at six a.m.

Kelsey let herself into the room. It smelled like must and pineapple, of all things. She switched on a lamp and threw her bag on the ugly yellow bedspread.

At least Dylan was safe. One potential heart attack down, one to go. Kelsey rummaged through her bag until she found her cell phone. Of course, it had no charge from sitting useless for weeks on end. She jammed the charger into an outlet by the bed and dialed Sattler's number with the cord plugged in. Four rings. Five. Kelsey toed off her Nikes and kicked them across the room. Finally, on the seventh ring, a deputy picked up. After a brief hesitation, he gave her Sattler's home phone number, along with the warning that the sheriff didn't like to be bothered at home unless it was an emergency.

Kelsey stripped off her soggy T-shirt and tossed it on the chair. She dialed Sattler with one hand while searching through her bag for some dry clothes. She still had the shakes, and she wondered whether discovering a covert border crossing and having her ass nearly shot off by men with machine guns constituted an emergency in Seco County. Apparently it did.

"I'll get out there first thing in the morning, have a look around."

The sheriff's patient drawl grated on her nerves.

"Are you sure that's the best approach?" she asked him. "I mean, shouldn't you call Customs and Border Protection or something?" She pulled off a bloody sock and tossed it in the trash can, along with its nonbloody mate. "It seems evident that these roadside deaths might be related and—"

"Why don't you let us worry 'bout that? You stick to your bones."

Kelsey managed not to hurl the phone across the room. "I'm only *suggesting* that—"

She heard a noise and turned around to see the door opening. Her pulse leapt as Gage stepped into the room, pulling a key from the lock.

"We'll take care of it, Dr. Quinn. I'll talk to you tomorrow."

The phone went silent in her hand. Gage tossed her car keys on the table and leaned back against the door. His gaze met hers across the king-size bed.

"That was Sattler." Her pulse pounded as she clicked off the phone and put it on the nightstand. "He's going to check out the tunnel tomorrow morning."

He pushed away from the door and moved toward her. She read the heated look in his eyes and her stomach did a flip. She stepped back, bumping into the wall, and for the second time tonight she felt foolish.

He stopped in front of her and just stood there, silently. She couldn't talk. Her chest was rising and falling much too quickly, and her legs suddenly felt like noodles.

His gaze dropped to her wet white bra, then lifted. "If you want me to get another room, tell me now."

She didn't say anything. He lifted a hand to her neck and rubbed his thumb over the line of her jaw.

Kelsey opened her mouth but she couldn't talk. His hand trailed down, lightly, and then the warmth of it closed over her breast. He dipped his head down and kissed her mouth, once, twice, three times, as his thumb traced her nipple.

"Kelsey?"

She twined her arms around his neck and pulled him against her.

His body was hard, warm. And she didn't realize how cold she'd been until he started rubbing the heat back into her with his hands and his mouth. He touched her shoulders, her arms, her hips, filled his hands with her breasts. He kissed her ear, the side of her neck. He trailed kisses down her throat, and she tilted her head back to give him a better angle.

"I need a shower," she managed to say.

"Not yet." His hands went around to unhook her bra and then he shoved it aside. His mouth closed over the tip of her breast, and the hot burst of pleasure made her moan and press against him. She closed her eyes and tipped her head back, and just when she thought she was going to melt into a puddle he lifted his head and found her mouth again.

There was an urgency to his touch now. He kissed her deeply, hard, and she tightened her arms around him and tried to give as good as she was getting. It was the way he'd kissed her earlier—raw and uninhibited—and she wanted him to keep kissing her like that and never stop. Her bra fell to the floor. She felt his hand at her waist, unbuttoning her shorts, and then they slipped to her feet, and she stepped out of them, never breaking the kiss. She reached for his shirt and pulled it from his jeans, and then he wrapped his arms around her and lifted her off her feet so he could walk her backward the few steps to the bed. They bounced onto it together and she yelped.

He covered her mouth with his and pressed his weight into her, and she twined her legs around him and squeezed. He dove for her breasts again, and she held his head in her hands, letting her fingers curl into his hair as he licked his way down her body.

She heard a low groan of approval and propped herself on her elbows.

"Red," he said, shaking his head and staring down at the bottom half of the only girlie clothes she'd packed for the summer.

"Sorry. Haven't done laundry in a while."

He glanced up at her. "Do not apologize." He kissed his way down her legs, then back up again, lingering over the lace with his warm breath. She closed her eyes and lay back, and then she felt him stripping that away, too.

She sat up and looked at him, feeling self-conscious. He was fully clothed, and she scrambled to her knees so she could balance things out. They knelt together on the bed, and she helped him off with his T-shirt. It was wet and cool, like hers had been, but the skin beneath it was smooth and warm. She sat back on her knees to marvel at his perfect chest, and she realized she was looking at the evidence of countless hours of pain and hard work and training, and suddenly her throat tightened. He was a soldier. He would leave soon. He was going to get on a plane and go somewhere and he might never come back.

His hand combed into her hair. He tilted her head back to look at him. "What is it?"

"Nothing."

He leaned her back on the bed again, and then the urgency was back, and she put everything out of her mind except the feel of his mouth on her and the hard, heavy weight of him between her legs. The bedsprings creaked as she wrapped herself around him and pulled him closer, and she sighed at the bittersweet pain of him pressing against her.

"Oh, man," he said huskily.

She rolled her hips, teasing, and he propped up on his hands and smiled down at her in the lamplight.

"You're trying to kill me, aren't you? I haven't done this in a while."

She felt a surge of happiness. A smile *and* a personal admission all in one moment. "You going to embarrass yourself?"

He huffed out a laugh, and she saw the strain on his face. She loosened her grip on him and he stepped away from the bed to peel off his wet jeans. Her stomach fluttered as she watched him. Oh, God. She was the one who was going to embarrass herself. He dug a condom out of his pocket and put it on, all the while watching her. Was that the errand he'd run? Suddenly his rejection at the dig site stung a little less.

He knelt between her legs, and then he was kissing her again, and she tasted his desire for her and none of it mattered, not his leaving or that this relationship was going nowhere. She just wanted to give herself to him and take whatever he had to give her in return.

As she opened herself up for him, their gazes locked and he pushed inside her. He watched her—his face taut—going slowly at first, and then harder, faster. Then his eyes drifted shut, and she wrapped her arms around him and urged him on with her hips.

"Kelsey, baby—"

She squeezed tighter. She lost her mind in a white-hot blaze of pleasure that went on and on and on until she thought she would die. And he held her through it, and then finally, amazingly, he gave a last powerful push and collapsed on top of her.

The moment stretched out. Neither of them said anything. Kelsey wasn't sure she could. She felt spent, boneless, too wasted to move. So she lay there with her heart thrumming underneath his and kept her eyes closed. Finally he lifted his weight off her and she took a deep breath.

He rolled onto his back and pulled her with him.

"They gave you a key," she murmured.

"I gave *you* a key." He tucked her head under his chin. "It's my room."

She gazed up at the meandering crack in the ceiling. This place was a dump, and yet she didn't want to be anywhere else. Maybe it was the way he seemed so comfortable, lying there with his arms around her. Or maybe it was the way her head fit so naturally against his collarbone. She never wanted to leave.

"You finally stopped shaking."

She tipped her head back to look at him. "You warmed me up."

He ran his hand over her hip and she closed her eyes.

"I get them, too, sometimes. The flashbacks."

She opened her eyes, shocked. She never would have expected him to bring that up again, and definitely not while they were naked together for the first time. She waited for him to go on but he didn't.

"Iraq?" she asked.

"Afghanistan, mostly." He cleared his throat. "Actually, one particular night in Afghanistan."

"What happened?"

Seconds ticked by, and the room was silent except for the low hum of the air conditioner.

"I got my teammate killed."

She rested her cheek against his chest, waiting. She couldn't ask.

"I did something impulsive. In the moment, you know?" He paused. "It didn't go like I'd planned, and pretty soon Adam—that was his name—he's lying on the floor of the helo with his face half blown off, screaming for his mom. I swear to God, I'll never forget the sound of it."

She covered his hand with hers and squeezed it. Neither of them spoke as she listened to Gage's heart beat. Images of *him* on the floor of some helicopter crowded her mind. For the first time, she understood why Joe had never been married. What woman could live with that sort of fear hanging over her head?

Kelsey's chest constricted as she realized what a terrible, irreversible mistake she had made. She'd let herself fall for a man who had the power to rip her to shreds. Even if by some miracle he didn't push her away when the job was over, he could still do it. Without even wanting to, he could still break her heart.

GAGE WAITED FOR her to say something, but she didn't. Even more surprising, she didn't pat his hand and start spouting platitudes about not blaming himself and time healing all wounds or some of the other crap he'd heard over the past three months. She just listened. He knew she was listening because he could feel her body tense under his hands.

He tried to imagine Kelsey at work in Iraq, digging up women and children and elderly people who had been executed by their own government. He didn't know a lot of people who'd sign up for a job like that.

"So"—he cleared his throat—"do you ever talk to anyone about it?"

"Not really. What about you?"

"Not really."

"I had some friends while I was there," she said. "One friend, really. I talked to him some. He was on a counter-terrorism task force, so he'd seen things. He understood."

Gage wasn't sure he wanted to hear this but he persisted anyway. "You talk to him anymore?"

"Not a lot." She sounded guarded now and he knew he'd guessed right. This was an intimate friend. "We run into each other every now and then, but it's not the same. Our relationship more or less ended when I left."

He filed that away for later. How did she run into him still if the relationship was over? A sour ball of resentment formed in his stomach. Which was crazy, he knew. How could he be jealous when she wasn't even his girlfriend? This thing was temporary, and they both knew it, so why should he care who the hell she ran into "every now and then"?

She sat up. "I'm going to take that shower now. Want to come?" She gave him a look over her shoulder that made his just-returning-to-normal pulse kick up again. Then she turned to face him, emphasizing the invitation with a view of her lush breasts.

He sighed. "How did I ever mistake you for skinny?"

She scowled at him and swung her legs over the side of the bed. He caught her around the waist.

"I meant that in a nice way."

"That was *so* rude." She swatted his hand. "You are *not* invited into my shower!"

He scooped her up and carried her into the bathroom, ignoring the way she pounded his chest.

"I'm serious!"

"My room, my shower." He put her on her feet in the tub, then climbed in with her. Blocking her exit with his arm, he reached over and turned on the water, and she squealed as an icy spray shot down from the faucet.

"Gage!"

He silenced her protest with a kiss, not letting her up for air until the water flowed hot and her arms draped over his shoulders and she was completely convinced of how attracted he was to her very amazing, unskinny body.

He pulled back to look at her. Lips parted, cheeks flushed, eyes glazed with desire—she was the most beautiful woman he'd ever seen, and he had the overwhelming wish to freeze this image, this moment, in his head so he could take a part of her with him when he left.

Nine

Mia knocked again and glanced at her watch. She tapped her foot impatiently. Finally the door swung back and her jaw dropped open at the sight of the gorgeous, half-naked man standing before her.

She cast a glance over her shoulder. Yep, it was Kelsey's Suburban, parked right in front of this motel room.

"I'm sorry." She turned back to face him, and he hadn't somehow managed to put on a shirt in the intervening two seconds. She concentrated on not drooling as he looked her over with a calm, blue-eyed gaze.

"Excuse me," she said. "I think I have the wrong room."

"Mia?" Kelsey appeared in the doorway. "What are you doing here?"

Mia took in the wet hair, the bare feet, the towel in her friend's hand.

Oh, damn. She cast an apprehensive glance at the parking lot. "Sorry to interrupt, but I wanted to let you know we're here. Obviously."

The man's eyebrows tipped up. "We?"

"Yes, me. And some . . . colleagues." She glanced at Kelsey.

"It's okay. He knows everything." Kelsey made quick introductions, acting as if it made perfect sense for a naval lieutenant to be out here in the middle of nowhere providing security for an archaeology dig.

"Kelsey, can I talk to you for a sec? Privately?"

The lieutenant disappeared into the dim room as Kelsey stepped outside and pulled the door shut.

"Oh my gosh, Kels."

"What?"

"Where do I start? The FBI is here. The CT task force out of San Antonio. There's a briefing in ten minutes and they want you there."

The blood drained from Kelsey's face. "Blake's task force?"

"Yes."

"But what does counterterrorism have to do this?"

"Come to the briefing in ten minutes," Mia said. "Behind the diner."

Fifteen minutes later, Mia was leaning against the fender of a black SUV as Special Agent in Charge Blake Reid updated his team. Kelsey and her lieutenant, both in jeans and T-shirts now, walked over and silently joined the group.

Mia watched Blake's reaction, but he didn't miss a beat, probably because Mia had already let him know that his ex-girlfriend and the man providing her security would be attending the meeting.

"I just got off the phone with San Antonio," Blake said. "The remains sent to us by Dr. Quinn have been positively

IDed as Khalid Rahim, who was working as a confidential informant for us before he went missing last January." Blake glanced at Mia. "Dr. Voss is here today with a mobile DNA lab on loan from the Delphi Center. She's going to try to get an ID on the second set of remains as soon as they're pulled from the ground." He glanced at Kelsey. "We'd appreciate your help with that."

"Of course."

"We expect to learn that the second body is that of an agent out of our Brownsville field office. He went missing at the same time as our CI while investigating a possible terrorist cell out of Mexico City."

Kelsey's brow furrowed. "Mexican terrorists?"

"Al-Qaeda," Blake corrected. "We believe this particular group is a sleeper cell that we've heard rumors about for years. At the time of his disappearance our agent had a lead on an attack they'd been plotting from their base in Mexico. Our theory is that the CI's cover got blown somehow, and then both he and our agent ended up murdered."

"Tell me about the attack." This from the SEAL.

For the first time, Blake hesitated. "We're still running a background check on you, Lieutenant Brewer. Until that's complete—"

"Then let me tell you what I know," he cut in. "Those two graves Kelsey found were located near a dirt road that makes a bend down near the border." He turned and held his hand out to Mia. "Borrow your pen?"

She handed him a ballpoint pen and the SEAL produced a small notebook from one of his pockets. He flipped it open to a page where he'd obviously been mapping something. Mia noted the GPS coordinates scrawled on the edge of the page.

"Here's the town." He drew a straight line from a spot marked "Madrone" to a spot marked with an *X*. "Here's where the road bends. Now watch this." He extended the line north and south. To the north, the line followed a highway until it intersected Interstate 10. To the south, it intersected a crudely drawn picture of a rock and some trees.

"What's that?" Blake wanted to know.

"The entrance to a tunnel."

Blake's gaze shot up. "A tunnel leading—"

"South, under the river. We were there last night, saw some traffic moving through."

"Foot traffic?" One of the agents asked.

"Motorized traffic. This thing's big enough for cars, SUVs, even a mid-sized rig."

"That fits with the intercept." The agent turned to Blake, who was regarding Lieutenant Brewer with a wary look. Blake wanted the SEAL's information, obviously. What he probably *didn't* want was a reason to cooperate with this man, who clearly had been doing a very hands-on job of guarding Kelsey.

Blake's gaze moved from the SEAL to Kelsey. From what Mia knew of Blake Reid, she predicted his professional ambition would win out over petty jealousy.

"We've intercepted communications about a truck bomb being smuggled into the U.S. via Mexico," Blake said. "We believe the intended target is the global economic summit being held in Houston this weekend."

"It's a straight shot to Houston on I-10," Kelsey pointed out.

Blake didn't acknowledge her. "At first, we had intel the bomb might be coming through a border crossing in Brownsville. Then we had reason to believe it was coming through Del Rio."

"Maybe it's not coming *through*. Maybe it's coming *under*," the SEAL said. "Whatever cartel controls the route could have granted access for a hefty fee."

Blake gave a curt nod. "Show me this tunnel."

KELSEY LOWERED HER binoculars and sighed. Two hours and still nothing. How long did it take to map a tunnel complex? With a sick feeling in the pit of her stomach, she trekked to the bottom of the hill and over to the mobile crime lab near the recovery site.

Kelsey stepped inside the air-conditioned trailer, which put her dilapidated camper to shame. "Any word?"

Mia glanced up from her work. Kelsey had excavated the skull first, and Mia now stood at a slate-topped table, extracting tooth pulp for her DNA test.

"Nothing." Mia glanced at the nearby sat phone. "That thing's been quiet. Go back to work. It'll get your mind off it."

Kelsey bit her lip. Nothing would get her mind off it. "I can't concentrate. I tried."

The phone buzzed and she lunged to answer it.

"Kelsey, it's Blake. Is Brewer with you?"

Her heart skipped. "I thought he was with you?"

"He peeled off to install a surveillance cam for us at some manhole he knows about on the U.S. side."

"And where are you?"

"On the Mexico side, checking things out. I just watched

a convoy go in——three white delivery trucks——and I think one of them is our bomb."

"But why——"

"Call it a hunch. Our bomb squad should be there any minute, but this convoy could be gone by then."

"Can't your team just block them off at the exit?"

"Yeah, and if all they're smuggling is dope or people, we spook our terrorists and miss the chance to intercept the explosive. Listen, Brewer's not answering his radio, which means he's probably underground, but I need him to set up a diversion somehow so we can get a tracking device on these trucks. If you hear from him, tell him to get in touch ASAP."

"I'll tell him," Kelsey said, although she knew Gage wouldn't call. But it didn't matter, because she also knew exactly where to find him.

GAGE WATCHED FROM the shadows as the men positioned the magnetic sign on the side of the truck: U.S. MAIL, complete with the official-looking eagle logo. As far as maintaining a low profile on American highways and maybe even pulling up to a government building, it was damn good cover.

Gage made himself invisible as he eased along the wall and positioned himself near the back of those trucks. Two of the three were locked with a padlock. The middle one had had its cargo door open ever since the drivers had stopped to retrieve the signs and disguise the vehicles.

Gage crept around back and peered inside. It was too dark to see, but his nose was giving him plenty of other information. He took out his penlight and shined it in the cargo space.

Holy, holy shit. Whoever bankrolled this op wasn't fooling around.

Adrenaline hummed through Gage's veins as he made his way back to one of the manholes he'd discovered today. He climbed the ladder and the instant he was above ground he was on the radio with the leader of the FBI's bomb squad. The guy was a former SEAL, which just proved Gage's theory that every frogman was really just a highly trained kid who liked to blow shit up.

"I got a visual ID on the cargo in one of those trucks," Gage told the man now. "Twelve metal drums. And based on the smell, I'm betting they're loaded with enough ammonium nitrate to wipe out a football stadium, over."

The team leader on the other end cursed.

"They're being disguised as mail trucks," Gage added. "We clear to proceed with the plan?"

"Affirmative. You got what you need?"

"Affirmative."

"Be careful."

Careful? This guy had been out of the teams too long.

Gage dropped back down the rabbit hole and crept deeper into the tunnel, moving purely by feel. The wall curved as he retraced the same route he and Kelsey had taken last night.

God, had it really been just a few hours since he'd flattened himself against her in a desperate attempt to hide her from that truck?

Gage shook off the memory. He couldn't think about Kelsey now. He couldn't think about her arms around him or her soft skin or the fact that he was leaving soon, and that he might never get another chance to touch her. None of that mattered right now. Because Gage wouldn't even be able to *look* at her, much less touch her, if he allowed some fucking al-Qaeda sleeper cell to slip through his grasp and kill a bunch of innocent people.

Gage reached the designated setup point, unloaded his supplies, and quickly got to work molding C-4 and attaching fuses, doing everything by touch alone because he couldn't risk a light. But he'd practiced this a zillion times. And less than a mile away, near the entrance to the tunnel, another guy who'd once worn the SEAL pin was busy doing the exact same thing. When Gage was satisfied he had enough explosive in place to completely seal off this tunnel and trap the trucks inside, he prepared to extract.

A commotion behind him made him go still. Two men yelling, followed by silence. He crept closer to the sound and saw a man standing at the front of the convoy, an AK-47 raised and pointed at something.

And then Gage heard a familiar voice that chilled him to the bone.

KELSEY STARED AT the machine gun, willing her feet to move. She was pretty sure that's what they'd said to her. *Move, bitch!* Or something equivalent in a language she didn't understand.

But their body language was loud and clear. And three nasty-looking guns underscored their point: *Move your ass or you're dead right here.*

Kelsey's heart galloped as she turned and walked toward the blinding lights. When they'd blinked on suddenly, she'd been paralyzed, like an animal in the headlights. Yet an animal would have had a much better chance of sprinting to safety. Where had they come from? Kelsey hadn't heard a motor, so they must have been parked there in the dark, not ten feet away from the ladder she'd climbed down looking for Gage.

The man behind her prodded her with his machine gun and she quickened her pace. Would they take her with them or would they execute her right here in this tunnel? She focused on her Ruger, now tucked into the tallest one's waistband. He seemed like the leader and she wondered how quick his reflexes were. Kelsey's fingers itched. If she snatched the gun back, what was the likelihood of getting three shots off before one of them managed to shoot her? About a hundred to one, she figured.

They passed the first truck. Kelsey glanced around for any sign of Gage or Blake or any of his agents. Were they down here or were they skulking around in Mexico?

They reached the back of the second truck and Kelsey saw that the cargo door was up. The leader let his machine gun dangle at his side as he grabbed Kelsey's arm and shoved her roughly toward the opening.

"You! Go!"

She glanced at the metal drums, lined up like soldiers. Her throat went dry. "You . . . want me to climb in there?" she croaked.

She got her answer as three machine guns lifted and pointed at her face. She hefted herself up on the bumper and crawled into the truck. Three pairs of deadly cold eyes watched as she scrambled to her feet.

The leader reached up.

"Please. Let me just—"

A rusty squeak, then the metal door crashed down.

THE FIRST BOOM knocked Gage off his feet. He jumped up and made a lunge for the truck where they'd stashed Kelsey. Concrete rained down around him. Men shouted. Doors slammed shut and someone fired up an engine.

Gage reached the second truck as it roared to life. He grabbed the bumper and hauled himself up. Clinging to the side of the truck, he pulled out his SIG and fired two shots at the crappy padlock, then jerked loose the remaining scrap of metal. He hefted the door just as the truck sped forward. Kelsey careened into him and he caught her around the waist an instant before she tumbled off the back. She was lit up by the headlights of the truck behind him, and Gage knew they made a perfect target. Would the driver dare shoot into a van full of explosives?

A bullet pinged off the metal wall beside him. He grabbed Kelsey's arm.

"Jump!"

He leaped from the truck, dragging her with him, then he hauled her out of the way and up against the tunnel wall. Dust and debris and truck exhaust swirled around them as he groped for the ladder they'd used last night. He spotted the telltale shaft of light coming down from the ceiling.

"Here!" she yelled, running for it.

"Go up!" Christ, he had to get her out of here. He boosted her up the ladder.

"But what about you?"

"*Go!*" He gave her one last shove, then dropped to the

ground and fumbled with his pack. Thank God he hadn't lost the detonator. He just hoped it wasn't too late.

KELSEY POPPED UP like a groundhog and squinted at the blinding sunlight. She glanced back down the ladder. Where was Gage? She stumbled to her feet as a muffled *boom* rocked the earth beneath her. She landed on her hands and knees in the dirt, coughing and sputtering as a plume of dust billowed out from the hole.

"Gage!"

She reached for the hole. A tremendous weight landed on her back. Something cool and metal pressed into her neck.

"FBI! You're under arrest!"

DUST FILLED GAGE'S lungs, his eyes. Wheezing and coughing, he yanked out a pair of zip-cuffs and wrenched back the arms of the man he'd just tackled to the ground.

"Truck one, driver down! Brewer, where are you?"

Gage recognized the voice of the bomb squad leader who had been on the radio with him just minutes ago. He must have come down the manhole.

"Driver two, cuffed and disarmed!" Gage shouted. "Where's driver three?"

Pain ricocheted up his leg as his captive landed a kick. Gage jabbed him in the kidney, then secured his ankles and rolled him against the wall. Then he ran to help the bomb tech grab the third terrorist.

"He's gone!" The bomb tech's flashlight beam swept over the truck half-buried in rubble.

Gage checked the cab. Even through the still-swirling

cloud of dust and smoke, he could see it was empty. One by one, they scoured each truck from top to bottom. Shit, where would he go? Both ends of the tunnel had been sealed off by bomb blasts.

"The ladder!" Gage jerked his SIG from its holster and dashed back toward the exit where he'd taken Kelsey. *God, please don't let this turn into a hostage crisis.* He raced toward the faint band of light that shone down from the manhole, then took the rungs three at a time and erupted into the sunlight.

It was mayhem.

Every emergency vehicle in west Texas seemed to have converged on the scene. Gage spotted the missing tango face down in the dirt, where a team of FBI agents had him pinned to the ground as they shouted commands.

"Brewer!"

He spun around to see Reid jogging toward him. Gage jumped to his feet and wiped the dust from his brow with the back of his arm. "Two tangos in the tunnel," he told the fed. "One cuffed, one dead. Your bomb tech's down there, too."

Several agents in SWAT gear pushed Gage aside and dropped down through the hole. Gage turned back to Reid. "Where's Kelsey?" he demanded.

At his blank look, Gage shoved past him and plowed through the sea of people. He saw firemen, federal agents, hazmat workers, but no baseball cap with an auburn ponytail sticking out the back. Cursing, he scanned the scene again.

And then he saw her. She was yelling at some guy in an FBI windbreaker as another one tried to restrain her. Gage moved toward her, and her gaze landed on him just as she looked like she was about to deck the guy.

"Gage!" She shook off the agent and charged toward him. "Oh my God! Are you okay? I thought you were *dead*!"

"God*damn* you, Kelsey!" Gage caught her by the shoulders and shook her. "What the hell were you thinking jumping into an op like that?"

Ten

Kelsey's hands were still trembling as she scooped her last bit of clothing off the floor of the motel room and zipped it into her bag. That was it. She had everything. She slid her hand into her pocket and pulled out the note she'd written before her shower. She'd leave it on the pillow, where Gage would be sure to see it when he returned from the debriefing.

But one look at the bed they'd shared last night had her pulse racing—not from fear but something else. On second thought, she'd leave the note on the dresser. As she put it there, the door opened, and Gage stepped into the room.

She took in everything at once—the grimy clothes, the muddy boots, the line of dried blood down the side of his face. It trailed down from a nasty-looking knot on his head, a knot she was fairly sure he'd sustained when the force of his own bomb blast had thrown him to the floor of that tunnel.

The same bomb blast that had caused Kelsey's heart to stop. And even after the dust had settled, and he'd come up from that hole and let loose a flood of curses, it still hadn't started beating again. It wasn't until hours later that her pulse finally returned to normal because she knew he was okay. Angry as hell, sure, but not dead.

Glaring at her now, he crossed the dumpy motel room and began stripping off his clothes.

"Going someplace?" He flung his T-shirt on the bed and glanced at the duffel slung over her shoulder.

"Thought I'd go back to the dig site, see if Mia needs a hand with anything."

His expression hardened as he leaned over to unlace his boot. He threw it into the corner of the room with a *thomp* that made Kelsey jump a little. The other boot followed. And an instant later she had a giant, sweaty SEAL glowering down at her.

"Why are you shaking?" he demanded.

"It's cold in here."

"Bullshit."

"It's been an emotional day. And night," she added, glancing at the window where the neon glow of the VACANCY sign now seeped through the flimsy blinds. The ordeal at the tunnel and the ensuing chaos and questions and formal debriefings had dragged on for hours. And still she hadn't managed to regain her equilibrium. Every time she looked at Gage she got the shakes all over again.

He could have died in that tunnel. He could have died because of her. And even without her, he could *still* die, on any day, for a thousand different reasons, and each one of them had to do with the fact that he was a soldier.

"You were going to take off, weren't you?" His voice was low and dangerous, and Kelsey stepped back.

He took her elbow and jerked her to him. "Weren't you?"

"I wrote you a note."

Anger and something else—hurt? disappointment?—flashed in his eyes. "Do you have any idea how much you scared me today?" His grip tightened. "Do you have any idea how much I care about you?"

She gazed up at him, wide-eyed, and gave a tiny shake of her head.

He pulled her up to him and crushed his mouth down on hers. She opened hers up to him and finally, *finally* found a way to tell him everything she hadn't been able to say in the note. She told him with her tongue, her teeth, her arms coiled around his neck as she clung to him. And he understood all of it, she knew, because he lifted her right off her feet and deposited her on the dresser, right on top of the note he didn't want to read, all the while jerking her shirt up and over her head and pulling her bra off and attaching that hot, angry mouth of his to her breast.

She leaned back and wrapped herself around him and let him take all that anger out on her, one kiss at a time.

KELSEY AWOKE TO find the sun casting stripes of light across the half-empty bed. Her heart gave a little lurch. She sat up and glanced around. She heard the low murmur of Gage's voice on the other side of the motel room door.

Soon the door opened and he stepped inside, wearing only his faded blue jeans. His gaze locked on hers as he tucked the phone into his pocket and came to sit beside her on the bed.

"That was my CO."

It took a moment to process. "You mean Joe?"

He nodded. "Our team's going wheels up at twenty-one hundred."

The numbers permeated her brain. She glanced at the clock. She looked up at his somber expression and knew he was talking about today. He lifted a hand to her face and brushed his fingers down her cheek, as if that would somehow soften the message.

"When do you . . . ?"

"I've got a flight leaving Midland in three hours."

"I'll drive you," she said.

Then she got up from the bed, walked into the bathroom, and closed the door. She showered, dressed, and packed her duffel—again—all without the slightest sign of emotion. She thought of Joe, the man who'd raised her to know what stoicism was, and held it together the entire time. Even her hands were steady on the wheel of her Suburban as she neared the dusty town of Midland and the first airport sign came into view.

"Where are you going?" she finally asked, breaking an hour of silence as she exited the highway.

"I can't tell you that." He turned to face her and she saw her reflection in his sunglasses.

"Is this training or . . . ?"

"I can't tell you that either."

Her chest squeezed. She focused her gaze on the road in front of her, concentrating on the little yellow stripes to keep from thinking about the emotions churning around inside her.

At last, the passenger drop-off area came into view and she pulled up to the curb.

"Kelsey."

She turned to look at him. He'd removed the shades and those blue eyes held hers.

"I can't tell you. Even if we were married, I couldn't tell you. That's the way it is in the teams."

"I know."

Married? The word put a giant lump in her throat. Why had he said that?

She glanced away and was proud to see her hands at least looked still on the steering wheel. He couldn't see that her palms were sweating, that her pulse was racing, that a cold panic was seeping into her chest. She took a deep breath and fixed a smile on her face.

"Good luck," she said, maybe a little too brightly.

He watched her as if he were trying to read her mind. She prayed that he couldn't, that he had no idea how she felt right now, or that she was about one kind word away from losing it at the door of this airport.

He leaned closer. "Kelsey . . ."

"Bye." She gave him a quick kiss on the mouth and pulled back, putting the car in gear.

She waited, nearly biting a hole in her tongue as she gazed into those unreadable eyes. Finally he eased away and opened the door. He reached over and grabbed his bag from the backseat. "I'll be in touch."

She held her breath as the door slammed, as he hesitated beside the car, as he stepped to the curb. Then she pulled away. She drove past the waiting passengers, the loading and unloading cars and trucks. She drove past the sign for a rental car company, past the orange cones marking a construction zone, and even the sign for the upcoming

Interstate 10 before she pulled over and let herself breathe again. And when she finally did, it felt like a thousand razors filling up her lungs, and she knew it was the ragged shards of her broken heart.

GAGE JOGGED UP to the Suburban that had stopped on the shoulder, and he knew before he even opened the door what he was going to find. But knowing it didn't make it any less painful.

"Hey." He climbed in and pulled her hands away from her face. She looked up at him with those soulful brown eyes and he felt like he'd taken a bullet in the chest.

"Come here," he said, and pulled her over the console and into his lap, and she made a keening sound like an animal. "Hey." He wiped the tears off her cheeks with his thumbs. "Don't do that. Hey."

"The thing is, I think I love you. And I can't stop thinking about"—her breath hitched—"what happens when you come back. And what happens if you don't."

She buried her face against his chest, and he held her head against his heart and wanted to absorb all that pain he'd seen in her face. He never wanted her to feel that. Ever. And especially not because of him.

His pulse was pounding now because of what she'd said.

He eased her back and lifted her chin with his finger, and he took another hit when he saw the anguish on her face.

"I love you, too," he said. "Only I don't think, I *know*."

Hope flickered in her eyes, but he could tell she still didn't believe him.

"And what happens when I come back is that I come see you. First thing. Because we're going to have a lot of catching up to do." He paused. "You up for me coming to Texas?"

She nodded.

"And what about San Diego? You up for coming to visit when I get leave?"

She squeezed his hand. "Will this work? Do people really do this?"

"It's hard, but yeah, some people do it. I've never understood why. Until now." He cupped his hand around her cheek. "I want to see you every chance I get. So don't go forgetting about me or picking up with that guy Blake or finding someone else, all right?"

She looked startled now. "How did you know about Blake?"

"Call it a sixth sense." He smiled. "Maybe because every time he looks at you or talks to you or gets within a hundred feet of you, I want to take his head off."

"Is this just about jealousy?" She looked worried again. "Because that's not love."

"It's not." He kissed her. "Jealousy, I mean. This is . . . I don't know, different than anything I've felt before."

"Me, too," she whispered, then she smiled up at him through her tears and he felt his own eyes filling up.

She laughed. "God, would you look at us? How did this happen?"

"Hell if I know. I think it happened for me when I first saw you out at that dig site, covered in dirt and bossing everyone around. Only I didn't know it then."

She laughed, but then her face grew serious. She glanced

over her shoulder at the airport behind them as the reality of what he had to do came back into focus.

"Are we really going to try this?" she asked.

"Trying isn't going to work." He took her hand and looked into her eyes. He hoped he could somehow make her understand. "If you want to do something really hard, you have to decide. And then make it happen. Are you up for that?"

She kissed him, and she was heat and sex and tenderness and *Kelsey*, and she was everything that had turned his world upside down and everything he'd come to care about, and she was the thing that had made his heart start working again when he'd thought it was dead.

And when she was done kissing him, he pulled back and looked down at her. "Is that a yes?"

She smiled. "That's a yes."

Turn the page
for a sneak peek
at the first novel in the new Belador series

Blood Trinity

from
New York Times bestselling authors
SHERRILYN KENYON AND DIANNA LOVE

Coming soon from Pocket Books

Uphold my vows *and die.*

Or break my vows and die.

Evalle Kincaid had faced death more than once in the past five years, but never with so little hope of escape. A citric odor burned her lungs, confirming that Medb majik shrouded the rock walls, high ceiling, and dirt floor of her underground prison.

Grace be to Macha, Evalle still couldn't believe one of her own, a Belador, had betrayed her.

Not just her.

Anger over the betrayal and her own stupidity for falling for this filled her deep. But she pushed it down, knowing it wouldn't do anything except weaken her more. And right now, she needed her full sense and bearings.

Peeking carefully from beneath lowered eyelashes, she took in the other two captives—male Beladors—also held upright by invisible constraints.

A human would be blind in this black hole but her vision thrived on total darkness. Natural night vision that allowed her to see in a range of monochromatic blue-grays. One rare perk of being an Alterant—a half-breed Belador . . . unlike those two purebloods with their backs against the glistening red-orange stone wall.

Did those men know each other?

Did she really care? They were either allies or enemies. And until she knew more about them, they were definitely enemies.

Similar in height and size, they were different as night and day in skin color and the way they dressed. The one with nothing on but jeans had been conscious when she'd regained her wits twenty minutes ago. Completely still, he hadn't made a sound since then—like a snake lying low until it saw an opportunity to strike. Arms outstretched and legs spread apart, his gaze now cut sideways at a rustle of movement.

The fair-haired guy on his left struggled to reach lucidity.

Being imprisoned with two Beladors would normally fill her with hope for escape, because of their ability to link with each other and combine their powers. When that happened, Beladors fighting together were a force few unnatural beings could win against.

But linking required unquestioned trust. And right now, she couldn't offer trust so easily. Not after a Belador's telepathic call for help had lured her into this hole—into the hands of Medb warlocks—her tribe's most vicious enemy for two thousand years.

Burn me once, shame on you. Burn me twice . . .

Die with pain.

Even so, could she refuse to help these two warriors—members of *her* tribe—if there was a chance to save them? Beladors were a secret race of Celtic people connected by powerful genetics and living in all parts of the world. She'd only met a few. Never these two.

But every member of the tribe had sworn an oath to uphold a code of honor, to protect the innocent and any other Belador who needed help.

If a warrior broke that vow every family member faced the same penalty as the warrior, even the penalty of death.

Evalle had no one who would be affected by her decisions—too bad her aunt was dead, but she'd still upheld her vows since the day she'd turned eighteen. Not because she had to, but because she wanted to. And—until now—she'd always supported her tribe without question.

Absolute trust was expected, demanded, among the Beladors.

Were those two Beladors across from her allies or foes?

She had one chance to answer that question correctly. Live or die . . .

What else was new?

"Anyone know who called for this delightful little meeting?" the fair-haired male grumbled in a smooth voice born of enhanced genetics and a hint of British influence. The sound matched the urbane angles of his European face, which could be Slovak or Russian. He straightened his shoulders as if that would smooth the creases in his overpriced suit, obviously tailored to fit that athletically cut body that James Bond would envy. She'd put him in his early thirties and close to six foot three.

Bad, black, and wicked next to him might be an inch or so shorter, but he balanced out the difference with a pound or two of extra kick-your-ass muscle.

"Introductions appear necessary . . . unless you two know each other." The blond guy looked in her direction, then at the other male, but she doubted he could see a thing in this blackness.

Then again, as a Belador, who knew what powers he had? That thought sent another chill down her spine.

Evalle fought a smirk over pretty boy's dry tone and well-honed nonchalance. She'd never met a Belador male who wasn't alpha to the core. But she had no intention of jumping in first to answer after blind trust had landed her here.

Trust had never come easy to her to begin with. She'd been a victim enough in her life, and one of these two could very easily be a Medb surveillance plant.

Tonight's betrayal had put a serious damper on her "team" mentality and it burned raw inside her.

"I suppose I shall have to open negotiations," pretty boy continued, undeterred by the rude silence. "I'm Quinn."

The other prisoner still hadn't twitched since being hauled into the cave by four Medb warlocks and slammed against the wall. He'd been the last one captured. Blood that had trickled earlier from gashes in his exposed chest was now dried . . . and the gashes were gone. Rumors had surfaced that a few of the more powerful Belador warriors could self-heal some wounds overnight, but she'd never heard of one healing so quickly. Odd.

His head was completely bald and sexy, that added a lethal edge to his face. Ripped muscles curved along his long arms. All that body flowed down to the narrow waist of his jeans. He cleared his throat and even that sounded dangerous. "I'm Tzader."

"The Maistir?" Quinn's gaze walked up and down the other warrior, sizing him up.

"Yes."

Truth or lie? Evalle had never met Tzader Burke, commander of all the North American Beladors. If he was Maistir that might explain why *he* was here. He would be a coup in any Medb's career.

She slashed a look at the self-appointed cave host, waiting on Quinn to make the next move.

He shifted his head in Evalle's direction. "I can see another faint aura glowing across from us. A woman I presume from the shape of it."

How come other Beladors could see auras, but not her? What had she done to tick off the aura fairy?

When she didn't pick up the conversation thread, Quinn said, "You would be?"

"Pissed off," Evalle answered, opening her eyes all the way.

He smirked. "Love the name, dear. Should I refer to you as simply Pissed?"

She ignored his sarcasm. "No offense, I'm going to need a little more information before I'm ready to buddy up to *anyone*. Especially two who could be lying to me."

First again to keep the ball rolling, Quinn nodded. "I had assumed only Beladors answered the call, but your aura is—"

"—not Belador," Tzader interjected.

Quinn's moment of hesitation spoke louder than his words. "I see."

Snubbed again by Beladors. What else was new? Even though she'd heard the traitor's call for help telepathically just like this pair of Beladors had, and felt the sizzle of their tribe's connection on her skin, they still didn't consider her one of them.

Raw fury roiled through her veins. What would she have to do to be considered one of the group? But then why was she surprised or even hurt? Her own family had wanted nothing to do with her. Why should anyone else?

Still, she refused to be discounted so easily. "You two may be able to see auras, but I doubt that either of you *see* anything else in this pitch dark. Not like I can."

"That explains it," Tzader murmured in disgust.

"What precisely does that explain?" Quinn allowed his annoyance to come through that time. Not the happy cave host after all.

"She's an Alterant." Tzader stared her way, studying on something. "The only one *not* in VIPER protective custody."

Evalle released a sharp stream of air from between clenched teeth. "Right. Protective custody sounds so much more civilized than being *jailed*, which is what really happened to the other five Alterants. I'm not there, because I refuse to live in a cage." She'd been there, done that, and burned the T-shirt reminder, and it would take more than the entire Belador race to put her back in one.

And she had no doubt how he'd vote if she shifted into a beast in front of him.

Thumbs down.

Yeah, the pendulum was buried on the side of them being her enemies.

Tzader frowned as he studied something. "You work for VIPER?"

VIPER—Vigilante International Protectors Elite Regiment—was a multinational coalition of all types of unusual beings and powerful entities created to protect the world from supernatural predators. Beladors made up the majority of VIPER's force and if that really was Tzader Burke across from her he'd know the only free Alterant worked with VIPER. Might as well cop to it. "I'm in the southwestern region."

Quinn said, "I'm with VIPER as well and was on my way to investigate a Birrn demon sighting in Salt Lake City when I heard the call. What about you two?"

"Meeting an informant in Wendover," Tzader replied, mentioning the small gaming town at the Utah–Nevada border. "What were you doing in this area tonight, Alterant?"

Following a lead I have no intention of sharing with you . . . dickhead.

When she didn't answer, Tzader chuckled in a humorless way that brushed a ripple of unease across her skin. "Listen, sweetheart. We might have another couple hours or we might only have a couple minutes. The Medb don't ransom. They trap, plunder minds, use bodies in hideous ways, and toss the carcasses into a fire pit. I could reach Brina even this far belowground, but I can't get through the spell coating these walls. So there's not going to be a Belador cavalry charging in to save us. You either join up and help us find a way to escape or prepare for the worst death you can imagine."

As if she didn't know the stakes . . .

And hadn't lived through a fate worse than death. They had no idea who and what they were dealing with.

"I quite agree, love," Quinn added. "I can understand your resistance to trusting anyone after being caught in this trap. I, too, want that traitorous Belador's head as a hood ornament on my Bentley, but none of us will have any chance to discover his identity if we don't survive and that endangers all our people."

Evalle would give him that, but hanging here manacled to a rock wall by majik didn't exactly instill a sense of camaraderie in her. More like, it brought back memories that made her seethe.

She held the key to possibly overpowering the Medb— a physical ability to shift into a more powerful form that might afford the three of them the combined energy to fight their way out of here. But using that ability would expose the secret she'd shielded for five years and give the Tribunal, the ruling body of VIPER, all the reason they'd need to lock her back inside a cage.

Adult Alterants did not get a second chance for any infraction. The five male Alterants with unnaturally pale-green eyes like Evalle's had shifted into hideous beasts over the past six years and killed humans—and Beladors— before being imprisoned.

When she'd turned eighteen and a Belador druid had appeared and informed Evalle of her destiny, she'd explained how the dark sunglasses she wore constantly protected her ultra-sensitive eyes. By the time the Beladors had realized her eyes were the pale green of an Alterant, she hadn't shifted or posed a danger. For that reason, the Belador warrior queen Brina had asked the

Tribunal to allow her warriors to train Evalle with the understanding by all parties of what would happen if Evalle ever shifted.

Transforming into a beast would mean immediate imprisonment.

These two Beladors in the cave with her had taken a vow to uphold the Belador code of protecting humanity, which also meant reporting any Alterant who shifted.

Evalle had almost changed into a beast once.

Almost.

Even now, she didn't know if she could do it and maintain control. Which meant she could shift and the Medb could still kill her.

So her only real option for escape depended on trusting these two men enough to link so the three of them could use their cumulative natural abilities to defeat the Medb.

If not . . .

Her choices narrowed by the heartbeat as the other two weakened, but Quinn had a valid point. She couldn't find the one who had betrayed her and make him pay if she died in this underground prison.

"I'm Evalle. My reason for being in this area tonight is personal." She shot her attention to the one who would clearly lead a charge against the Medb. "Got a plan, Tzader?"

"Working on it. They must have used water from Loch Ryve to coat the walls and hold the spell. That's the only substance I've ever known of that can drain Belador powers. I don't know how long we've been down here, but it's probably been working on us for a while—"

"Not my powers," she corrected, enjoying a moment

of satisfaction over another unexpected difference between her and the purebloods. "I'm at full strength."

Tzader paused for a moment, then nodded. "Good. That's one plus for us, but we're losing power, right Quinn?"

"Correct. I'm probably at half strength, which is why we must strike soon while we're still capable of battling."

"Either of you have an idea how many we have to fight to get out?" Evalle asked.

"Best I could tell, there were five Medb warlocks and the one traitorous Belador." Tzader's deep voice hardened on the last word. He was either just as pissed off as she was or very convincing. "Didn't get a good look at the fifth Medb, but he wasn't big and he wore a priest's robe. This is a war party of hunters. If they were taking us to someone higher we'd be gone. They plan to torture information out of us or maybe use us to bait another trap. I want blood from that traitor, too, but I won't let the Medb hurt another Belador regardless of what that bastard did."

Tzader's immediate concern for his tribe struck a note of guilt in Evalle, making her realize she'd been more worried about getting out of here alive than protecting her tribe. She'd fought alongside Beladors until she was bloody and spent to defend the tribe . . .

And to prove she was worthy.

Refusing to help another Belador now would destroy what trust she'd gained from some and give voice to the ones murmuring that she was little better than a trained animal.

Quinn cleared his throat. "I agree with Tzader."

Before she had a chance to say yea or nay, Tzader started

strategizing. "Let's do a quick check of resources. Since she's wary of us, I'll start. I've got kinetic, telepathic, and energy force plus two sentient blades they stripped from me with my body armor. If I can get out of here I'll call them to me."

Quinn said, "Ditto on the kinetic, telepathic, and energy force, plus I can mind lock."

Evalle had no idea what he was talking about. "What do you mean by mind lock?"

"I can reach into another mind remotely, lock into their brain waves, and see through their eyes. I can guide them as well . . . if they don't realize I've invaded their mind and resist. Then I'd have a battle on my hands."

"I thought the spell coating the walls was blocking us from reaching anyone. How can you access someone's mind from here?" She hadn't lived this long by accepting anything at face value.

"I can't reach beyond this facility, but I feel air movement. The Medb must have air passages running between the caverns or we'd have already died of asphyxiation. I can access anyone in another space connected to this one by even a thin gap in the rocks."

Tzader perked up at that last bit. "Can you destroy a mind while you're inside a person's head?"

His question had been asked purely for battle strategy, but Evalle wanted to hear the answer for another reason. Could Quinn tamper with her mind if they linked? She didn't like the thought of that at all.

Quinn's pause indicated he'd given Tzader's question some thought. "Not without our warrior queen's approval."

On the other hand, Evalle had hoped he'd share something no one knew about him, a secret that would make Quinn as vulnerable as she was if she had to shift.

Fat chance either of these two men would make that mistake.

"Are you . . . dressed, Evalle?" Quinn asked that with sincere concern that surprised her. He thought they'd stripped her?

"Yes. I'm in jeans and a shirt." The dark brown cotton shirt hanging open over her running top was one of the two changes of clothes she owned—she preferred to live her life unencumbered by anything, even wardrobe. She'd twisted her shoulder-length hair up beneath a frayed ball cap to spend a night of surveillance in Wendover. She had lost the cap when she was captured.

"What about your powers, Evalle?" Tzader clearly wanted all the weapons laid out so they could make a solid plan.

"I have exceptional vision, similar to infrared-illuminated night-vision optics. I have kinetics, telepathy, energy force . . . and the Medb failed to remove my boots, which conceal blades." *And I might be empathic, but that was a recent surprise and unimportant right now.*

Quinn gave a low laugh. "Can't wait to get a look at you."

"Your optics are another plus." Tzader's eyes stared her way. "The next step's gonna take some trust. You willing to link with us so we'll have your full power and night vision?"

Not if Quinn could overpower her mind.

"Evalle, I sense hesitation on your part after learning I

have the capability to take control of your mind." Quinn's voice was smooth as though he'd lifted her thoughts. Could he? "But do realize that I could have already done so and locked on to your vision if I'd so chosen."

He was right.

She considered her dwindling options and had no choice but to relent. "Linking is our only chance, but first I want an agreement from both of you."

"On what?" Suspicion filtered into Tzader's commanding voice.

"That no matter what we have to do to get out of here you vow that we keep any secrets shared between us. You swear on the life of our goddess Macha."

"You get a head injury when they caught you, woman?" Quinn lashed back, not sounding quite so cultured, as if he hid a less than polished background behind that suave voice. "Swearing on Macha's life's a good way to see the last of yours."

"You think that's any crazier than me making a leap of faith with you two after one of our tribe tricked me?"

"*Our* tribe?" Quinn asked.

"Yes." Evalle was tired of always being doubted. "I swore the same oath you did. I've put my life on the line many times for other Beladors, even though—" She bit off her last words, stopping before she finished with *even though I'm treated like some mutt with tainted blood*. Never let them know how much their biased stares and constant spying slid under her defenses like a fresh habanero pepper rubbed on raw skin.

Beladors might tolerate an Alterant but any trust she'd received in the past had been an uneasy alliance in tense times. She'd admit that the tribe had reason to be suspicious of Alterants after the last male who shifted two months ago had killed nine Beladors trying to contain him. But she'd proven herself for five hard years and deserved respect.

Too bad they didn't see things the way she did.

"No deal." Tzader's unmerciful gaze arrowed through the dark in her direction with the intensity of a lightning bolt.

"I think not as well," Quinn concurred.

Now what was she going to do?

The stretch of curved wall on her left that ran between her and Tzader began to fade.

Evalle tensed. She had no offensive edge. Not until she either linked with the two men or was released from the shackles where she could shift. Both options twisted her stomach into a sick knot of terror.

When the rock disappeared, leaving a hole big enough to drive a small automobile through, a diminutive Medb figure wearing a pale gray robe entered. Light glowed from inside the hood. Where were the four brutes who had hauled Tzader into this chamber?

"You shouldn't be here." Quinn's soft voice was full of tender feelings.

Evalle glanced at him. Was he talking to that warlock?

The person in the robe moved toward Quinn, as though floating across the floor. Evalle debated the risk of linking with Quinn and had just about talked herself into helping him when the hood fell away from the Medb's head. Not a warlock, but a stunning witch with hair so bright it had to be the color of a flame in natural lighting.

The witch stood a head shorter than Quinn, angling her

chin at him. Without saying a word, she lifted up on her toes and cupped his face with her hands then kissed him sweetly on the mouth. Quinn didn't just let her kiss him, he joined in until she finally pulled away. "When my men described the three Beladors they'd caught I didn't want to believe what I heard. I had to see for myself. What are you doing here?"

"Protecting my tribe." Quinn's heavy sigh bulged with regret. "Leave before your men find you here."

"I don't know how to help you," she whispered desperately.

"You can't. If you do, they'll kill you for treason, regardless of your being a priestess."

"You shouldn't have been caught in this trap," she whispered. "They weren't looking for you—"

"*Who* do they want?" Quinn's voice sharpened.

The witch shook her head. "They'll take you last. I'll come up with a way to free you. I have to go." She turned to leave.

"Kizira."

When the witch turned around, Quinn said, "Don't try to save me. I'm bound to my tribe and will die with these two if they can't also be saved."

"Ever the fool." She shook her head. "You should not have protected me that day."

"I must uphold my oath of honor in *all* situations."

Quinn's reply renewed Evalle's hope at gaining an ally in keeping secrets. If she had to shift to escape, would either of these two be willing to say she'd done so with honorable intent?

The Medb witch visiting Quinn lifted her hood back

into place and started to leave then hesitated. "Your time nears." She vanished and the wall was solid again.

The tight muscles in Evalle's chest relaxed after that bizarre scene. Quinn was friends—more than friends— with a Medb priestess. Not kosher in the Belador world, but she couldn't fault him if he'd acted out of honor and spared an enemy rather than kill without thought as their bloodthirsty ancestors had. Their goddess would respect that, but Quinn had a secret to protect as vigorously as Evalle shielded hers.

Now, if only Tzader had something to hide.

But he was a warrior who would die before exposing any vulnerability. She'd bet he hadn't shared all his powers either.

"Want to explain that visit, Quinn?" Tzader asked.

"Sorry, chap. Rather not."

Evalle smiled. "Maybe you should both reconsider my offer to hold each other's confidence in order to escape."

Quinn gave a quick shake of his head. "I won't ask either of you to put yourself in jeopardy with Brina or Macha. Not for me."

Damn. Damn. Damn. What was with these two? Why couldn't they bend an inch? Evalle wouldn't admit defeat, but winning their freedom wasn't looking too promising either. The witch had said they were running out of time.

Quinn narrowed his eyes. "I'm roving mentally through the tunnels for a mind."

Evalle was starting to like this guy in spite of his being cozy with a Medb. He knew his ass was in a sling if word of his association with a Medb made it to Brina, but he was still determined to help. Maybe she could trust *him*.

Tzader still didn't have her vote, though.

"Got one . . . don't think he's the leader." Quinn's voice changed to a monotone. "He's listening to one of the other warlocks . . . they can't wait on the spell to drain the Beladors . . . Kizira arguing they should wait . . . Beladors dangerous even one at a time . . . leader says . . ." Quinn's head jerked back. His shocked eyes swung toward her. "You're the one they want, Evalle, and you don't want to know what they plan to do to you."

"Bring it," she said with more arrogance than she felt capable of backing at the moment.

Quinn's eyebrows tightened, his eyes staring at nothing as he concentrated. He sucked in a breath. "I hope you can take on four warlocks alone, because that's what's coming for you . . . Right now."

The warning in his voice spiked chill bumps along her arms.

"Link with us, Evalle. *Now!*" Tzader's tone brooked no argument or questions.

She had seconds to make up her mind. Tzader and Quinn couldn't link unless she lowered her mental shields. "How do I know you aren't lying just to trick me into linking?"

"You don't." Quinn shrugged. "Just like I don't know what I'm in for when I link with an Alterant, but I'm willing to trust you for a chance to escape."

The wall to her left started fading again, slowly widening as though to accommodate more people this time.

Grace be to Macha, it was time to decide if she'd live or die.

As the cave wall disintegrated under Medb majik, Evalle realized she only had to answer one question.

Could she let even one Belador die after vowing to protect her tribe?

The answer was an unfortunate one for her . . .

No.

She sighed softly. "Let's do it."

Flexing her fingers quickly before the warlocks entered, she opened the channel to her mind for Tzader and Quinn.

The immediate synergy that shot between the three of them sparked the air with combined power. She flagged physically for a couple seconds, experiencing how drained the other two were, then she focused only on sending energy to them.

You got some screamin' optics, babe, Tzader's voice whispered in her mind.

And her vision isn't her only asset, Quinn muttered through her thoughts like a warm flood of fine whiskey.

If she wasn't so concerned over the threat entering as soon as the wall disappeared she'd have smiled at the flirt.

Don't move until I give the signal. Tzader gave that order with enough heat to let everyone know he was in no mood to joke.

Guess we'll allow him to lead this one, eh? Quinn's sarcasm took the edge off Evalle's anxiety and filled her with a flush of confidence.

She glanced over at the rogue and winked then sent them a message. *I'll wait for the word to attack, but let them unshackle me before you do anything if you want the full force of my power.*

Tzader gave a curt nod of his head.

Quinn lifted a finger in acknowledgment.

The wall cleared. Four warlocks in swirling gray robes with no hoods carried torches into the room, all headed for Evalle. Without her shades on, she squinted to be able to see in what for her eyes was brilliant light.

A serpent tattoo wrapped their thick necks then swept around each bald head until the pointed tip of the viper's head stopped at the bridge above the warlocks' wide noses. Yellow-orange eyes with narrow black diamond centers glowed brightly above their smooth cheeks. When one warlock stood in front of each of her arms, they chanted in unison, releasing the shackles.

She dropped to the floor.

One of the other two warlocks extended his hand, not touching her. His fingers kinetically circled her throat and lifted her off the dirt floor.

She fought to breathe. *Tzader? What the hell are you waiting on?*

"She is secure, Priestess," the warlock choking Evalle called out in a loud voice.

Kizira appeared at the entrance, her face stoic.

Quinn answered Evalle. *Tzader was waiting on Kizira to enter. I'll deal with her.*

Kizira closed her eyes and held her hands in front of her with the palms turned up. Her eyes glowed yellow. She began murmuring foreign words that sounded ancient and deadly.

Now, Evalle, Tzader roared in her mind.

Evalle willed herself into battle form, a minimal physical change all Beladors were approved to use when engaging with an enemy. She tightened her fingers into fists. Spiked cartilage raised along the length of her arms. Power surged throughout her, expanding muscle tissue and driving her adrenaline to a volcanic level.

She gripped both hands around the invisible arm holding her and bared her teeth. "You're dying first, just to kick this party off on a high note."

The blunt-nosed warlock smiled and squeezed tighter, drawing tears to her eyes.

Using her kinetic ability, she knocked the torches into the dirt, killing the flames. The warlocks howled in anger.

She shouted *Ready?* to the Beladors.

Tzader and Quinn broke free of their shackles, drawing the other three warlocks around to face them.

Battle screams ricocheted off the walls, gathering force like the wail of a banshee.

Pulling in opposite directions with each hand, Evalle snapped the force holding her throat. The warlock screamed in agony, his arm falling uselessly to his side. Released from his power, Evalle dropped to the dirt floor. Blunt-nose snarled with pain and dove at her. She shoved her hands up, palms out, blocking him with shield of power. He bounced back, falling to the ground.

Kizira swayed, caught in a deep trance.

Evalle stomped each foot and silver spikes with razor-sharp tips shot out from around the boot soles. She took a step toward Tzader who fought two warlocks.

Quinn snapped the neck of the Medb he battled, tossing the body aside quicker than yesterday's trash then snatching one of Tzader's opponents away.

The warlock Evalle had knocked out gained his feet. He charged her, his mouth opening wide to release demonic curses on a stream of black breath.

She spun, whipping her boot high, the lethal tips slicing his neck like a buzzsaw. Purple liquid bubbled from the mortal wound, filling the air with a soured orange stench. Evalle whipped her boot up again in a crosskick. The warlock's head flew off sideways, hitting Kizira in the chest. That jolted the priestess out of her trance. Her glazed eyes started clearing.

Oops.

Evalle swung back to the fight, but she couldn't jump in kicking and risk killing the Beladors who now fought the only two warlocks still alive. Of the two dead, one lay facedown on his chest with his head spun around to stare at the ceiling.

Tzader battled a warlock armed with a three-pronged sword he hadn't possessed a moment ago.

Quinn blasted the fourth warlock backward with a shot of energy, then produced three Celtic Triquetra with jagged blades and threw them with deadly accuracy. The blades struck the warlock in his throat, heart, and eyes, killing him instantly.

"Not my brother! No!" Kizira screamed. She looked at Quinn, her agonized face a mix of shock and betrayal. When the priestess lifted her hands at Quinn, Evalle dove at her.

Quinn shouted, *"No, Evalle!"*

She slid to a stop at the side of Kizira who froze in midmotion with arms extended, eyes stuck open, full of fury.

Quinn appeared next to the priestess. "I've locked her mind, but I can't hold her long without harming her." He cut eyes teaming with sadness at Evalle. "Help Tzader."

She nodded then felt a blow to her midsection and

doubled over. Quinn groaned but held his position with his back to the room. When she turned to Tzader she found him on the ground, the three-pronged spear staked through his chest.

Tzader looked over at her. His face twisted with pain. *Unlink . . . before I die and leave me,* he called into her mind. *You can't kill this one.*

Evalle looked at the last warlock who laughed in triumph until he eyed Kizira immobilized. That's when the eyes on the serpent tattoo on his head came to life. That meant he carried the same blood as the Medb High Priestess.

We stand together or we die together, Evalle told Tzader.

Agreed, Quinn confirmed on a gasp. *But I can't help you and hold Kizira immobile.*

Evalle faced the warlock. Intimidation played a role in every battle won. "You don't look so hard to kill."

The warlock whispered a chant, lifting his hands to his lips and blowing across the palms. Both hands tripled in size, extending into claws. He swiped one long talon at the nearest wall, digging a trough through stone that crumbled as though cutting butter with a cleaver. He crooked the same claw, smiling when he goaded her to attack.

Well, crap. She hadn't really expected to get out of this mess without facing this decision. But she'd only shifted once—part way—and that had been a reaction to terror. Returning to her normal physical state had been a struggle.

No time to worry about what might happen.

It was time to live . . .

Evalle mentally reached inside herself, deep into the core of her life source. She urged her body to free itself. Power rolled through the center of her, surging into her legs and arms. Bones cracked and popped, skin stretched tight. Her clothes split, shredding into tatters that fell away from her body.

Quinn would get an unobstructed view of all her assets later if they survived this. Leather ripped with a squeal when her feet thickened, toes growing the length of a human hand. Her jaw expanded to accommodate a double row of teeth that sharpened into jagged fangs.

Nerves and tendons cried out in pain, but she roared, now able to stare down at the warlock from ten feet off the ground.

He dared to laugh then threw a ball of energy at her.

She batted it away, blowing a hole in the rock wall.

The warlock cocked his head, still smiling, but with a little surprise. He flew at her, arms drawn back to swing a clawed hand at her neck. Before he could sever her head, she blocked him, using an oversized arm that sizzled with unspent power.

He bounced back, stunned for the two seconds she allowed him to live.

She curled her leathery fingers into a fist and smashed his face, slamming him backward to the wall where his body clung, shaking. Bolts of energy popped and sparked around him before he dropped to the ground. When she stepped close to the warlock he gasped, "You shall pay for this. I call upon the gods of—"

She lifted a foot heavy as two cement blocks and slammed down on his midsection, crushing him into two halves.

His last breath screamed out of him, a sound of agony Evalle never wanted to hear again.

Brilliant orange light blanched the inside of the cave. His body foamed purple then disintegrated into a puff of brown smoke. A sure sign he was Medb royalty.

Evalle took several breaths, calming the power pulsing through her. She begged her body to pull back into itself now that they were safe. Each breath she drew forced another part to tighten and shrink, but hallelujah, she was reversing the change. Sweat covered her skin. Pain daggered her arms and legs, sickened her stomach. Her head felt as though a stake was being driven through her temples, but she'd end up facing worse if the Tribunal found out she'd shifted.

Feeling the last of her body return to human form, Evalle swung around to Tzader who lay perfectly still. When she reached him, she yanked the spear free. Blood gushed out the three holes. Ignoring her naked state, she dropped down on her bare knees and pressed her hands over the gaping wounds to stop the flow of blood. But she had no power to save him from all the internal damage.

"He can't be dead, because we're alive," Quinn said in a wheeze over his shoulder from where he still controlled Kizira.

"You're right." Evalle and Quinn had a chance to survive if they unlinked and escaped, but she couldn't walk away from Tzader. He was not the traitorous Belador. If she unlinked, he'd lose the strength she still gave him. Her abdomen hurt, too, but . . . not as though she'd been stabbed. Why didn't she feel like she was dying?

Could an Alterant linked to a Belador not die?

Tzader's eyes fluttered.

"I'm here," she assured him. "I won't leave you."

He gasped hard for air, chest heaving. His hand shot up to grab her arm with a strength that surprised her.

"He's living . . . I feel him getting stronger," Quinn said.

Evalle glanced over her shoulder at Quinn. "Me, too."

"You can move your hand now," Tzader told her.

When she looked down his face was robust with life. She pulled her hands away. The holes in his chest were shrinking. "What'd you do?"

Tzader sat up and stretched, then his shoulders slumped with the effort. "You saved my life, Evalle."

"Oh, hell no I didn't." She stood up and backed away from him. "I do *not* have those powers."

Pushing up to his feet, Tzader turned to her, politely avoiding her naked body. "You ought to grab a robe."

She yanked a robe off the closest dead warlock, one of the three that hadn't disintegrated, and shoved her arms through the sleeves. "Now. What happened to you, Tzader?"

He moved slowly, still recovering. "Best I can tell, the spear tips were made of lava from a volcano I'm not telling either of you about since it's the only thing that can kill me. But the tips have to stay in place while I die a slow death. If you hadn't defeated the last warlock and pulled out the spear I'd be dead."

Beladors were not immortal, as a rule, as far as she knew. "Why can't you be killed?"

When Tzader didn't reply, Quinn did. "Might as well tell us. Then Evalle can share what it takes to kill her, too. I'm not leaving here without knowing more about both of you."

She gave him an arch stare. "I think you two know all you need to know about me right now."

Tzader shrugged. "Let's just say I'm the descendant of a Belador who had me blessed, or cursed, depending on your point of view, and leave it at that, okay?" He walked over to Quinn. "Can we get outta here?"

"Yes. I withdrew the exit route from Kizira's mind."

Evalle stepped up to both of them. "I doubt she's going to let us go without a fight once you unlock her mind."

"I won't kill her," Quinn said with quiet conviction. "I can leave a blank place in her thoughts when I release her that will last maybe a minute after she comes out of this state. That's enough time to reach the surface."

"Then do it." Tzader glanced at the wall still open. He whistled shrilly. Two spinning knives with Celtic designs on the handles flew into the room and circled him, landing at each hip. The tips of the blades snarled and hissed.

Evalle missed her boots more than her clothes, but she had bigger worries. She knew better than to believe these two would protect her secret unless they gave her their word. But what Belador would risk his existence *and* his family for an Alterant?

"We have to go now," Quinn ordered, stepping away from Kizira who stood silent as a statue. He led the way, racing through a maze of dark corridors that climbed upward to the surface.

Tzader followed Evalle who kept pace with Quinn.

"We're all good with keeping a few secrets, right?" Evalle was dying to know why neither of the men had commented on her shifting. She'd do anything to protect her tribe, but she would not go willingly into a cage again.

Not after spending her childhood locked away as a freak.

Tzader's steps pounded close behind. "Let's get outta here first, then talk."

"You can talk and run," she argued. "Admit it, I changed right back into my normal state. I only did it to help us escape."

"It's complicated, Evalle." Quinn had led them with confidence, choosing turns without hesitation and running all out.

Until he reached a pile of rocks that blocked their path.

Everyone skidded to a stop.

Neither of the men made a move to clear the rocks and their minute of a headstart was close to ending. Evalle looked at them. "Let's get kinetic, shall we?"

Quinn shook his head. "We can't move these rocks that way. I pulled several chants from Kizira I believe are connected to this route, but—"

"But what?" Evalle asked. Anger mixed with fear inside her. "Start freaking chanting before your crazy priestess wakes up from her litte nap."

"I might *kill* us if I use the wrong chant. And she's *not* crazy." Quinn's tone told her his patience was strained.

An unearthly shriek right out of a B horror movie rocked the underground tunnel.

"Sounds like Sleeping Beauty's awake." Evalle stoo hands on hips, robe falling open.

"I liked you better when you didn't talk," Q snapped, losing all hold on his composure.

"I don't like either one of you right now,"

snarled. "Open the damn exit or we gotta kill one seriously pissed-off priestess."

Kizira's shrieks grew in volume.

Quinn faced the rocks and spewed out a rapid sequence of mumbo jumbo Evalle couldn't begin to translate or remember.

Boulders started falling away to each side, parting to make an opening. Evalle took one quick look back to watch behind them for Kizira. Quinn might not want to hurt his evil-eyed honey, but Evalle did. If not for the Medb she wouldn't be facing imprisonment—or worse—for shifting.

"Let's go," Tzader ordered Evalle, snagging her arm and dragging her through the opening. *"Seal that mother, Quinn!"* Quinn's chant was lost in the sound of rocks piling in behind them.

When Evalle caught her footing she was aboveground.

In daylight. No shelter within a mile.

An August sun blistered the desert landscape.

"No!" She curled inside the robe, pulling the thin protection around her. Skin on the back of her exposed hand that held the robe closed started turning a nasty ~~gr~~een color.

Tzader and Quinn shouted something, but her screams ~~drow~~ned them out. Heat scorched through the blood vessel~~s in~~ her arm and into her body, carrying the poison ~~into her~~ system.

~~She woul~~dn't face imprisonment after all.

~~The sun w~~ould kill her first.